A PENGUIN MYSTERY

Death at the Château Bremont

M. L. LONGWORTH has lived in Aix-en-Provence since 1997. She has written about the region for the *Washington Post*, the *Times* (UK), the *Independent* (UK), and *Bon Appétit* magazine. She is the author of a bilingual collection of essays, *Une Américaine en Provence*, published by La Martinière in 2004. She divides her time between Aix, where she writes, and Paris, where she teaches writing at New York University. This is her first novel.

Death at the Château Bremont

A VERLAQUE AND BONNET MYSTERY

· M. L. LONGWORTH ·

PENGUIN BOOKS

PENGUIN BOOKS
Published by the Penguin Group
Penguin Group (USA) Inc.,
375 Hudson Street, New York, New York 10014, U.S.A.
Penguin Group (Canada), 90 Eglinton Avenue East, Suite 700, Toronto,
Ontario, Canada M4P 2Y3 (a division of Pearson Penguin Canada Inc.)
Penguin Books Ltd, 80 Strand, London WC2R 0RL, England
Penguin Ireland, 25 St Stephen's Green, Dublin 2,
Ireland (a division of Penguin Books Ltd)
Penguin Group (Australia), 250 Camberwell Road, Camberwell,
Victoria 3124, Australia (a division of Pearson Australia Group Pty Ltd)
Penguin Books India Pvt Ltd, 11 Community Centre,
Panchsheel Park, New Delhi – 110 017, India
Penguin Group (NZ), 67 Apollo Drive, Rosedale, Auckland 0632,
New Zealand (a division of Pearson New Zealand Ltd)
Penguin Books (South Africa) (Pty) Ltd, 24 Sturdee Avenue,
Rosebank, Johannesburg 2196, South Africa

Penguin Books Ltd, Registered Offices:
80 Strand, London WC2R 0RL, England

First published in Penguin Books 2011

5 7 9 10 8 6 4

Copyright © Mary Lou Longworth, 2011
All rights reserved

LIBRARY OF CONGRESS CATALOGING IN PUBLICATION DATA
Longworth, M. L. (Mary Lou), 1963–
Death at the Château Bremont : a Verlaque and Bonnet mystery / M.L. Longworth.
p. cm.
"A Penguin mystery."
ISBN 978-0-14-311952-4 (pbk.)
1. Judges—France—Fiction.   2. Women law teachers—Fiction.   3. Brothers—Crimes against—
Fiction.   4. Murder—Investigation—Fiction.   5. Mafia—Fiction.   6. Aix-en-Provence (France)—
Fiction.   7. France, Southern—Fiction.   I. Title.
PR9199.4.L596D43 2011
813'.6—dc22   2011007573

Printed in the United States of America
Set in Adobe Caslon · Designed by Elke Sigal

For Mum and Reini

Death at the
Château Bremont

~

Saint-Antonin, France
APRIL 17, 12:05 A.M.

*T*he attic light was burnt out. He'd talk to Jean-Claude tomorrow. Étienne sensed that the caretaker had never really liked him, or perhaps his coolness was out of respect for their difference in class; Jean-Claude was polite but never looked his employer in the eye. They had easily avoided each other while Étienne's parents were still alive, but as Étienne was now the only Bremont living in Aix, the château's enormous upkeep required that owner and caretaker have more frequent contact. Jean-Claude was a huge man but clumsy. His size had never caused Étienne much worry, but there was something in the way Jean-Claude looked at him sometimes that made him uneasy. Étienne de Bremont had recently found himself fascinated by the caretaker's enormous hands, which would lie stiffly at his sides as he received his employer's blunt instructions; after a few seconds his fat fingers would slowly, and then quickly, begin to twitch, as if they were waiting for messages from the brain that would call them into action. At any rate, the fingers seemed to be thinking ahead of the slow, still hands.

Luckily Étienne had brought a flashlight with him, out of habit. There was always a burnt-out lightbulb somewhere in the crumbling château—a home that no one lived in, more trouble than it was worth. He shone the light around the dusty room, one of the only rooms of the twenty-odd that brought him some good memories. His first ten-speed bike was propped up in a corner: it had taken him downhill into Aix-en-Provence in forty-five minutes, the return trip took almost double that. He was fit then, and still was, considering in five years he would be forty.

Next to the bike, a rosary hung on the post of a nineteenth-century iron bed, as it always had, and he thought of her laughing face and green eyes. He missed her, but it wouldn't do to call. Their lives were too different, their friends too different. Especially their friends.

There was a full moon that night, and Étienne walked over to the window. It was covered by a wooden shutter a meter wide and two meters tall. He swung it open, careful to latch it against the stone wall with his left hand as he held on tightly to the inner wall with his right. The window was open to the elements: years ago the hay had been brought in through this opening for the winter. They had never bothered to put glass in the window. Each Bremont family member learned, as soon as they were tall enough to be able to reach the wrought-iron latch, how to open the window without falling out. The moonlight now filled up the room and would give him enough illumination to read what he had come for. The Louis Vuitton suitcase was on the floor near his right foot, and he picked it up and set it on the wooden dresser that was filled with moth-eaten blankets. The lock on the suitcase had been opened, probably by his brother, François. He quickly opened the suitcase and grabbed the first papers that lay on top, flipping hurriedly through the documents. He didn't understand why he suddenly felt so rushed—Jean-Claude was gone, an hour and a half away, until tomorrow—but he was anxious all the same and couldn't stop his hands from shaking. The lawyers' and notaries' documents were handwritten, in the graceful script he and his brother were taught to use in the first grade, with fountain pens his father had bought at Michel on the cours Mirabeau. The papers were out of order, and mixed in with the legal documents were odd bits of paper that characterized his noble family's disregard for money, for filing, and for organization in general. Receipts had been kept in flour tins; hundred-franc bills were dropped or hidden under the library's faded Persian carpet; the electricity and telephone companies had to call regularly because of late payments, but they never dared to cut off the château's power.

He began separating the papers, dividing twenty-year-old bank statements and shopping lists from important legal documents. He laughed as he picked up a yellowed receipt from Aix's best pâtisserie, still in operation, with a fourth-generation chef doing the baking. The receipt was for two brioches, which could have been for him and François, or Marine, except that it dated from the 1950s, years before any of them had been born. He held the receipt in his hands, calming down a bit and allowing himself to think again of Marine and their friendly preadolescent arguments over the merits of brioches versus croissants, or the chocolate powder Banania versus Quik. She could always outargue him.

Étienne de Bremont's smile froze when he heard the château's front door open. Instinct told him to stand closer to the wall, partly hiding his thin frame in the shadows. He took off his reading glasses and rested them inside his V-neck sweater. Footsteps quickly ran up the first flight of stairs, and then down the hall and up the second flight, down the next hall and up the last set of stairs, these narrower and wooden rather than stone. Holding his breath, Étienne reasoned that the footsteps probably belonged to Jean-Claude, who must have gotten it into his head that he couldn't possibly spend a night away from the château. His stupid plants would miss him too much. When the attic door opened, Étienne pointed his flashlight at the figure in the doorway; he sighed and said, "What are *you* doing here?"

The shutter rattled intermittently against the stone wall as Étienne spoke to his uninvited visitor; a strong wind had begun to blow, carrying their voices out the open window, over the pine trees, and up the hill toward the field of lavender.

As the wind grew louder so did their voices, now tinged with anger. Étienne, oddly enjoying the insults, imagined that he could smell lavender. He was getting bored with this exchange. For a split second, he turned his face toward the open window, in order to inhale the night breeze, and as he turned back around, he heard a rushing sound on the attic's wooden floor and felt hands on his chest. The mistral blew around his body as he fell. He looked up at the attic window and saw the faint light from his flashlight, and he heard the wind, not whistling, but groaning. Even in the few seconds before his death, all Étienne de Bremont could think of were those two brioches and how he had always preferred brioches to croissants.

Chapter One

❧

Saint-Antonin, France

APRIL 17, 5:30 P.M.

Verlaque stood in front of the caretaker's house. It was a medieval cottage; its thick walls made of a golden, rough-hewed stone that glowed in the late afternoon light. The windows were small, to keep out the summer heat, and their wooden shutters were painted a faded gray-blue. Behind Verlaque loomed the mountain. He remembered what Paul Cézanne had said of the montagne Sainte-Victoire—that he could move his easel half a meter and see a totally different mountain. Verlaque tried it now, shifting his heavy body slightly to the right. It worked. The spiky top of one of the mountain's many limestone knobs—its south flank resembled a dinosaur's back—came into view. A shadow suddenly floated across the peak, and its color changed from dusty rose to gray.

He turned back around and looked at the château... vence's château but a *bastide*—a country home built by ... would wealthy seventeenth-century citizens, ...

leave their downtown mansions and make their way, servants in tow, to the cooler countryside. It *was* cold up here—although less than ten kilometers from Aix, Saint-Antonin was five hundred meters above sea level—and Verlaque realized that he had left his jacket in the car.

The *bastide*, like the cottage, was built of golden stone, but this stone had been smoothly cut. Giant yellow-and-green-glazed earthenware pots, now chipped and cracked, lined the pebbled walk that led to the front door. He noticed that despite the poor shape of the pots, each one contained a healthy oleander, not yet in bloom. Another pebbled walk, lined on either side with rows of lavender, cut across a manicured lawn and led down to a centuries-old ornamental pool. Verlaque walked down the path, aware of his newly acquired kilos and his stomach pushing against his Italian leather belt—living alone didn't mean that he now ate less, as he imagined other bachelors did after a breakup. He sighed and promised himself that he would start running tomorrow, trying to think where his trainers might be. "Trainers," he said aloud in English, and smiled. His English grandmother had called them "trainers," and his French grandmother wouldn't let him leave the house with them on. "Seulement pour le tennis," she would say.

The pool's water was green and murky and covered with leaves that had fallen from the plane trees that towered above it. At the far end was a fountain made from the bright orange and yellow marble that came from the mountain. It was in the shape of a lion's head whose mouth spewed water into the pool. When he first came to Provence, Verlaque didn't like the mont Sainte-Victoire marble—he thought it too bright, almost kitsch—but now loved it. Marine's bathroom sink was made of the same reached down and put his hand under the running water and thought of some lines from a Philip Larkin poem, his preferred grandmother's preferred poet: "I put my mouth / Close to running water: / Flow north, flow south, / It will not matter, / It is not love you will find." He had found love with Marine, but not contentment, and so he let the love go. His past was too difficult to explain to Marine, and the more she tried to get Verlaque to talk about it, the more he withdrew. It was easier to be on his own, in his loft, with his books and paintings and cigars. They hadn't spoken for over six months now.

"Monsieur le Juge!" cried a voice from the cottage. The caretaker was standing in the doorframe, his height and breadth filling it completely. "The coffee is ready!" Verlaque walked toward the cottage, at the same time slipping his hand into his pocket and turning on a tape recorder.

He tried not to shiver as he stood in the chilly kitchen. The caretaker, Jean-Claude Auvieux, began to serve coffee for the two of them. Judge Verlaque glanced around the frugally furnished and spotless room, taking time to admire the perfectly preserved flagstone floor. A stove dominated the room—an old burgundy red La Cornue of the sort amateur chefs like Verlaque dreamed about. He would like to have one, with two ovens, at his home in Aix, but then he'd have to redesign his entire flat. He rubbed his big hands together and resisted the temptation to blow on them.

Auvieux turned away from the stove and spoke to Verlaque, as if sensing the judge's discomfort. "I'm sorry that it is so cold in here. I turned the heat off before I went away this weekend. It's warm enough during the day, but at night we still need to turn on the heat a bit, *non*? It will warm up soon." Auvieux was older than Verlaque, perhaps in his late forties, but his weathered face made him look even older. He was a huge man: tall and wide shouldered, with full lips and big brown eyes. He wore the usual dress for a Provençal in his line of work: blue overalls and a quilted green hunting vest.

"You've had a rough Sunday," said Verlaque, pulling out a wooden chair and sitting down without invitation. "What happened exactly?"

Auvieux looked down at the floor, and then back at Verlaque, whose dark eyes were staring at him. "Well . . . I found the body and called the police straightaway, and then—"

"Were you alone?" Verlaque interrupted. The caretaker froze; "Yes, I was," he answered. He kicked at some imaginary dust on the floor.

Verlaque sighed and said, "I realize that it must have been a terrible shock when you found Count de Bremont's body. I don't know if you were close to the count, but I know that you grew up here, with him and his family. Can you please tell me precisely what you did when you got back from the Var? Be as detailed as possible."

"I got back to Saint-Antonin around noon today," answered Auvieux, after a short pause. "Alone. I left my sister's house in the Var, near Cotignac, around ten thirty."

"I'll need your sister's name and address, for our records," Verlaque interrupted.

"Fine." Auvieux swallowed a bit, then breathed in and continued, "I parked my car beside the cottage, to the right of the château. The car is still there. I brought my suitcase inside and then began to prepare a lunch for myself."

"What exactly?" asked Verlaque.

"My lunch?" Auvieux stared at the judge for a few seconds, trying to understand the line of questioning, and then shrugged. He had long ago given up trying to understand people. Plants were so much easier. Verlaque, in fact, had already noticed a bowl full of strawberries and some thin green asparagus sitting on the counter, waiting for that night's dinner. When Auvieux opened the fridge to get the milk, Verlaque had quickly taken an inventory: eggs, a half-eaten goat's cheese, a salami wrapped in plastic, butter, mineral water, and white wine. Just about the same things that were in Verlaque's fridge at home. Minus the Pol Roger champagne. The caretaker finally answered, "Um, I fried a steak, an entrecôte, and I had a salad, a green salad. Plus two glasses of red wine. I buy the wine in bulk from the cooperative in Puyloubier. It's not bad, you know."

Verlaque smiled a warm, genuine smile. He knew that cooperative's wine, and the caretaker was right—for a wine that cost less than three euros a liter, it really wasn't bad. "What time did you finish eating?" Verlaque continued.

"Around two o'clock. After lunch I changed into my work clothes, and I took my walk—I like to walk after lunch, even a fifteen-minute walk is beneficial to the health. My sister saw a *reportage* on it. Fifteen minutes is all you need."

"Yes, that's what they say," Verlaque answered, starting to grow impatient again.

"And so I walked along there," continued Auvieux, gesturing with his hand toward the château, which could be seen from his kitchen window, "through the olive grove. I took a few minutes to check the trees—I'd cut them back in February. Count de Bremont, that is, Mr. Étienne's grandfather, used to tell me that the branches should be pruned enough so that one still had a clear view of montagne Sainte-Victoire through the trees."

At this point the caretaker stopped and looked at the judge, as if waiting for an answer.

"I've heard that too," Verlaque found himself saying. It took him a few seconds to realize that it was Marine who had told him, while clipping the olive tree on her terrace one sunny morning. There wasn't a view of the mountain from her downtown apartment, but in the early twentieth century there had been glorious views, before the tall apartment buildings were built on the outskirts of Aix, and so the expression had stuck. Verlaque remembered seeing Cézanne's many studies of the mountain, done from his studio located on a hill north of Aix. Today those views were hidden behind cube-shaped concrete apartment blocks. It seemed fitting to Verlaque that not only could Cézanne's mountain *not* be seen from the painter's studio, but the town itself now possessed only two or three small paintings by its famous son— arguably one of the most important painters in the history of art. Verlaque thought about Aix's small musée Granet, and tried to think if he remembered seeing a Cézanne painting there. The nineteenth-century Aixois had scoffed at the painter's work, it being too modern for their provincial tastes. The twenty-first-century Aixois still had the same conservative taste as their ancestors, Verlaque thought. Despite all the new, and old, money in Aix-en-Provence, today they still lacked the contemporary art galleries and modern restaurants that filled other cities, like Toulouse and Lille.

Verlaque looked out the window toward the château and suddenly asked, "Whose car is that with the Côte d'Azur plates?"

Auvieux leaned down so he could see out the small cottage window. He answered, "It's an old car of François's—François is Étienne's brother—he lives in the Riviera. He and Étienne shared it. They used the car for odd jobs or for driving into Aix."

"All right," Verlaque said. "Continue." Seeing the bewildered expression on the caretaker's face, Verlaque added, "You were in the olive grove."

"Ah, *merci*. So after about fifteen minutes in the olive grove, I walked behind the château, intending to go up into the pine forest to the south of the house. But just before I headed up the hill, I looked to my left and saw Mr. Étienne's body lying on the ground."

"So it was between two fifteen and two thirty. And that's when you called us?"

"Yes. I looked at the body, of course, but I didn't touch it—him. I knew he was dead. I ran back to my house and called 18 right away."

"What time did you leave Saint-Antonin on Friday?" Verlaque asked.

Auvieux sipped a bit of coffee before answering. "I left well before dinner, because my sister was making me a *blanquette de veau*. I left here at about five o'clock."

"And you didn't see anything unusual?"

The caretaker's body twitched and his eyes widened as he asked, "What do you mean?"

Verlaque noticed Auvieux's uneasiness. "Well," he replied, "I know that the police have already asked you if anything was missing. But did you notice anything out of place either before you left for the Var or when you got back?"

"No," the caretaker slowly replied.

"Have there been any break-ins at the château?"

The caretaker rubbed his hands together fretfully. "Only once, two years ago. Some kids from Marseille, three of them. They tried to break in through one of the shutters in the dining room. I heard the racket they were making and scared them off with my hunting rifle. I called Mr. Étienne the next day, and he had someone come out and repair the shutter."

Verlaque did not ask Auvieux how he knew that the kids were

from Marseille, but he could guess that the color of their skin had something to do with it.

As Verlaque got up to leave, he gestured toward the asparagus and strawberries. "Did you buy those at that roadside fruit stand on the *route nationale?*"

The guardian, wide-eyed, looked at the table and then at Verlaque, and answered, "Yes, on the way home."

"How is their produce?" Verlaque asked.

"Quite good!" the caretaker exclaimed. "And cheaper than at the market in downtown Aix."

Verlaque rolled his eyes up to the ceiling. "Yes, it's funny how the price of an apple at the Aix market is double the price of one in Gardanne." Gardanne was an old coal-mining town fifteen minutes south of Aix. The mine was closed, but the power plant's imposing chimney, now fired with coal from China, could be seen south of the highway as one approached Aix. It was an ugly, sinister town, and the buildings, and even some of the inhabitants, looked as if they always had a fine layer of soot shrouding them. Verlaque wasn't about to do his shopping there. In fact, he wasn't even sure about the prices—it was just what everyone in Aix said.

Now that they'd had their chat about food, Verlaque asked, "Did you like Étienne de Bremont?"

The caretaker seemed surprised by the question. "He was my boss."

"But," the judge continued, "did you like him?"

Auvieux looked down at the floor. "No, sir, to be honest with you. Not very much."

Verlaque saw that the caretaker was tired and overwhelmed. He finished his coffee and said good-bye, telling Auvieux that a team of policemen was still in the attic, inspecting, and when they had finished they would let him know so that he could lock up. "Should I come with you, Monsieur le Juge?" Auvieux offered.

"No, that won't be necessary, but thank you."

Auvieux asked the judge to make sure that his men didn't leave a mess, and that they turn off all the lights. Verlaque reassured him, and thanked him for his time and the good strong coffee.

As Verlaque walked back to the château, he thought that despite the family's obvious lack of funds the caretaker Auvieux took great pride in the estate and his work. He wished that some of the civil servants who worked at the Palais de Justice had the same attitude. He hadn't been the examining magistrate long—less than two years. He had in fact jumped from prosecutor to head district judge in record time and at an extremely young age—he had been thirty-nine years old at the time of his appointment. He was known as being incorruptible and was extremely well spoken—both in French and in English—and outspoken as well. Verlaque made it clear that in his new position he would be taking a hands-on role in the investigations, something examining magistrates were entitled to do, though they seldom took advantage. In July of that year he had been interviewed by various newspapers, including *Le Monde* and *Le Figaro*, and his portrait had appeared on the cover of the Marseille edition of *L'Express*. The oddest piece of publicity had come in the form of a short article in *Elle* magazine. A black-and-white photograph of the judge had been taken by an extremely popular young Czech photographer living in Paris. The photograph, shot from below, exaggerated Verlaque's already large shoulders and powerful chest, while disguising his paunch and the fact that he was only five foot eight. His dark brown eyes, almost black, stared directly at the camera; his hair, thick and black and streaked with gray, was—as it always was—disheveled. The photographer had said, "I love your nose, man." Verlaque, while at law school, played rugby for a club team at Château de Vincennes, and his nose had been broken and was still very crooked. During that game, he had knocked heads with another player in a scrum; that night, while studying a law case, he had the frightening realization that he could only read the bottom half of the text—the upper was black. The impaired vision lasted only a few hours, but it marked the end of his rugby playing. The editors at *Elle* had obviously not minded the crooked nose. The eventual article ran with the headline "We Surrender!" The sudden fame didn't suit him well, but the power given to examining magistrates did: the exclusive right to authorize searches and to issue subpoenas and wiretaps, the results of which could be used in criminal proceedings.

He pounded up the château's stone stairs and could hear some police officers laughing and chatting in the attic. It was a routine job for them—it appeared that the young count had fallen from a window and broken his neck. What Verlaque wanted to know was why Étienne de Bremont had been leaning out of the window in the first place—he had met Bremont a few times and had liked and respected him. He felt that he owed it to the count, and to his wife and children, to thoroughly inspect the place where he met his death. The judge had also detected Jean-Claude Auvieux's anxiety under questioning: his slow, nervous pauses when asked if anything had been disturbed in the château.

The policemen's chattering immediately stopped when Verlaque entered the attic. It was late afternoon, and the sunlight shining through the window was fading. "Why hasn't anyone turned on the lights?" he asked no one in particular.

One of the policemen answered back, "They're burnt out, sir."

Verlaque crossed the room and smiled when he saw *le commissaire*. Verlaque had been away for the past six months—a month in Luxembourg with the European Court, a month's holiday in England, and a four-month research sabbatical in Paris—and although he had only worked with the commissioner once or twice, Bruno Paulik was one of his favorite colleagues, a no-nonsense man with a thick Midi accent. Paulik was full of contradictions—he was born to farming parents in a small village in the Luberon, was now one of Aix's best detectives, and was an opera buff. His wife, Hélène, was the head winemaker for a prestigious, privately owned winery north of Aix. Paulik normally took a full-week's holiday during the Aix opera festival, and his nine-year-old daughter was already an accomplished singer at Aix's prestigious music conservatory. Paulik was also a former rugby player and, like Verlaque, had an undying love for the game.

"Hello, Commissaire," Verlaque said, holding out his hand.

"Welcome back, sir." The commissioner's smile then turned to a perplexed frown. "You haven't already received the prosecutor's dossier, have you? She only just left."

"Simone Levy from Marseille? Is Roussel still away?"

"Yeah, he's still on holiday, but he's due back any day."

Verlaque tried to hide his disappointment at missing the striking prosecutor Levy from Marseille, but also at the news that Roussel, Aix's prosecutor, would be back soon. "An inquest was formally requested by the family about an hour ago, so here I am."

"Ah," Paulik replied. "The widow?"

"Actually, no. Charles and Eric Bley, the deceased's first cousins."

"The lawyers Bley? Ah, I didn't realize they were related to the Bremonts. So did Bremont's widow cosign the request?"

"No, she refused," Verlaque answered, raising an eyebrow. He surveyed the room. "Anything?"

"Nothing, Judge," Paulik answered. "The area in front of the window has recently been swept; the caretaker told me he sweeps and dusts up here often. In fact, we had trouble getting rid of him; he was following me around like a lost sheep."

Verlaque noticed the broom propped in a corner. "Make sure you get that dusted for prints."

"I've already told them to. So far we haven't found any signs of a disturbance. The attic door was wide open, and the key to the door was sitting here on this suitcase. We're getting the fingerprints off it. The caretaker has given us one of his keys, and I've told him not to let anyone in."

"Good," said Verlaque, glancing down at the suitcase. It was a vintage Louis Vuitton, probably from the 1930s, with a label from the Ritz Hotel in London still attached to it and the name Comte Philippe de Bremont written in black ink across the tag. Philippe de Bremont would have been the dead man's grandfather, Verlaque thought—the man the caretaker had spoken of.

"Quite a room isn't it, sir? They have more stuff in here than I do in my whole house," Paulik said, looking around the attic and rubbing his bald head at the same time.

"The French nobility aren't so bad off as they want us to believe, *hein*?" Verlaque asked, trying to joke. He did not like the police officers to know that he came from money, although it was fairly obvious since not many judges, who were after all civil servants, could afford to drive an antique Porsche and eat out almost every night. But he didn't come from nobility—far from it.

Paulik didn't reply but was busy frowning and leaning out of the open window. The commissioner was humming what Verlaque believed to be an opera aria, but Verlaque's knowledge of opera was embarrassingly nonexistent. Paulik stopped humming and told the other officers they could leave the attic. He then frowned and asked the judge, "Do you think that Bremont could have lost his footing and fallen through that opening?"

Verlaque shook his head back and forth. "Not very possible—he grew up here. He must have opened that window thousands of times. That's what Eric Bley told me on the phone and why he and his brother asked for the inquest. What's your theory?"

Paulik considered before answering. "He could have been pushed, but there are no signs of struggle. Or he was taken by surprise—it could have happened in seconds." Then he added, "If there was a struggle, the mess may have been cleaned up. Suicide?"

"Suicide seems unlikely from what I know of the count, but we'll need to ask those uncomfortable questions of his family members. Both of the Bleys thought it highly unlikely. Besides, Bremont's glasses were found next to his body. Wouldn't you take off your glasses if you were going to jump?" Verlaque asked, and he grabbed his reading glasses, which had been hanging permanently from his neck since he was in his early thirties.

Paulik nodded and replied, "Yeah, I see what you mean. It's like those suicides on the Mediterranean. The distressed will carefully fold their clothes and leave everything in a neat pile on the shore, and then quietly walk into the sea."

Both men stayed silent for a few seconds, each one lost in thought. Verlaque then finally said, "As for theft, the caretaker did a thorough check of the château and everything seems to be in place. Talk to him tomorrow and get a second report, just in case. I've already talked to him. We'll need to go visit his sister in the Var. As I understand it, they both grew up here."

"And the count's brother?" Paulik asked. Verlaque silently

noted that Paulik, as usual, had done his homework before visiting the accident scene.

"François de Bremont is expected tomorrow," answered the judge. "Let me know as soon as he arrives—he was sailing off the coast of Corsica and will be driving here from Toulon."

"What about Count de Bremont's work? Could he have made an enemy during the filming of one of his documentaries?"

Étienne de Bremont had made his name as a filmmaker. He'd shown several documentaries at festivals over the past five years, including one that focused on organized crime in Provence. It was during the production of that film that Verlaque first made his acquaintance.

Verlaque thought of the film and the earnest young man behind the camera. He remembered Étienne de Bremont, from their interviews together, as tall and thin, with jet-black hair that always seemed a little greasy. For each of the interviews, Bremont had been wearing one of those safari-type vests that *National Geographic* photographers seem to prefer. Verlaque thought it was a little *curieux*, until the interview began and Bremont's sincere gray eyes didn't, for a second, leave Verlaque's face. Bremont had delicately posed his questions to Verlaque, who in turn answered as truthfully as he could without pointing fingers. The director and the judge both knew that high crime in the Marseille area had its origins in Corsica, but there was little either of them could, or was willing, to say. Verlaque had liked the film very much. It was stunningly photographed, in a light so bright that it made the viewer uncomfortable, which Verlaque thought suited the Corsican Mafia and the criminal world in general. The judge's prejudices about noble gentlemen with no serious professions, only titles, had lessened after his three interviews with

Bremont, and especially after seeing the documentary, which had just won an award earlier that year.

He answered Paulik's question: "It's possible. Send one of the other officers, perhaps Flamant, to talk to the CEO of the film production company he worked for, Souleiado Films. They're in a renovated factory in the Belle de Mai neighborhood in Marseille. On second thought, why don't you head down there yourself tomorrow morning?"

Paulik shook his head. "Sorry, sir. I can't. I'm testifying in court tomorrow and Tuesday."

"Merde. All right. Well, it's not urgent. Later in the week will be fine."

The two men were jolted out of their respective thoughts when they heard a pair of hurried footsteps on the stairs leading to the attic, and a young officer rushed into the room. Verlaque had seen the red-haired, freckle-faced youth around police headquarters, but his name escaped him.

The young officer let out a long and weary "*Putain!*" as he mopped his brow with the back of his hand. He then, to his horror, saw his superior officer and the *juge d'instruction*, and apologized for his six-letter word. "Sorry, Judge, but there's a bunch of reporters gathering outside the front door."

"Tell them I'll be right down to give my statement," Verlaque told the youngster.

On his way out, the young officer dropped his notebook and pen on the stairs, swearing again as he picked them up. Paulik, trying unsuccessfully to hide his smile, coughed and asked the judge, "What *is* our statement, sir?"

Verlaque shrugged. "Death from an accidental fall. That's what the coroner has said, and until I can talk to Bremont's wife and find out why he was up here on a Saturday night, that's all we can say." He then added, "If you're through in here, we can leave and lock the door."

"Yes, sir."

The two men locked the attic door and headed downstairs, passing bedrooms that had already been inspected by Paulik and his team. On the ground floor, Verlaque turned to the commissioner before opening the front door and asked, "Are there any rooms in this place that *have* been used in the past decade?"

"The library, and a first-floor bedroom that has an adjoining bath. That's about it. The library is through the salon, in the rear of the château."

"Let's have a look. The reporters can bloody well wait." The salon's furniture was covered, not with fresh white sheets like those that now protected Verlaque's grandmother's furniture, but with psychedelic flowered sheets—no doubt itchy polyester, thought Verlaque—that were the rage in France in the 1970s. Verlaque winced when he realized why he hated those sheets—he hadn't thought of Aude in months—and his mood turned sour.

Double doors opened into the library, its shelves covering two walls. The books were a mixture of leather-bound editions of classics, in French, English, Russian, and German, and thousands of paperbacks, in English and French, most of them murder mysteries and westerns.

"What's in the desk?" Verlaque asked.

"Almost nothing, sir. Some paper and pencils, tape, a stapler. No documents."

"A safe?"

"No, sir."

Verlaque approached the desk. A small collection of silver-framed photographs sat on its polished wooden surface. "This room is spotless, and the silver frames shine. Who cleans this room?"

"The caretaker, sir. I noticed the lack of dust and asked him about it. He told me that he insists on cleaning the library himself, while a young girl from the village comes in to clean the rest of the rooms whenever François de Bremont is in residence, which is only a few times a year and at Christmas."

Verlaque leaned down and put his reading glasses on. "The old couple in this picture taken in front of the house, they must be the grandparents?"

"Yes, Philippe and Clothilde de Bremont. In the next photo, taken in the 1970s judging by the guy's wide tie and her hair, are the parents of Étienne and François de Bremont, both dead now as well."

"And the third photo, the brothers in their teens, perhaps fifteen and seventeen it looks like," Verlaque stated. "I recognize Étienne de Bremont as the skinny guy on the left. The handsome one with the big shoulders and wide toothy grin looks like a Kennedy. That must be François. And who is the girl in the middle? I thought there were only the two sons."

"You're right. There was no mention of a daughter in the report. It must be a cousin or a girlfriend."

Verlaque leaned in closer to look at the laughing girl, her thick auburn hair a mess, her green eyes sparkling, and a slender freckled arm around each of the boys' shoulders. Verlaque began to smile, despite himself. "Take a closer look at the girl," he said to Paulik. "I think we both know her."

Verlaque looked away from the photograph and walked over to a shelf that held a collection of leather-bound editions of French classics. His eyes glazed over as he scanned the titles, and he realized that he would call her as soon as he could, in fact as soon as he stepped out of this cold old house. She had made him smile and laugh—not many women could do that. He had been comfortable with her. A few nights ago a mutual friend had told him that she was now seeing an overly handsome young doctor, and he felt a pain in his stomach that he had never had in connection with a woman before. At first it had been easy, with work and travel, and his nose buried in law books in Paris for four months, to ignore her absence, and he knew from experience that the desire would, with time, disappear. But instead of forgetting about her, as he had so easily done with other lovers, he found himself thinking of her more and more. The poetry didn't help, nor did the whiskey. One evening, late, he had walked across town to her apartment and rung the bell, but there was no answer.

"*Ah bon?*" Paulik too leaned in and looked. "Since you say we both know her, she must still live in Aix," Paulik said as he looked at the girl. She was laughing despite her picture being taken— and he could almost hear her infectious laugh. Then it clicked. "It's Professor Bonnet, *non?*" Marine Bonnet, always one to shake up the conservative law faculty at Aix's university, loved to invite guest speakers into her classroom, and Verlaque remembered that one of her most well-received guests had been the commissioner. Paulik had enjoyed speaking to her class and thought it hilarious that the law students had gathered around him afterward as if he were a rock star. Verlaque and Marine had also been invited to a dinner hosted by Hélène Paulik's vintner-boss, and the Pauliks had been briefly present. They left early, Hélène feigning an oncoming flu, though the real reason was Bruno Paulik's uneasiness about being at a social event with his boss, the examining magistrate.

"Yes, I think it's Marine. I'm going to phone her and tell her to come up here tomorrow morning. She obviously knows—or knew—the family intimately."

Paulik raised an eyebrow at the suggestion that a layperson, even a law professor, would be invited to the scene of the accident, but he said nothing. Verlaque noticed his expression and shot the *commissaire* a look over his reading glasses. "I'm the examining magistrate and can invite whoever the bloody hell I want up here. Now," he said, changing the conversation, since he realized that he was in a foul mood for other reasons—the flowered sheets. "Let's deal with the reporters out there. The poor sods have been pulled away from their pastis-filled Sunday barbecues."

"Yes, sir." Paulik respected Verlaque and pretended not to hear when other policemen in Aix called him a snob and an elitist. The judge was thorough and had an encyclopedic knowledge of the law, and although Paulik was very confident in his own knowledge, after each case with Verlaque he came away with new insights. They worked well together, and he knew that the judge felt the same way: Verlaque wasn't afraid of criminals or of sitting up for hours questioning them, nor was Paulik, whose intimidating physical appearance usually got him respect from the accused. Verlaque didn't waste time with Paulik, making off-color jokes or referring the women as *poulettes*. So what if Verlaque drove an expensive car and drank fine wines? But his comment about barbecues *was* a slight directed at another man's enjoyment, and Paulik didn't like it—for he too had been called away from a family lunch in the Luberon, complete with pastis and a barbecue.

Chapter Two

⁊

*T*he bells at Saint-Jean-de-Malte had already started ringing, as they did each morning at 7:50. In the past the bells served as a warning to churchgoers that they had ten minutes to get to mass. Marine now used them as an alarm to help get herself out of the apartment on time—off to the university or, if she had a late class, to her favorite café.

When the bells had finally stopped their pealing and she was dressed, Marine opened her bedroom windows and a gust of wind blew in, whipping around the room the pages of the newspaper she had been reading. She leaned out and fastened the shutters against the outer stone wall. The wind temporarily died down, and she looked up at the four stone creatures that jutted out from the corners of Saint-Jean-de-Malte's medieval tower. They hung on to the church by their rear claws, the rest of their bodies reaching out into the sky, poised to spring away from their foundations at any moment. Marine worried about them sometimes—especially during the mistral, which had started blowing in the middle of the night. Eight hundred years of hanging on—and in an instant the gargoyles could be gone, shattered in a heap on the cobbled square below. Satisfied that the stone creatures were safe, Marine noticed that her neighbor across the courtyard had just opened her shutters and windows too. And before Marine could duck out of the way, Philomène Joubert yelled, across the fifty meters that separated them, and through the blowing wind, "*Coucou,* Mlle Bonnet!" Not waiting for an answer from Marine, Mme Joubert—or Mme Saint-Jean-de-Malte, as Marine secretly called her, for she'd been a member of the church's choir since Marine was a little girl—continued to yell as she quickly hung her laundry from wires suspended below her apartment windows.

"This wind would blow the hair off a bald man!" Mme Joubert shouted, and then laughed heartily. Marine smiled and waited for the line she knew would come next. "Although it doesn't blow as much as it used to when I was a girl! I can remember having to be pushed up rue de l'Opéra by my mother—the wind was that strong! But the weather is changing, you know. It's that climate change they're calling it! But it will dry our laundry quickly all the same, won't it, Mademoiselle?" Marine nodded furiously this time and got in an "Ah oui!" But before she could add anything else the old woman had finished her hanging, said good-bye, and popped her head back inside, closing her windows with a well-practiced bang. Mme Joubert had obviously never noticed that Marine seldom hung laundry outside—she had cheated and installed a clothes dryer when she renovated the apartment. She used the excuse that she didn't have time to hang her laundry, but she hated housework and was too embarrassed to hire a maid. Mme Joubert, on the other hand, was so organized that she did her washing by category. Today was nightgown and pajama day, and there they were: six pairs of men's cotton pajamas and three or four almost-transparent white nighties, hanging in a row. Tomorrow was what? Maybe tea towel day. Marine had never really been taught how to keep house and believed that while other women all knew the secrets of laundry, wood polishing, and ironing, she was the only one left in the dark. Mme Joubert's system seemed like an organizational nightmare to Marine. Did she have seven or eight laundry baskets, one for each type of garment?

Marine looked down at the almond tree, which was beginning to flower, and breathed a sigh of relief that she bought the apartment when prices were still reasonable and Aix-en-Provence wasn't yet known as "the twenty-first arrondissement of Paris." She had lived here for over ten years. Still, somehow she couldn't help but associate Antoine Verlaque with the apartment, as if he had been here for ten years as well, and not just one. He'd enjoyed the time he'd spent here, of that she was fairly certain. After six months of dating, he had moved most of his clothes over, although he'd kept his loft on the other side of Aix. And so if the two hadn't officially lived together, they had shared some wonderful moments in this apartment: the long summer dinners on the terrace, mesmerized by the church's illuminated steeple, and sitting in front of winter fires in the living room, while Antoine smoked a cigar and they drank Armagnac and argued law—or anything. He used to rub my tummy, she thought, even when we argued.

Marine cursed to herself, out loud this time. She had spent too long looking out onto the courtyard and would now have less time for coffee with Sylvie and other friends at Le Mazarin, their preferred café, named for the elegant eighteenth-century neighborhood she lived in. She grabbed her purse, keys, and briefcase and made for the front door, only to turn around, unplug her cell phone from its charger, and throw it into her purse. Locking the door behind her, she skipped down the three flights of steps to the street below, saying good morning to the street cleaner,

Sami, who washed her street every morning at eight fifteen. Sami said hello and then pretended to chase her heels with the water hose, and she ran away giggling. It was their morning routine, and it made both of them laugh every time, and for that she was grateful.

She walked quickly up the rue Frédéric Mistral and paused, as she always did, when she got to the cours Mirabeau, Aix's celebrated main street. One hundred years ago double rows of plane trees had been planted on both sides of the street, and by summer they would shade the sidewalks and the street itself. But the *cours* had been in a state of construction, or "deconstruction," as Sylvie, Marine's best friend, a photographer and art historian, liked to say. No sooner was the top of the street completed than the workmen would start jackhammering the bottom, and then someone at city hall would change his or her mind and the bottom would be hurriedly finished so the construction team could tear up the newly finished work at the top. This had been going on for four years, and Marine had overheard one American tourist say to her husband, "I just can't get a good picture of the street from any angle!" Marine wanted to tell the woman that it was a good thing she hadn't seen the *cours* this past Christmas, when the city's new mayor, Yvette Tamain, had allowed a private company—owned by her brother-in-law—to line one side of it with Alsatian-style wooden chalets. It might have been a good idea if the chalets had sold handmade Christmas objects, like at the winter festival in Strasbourg. But instead each chalet was tackier than the next, full of mass-produced objects that could've been found at any carnival. Sylvie had been furious, and Marine had had to walk a bit ahead of her, embarrassed at her friend's loud string of profanities, mostly aimed at the mayor. The showstopper, and where Marine had stopped, openmouthed, and begun to swear as well—although not as loudly or as profanely as Sylvie—was a large, orange, plastic kiddie slide that had been parked at the top of the *cours*. It completely blocked the view of the fabulous sixteenth-century goldenstone mansion, the Hôtel du Poët. While Sylvie marched off to yell at the proprietors of the plastic slide, Marine walked over and looked up at the statue of King René, Aix's beloved medieval ruler, smiling and holding a cluster of grapes in his hand, thankfully unaware of the changes the good mayor Tamain was making to his fine city.

This morning the *cours* seemed strangely quiet: the construction workers had not yet begun their noisy work, and there were fewer cars on the road than usual. Marine ran across the wide avenue, holding down her skirt in the wind, and happy to see her favorite café. Cafés lined the west side of the street, where they received the morning sun, and banks and estate agents occupied the east side—one side gave you pleasure, the other side was interested only in your money. She walked across Le Mazarin's terrace, pulled open the heavy wooden door, and was greeted by the café's interior—its burnt ocher walls, the black-and-white tiled floor covered with a light carpet of sawdust, the long wooden bar with its dented copper countertop. Le Mazarin was her morning's delight, and it had been even when she was with Antoine. She loved the smoky, noisy room that smelled of espresso and was filled with people who wanted to be in the company of others before their day began. To start the day there was, she knew, a pleasure and a privilege, one that could be enjoyed by only those who had flexible schedules or were lucky enough to work in downtown Aix. But today there was something wrong, and she noticed it instantly. Inside, the café was unusually hushed, just as it had been out on the street—the waiters whispered to clients, instead of barking at them, and her friends, already seated at their corner table, weren't noisily arguing about European politics or the Marseille soccer team.

"What's going on?" asked Marine, when she got to the table scattered with croissant crumbs, thick porcelain coffee cups, cigarette packages, cell phones, and newspapers. Marine glanced at the table and at her two best friends and smiled. I am lucky, she thought.

"You haven't heard, then?" replied Jean-Marc, a fellow lawyer. He took Marine's arm, guiding her to a chair beside his own.

"Heard what?" Marine repeated.

"About Étienne de Bremont," answered Sylvie, taking a huge drag on her cigarette and looking smug. "Nice hair, by the way." Marine looked at herself in the mirror on the opposite wall and saw that the mistral had given her hair a vertical touch. She flattened it with her hands, put down her purse, and looked at Sylvie and then at Jean-Marc. "No, I haven't heard. What is it?" she asked, despite the answer that she feared was coming.

"He's dead," whispered Jean-Marc, who seemed to have been chosen as the spokesperson for the morning's bad news. Sylvie raised her eyebrows to an impossible height, expertly flicked her ash into the ashtray, and crossed her well-toned arms across her breasts.

Jean-Marc continued, leaning even closer to Marine. "He fell from one of Château Bremont's windows, sometime late Saturday night or early Sunday morning. His body was only found yesterday, when the caretaker came home from a weekend visiting his sister, Colette, Cosette, Yvette—something like that."

Marine looked toward the large oil painting on the wall, a nineteenth-century portrait of an unknown male sitter. "How horrible, horrible," were the only words that managed to get out of her mouth. "Cosette," she suddenly said. "Cosette is the sister's name." She hadn't thought of Étienne in a long time and couldn't believe that he was dead. She stared down at the grain of the wooden table.

"Had you seen him recently?" asked Sylvie, who hadn't grown up in Aix but had met Étienne. She loved gossip of this sort, especially bad news.

Marine thought of the young Étienne de Bremont—the Bremont family was one of Aix's oldest noble families. Étienne and Marine used to play for hours in the château while their mothers worked together on church projects. And then later, in high school, Marine and Étienne had labored over the small newspaper that served their two respective schools—the sexes were still separated in those days. Sincere, dedicated, careful Étienne—he had driven Marine nuts over fussy details. But she had enjoyed his quiet enthusiasm, and they had made a good team that spring: he the writer and she the researcher. Étienne's older brother was always around as well, but Marine had always thought François a bully, and she tried to avoid him when she could.

Étienne had moved away for university. He had become a filmmaker and now lived—no, he's dead—had lived with his wife and small children in a faded but very elegant mansion, *un hôtel particulier*, on the cours Mirabeau. The family also owned the crumbling château in the hamlet of Saint-Antonin, just east of Aix. Poor Étienne, she thought. His poor children.

She looked up from her coffee and realized that Jean-Marc and Sylvie were staring at her, waiting for her to respond. "No, I haven't seen him for ages. What happened?" Marine asked.

"Antoine was out there yesterday, and he's there again this

morning. He called me to cancel a meeting we had planned. All he told me was that it appears to have been an accident—nothing was disturbed in the attic where he fell from or in the rest of the château."

"If it was an accident, why was Antoine called? Isn't that a job for the police?" Marine asked. She was annoyed that Verlaque had already called Jean-Marc. He wouldn't bother to call her, but he would call Jean-Marc. Perhaps Verlaque didn't know that Marine was an old friend of the Bremont family. She knew from Jean-Marc that Antoine had been back in Aix for two weeks now, his sabbatical in Paris over. But still he hadn't called her.

Jean-Marc didn't let on that he noticed Marine's voice crack when she said Antoine's name aloud. "Eric and Charles Bley have asked for a formal investigation."

"You're kidding?"

"No. Procureur Roussel is in Scotland, golfing. He's due back any day now. Procureur Levy came from Marseille and went to the château to inspect, but as soon as Antoine received the family's request, he went up."

"Wait a minute! Fill me in a bit, would you? Why didn't the prosecutor stay? And who are these Bley guys?" Sylvie asked, looking back and forth between Marine and Jean-Marc.

"The Bleys are first cousins of Étienne," Marine answered. "They're both lawyers."

"The prosecutor is always the first official, with the commissioner, on the accident scene, but if an investigation request is made by the family, the examining magistrate immediately enters the picture," Jean-Marc added.

"Thanks," Sylvie replied. "Next question: why did they name the château after the family? That's completely bogus."

Marine sighed. "It's just always been called that, Sylvie. It's unusual, I'll admit. But the château has been in the Bremont family since it was built, in the seventeenth century, I think."

"Still bogus."

"It's awful, isn't it, a sudden death?" Jean-Marc said, looking from Marine to Sylvie, hoping to distract Sylvie from one of her antinobility tirades. "I didn't know Étienne, but I liked his work. Did you ever see the documentary he made on crime in Provence, the one where he interviewed Antoine?"

Sylvie shot a worried look across to Marine, as if again the mention of Antoine Verlaque's name would reduce Marine to tears. Marine returned her glance with a determined gaze: no tears, Sylvie, don't worry.

"Yes, I did see it, I showed it to my third-year class," Marine answered, not mentioning that she had actually taped it and watched it alone about a dozen times, for it had been released just after Antoine ended their relationship. She and Sylvie had also watched it, together, and had picked the film to shreds, critiquing every aspect of Verlaque's "performance," with the help of a half bottle of whiskey. Marine looked across the table and saw the huge grin on Sylvie's face and tried not to laugh. "It was a good film, and a realistic one," she said. Sylvie snorted.

Jean-Marc nodded sincerely, and Marine remembered how it had irked her to see her normally sensible female law students swoon over the bewitching new examining magistrate of Aix. No, Verlaque wasn't classically handsome—he was short and thick, with a tummy that revealed his love of food and wine, but he had dark intense eyes and was fully aware of his power of seduction— and he was very young to be one of the most powerful judges in the south of France. Marine had answered her students' questions about Verlaque as best she could, explaining to her criminal law class the responsibilities of the judge, who, according to French law, advises the commissioner of police regarding crimes and their examination. She tried to sound as indifferent as possible, not revealing the fact that they had been lovers. In fact, it was easy not to let on that she knew Verlaque intimately, because there wasn't much to reveal—despite almost a year of dating, what did she really know about him? She often thought that the real Antoine could be found lurking around a certain villa in Normandy, where he used to spend all his vacations with his English-born grandmother. The real Verlaque certainly wasn't in Aix.

"Speak of the devil," Jean-Marc whispered, as he looked up from his coffee. Marine froze, her hand trembling so much that she had to set down her *café crème*. She stared at the thick white porcelain cup and held it tightly, as if the cup itself could give her strength and keep her centered. She slowly lifted up her eyes and looked at Sylvie, who had a seat against the wall, with a full view of the café, but the look on Sylvie's face revealed nothing. Marine then heard her name, and the speaker was not Antoine Verlaque. Her whole body relaxed, her shoulders falling. At that point Sylvie noticed her friend's anxiety and reached out and quickly tapped her hand, smiling.

"Hallo, Marine. Hallo, Jean-Marc." Marine turned around and saw Eric Bley. She had gone to primary and secondary school with the Bleys—all eleven of them—and Eric and Charles Bley had their law practice on, she was fairly certain, the rue Thiers. She quickly got up and embraced Eric Bley, whom Sylvie was just as quickly assessing: thick, premature gray hair; the wide shoulders of someone who worked out; designer clothes but with a touch of originality—a big red Paul Smith watch instead of the Rolex that other wealthy men usually wore. Condolences were made, and Sylvie was introduced.

"You've heard that we requested an inquest?" Eric asked, looking at Marine. Marine nodded, and was about to speak, when Eric quickly went on, "There's no way Étienne just *fell* out of that window!" He realized that he had spoken too loudly, and looked over his shoulder as if to apologize. But the other Mazarin patrons just went on quietly drinking their coffees and reading their papers. If they had heard, no one acknowledged it. He sighed, running his hands though his hair—the hair that Sylvie was still admiring—and then said, "I'm sorry about that. I've been going over and over it . . . The attic . . . Étienne. You remember it, don't you Marine?" Again, before she could answer, he said, "How could Étienne have just fallen? No. No!"

The espresso machine let out a piercing cry, as if a steam train had been parked next to their table, and Eric Bley looked at his giant watch and mumbled good-bye, walking so quickly out of the café that he almost ran into a waiter who was balancing a tray of coffees and orange juices.

"Funny," Marine said, wincing a bit, "that's a sound we hear a dozen times a day, but today it seems too loud."

"Yes, today it's annoying," Jean-Marc replied, lifting his black judicial robe off of the chair beside him and throwing it over his shoulder. "Are you in court today?" asked Marine, seeing the robe.

"All week," Jean-Marc replied. "Well, time to go and start the day. Ciao, ciao."

"Good-bye," said Marine, giving Jean-Marc a kiss on each cheek—the *bises*. Marine got up to go as well; she had a class in thirty minutes. "Here, tonight," she whispered into Sylvie's ear. Sylvie's big smile was an affirmative response, and while lighting another cigarette, already poised in her mouth, with her free hand she gave Marine the universal "I'll call you later" signal—her extended index and baby fingers held up to her left ear.

Marine crossed Le Mazarin's terrace and headed south on the rue du 4 Septembre toward the *faculté*, the same route she took every day. Only today Marine knew she wouldn't see Isabelle de Bremont, on her way back from school or the market, with her children in tow. The Bremonts, like other good young Catholic families, seemed to have hordes of children, and Marine remembered at least four—one just school age, a set of three-year-old twins who were always running in opposite directions, and a baby. Although the two women moved in very different social circles, Isabelle always stopped when she saw Marine, and they would take the time to give each other the *bises*. Marine thought about the life of Isabelle and the children, and how from now on it would never be the same.

A young girl walked around Marine, busily chatting on her cell phone while managing to navigate the cobblestone sidewalk in heels at least six inches high. Marine realized she hadn't turned on her own phone yet this morning. When she pressed the on button, the phone began to ring at once with one recorded message: "It's me. Call me as soon as you get this message."

Antoine Verlaque never bothered to say his name when he called Marine, or when he called other people for that matter. She wondered if he introduced himself when he called people on court business. Did he assume that he was the only male between the ages of thirty and forty who would leave a message on Marine's phone? But he had always been more polite to men than to women—at least, Marine had sensed, more comfortable with them. Sylvie had gone so far as to suggest that Verlaque was gay: her final proof, and one she loved to dwell on—as if she were the only one in the world to have thought of it—was the fact that Verlaque had been privately schooled *en pension*. Marine would then jump to Verlaque's defense: she did not accept the theory that men who attended boarding schools grew up to be frustrated homosexuals; his unwillingness, or uneasiness, in sharing his emotions with a woman, Marine thought, must be due to his strict upbringing or perhaps some drama in his past—he had once hinted at a tragic incident, on the night after his grandmother died, but Marine had never been able to get him to tell her the details.

The man she had been recently dating, an intern eight years her junior, who worked at the hospital with her father, was unusually kind and considerate, at times annoyingly so. Arthur was the opposite of Verlaque in every way. Where Verlaque commanded, Arthur questioned, unable to decide, as if he had no preferences. "Wet" is how Sylvie had described him. Marine tried to remember if Sylvie had ever liked anyone she had dated, and yet Sylvie's own track record with men was dismal. Marine defended Arthur in the same way that she had defended Verlaque: they had a good time together; she enjoyed Arthur's stories of working at the hospital, which were so different from her work as a university professor. She was physically attracted to Arthur as well, but it was not the same wild lust that she'd had for Verlaque: she was embarrassed by how much she had enjoyed sex with the judge, and how often, even now, she thought about it—she had always assumed that intellectually she was above such basic emotions. She had recently read an article, in a copy of *Paris Match* at her dentist's office, about an aged film star who described his on-again, off-again, long-term relationship with his girlfriend as "an obsession" and said that even after thirty years of dating they still "went at it like twenty-year-olds." She had felt herself blushing and quickly put the magazine down, thankful when the dentist's white-jacketed assistant poked her head around the door and called her name.

She walked on toward the university, preparing herself for the call. She dialed his number, and he answered immediately.

"Where are you?" he asked.

No "hello, how are you?" she thought. Her hands began to shake.

"I'm just in front of the law school," Marine answered.

"I need to see you," Verlaque demanded, sounding out of breath.

"I have a class until eleven thirty," Marine answered, trying to be as curt as he was. She thought she was doing a good job. She was pleased.

"Come out to the Bremont château after that."

Marine was shocked. "Why?"

"Didn't you hear about Étienne de Bremont?" Verlaque asked. The tone of his voice made it clear that Verlaque thought only an idiot wouldn't have heard about the death. What if she hadn't gone to Le Mazarin and instead had gone straight to the university?

"Well, yes, this morning at the office," Marine answered. Her friends used to joke that her office was at the Mazarin café—the university had very little funding, and only very ancient professors had their own offices. But even just mentioning the café, and referring to it by its pet name, made her feel better. She went on, "Jean-Marc told me that Étienne fell from one of the attic windows."

"I want you to come and look around the place," Verlaque interrupted. "You played up here, didn't you, as kids? I saw a photograph of you and the two sons in the château's library."

Marine wasn't sure if this was another of Antoine's slight jabs pointed at her privileged, very conservative Catholic upbringing. His was a very different *enfance*, a childhood that despite lots of, loads of, family money would never have included an invitation to play at the Bremont's château.

"Yes, I was friends with the boys, mostly Étienne though. I do remember parts of the house, and the attic," she answered. "But why should *I* come up?" Marine did not want to see the château again, especially now, a day after her friend had died there. And did she want to see Verlaque? She wasn't sure.

"I'll explain more when you come up. See you at noon." He hung up.

The law school bells rang out, and Marine felt overcome by noises—bells, espresso machines, chattering students. She walked into the doors of the *faculté*, through a cloud of student cigarette smoke, feeling dazed but thankful that she had only one class, a first-year course on French legal history that she could probably teach with her eyes shut. But she would keep them open and force herself to concentrate on the twenty or so pairs of eyes that would be looking up at her—some fascinated, some bored, some wondering where they would eat lunch. Because if she closed her eyes, even for a moment, she would start thinking of Étienne and the Bremont family, and of her childhood, and Antoine Verlaque—whom she would be seeing in two hours, after an absence of six months.

Despite herself, Marine's hands trembled as she turned to the first page of her notes. She began to write the date of the court case on the blackboard and stopped, looking at her shaky, spindly scrawl. She erased the letters and turned around to face the students. "Close your books. There will be no need to take notes today." She sat on the edge of her desk, facing the students, who now looked wide awake and eager. Some even smiled. "This is the fascinating case of Marie-Pierre Bessone, found stabbed to death meters away from her barge on the canal du Midi in July 1882. The murder was never solved."

Chapter Three

❧

Marine had considered calling Verlaque back and canceling, but her natural curiosity had gotten the better of her. She also felt that she owed it to Étienne. Her eyes filled with tears, and she tried to keep them on the winding road, but she couldn't stop thinking of her childhood friend. In her head they were always twelve, thirteen, fourteen years old and never adults, a law professor and filmmaker. They had been inseparable during those years. They loved to argue, and discussed anything—food preferences, the best soccer teams, current politics—politics as their young minds understood it. While many of their classmates, including Étienne's brother, François, were already experimenting with smoking and sex, she and Étienne still climbed trees and played war games. If they were aware of their slow, innocent development, neither of them mentioned it to the other. They knew only one other youth who was not trying to race on to adulthood—Jean-Claude—and he would sometimes join their games. He did, because of his size, make a good prison-camp guard, and he could be convinced at times, with promises of stolen food, to play this role. Marine remembered sticking up for Jean-Claude—not specific scenes, just a general impression that now, for some reason, in the car on an April morning, stuck in her mind. Étienne had always treated Jean-Claude as though he was hired help. Marine had never felt that way toward Jean-Claude, nor his mother, and although Mme Auvieux cooked and ran the household, it was obvious to Marine, even as a child, that the Auvieux were treated as part of the Bremont family. Jean-Claude and his sister even attended their school, La Nativité, instead of the free village school down the hill in Beaurecueil. She realized now that it must have been the Bremonts who paid the fees for Cosette's and Jean-Claude's textbooks and uniforms.

Étienne, whose German was quite good, taught Jean-Claude some keys phrases and insisted he yell orders in that language, while Marine and Étienne spoke French with broken Anglo accents, pretending to be American or English or Australian. After a few months of being instructed about what to say and do, and being bossed around by Étienne, Jean-Claude abandoned the games and returned to the garden.

Étienne had only once made a pass at her—when they were eighteen and celebrating their high school graduation, with the aid of cans of cider. She did not return his kiss but had been gentle with him: Étienne had been more like a brother to her, never a love interest. She knew that Étienne was disappointed and embarrassed. From that day on they gradually drifted apart, as if the magic innocence of childhood was officially over.

Her grief for Étienne combined with the fear and excitement of seeing Verlaque caused Marine to feel ill. *Arrête-toi*, she said to herself, and she rubbed her tummy the way she did the first day of classes or before she entered a room full of people she didn't know. She would go to the château. She was curious, as she always was about events like this—she had even once, long ago, considered the police force as an occupation, but her love of research combined with her love of regular hours and long vacations helped her to choose academia.

It was normally a pleasant drive for Marine, la route de Cézanne. The road gently twists its way out of Aix toward mont Sainte-Victoire, Cézanne's obsession. The earth is red, a brick red that contrasts naturally with the dark green foliage and azure blue sky. "*Somebody* was designing brilliantly when they combined these colors," Verlaque used to say when they'd go for a walk or a drive around the mountain. It was one of the few times that he ever got remotely religious.

She drove past some of Aix's most prestigious properties, most of them hidden from view behind pine trees and iron gates. She slowed the car down as it maneuvered two hairpin turns that led uphill to Saint-Antonin, a tiny hamlet that stood at the foot of the craggy white mountain. Like other hamlets in France, Saint-Antonin was too small to have a *boulangerie* or a café but big enough to have a World War II memorial with thirteen names on it. She made a habit of reading the names to herself when she saw such monuments—the turn-of-the-century names were beautiful: Gaspard, Arsène, Isidore.

Verlaque's words, "You played up here, didn't you, as kids?" had stayed with her all morning. Jean-Marc said there were no signs of a break-in, and anyone who lived in Aix knew that the Bremont family had no money left. One only had to look at the weathered stone façade of the château, the missing roof tiles, the broken shutters on the upper floors. In some cases this was deliberate, a ruse for burglars, and the family still had hundreds of thousands of dollars hidden away in cash and bonds. But this couldn't be true of the Bremonts, and she thought of the broken baby buggy that Isabelle de Bremont pushed through Aix. Her eyes filled with tears.

Taking a breath and wiping her eyes, Marine parked her car behind a blue police cruiser. As she got out of the car, the sharp, cold wind took her by surprise, and she dropped her keys and cell phone on the pebbled drive. She bent down and picked them up, throwing them into the bright green Furla purse that Verlaque had bought her in Venice. As she stood up, she was stopped by a young, freckle-faced policeman.

"Who are you, and what you are doing here?" he asked suspiciously.

"I'm here to meet with Judge Verlaque. I'm Marine Bonnet," she answered, shaking the officer's hand. She then smiled and added, "I teach law at the university."

"Oh, yes," answered the wide-eyed policeman apologetically. "Judge Verlaque told me to expect a law professor, but . . ." He stammered, not finishing his sentence. Marine took that as a compliment, one she could tell the girls this evening over a drink. But then she saw why the policeman hadn't finished his sentence—Verlaque was marching across the château's manicured lawn, coming toward them. The young policeman quickly strode off in the opposite direction.

"Hi," said Verlaque, in English, as he leaned forward to exchange *bises* with Marine. He smelled of cigar smoke and Hermès cologne, a combination of scents that she would always associate with him and, despite herself, she still found intoxicating. Stop it, Marine slowly admonished herself. I'm here for Étienne.

Verlaque led her away from the police car. "It's nice to see you," he said, without smiling. Marine supposed that his professionalism reflected the situation and the seriousness that she knew shrouded such places. She hoped that he was happy to see her, and no matter how hard she tried she couldn't help but break into her famous wide grin. She took his upper arm, squeezed it, and then let go. "I'm happy to see you," she replied honestly. "Even here." Suddenly her voice was full of tears.

Verlaque reached out and swept back some of the curly bangs that had fallen into her face, his hand grazing her cheek. They looked at each other in silence for a moment; then a door slammed—it was the young policeman going back into the château—and they stopped smiling, reminded of what had brought them there.

"Is anybody around?" Marine asked, referring to the Bremonts. She realized that her voice had an edge to it that was too direct, but she wanted to get down to the business at hand.

"No. We had a team of police here yesterday, and the body is at the morgue until the funeral. He died of a broken neck," Verlaque replied, ignoring the way Marine's body sensually curved under her turtleneck.

"Who told Isabelle de Bremont?" Marine asked.

Verlaque stared at her, and then looked over her head toward the mountain. "A female officer told her, yesterday afternoon," he answered. "I waited an hour and then visited her."

"How was she doing?"

"Poorly," Verlaque said, looking now at Marine. "The kids weren't there, thank God. Her parents had them for the weekend."

"Étienne has a brother, I think in Cannes," Marine offered.

"Yes, François. He's on his way," Verlaque replied. "Do you know him?" Verlaque studied her in a way he hadn't allowed himself to do earlier. Something about her had changed.

"I haven't seen him in over fifteen years. I only know what people say about him, which may or may not be true: playboy, gambler, very good polo player." Marine let her distaste cut through her words. She had never been comfortable around François. It was as if he was always trying too hard.

"That's what I've heard too. One of the officers in Cannes plays polo with the Cannes team. He says that François is a good player but dirty."

Marine laughed at this. "Yeah? He was like that as a kid. He was always cheating Étienne and me. Étienne was fast, but François was stronger. And me, well you know . . ." Marine felt immediately embarrassed—Verlaque used to chide her because she was so unathletic. She had to force herself to go to a local gym, but she actually enjoyed the aerobics classes once she was there— she liked loud music and dancing. Skiing frightened her, as did swimming in the sea.

"La belle professeur!" Jean-Claude Auvieux bellowed as he walked quickly out of his cottage toward Marine and Verlaque. He was smiling from ear to ear and took Marine's shoulders and shook her with delight. Marine embraced the caretaker and let out a happy yelp. "Jean-Claude! It's been years! You look fantastic! The fresh air up here certainly suits you!" Verlaque marveled at the genuine, natural pleasure these two took in seeing each other after such a long absence. Their happy reunion was such a contrast to the awkward, stunted one that he and Marine had just had.

"*Ah oui!* Aix is so polluted now!" he answered, still smiling. Marine and Verlaque nodded in agreement—some days Aix's pollution hovered over the small city like a blanket.

"I haven't seen you since François broke the living room window!" Marine said, laughing and having to yell over the wind. "Do you remember that? He was grounded for a month!"

Auvieux laughed and slapped his forehead. "*Ah oui!* But it wasn't even François who broke the window! It was Étienne!"

Marine shot Auvieux a puzzled look and was about to protest when Verlaque interrupted—cold, and bored by the trip down memory lane. "Let's get out of this wind. Though I don't know if it's any warmer in the château. We'll drop by your cottage on our way out, M. Auvieux," he said, leading Marine into the château's tiled entryway.

The thick stone walls made for perfect architecture in August, but in April central heating was still needed. The walls leaked a damp smell—the same smell she associated with the château when she was a girl, only now, amplified by neglect, it was worse. The heating probably hadn't been put on since the death of Étienne's parents, some years ago. She already associated this damp smell with death, and she realized that from now on it would remind her of someone dying. Someone dying too soon.

A massive stairway faced the front door; the walls heading up the staircase were ornamented with hunting trophies—mostly deer and wild boar heads. Marine squinted and searched the trophies, to see if it was still there. And then she saw it, halfway up—an owl, about to fly, that had frightened her as a girl, and she shivered. It still did. Verlaque saw her looking at the owl, but if he sensed her fear, he said nothing.

On the first-floor landing, next to the bedrooms, hung large oil paintings of family members—rigid children in blue silk suits, unhappy-looking women staring at the viewer or the painter or both. The pictures Marine had always liked when she was young covered the walls on the next flight up, which led to the attics and servants' quarters. They were caricatures done in watercolor, dozens of them arranged haphazardly, of Étienne and François's grandparents in the 1930s in Cannes, appearing much less stiff than the sad women in the portraits on the landing below. The handsome couple, Philippe and Clothilde de Bremont, posed with persons of great importance—a young maharaja, for example, or the Prince of Denmark, or second-rate stage stars and singers of that decade.

Verlaque said nothing as they passed the cartoons, but Marine thought she detected a slight snort coming from his direction. They arrived at a small stone staircase that Marine remembered well—it led to the attic, and it smelled of dust and wood and boxes. Verlaque reached for a large key that was in his suit coat and began to open a heavy wooden door. The fact that the door was kept locked was a bit of a joke, since it was ready to fall off its hinges. A strong tug would have been enough to pull it from the wall. Just before he opened the door, Verlaque turned to Marine and said, "They fingerprinted and dusted up here yesterday, especially near the window where he fell. But still, try not to touch anything."

"Antoine," Marine replied. "Do you want me to look for anything in particular?" She still wasn't sure why he had asked her to come. She couldn't help thinking that perhaps he was using Étienne's death as an excuse to see her again. But, if that's what he wanted, all he had to do was walk past Le Mazarin on any given morning or evening, and he knew he would find her there.

"Yes and no," he answered. "Just look around and tell me if it's the way you remember it."

With that, Verlaque pushed the door open with his left shoulder. The attic was flooded with light that entered the room from the sole window whose shutters were open. Dust particles floated happily in and out of the shafts of light, as if unaware of the tragedy that had recently taken place. Sort of like King René and the terrible Christmas shacks, she thought. Marine wanted to hold on to the doorframe, as she was feeling lightheaded. She rubbed her eyes as a flood of childhood memories and voices filled the room, and as she saw what she knew must be the window, the thought of Étienne falling out of it brought her back into the present.

There appeared to be two people standing at the far end of the room, but Marine quickly realized that it was a reflection in a three-meter-high gilded mirror that stood leaning against the stone wall. She grabbed the sleeve of Verlaque's suit. "Oh God!" she cried, and buried her head in his arm.

"Do you have the spooks?" Verlaque asked, not meaning to tease.

"I just saw us reflected in that mirror," Marine answered, at once regretting her honesty and her reference to them as a couple.

Verlaque smiled. "Ah, the beauty and the beast. Come on, let's have a look around."

The attic looked as it had twenty years ago, as far as Marine could tell. Some of the larger pieces of furniture were missing—she imagined them decorating the apartments of the younger Bremonts. The great gilded mirrors she remembered well. Their sheer size and weight relegated them to staying in the attic indefinitely. In one corner of the room stood an old iron bed that had a wooden rosary hanging on the end of it. She bent down to look at the rosary and resisted the temptation to finger its smooth beads. It had been years since she had thought of Étienne or her childhood. She closed her eyes and remembered the hospital game she and Étienne had played—Étienne a World War II résistance soldier and Marine the nun who was nursing him. "I keep hearing loud booms," he would say, shaking his body back and forth, and she would answer, "There, there—think of something else, young man," and she would mop his brow, and he would pretend to fall asleep. They were nine, and Étienne wanted to grow up to be a soldier, and Marine a nun, or a nurse—she couldn't decide. She realized now that their games were based on that monument, for it was inscribed that the résistance fighters had been assassinated by "Hitlarian Hoards" while hiding in the woods. Etienne and François's father had told them that; although he had been a young boy, he had remembered each of the thirteen men.

Marine stood up and looked over toward the window. She finally spoke, choking a bit on her words. "Why do you think Étienne was looking, or leaning, out that window?"

"My guess is that he was reading—his reading glasses were found beside his body—and the attic's sole lightbulb was burnt out, so he would have opened the shutter on the biggest window to benefit from the moonlight. How he fell . . . I just don't know," replied Verlaque, who was now looking carefully at Marine. "Come and look out of it with me," he said, his voice full of tenderness.

Marine approached the window, which was wide and taller than she was, perhaps two meters high. It had no glass; it was more like an open doorway. A heavy wooden shutter, now fastened open to the outside wall, was the only way to close it. She was careful not to get too close to Verlaque as she leaned out the window. He's irresistible, she thought. And there's nothing I can do. In her effort not to touch Verlaque or touch the window frame, and driven back inside by the mistral, she took a step back and bumped into a suitcase, and it slid a few inches across the wood floor. "Careful!" Verlaque said, half scolding her, but she ignored him and knelt down.

"My God, it's the old Louis Vuitton suitcase—it's still here!" She stood up and continued, "Étienne obviously wasn't looking at the view, unless he wanted to see the hill and hundreds of pine trees. The great view from the château is of mont Sainte-Victoire, which can only be seen from the north-facing windows. My favorite view was always from Étienne's parents' room."

"So the attic is the same to you, as you remember it?"

"Yes, the mirrors are still here, the old bed, the flour sacks full of goodness knows what, the old radios, the broken chairs. Even this suitcase."

Someone coughed, and the pair turned around to see the freckle-faced policeman standing in the doorway. "Come in," Verlaque demanded.

"I'm sorry to bother you, sir, but I found this . . . near the bushes . . . near where they found the count's body." The young man held out a small, yellowed piece of paper in his gloved hand. Verlaque took a handkerchief out of his jacket pocket and took the paper. "Thank you," he said. "What's your name?"

"Terrier, sir. Nicholas Terrier."

"Good work, Terrier. Why don't you continue looking around the grounds? The first team obviously didn't do a thorough job."

"Yes, sir!" said the youth, turning quickly on his heels and walking out of the attic.

"The wind probably blew the paper into a place where it was more visible," Marine suggested. Verlaque held out the piece of paper for both of them to see. Marine leaned over and gasped. "Wow. A receipt from Pâtisserie Michaud. It's old."

Verlaque put on his reading glasses and looked closely at the receipt. "Nineteen fifty-four. It obviously hasn't been lying in the shrubs for forty-plus years; it must have fallen out this window . . .

probably Saturday night, when Étienne was up here. What were they doing saving receipts for—" Verlaque paused and looked again at the receipt—"*deux brioches?*"

"Oh," Marine replied. "My parents and grandparents keep all those old receipts. *C'est normal.*"

Verlaque looked at her, rolling his eyes and shaking his head. "You've got to be kidding? Even for two bloody brioches?"

"Oh yes."

"Have you seen any of Étienne's films?" Verlaque asked, seemingly out of nowhere. Marine once again felt like a dunce, as if she didn't understand what Verlaque was trying to get her to see. It also reminded her of his annoying habit of abruptly changing the subject: it irritated her and threw her off guard at the same time. It was, she thought, perhaps a technique he used in the courtroom.

Marine felt herself blushing. "I saw the one where he interviewed you, on crime in Provence. I showed it in my third-year criminal law class. And I saw the film on Marseille rap music that he did. I liked it so much that Sylvie and I went out and bought CDs by some of the groups."

Verlaque laughed. "You're a little too old for rap, no? Did you see his documentary on traditional building techniques?"

"No, I didn't see that one," Marine answered, ignoring his rap-music joke and beginning to lose her patience. They had been together over half an hour, and Verlaque hadn't asked a thing about her, and yet he had been gentle with her, and had touched her cheek, sending electricity, as his touch always did, down her body.

"It was something I would have normally considered pretty boring," Verlaque continued, "but Bremont managed to make it exciting, especially the roof scenes. They were laying different kinds of roofs—you know, thatched ones, in Normandy and Brittany, slate ones in the middle of France, and so on. What I remember clearly is Étienne: while interviewing the builders, he was running along the rooftops. The roof guys, they were far more used to such heights, but there he was, like a mountain goat."

Marine saw what Verlaque was getting at. "Yes!" she exclaimed. "He *was* a mountain goat, even when we were kids. Both of the boys were natural athletes, but Étienne was always the better of the two, something that made François writhe with jealousy. I had forgotten that." Étienne climbing olive trees; Étienne running down the château stairs three at a time; Étienne skiing like a god in Chamonix—Marine stared at Antoine's dark brown eyes and, composing herself, grabbed his arm and said, "And so it seems unlikely that he would lose his balance and fall out of an open window."

"Unlikely, indeed."

Chapter Four

❧

*L*unch was pleasant, Verlaque thought as he drove back into Aix. They had arrived at Chez Thomé in Le Tholonet at 1:45 p.m., just in time to place their lunch order before the kitchen closed. The young waiter recognized them at once and gave Marine the *bises* and shook Verlaque's hand. A year ago Marine and Verlaque had rescued the waiter when he was stranded by the side of the road beside his broken-down car. From then on, a bowl of olives and two pastis were always set on the table as soon as they took their seats. Today was no different, yet they sipped their pastis in silence. Verlaque smiled as he watched Marine—she was one of the few women he knew who actually enjoyed pastis. He missed that about her.

Marine moved an olive around in her mouth and finally spoke. "So," she said, taking the pit and placing it in the ashtray, "when will you talk to Isabelle de Bremont again?"

"After lunch," Verlaque replied, pricking an olive with a toothpick and putting it into his mouth. He was having a hard time not staring at Marine. She was wearing a pale blue turtleneck—it looked like cashmere. In fact, he seemed to remember buying it for her. Over that she wore a tight-fitting black sleeveless dress made out of a thick, synthetic material that looked like it would make a great parachute. The effect of the man-made fabric over such a natural one was striking—an imaginative combination of the sort that Marine was so good at and part of why she often turned heads while walking down Aix's streets. No twinsets for this girl, Verlaque thought.

Marine caught Antoine staring at her, and she nervously twisted in her seat. "You'd better chew some gum to hide the pastis and the wine," she said.

"I'll just have a cigar after lunch, and that will fix all other lingering smells." He smiled, and realized that in the short time they had been sitting there Marine had finished almost all the olives. He tried not to let it bug him, her lack of awareness while at the dinner table. Verlaque had very specific opinions about etiquette, and Marine's small habits, like this one, had often bothered him when they were together. He asked her, "How have you been?"

"Fine, Antoine, fine," she answered, trying to sound light-hearted. "You know—work, research, grading papers, and too many aperitifs with Sylvie."

"Not much has changed then, has it?" Verlaque said, quickly realizing his blunder. For Verlaque had brought a welcome change into Marine's small-town life—she had told him time and time again how happy she was that he had entered her little world in Aix. She had grown up there and sometimes winced when she saw familiar faces on the cours Mirabeau, faces that thirty years before were collecting bugs on the school playground. She had been shocked when she was offered a full-time teaching job in sought-after Aix; she so would have preferred Paris or Lyon.

"No," Marine said, smiling, pleased by his insensitivity. "Life is good." His ability to say the wrong thing at the wrong time hadn't changed. Fucking confirmation, she could hear Sylvie's voice, telling her, that you are better off without him.

Verlaque sensed that Marine was beginning to get defensive, and he shifted the conversation. "What do you know about the family? Do people in Aix talk much about the Bremonts?"

Before she could answer, the waiter came and they placed their orders. Verlaque tried not to wince when Marine took too long to make her decision, and then ordered an entrée and main dish that were not compatible—a fish soup with rouille paste followed by yet more fish and garlic, an aioli platter. He could not order for her, he knew from past experience: she would only get silent and sullen. Astounded, he wondered how could she eat rouille and aioli at the same sitting and still have taste buds left for dessert.

He caught himself daydreaming, remembering a birthday dinner they once shared in Marseille's most exclusive restaurant, Le Petit Nice, when every dish Marine ordered had foie gras. During one of their fights, Marine said that he was too bourgeois and that she was simpler than he was. Marine was at times— many times—a country girl, not even sure of how to order a meal in a restaurant. How funny it was that she was the one with the respected Provençal family—her parents both strict Catholics, her father a doctor and her mother a theology professor—and yet Marine seemed to know so little about manners and etiquette. He blamed it on socialism.

"They've no money left, but I can verify that for you with Marie-Pierre," Marine answered.

She hasn't properly tasted her wine, Verlaque thought. He had forgotten that Marine could drink any old plonk.

"She's your friend that works at the Crédit Mutuel?" Verlaque asked.

"Yes, the Bremonts have had their accounts there forever. Other than that, there's Étienne's brother, but I've already told you what I know about him. The parents died a few years ago, months apart, both of cancer. They were heavy smokers. I can imagine that Étienne's father didn't leave much in the way of an inheritance."

Verlaque tilted his head and asked, "Why do you say that? He wasn't a big spender, was he?"

Marine struggled with the last olive, which was too slippery and kept managing to avoid her toothpick. "Oh, no. Quite the opposite. He was a philosopher. He wrote a few small volumes that I tried to read once, but they put me to sleep."

"More than law books do?" Verlaque asked, smiling. An image of Marine, asleep, with a Dalloz civil law text covering her perfect face, flashed through his mind.

"Ha-ha. Yes, even more than law. And you enjoy reading law just as much as I do—that much I remember. Anyway, he just didn't seem like he would be very money-minded, not someone who would set money aside for later, if you know what I mean."

"Why haven't they sold the château? It must be worth a fortune, even if it is a ruin."

"I have no idea. Family pride? The château was always a sign of their nobility. Étienne's mother was very attached to it—she was a great gardener. But now that the parents are dead, I don't know. Maybe they—I mean Étienne and Isabelle—just didn't care about the money. Étienne was really sensitive—maybe he wanted to hold on to the château for sentimental reasons. They lived in a great place in downtown Aix; they had four beautiful kids; they went to church on Sundays and the market on Saturdays—what more did they need?" Marine said.

Verlaque wasn't sure if this was a jab at him, at the chance he had turned down: a comfortable life with a beautiful woman, a professor to boot, and a life with children. He decided not to pursue it and went on with his questioning. "But the château would have been more of a burden to him than anything else, so why not sell it? I can imagine that his brother, François, would want the cash."

"I don't know . . . The aristocracy is very attached to land. Sometimes it's all they have," Marine suggested. "Are you going to finish your duck?"

Verlaque smiled. "Yes, I am, but thanks for offering to help." Sometimes it was so easy between them. And when it was, like this, Verlaque forgot about the old fights, the biting words that had broken them. But too often, just like that—the moment was gone.

Verlaque had forty minutes to kill before his appointment with Isabelle de Bremont. Enough time for a coffee and part of a cigar at Le Mazarin. He slipped into the *tabac* across from the café and bought a Cohiba Siglo II from the owner's daughter, a dark-haired, dark-eyed, big-chested girl with whom all of the cigar smokers in town flirted. Their agreeable exchange was interrupted by Verlaque's cell phone ringing, and, seeing the number, he stepped outside to take the call.

"Mayor Tamain just called me," a voice said in a high-pitched whine. "What's going on up in Saint-Antonin?"

Verlaque could hear noise in the background—voices and the tinkling of glasses. He answered, "I was up there yesterday and this morning. I just got back. Étienne de Bremont fell from an attic window, breaking his neck, sometime late Saturday evening."

"Terrible, terrible. It's a blessing that both of his parents have passed on, *non*? Have you spoken to his wife?"

"I'm on my way to a second appointment with her."

"Second?" the voice yelped. "Why do you need to visit her again? There's no reason to remind the poor woman over and over again of what happened!"

Verlaque closed his eyes, knowing that the prosecutor was right but annoyed at being told how to perform his job. "The Bley brothers have submitted a formal request for an inquest." He also didn't know how to explain to Yves Roussel that he was working on a hunch, roughly based on a few childhood souvenirs and a bit of film footage. "Mme Bremont was in no state to talk on Sunday. I need to ask her if her husband was depressed. I've ruled out foul play," he said, lying, "but not suicide."

Roussel took what sounded like a long sip of something and said, "Suicide! If that's what it was, you'll keep that quiet, right? Nobody wants that posted all over town, and if those sleazes at *La Provence* get a hold of it, it will be front-page news. *Putain!*" Roussel seemed to then remember who he was talking to, and added, "I'll be back in Aix tomorrow. Good luck with everything."

Verlaque mumbled good-bye and looked toward the cours Mirabeau, where the afternoon light shone through the branches and was dappled by the broad leaves of the plane trees. He looked up at the trees and sighed, putting his BlackBerry in his pocket: one of his first lessons on the job was to learn how to cooperate and work calmly with Aix's prosecutor. Yves Roussel, despite, or perhaps because of, his small-town attitude, was extremely well connected, something highly desirable in a prosecutor, who represents the people. The son of a Marseille fisherman, he had by pure hard work finished Aix's law school with average grades, but then excelled at his postdoctoral examinations in Bordeaux. The fact that his wife was the mayor's cousin had also helped his career. To his credit, he had won, for the region, some high-profile cases, and two years ago, during a kidnapping incident, had become a national hero when a group of elementary school children and their teacher were held hostage by an armed lunatic. The then-*commissaire*, before Paulik's appointment, had done all he could—both he and a forensic psychiatrist had talked to the man by telephone for three hours. Roussel, in frustration, walked through the police brigade and straight into the school, unarmed. Minutes later the two men were heard laughing, and less than an hour they walked out together, the kidnapper with tickets for the next Marseille soccer game in his pocket, which he had been promised in exchange for the release of the children and their weeping teacher. Verlaque knew that Roussel had been reprimanded by his superior in Paris for taking such a risk, but he had also been called by *le président de la République*, who had congratulated him.

Loads of yellow pollen thickened the air, and people walked up the *cours* blowing their noses or rubbing their eyes. A group of tourists stopped in front of Le Mazarin to take pictures. "Frédéric, don't they have cafés in the States?" Verlaque asked the waiter. "No," the waiter replied, straight-faced, only his handlebar mustache twitching. "I really don't think they do." Verlaque sat down and ordered a coffee and thought of New York and California, two places that, for very different reasons, he loved. Trips to Chicago and New Orleans had been planned at various stages in his life but had never materialized. He was fascinated by Chicago—his favorite jazz musicians usually hailed from that city, and he was passionate about the architecture of Frank Lloyd Wright.

Verlaque's cell phone rang. Paulik's voice was on the other

end. "We've done a check of François de Bremont, Judge. He's clean, from what we can tell, but I haven't checked everything yet. He's part owner of a couple of mediocre restaurants in Nice and Cannes, and he makes money off a string of luxury studios he rents out. He gambles a fair bit in Cannes, but then everyone does on the Côte. We're looking into his bank accounts now. The rest of the time he sails or plays polo. Never been married, no children. Spends a lot of time with blondes, really tall blondes."

"Poor devil," Verlaque replied. "Maybe the blondes are opera singers, Bruno."

"Ha-ha. I seriously doubt it. Another thing—Bouvet called me from the lab. The only fingerprints in the attic were those of Étienne de Bremont, and there are a few of the caretaker's, but not around the window. On boxes and stuff. The broom had no prints on it whatsoever—weird, *non*? Will you be back at head-quarters this afternoon? François de Bremont said he would get to the office in Aix by seven this evening."

"I'll meet you in my office just after six thirty," said Verlaque before hanging up.

Paulik was right, the clean broom was suspect. The caretaker had said he swept the attic regularly. So why didn't the broom have his fingerprints on it?

Verlaque finished his coffee, took a last drag on his cigar, and, carefully brushing off the ashes, put it in his leather cigar carrier, which was small enough to fit inside his jacket pocket. He left some money on the table and went upstairs to the toilets, check-ing his teeth and three-day growth in the mirror before he paid his visit to Mme de Bremont. He quickly left the café, not want-ing to get caught having to drink another coffee and talk with any of his acquaintances that may have been standing at the bar. He walked down the cours Mirabeau, looking up at the addresses until he got to number sixteen. This was, of all the nasty things he had to do on the job, his least favorite task. Questioning the spouse of someone who was recently deceased—it was one of the few occasions in Verlaque's life when his talent for seduction didn't help him. People recognized early on that he had a gift for seducing people—men, women, old and young. Had he not studied law, he would have gone into business, sales most likely, but there were too many businessmen in the family already, and Verlaque yearned to break out of that mold. Since becoming the examining magistrate, he had rarely spoken to his parents, whom he imagined were still sitting at opposite ends of their immense dining room table, not talking, continuing the behavior he had experienced as a child.

He rang the buzzer labeled "Famille Bremont," and a maid came to the door. He introduced himself, as the maid had not been working on Sunday afternoon, when he made his first visit to number sixteen. She led him through the great foyer, with faded paintings on the walls and a massive stone staircase. Parked at the bottom of the stairs were two beat-up baby carriages and a soccer ball. They went up to the first floor and entered tall wooden doors that lead to the Bremonts' apartment.

This time he was prepared for the visual delight upon entering. The walls, fourteen feet high, typical for the first floors of Aix's *hôtels*, were painted a smoky tobacco color that Verlaque had immediately liked. The walls were lined with oil paintings, big and small, children's drawings, and a series of nineteenth-century etchings following some sort of mythological theme. The furniture was a bizarre collection of old and new. There was an Empire desk against the far wall that Verlaque particularly liked, various nineteenth-century cane-seated wooden chairs of the kind seen in many of Cézanne's paintings, and two battered love seats, facing each other, which looked like they had been bought at Ikea not long before. A large wooden bookcase covered one wall—it was haphazardly arranged with old books, new paperbacks, dozens of seashells, feathers, bright red coral, and butterflies pinned to boards. He felt someone's presence in the room and turned around to see a petite red-haired woman in her midthirties. "We lived for two years in Guadeloupe, when we were first married," she said, almost whispering. "That's when we collected all those things."

"It's a beautiful collection," Verlaque replied. Carefully walking up to the woman and offering his hand, he asked, "How have you been, Mme de Bremont?"

"Terrible," she replied. Her eyes and nose were red from crying.

"I'm sorry. And I'm sorry to be back here so soon, but I need to ask you a few more things about your late husband."

Isabelle de Bremont looked surprised. "What do you need to know?" She gestured for him to sit down on one of the small sofas, quickly removing a plastic airplane before Verlaque sat on it. She took a seat opposite him. Verlaque noticed that her legs were bare and very freckled. She wore bright pink, expensive-looking, low-heeled shoes.

"I want to try to understand how your husband fell from that attic window." Seeing the fright in her green eyes, he quickly added, "The château at Saint-Antonin is well known, and I want to be sure there weren't intruders—burglars, perhaps—that night, who may have frightened your husband or even pushed him."

She got up and walked across the room and sat down in an armchair, its upholstery faded and threadbare but its wood frame and proportions graceful. She continued, "I thought there weren't any traces of an intruder, Judge. There were some kids, a few years ago, who tried to break into the château, but they were scared off by the caretaker."

"No, that's true. Nothing was disturbed or stolen. But I'd like to understand why your husband was there. Did he tell you why he was going?"

"Only briefly," she answered. "He needed to look for some papers his parents kept, something like that. He left here late, around eleven at night." Verlaque noted to himself that Étienne de Bremont may not have gone directly to the château.

"But don't you think it's strange that your husband could fall out of a window in a place he knew so well, Madame?" Verlaque asked.

Isabelle de Bremont looked straight at the judge and replied, "Yes, to be frank, I do think it's strange. But life is like that, isn't it? There are so many strange things that happen, so many things I find difficult to explain or understand. I think he could have just lost his footing, and that, perhaps, it was his time to go, his time to die. His destiny." This seemed to Verlaque almost too easy a way to accept the death of one's husband. Why wasn't she jumping up and down, pounding her fists on the wall? That was the way that, last year, the wife of a convicted minor felon had reacted to the news that her husband had been killed. And then Verlaque saw the gold crucifix and baptismal medal hanging from Isabelle de Bremont's slender neck. He glanced around the room and saw a replica of a Russian icon and, finally, yes, there it was: a crucifix above the salon doors. Faith was something he didn't understand, but it might explain the woman's silent acceptance of this atrocity.

Verlaque was almost certain that the death wasn't a suicide, but he still needed to ask. "I would also like to know if it is possible that your husband may have jumped out of the window by choice."

"No way, never," Isabelle said flatly. "Impossible." She wiped her eyes with an antique handkerchief—white cotton embroidered with poppies. Faith again, thought Verlaque. Suicide would be a sin.

"Why did you refuse to sign the inquest demand?" Verlaque asked.

Isabelle de Bremont looked at the judge as if the answer was an obvious one. "He fell," she said, raising her hands in the air. "That's it. I want his death put to rest."

"The Bleys don't agree with such a straightforward explanation of a sudden death."

"The Bleys?" Isabelle de Bremont hissed. "What do I care about the Bleys? What do *they* know about us? We saw them twice, maybe three times a year! I was his *wife*!"

Verlaque remained silent. He had no way of knowing how close the Bleys were to Isabelle and Étienne de Bremont. But the speed of their inquiry request, just hours after the death was announced, had surprised him. He then answered, "Still, Madame, with all due respect, they have asked for an inquest."

A slight smile formed at the edge of her lips. "The Bleys are lawyers."

"Were you happy?" he asked, abruptly changing the subject.

The widow looked at him, slightly irritated. "We were very happy." When Verlaque didn't reply, she continued, "We had our problems, like many married couples—four children and no time to be alone together, money and business worries, that sort of thing. But he was happy recently, Étienne."

Verlaque picked up on the money and business worries and

the word "recently." He asked, softly, "His career, Madame? Was he satisfied?"

Isabelle de Bremont looked at him steadily for a few seconds. "Yes and no," she replied. "You see, he had been hoping to get into commercial cinema, but a few months ago he received news that the Parisian producers had pulled the funding for his latest project. Étienne had written the screenplay—it takes place in Saint-Antonin—so he was terribly disappointed. But not enough to . . ."

"Didn't he try to find other sources of funding?"

"He had already tried, with no success. But in the past few weeks he seemed upbeat about it, and he began talking about the film again, as if it might happen."

"What was the film about?"

"I don't know . . . a story of lost youth, I think. I never read the script."

"Really?" Verlaque asked. "Weren't you curious?"

"I have four children, Judge." She sighed, as if beginning to lose patience. Verlaque found it difficult to not stare at Isabelle de Bremont. Her wavy red hair and freckled shoulders reminded him of both Isabelle Huppert and the women in Pre-Raphaelite paintings he loved to visit at the Tate Britain in London. Her ankles and wrists were fine and delicate, and matched her soft voice. He then asked, "Aren't your three small children at the crèche?"

Isabelle de Bremont sat up straight, her voice now raised. "Certainly not!" Although Verlaque didn't have children, he knew that most of his friends put their children in state-funded day care as soon as they were potty trained. When he only nodded, she continued, "I don't work, and so I don't agree with someone else raising my children. So you see, Judge, why I don't have the time to read every one of my husband's scripts." At that point she realized that she had referred to her deceased husband in the present tense, and Verlaque thought she might break down, but she continued staring at him.

"Was he normally a bit clumsy?" asked Verlaque somewhat abruptly.

"No, that's the funny thing. He was very coordinated," she answered, with a slight look of perplexity on her face. She too had been lost in thought. "Our eldest son, Raphaël, is just like him. Étienne was teaching Raphaël to climb mont Sainte-Victoire, you know—the south face that everyone climbs. But I've already gone over the accident, how it could have happened, a million times in my head, and now I just can't think about it anymore."

She laid her head in her hands and began to weep. Verlaque started to walk across the room—he wanted to be near her; he wanted to be beside her, touching her. But a thin woman in her thirties came into the room at that moment and ran over to Isabelle, reaching her before he could.

"Are you finally finished with the interrogation? This is the second time you've come . . . I really don't understand. There were no robbers in the château Saturday night, right? So why do you keep harassing her?" the thin woman's voice demanded.

"No, there wasn't any theft, but there may have been someone else with the count in the attic," Verlaque answered. Both of the women looked at the judge, wide-eyed.

"What is that supposed to mean? Who else would have been there?" the second woman demanded.

"I am suggesting that the count may have been pushed to his death. I'm sorry if this idea upsets you and your . . ." Verlaque answered, waiting for Isabelle to fill in the blank.

"Sister," the other woman answered. Then, remembering

some kind of manners, she held out her hand and added, "My name is Sophie, Sophie Valoie de Saint-André. I'm Isabelle's sister."

She was the kind of woman Verlaque disliked—too thin and brittle, too bourgeois. He noted that her posh surname was the same as one of his colleague's, an examining magistrate in Marseille. It was very possible that this woman was related to the judge, and Verlaque silently noted to himself to check later. "Thank you both for your time. I'll let myself out. Oh, Mme de Bremont—did your husband wear his glasses all the time?"

"Only for reading, especially when he was tired," answered Mme Valoie de Saint-André for her sister. A little too quickly, Verlaque thought. It was the response he had been fairly sure he would get. The fact that Étienne de Bremont was found dead with his glasses next to him bothered Verlaque. Strange place to read, a dark attic—the papers that he was looking for surely must have been kept in an office in the château? But then that young policeman had found the ancient receipt for two brioches . . . No, the papers must have been in the attic. He saw that Isabelle had already stopped listening.

"And, Mme de Bremont, if you think of anything else that might be helpful, would you please call me?" Verlaque added, looking one last time at the redhead as he opened the doors to leave the now overcrowded room. "Yes," she answered, looking up at him.

No one moved to accompany Verlaque to the front door, so in the apartment's spacious entryway he had time to gaze around. He saw an overnight bag sitting on the floor, next to the door, with the familiar blue TGV address label hanging from its leather handle. He quickly bent down and read Isabelle de Bremont's name. Lifting the bag up slightly, he noted that it was full. Verlaque walked back into the salon, where he saw the two women in fast discussion with heads bent close together. "Now what?" demanded Isabelle de Bremont. Verlaque looked at her, surprised, but tried not to show it. He had expected that sort of voice from her sister but not the soft-spoken widow.

"I noticed a full overnight bag in the foyer. Were you here this weekend, Madame?"

"This is outrageous!" replied Sophie Valoie de Saint-André. "She told you she was. Étienne told her he was going to the château." Verlaque now realized that Mme Valoie had been listening at the living room doors when he was talking to her sister.

Isabelle de Bremont stood up and looked straight at Verlaque. "Yes, I was here, with my sister, all night. Saturday night, I assume, is the night you're asking me about. I used that bag last week, for a quick trip to Paris. I haven't had time to unpack it."

"Right," Verlaque replied. "Four children."

Isabelle de Bremont's face fell for a moment, and then she ran her fingers through her hair and said, with a slight smile forming on her lips, "Please, let me show you out." She walked through the living room and into the foyer with him, opening one half of the massive wooden doors. Whether she was conscious of it or not, she put her slender hand on his shoulder and said, "*Merci.*"

Verlaque walked back up the *cours* feeling strangely attracted to Isabelle de Bremont, which was neither ethical nor comfortable, especially since he was certain that she was lying. He thought it unlikely that the overnight bag would have been left in the hall for days, especially since the Bremonts had a maid. Sophie Valoie was, conveniently, her sister's alibi.

He stopped and quickly rang Officer Flamant on his cell phone, remembering that Paulik was in court all day. "*Salut*, Flamant," he said. "Could you call the SNCF and check train tickets purchased last week and this weekend from Aix to Paris, under the name of Isabelle de Bremont?"

"There's nothing I like better, *Juge*, than to make the SNCF employees work a little for me. The last time they went on strike, I missed my grandmother's birthday in Lille. A month later, she was dead, and I missed her funeral. Another strike!"

Verlaque smiled, not because Flamant had lost his grandmother, but because the officer felt comfortable enough to tell Verlaque the story. Verlaque then said, "But wait, she could have traveled under an assumed name."

"Possibly, but most people buy their TGV tickets on the Internet now, and when using them you have to show photo ID when you get on the train."

"Good point," Verlaque answered. He remembered seeing a new Apple computer in the Bremont salon. Verlaque thanked the officer and rang off.

He walked past Le Mazarin's terrace and didn't see anyone he knew—no, it was too early for aperitifs. The lunch with Marine had gone nicely, he thought. He had complimented her on her blue sweater and how it set off her green eyes. She appreciated that, he knew. She would go away thinking of him, hopefully thinking well of him. He realized now how important that was. At the same time he sighed aloud: he had wasted six months not explaining to Marine why he had left her, purposely hiding himself away, after Luxembourg and England, at the law library in Paris. Sometimes he wondered about it himself. There was no easy answer he could come up with. But perhaps they could be friends again? He'd invite Marine over for a dinner soon, on his terrace if the weather was fine. Strange that a death would bring them back together. Marine was so patient and diplomatic—so unlike him in that regard—and she didn't judge. He once again made a silent vow to try to be more patient; it was his worst character flaw. He could see her now, closing her lovely almond-shaped eyes and listening to him talk, her head tilted to one side. Surely that was worth something. Maybe something worth holding on to after all.

He stopped in the street to relight his cigar and realized that he was smiling to himself.

Chapter Five

꙳

"*T*he lunch was just awful, such a typical Antoine Verlaque lunch!" Marine told Sylvie as they sat on Le Mazarin's terrace. Arriving as they did at seven thirty, they had been lucky to get a table, squeezing in between an old woman who was feeding her miniature dog the bar's curried chickpeas, which come, free of charge, with an aperitif, and a group of German tourists who were poring over maps. Marine sat with her arms folded, ready for the blast that would come her way from Sylvie.

"He's a big dick. Forget him," Sylvie said. "Besides, you now have your twenty-seven-year-old boy toy." Although the sun was setting, Sylvie Grassi still wore her sunglasses—black Armanis with huge, round lenses like the stars wore on the Côte d'Azur in the 1960s. Her hair was dark black, neatly cropped short, her eyes a pale blue. She preferred clothes that showed off the contrast between her hair and eyes—bold colors like apple green and neon pink. Approaching forty years of age, she had recently toned down her appearance, a bit, but she was still a familiar figure, walking around the streets of conservative Aix wearing designer Japanese clothing and carrying brightly colored handbags. She taught photography and art history at the Beaux-Arts school in Aix and had participated in numerous photography exhibitions around Europe. Thanks to the sales of her photographs, and to photography's rise in status as an art form, she could afford designer clothes, and she had recently paid off the mortgage on her two-bedroom downtown flat. She had an eight-year-old daughter, Charlotte, who was Marine's godchild; the father was a German photographer who had no idea that he had a child in Provence.

"I thought I was doing a good job of forgetting him. And then he calls me out of the blue," Marine said, sighing. She hated herself for uttering the words out loud, even to her best friend. She wished that they were untrue, but knew better.

"But it wasn't exactly out of the blue, was it? He asked you to go to Saint-Antonin to help with the investigation," Sylvie answered. "Or *was* it for that?" she asked, lifting her eyebrows in question.

"You think it was just an excuse to see me?" Marine asked.

"What else?"

"No, Antoine's too selfish for that. I think he really did need me—in his 'I don't need to say please or thank you' kind of way. He seemed really troubled by Étienne de Bremont's death—about how Étienne could have fallen from an open window."

"What do you think?"

Marine mulled for a moment. "I agree with Antoine. I can't imagine anyone as sure-footed as Étienne falling from a place he knew so well. And suicide? That's hard to imagine for anyone, isn't it?"

"Yeah, but you guys will need some hard evidence to prove that, won't you?"

Marine paused, embarrassed when Sylvie tried to become an

expert at something she knew nothing about. "There was a Michaud receipt, for two brioches, that was found near where Étienne fell."

"Brioches?" Sylvie asked, drinking some wine, not taking her eyes off a group of three men who had just taken a table near to them.

"Yes. The receipt dated from the fifties."

Sylvie turned her head away from the men and looked at her friend. "*That* is interesting."

Marine nodded and looked down at her hands. Sylvie sensed Marine's sadness and tried to get her back on of the subject of the horrible lunch. She preferred trashing Antoine. "And then he took you out for lunch," she said, encouraging Marine to continue.

"Yes. And the whole time he kept staring at me—watching how I ate the olives—I was so nervous that I think I ate the whole bowl."

Sylvie laughed. "Marine! You didn't!" The two women laughed out loud, and Frédéric, the waiter, came over to their table, resting the tray on his hip. "You two are constantly laughing. It's good to see. Two more glasses of white?" he asked.

"More white!" Sylvie hollered, pointing her finger in the air in mock pretension, and then added, "And a bowl of olives please, Fréd!"

"I know that the whole time he was watching me, rating me," Marine continued, ignoring the olive joke. "He's such a food snob."

"He's such a snob, period," Sylvie said. "But your eating all the olives is way too funny. And it's true—you don't appreciate good wine and good food, and that's always driven him nuts."

"This wine," Marine said, holding up her glass, "is very fine."

Sylvie laughed. "You liar, you hadn't noticed. It does happen to be a very fine wine—Château Revelette, a winery just north of Aix." Sylvie took a sip and then added, "And with a very cute German winemaker-owner."

"Married?"

"Yep, unfortunately," and they both laughed, as they knew that Sylvie had a habit of getting tangled up with married men. Marine wanted to forget—Étienne's death, Antoine, old memories, all of it—and laughing felt good. You ass, Marine, she told herself. What about Étienne? Poor Étienne. He'll never again walk through the woods near mont Sainte-Victoire, never again see his children.

Sylvie brought her back to reality. "Oh, Marine, I know that lunch today must have been hell for you. You know I never liked *le juge*, except when he bought some of my photographs," Sylvie said, laughing. "It's that stare of his—I never knew if he was rating me, as you put it, or trying to see through my clothes."

"What? He flirted with you?" Marine asked.

"Oh no, don't worry. He never flirted openly, but you know him, his whole thing is seduction—flattering and charming people, women and men, but at the same time never giving himself away. He says the right things about wine and cigars or soccer, if he's with soccer types, or politics, if he's with political types. All the while never letting anyone know the real Antoine, the Antoine he is when he is alone. The vulnerable Judge Verlaque."

"I know," Marine replied, getting annoyed with Sylvie's overly simple assessment of Verlaque. "I guess that's what broke us up in the end. Even I couldn't get near him. But you already know all this. Plus, he was constantly criticizing me, telling me what to do. He didn't like how I dressed, what I ordered from a restaurant menu, and he never complimented me, except when we were making love, but then you have to compliment your partner, otherwise you're a total jerk. He never said congratulations when I published a paper, only little critiques, little jabs. I guess in the end I never really got comfortable, and when he left me, it was almost a relief."

"It was hard work with him," Sylvie offered.

"Yes," Marine replied, looking far away, lost in thought. "Hard work, but I can't help thinking it would have been worth it in the end."

"The idiot," Sylvie said, wanting to bring Marine back to the world of the living. "Forget about him. Let's go up to Paris next month for my art opening, okay?"

"Great, just what I need, to be surrounded by a bunch of gay guys," Marine said, as she watched the crowds of people who walked up and down the *cours*, past the café.

"No, not this time, the gallery owner is straight—an ex-businessman who made a ton of money in London and has semi-retired to Paris and the Loire and sells photographs. He may have some friends there—you know, other rich, handsome Englishmen. I know you have a soft spot for the British, heaven knows why."

"Hmm, it's starting to sound better. I could use my college English," Marine said, laughing. "That's *another* thing Antoine would chide me about—my bad English! You're right. What a fuckup!"

Sylvie reached across the wine-splattered table and grabbed Marine's hand. "So what? Antoine is half British—of course he speaks perfect English! And, if I remember correctly, your Italian is pretty flawless. Just think," she continued, "those London businessmen will go crazy over you at the gallery—a beautiful, young, well not *so* young, university professor, never married, with no kids, and a little French accent." Sylvie said the words "little

French accent" in her own heavily accented English. They began laughing, and Frédéric smiled at them from across the terrace. "Ladies! Keep it down!"

"Let's pay up. I have a class to prepare for tomorrow," Sylvie said.

"Yeah, good idea. I think I'll get to bed early," replied Marine. But when the two women gave each other farewell *bises*, Marine did not head straight home via the rue Frédéric Mistral but instead walked up the *cours* and slipped into the passage Agard, a narrow pedestrian way that emptied into the place des Prêcheurs, where the church of her childhood, the large half-neoclassical, half-Baroque église de la Madeleine, stood guarding the square. The doors were still open, and she walked into the cold church. It was the same one where she had attended mass as a child—a church she knew well but had never liked. She preferred the smaller Saint-Jean-de-Malte, its architecture somewhere between Romanesque and Gothic and built out of the warm golden local stone. But she had come into la Madeleine for the same reason she had been visiting it since she took her first high school exams—for good luck. And there was a particular painting on the left-hand side of the nave that she loved. It was an annunciation scene, a northern Flemish one by some van Eyck, not Jan van Eyck but possibly a relation, Sylvie had explained. Marine liked to stare at the details in the painting— all the symbols that Sylvie had taught her to unravel in such paintings—how there were always white lilies present, and a dove that usually came flying toward Mary through an open window. Marine and Sylvie had made two "annunciation vacations," one to Florence and another to Venice, trying to track down as many annunciation paintings as they could find. The many moods of Mary, as Sylvie liked to say, fascinated them—how at times she could be frightened by the news that she was about to carry the Son of God, or proud or pensive or sometimes even bored, depending on the painter and his background.

Marine stared at the painting she knew so well and tried to ignore the sound of skateboarders outside the church. She moved closer to the painting, and, glancing around to make sure nobody was near, she stood up on one of the pews to get a better look. She probably never would have done this had it not been for the wine—Château Revelette, was it?—at Le Mazarin. She wanted to get a better look at the golden dove that flew in through an open window, about to impregnate the young virgin. Squinting, she saw, after all these years, that it was not a bird, as she had thought, but a fat little baby, only millimeters long. She inched along the pew and got a better look—yes, it was a baby, a fat little jewel of a baby.

She slid down off the pew and walked out of the church, smiling, walking across the place des Prêcheurs, and then its neighbor, place de Verdun, stepping out of the way as cars drove into the squares much too quickly, their drivers desperate to find parking places. When she reentered the dark and damp passage Agard, she thought of the Bremont attic and all the details that could so easily be missed, crowded into that one room. What did Antoine want me to see in that attic? she wondered. They had talked about the view, and she had agreed with him that Étienne was probably not standing at the window to take advantage of it. And then Antoine had scolded her for bumping into the Louis Vuitton suitcase, when the policemen had already dusted and there was not much harm in the tattered suitcase moving a bit. Another Verlaque scolding, another raised eyebrow. But what was it about the suitcase that bothered her, even more than Antoine's remark? As children they had tried to play with it, especially Marine, who was aware of its prestige and value. But the suitcase was always so heavy that it took two of them to pick it up, and the boys would usually lose interest, not wanting to play Marine's hotel games.

"That's it!" she said aloud, causing a beggar who sat in the passageway to look up at her hopefully. She entered the busy *cours* and walked toward her apartment, dialing Verlaque's cell phone at the same time.

Chapter Six

꙼

Verlaque got back to the courthouse at six thirty that evening and found Paulik waiting for him in the outer office, sipping an espresso and reading the local newspaper. "Anything interesting?" Verlaque asked. *La Provence* was the paper one read for soccer scores or for the times and locations of local *pétanque* games, but not usually much else.

"Actually, quite a lot today," answered Paulik. He took a sip of coffee and made a face—the office coffee remained as terrible as usual, despite Verlaque's constant complaints. "Nicole Kidman a real star on the Croisette," Paulik said, reading the headlines. "But also two things of a more professional nature, sir. They've sent fifteen policemen down to Casablanca to investigate that suicide bombing at a hotel that killed four French citizens. And, the cut-up remains of a body were found in some garbage bags in a park in Marseille."

"Man or woman?" asked the judge.

"A man. Dead about a month," Paulik replied.

Verlaque imagined Procureur Roussel's disappointment at missing such a grisly find, even if Marseille was out of his jurisdiction. He didn't like Roussel—a short, annoying man who thought authority came to those who yelled the loudest. Verlaque was reminded of Marlon Brando in *The Godfather* and how the actor had told Francis Ford Coppola that a man with power needn't yell and, in fact, could almost whisper, which is exactly what Brando did.

"Well, if the *commissaire* in Marseille needs extra police, he'll be calling here," Verlaque said.

"We're very busy," Paulik replied, tapping at the newspaper.

"Hey! What happened in court today?"

"Case thrown out," Paulik replied, leaning back in his chair.

Verlaque raised his eyebrows. "Let me guess . . . on a technicality. Who's that punk's lawyer? Philippe Castel?"

The commissioner nodded ruefully.

Philippe Castel, a lawyer from Marseille, charged an hourly rate well beyond the means of petty criminals.

"I wonder which branch of the family paid Castel's bill?"

The door opened, and Verlaque's secretary, Mme Girard, came in. "They've just buzzed me from downstairs. M. François de Bremont is here," she said. Verlaque smiled at Mme Girard and noticed that, although always dressed impeccably, as were most women of her age and position in Aix—somewhere between fifty-five and sixty years of age, married, with three grown children—she was today especially striking in an emerald green suit with a short skirt that showed off her muscular, tanned legs.

"Send him up," answered the judge. And then he said to Paulik, "You can sit in on this, unless you still need the soccer scores."

"I've got them. Thanks, though, sir," Paulik answered, smiling.

Furnished with a large glass-topped desk that Verlaque had ordered from Conran in Paris, the office belonged to a man with an authority that inspired either confidence or fear, depending on the visitor's state of mind and their level of culpability. A *juge d'instruction* was supposed to be impartial. A bookshelf was up against one wall, heavy with law journals and casebooks. Two windows faced south and west. For the walls he had chosen an olive green, or "Empire green," as Mme Girard had insisted on calling it. Green was a color known to calm and reassure people, and Verlaque had thought it a good idea. Sylvie had furnished the only wall decorations: four large black-and-white photographs that Verlaque had bought at one of her openings.

Paulik took a corner seat, and Verlaque sat behind his desk, looking up at one of the photographs—a detail of three leaves floating in one of Aix's fountains. Infrared film dramatized the photographs, turning the leaves bright white and the water in the fountain black, jet-black, like ink. The photograph reminded him of a scene from his childhood: one bright morning when he had been playing by himself in the Tuileries gardens, not far from the Verlaque family mansion. He had come across some perfectly formed leaves floating in a fountain. He called over his English nanny, hoping to show them to her, and when she heard Verlaque, she merely lifted her head slightly in acknowledgment of his excitement. "Don't get yourself wet before lunch," was all she had said, in English.

Mme Girard stepped into the doorway and gestured for the young man to step into the room. "M. François de Bremont," she announced. "Judge Verlaque and Commissioner Paulik."

"Hello," Bremont said, giving the judge a herculean handshake. He turned to Paulik and delivered the same grip. Verlaque was blown over by his resemblance to Étienne—the only difference was that François's hair was a bit lighter, and he had the tan and big shoulders of a serious sailor.

"Thank you for coming straight here," Verlaque said.

"You were very insistent," Bremont replied. "I can't stay long, though. I'm anxious to get to the house in Saint-Antonin and check on things . . . especially on Jean-Claude."

"Fine. Please sit down," the judge said. "I'm sorry about the death of your brother. I only met him a few times—he was filming a documentary in Marseille—but I liked him very much."

"Everyone liked Étienne," Bremont said pointedly. "He was always affable and very good at his work."

"You're probably wondering why we called you here," Verlaque said. "The death of your brother was, as far as we can tell, accidental. But because of the nature of his death, falling from a place so familiar, and because there were no witnesses, we have to be as thorough as we can."

Paulik then added, "And, to be frank, given your brother's notoriety in the filmmaking world, and his stature in Aix, we would like to be extra thorough."

"Sure," replied Bremont, sitting up straighter, proud either of his brother or the family title. Verlaque quickly looked at the commissioner in acknowledgment of his tactic: Paulik, the farm boy, couldn't care less if the deceased had been rich or famous. François then asked, "What went on up there anyway? Was it a break-in?"

"No. Nothing was disturbed or taken from the château. The caretaker went through the place with me on Sunday."

"How sure can you and Jean-Claude be?"

Verlaque looked at Bremont and answered, "Quite sure, M. Bremont. Our policemen also made a thorough search. Why do you ask?"

"No reason," Bremont answered.

"You seemed worried. You must have a reason," Paulik challenged.

"It's just that the château is so remote. Anything could happen up there." Paulik noticed the sailor slowly rubbing his hands together, the way his grandmother had at his grandfather's deathbed.

"Do you think that your brother was capable of suicide?" Verlaque asked, changing the subject. He had noticed the wringing hands as well and thought François de Bremont had something in his voice that resembled fear.

"No way," answered Bremont, in a strong, clear voice. "Not Étienne. Judge Verlaque, I believe that my brother was a happy man. We may not have been close over the past few years," he paused, and looked at the judge and the commissioner, and then added, "You probably know that we live very different kinds of lives."

Paulik thought of the tall blondes on the sailboat. Bremont continued, "But I knew him well enough to know that he would never kill himself. He was too dedicated to Isabelle and the kids." François's voice broke slightly, and he took a handkerchief out of his pocket, dabbing the corners of his eyes. He sniffed. "I'm sorry," he said. "Étienne's death is a shock. I didn't sleep all night." Verlaque couldn't tell if the tears were forced or real, but the dark circles under the nobleman's eyes were genuine.

"I understand. Do you think that anyone had any reason to regard Étienne as an enemy . . . or vice versa?" the judge asked.

"Not likely," Bremont answered, then adding, after a pause, "but who knows?"

"Your brother never mentioned being worried about something? Or upset?"

"No! I already told you that we rarely spoke. And now, if you don't mind," François said, getting up quickly from his chair, "I really need to be going." The nobleman looked past Verlaque and out the office window, as if he was worried that the weather would suddenly change.

"Thank you, and again, I'm sorry for your loss," Verlaque said, extending his hand to say good-bye. Bremont, glancing at his watch, left the office.

"Not much, eh? He was in a hurry," Paulik said.

"So I noticed. He seemed almost frightened. Would you mind doing some further checks on him, since you've become such a computer whiz these past few months?" The police officers in Aix and Marseille had been given free computer-training sessions, and Paulik had offered to go on behalf of himself and *le juge*. Verlaque would have done it as well, but the first weekend of training sessions happened to coincide with a wine festival in Bordeaux, where friends of Verlaque's had a winery, and the second fell on the weekend of an important corrida in Nîmes, and Verlaque had managed to get, thanks to his position, two exclusive seats for the bullfight. He admitted to himself that his lack of patience had much to do with his avoidance of computers.

"And while you're at it, check with Officer Pellegrino, the polo player in Cannes, and see what he can tell you about François de Bremont."

"Right," Paulik said.

A loud laugh echoed down the corridor, and the closer and louder it got the quieter the judge and commissioner became, as if both knew that their conversation would soon be over. They could hear some officers laughing politely, while others guffawed, genuinely having a good time. The comedian had a heavy Midi accent, so that *putain*—his favorite word—became "putainge," with the famous southern emphasis on the last consonant.

"*Ma belle!*" Procureur Yves Roussel exclaimed, approaching Mme Girard's carefully decorated desk. "It's so good to see Provence's sun shining. *Ce putain d'Écosse!*"

"Didn't you have a good time in Scotland, Monsieur le Pro-cureur?" Mme Girard asked, puzzled.

"Good time? It was *ex-tra-or-din-aire*. Just not enough sun for a southern boy."

Paulik and Verlaque both stayed silent. Paulik looked out of the window, and Verlaque sat at his desk, with his hands behind his head, leaning back in his chair. They both knew the routine: Roussel would go into his office—he had been named prosecutor before Verlaque had arrived and had snagged the bigger one, next door—and take a tour of it, like a dog, making sure that nothing had been moved or touched in his weeklong absence. He would then knock loudly on Verlaque's door and, before being asked to do so, enter. The tour of his office was very quick this time, for almost immediately he was back with Mme Girard, his conversa-tion peppered with loud laughs and phrases describing Scotland, most of them beginning with *putain*. Just before he knocked on Verlaque's door, the words "*putain* haggis" were overheard. Paulik looked at the judge and said, "I've always wanted to try that. Haggis, I mean. Not *putain* haggis."

Verlaque laughed. "It's delicious, actually, especially with a single malt or a good strong ale, but the butcher should be re-commended to—" Before he could finish there was a loud knock and the door immediately swung open, revealing a short man made two inches taller by his turquoise cowboy boots.

"Mates!" Roussel bellowed in English, his hairy arms out-stretched. Verlaque smiled and got up from behind his desk and shook Roussel's hand, the prosecutor's oversized watch and thick silver bracelets sliding down his wrist as they did.

"How was your trip?" Verlaque asked. Roussel was obnoxious and had terrible taste, but Verlaque knew that he loved his job and the citizens of Aix and would protect them to the ends of the earth. Verlaque had been in such a slump lately that he wondered if he had actually missed Roussel's joking presence in the office.

"*Su-per. Fan-tas-tique.* What a beautiful country! They love the French, you know!" Roussel answered.

"Yes, because we're not English," Verlaque replied.

"How was the grass?" Paulik asked.

"*Su-per. Beau, beau, beau,*" Roussel replied, not picking up on the rugby man's tease aimed at golf. "Great golfing. Terrible food. Overpriced wines. Good whiskey, though."

Verlaque shot a glance over to Paulik, who smiled. Both men amused by the three sentences that summed up a country for Yves Roussel.

"So, what's this mess with Étienne de Bremont, eh? Suicide, eh?"

"No, I think not," Verlaque said.

"Ah, then he fell, poor lad. I knew his father. We'd best keep this quiet, eh? Such an important family." Verlaque now remembered why he couldn't stand Roussel: he was constantly trying to ignore, or forget, his humble background. Paulik, on the other hand, wore his with pride.

"I'm investigating it, actually," Verlaque said.

Roussel looked down at him sharply. "What the hell for? You told me on the phone that you had ruled out foul play."

"Because, just as you say, they are such an important family."

Paulik turned and looked out of the window, hiding his smirk.

"More important, Eric and Charles Bley have demanded an inquest. Procureur Levy came up from Marseille in your absence."

"Levy?" Roussel asked with a smile. "Nice gal. Fine legs."

Verlaque stayed silent, and Roussel stopped daydreaming about his fellow prosecutor and asked, "Do you have any evidence that Bremont was murdered?"

"Zero," Verlaque answered. Verlaque didn't tell Roussel about the caretaker's nervousness, the brother's fear, or the widow's dishonesty. He wanted to work on this alone, not because the Bremonts were "such an important family" but because Aix was such a small town.

"Death threats?"

"No."

"You see! Who would want to kill a filmmaker? Besides, he just made documentaries, not even interesting films!" Roussel looked over at Paulik, hoping to get a laugh from the commissioner. Paulik was smiling, but not for the reasons that Roussel assumed.

Verlaque stared at the prosecutor, suddenly realizing that he had not missed Yves Roussel at all and now wanted him out of his office.

"You're probably right, Yves." Verlaque left it at that, not mentioning when he planned to close the investigation. He knew from experience that Roussel had a short attention span. Verlaque had just bought himself a day or two, max. "I'll give the Bleys their report as soon as possible."

"Good. I'm off, boys! Time to take the Harley for a spin. She's been sitting in the garage for too long! I'm still officially on vacation until next week, but I'll be in and out!" Roussel turned on his slanted, raised turquoise heels and left, yelling a "*Salut*, Madame! Be good!" as he passed through Mme Girard's cubicle.

"Fancy a road trip tomorrow afternoon?" Verlaque asked Paulik, before switching off the office lights and closing the door behind them.

Paulik looked pleased. "Why not? I have a free day tomorrow, now that the court case has been postponed. What's the destination?"

"Cotignac. I thought that we could pay a visit to Jean-Claude Auvieux's sister. Let's walk out together and I'll fill you in on my visit with the caretaker and my interview with Isabelle de Bremont."

Once the two men had compared notes, Verlaque left the precinct and headed north, walking up past the cathedral. He glanced at his watch—it was just after 8:00 p.m., and he was feeling hungry. The contents of his refrigerator—half a bottle of red, some bits of Roquefort cheese, lettuce, lemon, and Parmesan— would be his dinner. He then remembered that his cigar club was meeting tonight, at Fabrice's house in the country. He turned left and began walking toward his garage to pick up his car when his cell phone rang and identified Marine as the caller.

"Oui?" Verlaque said.

"Hi, Antoine," said Marine, sounding out of breath. "I've just been thinking, inside la Madeleine."

"La Madeleine the café or la Madeleine the church?" asked Verlaque.

"The church," said Marine. "Do you remember the Louis Vuitton suitcase in the Bremont attic?"

"You mean, the one you made slide halfway across the attic?" Verlaque teased.

"Yes," Marine said, ignoring the jab. "It was empty."

"So?"

"It was always full, and locked, when we were kids. We used to play travel games, and I always wanted to play with that suitcase, but it was so heavy that we had to drag it with two hands across the floor. Étienne and François were always weird about that case—they didn't like to play with it like I did. Perhaps it was just because they were boys. Anyway, maybe it's silly of me, but I have a funny feeling about it. Once Étienne's mother came upstairs to check on us and saw that we had moved it, and she flipped out. It's entirely possible that after all these years one of the family members may have opened it and took out whatever was in there, but—"

"I'm planning to visit the caretaker tomorrow morning. I'll definitely ask him about the suitcase. Perhaps there was money in it. He told me he knew the attic by heart. Can we talk about this more then?"

"Sure, good night," Marine said, a bit disappointed that Verlaque had not been more grateful or optimistic about her news. She started to move her thumb to end the call, and as she did, Verlaque said one more thing.

"Marine?"

"Yes?" she answered.

"Would you like to . . . Ah, never mind . . . Thanks for this information."

He hung up the phone.

Chapter Seven

*T*here were already six or seven cars parked in front of the restored stone farmhouse when Verlaque arrived just before 9:00
p.m. He turned off the jazz, and his car engine, and got out of the
Porsche, and did his usual tour, looking to see who had a new car.
A Lexus that he hadn't seen before was parked off by itself, taking up what should have been two spaces, and causing him to
frown. He moved on and smiled when he saw a pale blue Deux
Chevaux, immaculate thanks to meticulous care by its owner, a
petit, well-groomed bookstore clerk, every bit as neat as his car. A
light came on above the front door, and a voice called from the
lit-up doorway. "We heard your Porsche. Are you going to come
in sometime?"

"I'm just admiring Pierre's Deux Chevaux. Tell him I'll buy it
whenever he's ready."

"I've got first dibs, sorry."

The two men gave each other affectionate *bises* as Verlaque
stepped into the low-ceilinged living room, warmed by a lit fire in
the hearth—necessary even in April in the centuries-old stone
house that stood in a clearing, wide open to the elements, surrounded by only vineyards. His host, Fabrice Gaussen, had grown

up in Marseille and had made his fortune in the plumbing business, with stores that bore his name across southern France. He had purchased the farmhouse in Le Tholonet, Aix's chicest neighborhood, in the early 1990s, before the TGV had arrived in Aix and real estate prices soared. Fabrice's introduction to cigars had been simple—his brother, Rémy, had married a Cuban, and Maria Gaussen was responsible, much to the chagrin of Fabrice's wife, for her brother-in-law's love of Cuba, its music and history, and especially its tobacco.

Verlaque smiled as he saw his friends and was immediately thankful that he had made the effort to come, despite his fatigue. It took about five minutes to make the rounds, each man kissing the judge on the cheek twice and warmly grabbing his shoulder or arm, except for Julien, who gave four kisses, two on each cheek, as was the tradition in his home town of Avignon. A box of cigars was thrust into Verlaque's hands.

"A little cigar for the aperitif," said Fabrice, also the club's president. "Get Monsieur le Juge a glass of champagne, would you, Gaspard? And no one is to ask Antoine about the Bremont case, all right? He's here to relax." Fabrice pointed to a flowered chintz chair obviously purchased by his wife—who tonight had escaped to her sister's house in Marseille—and he fluffed up a small pillow that was embroidered with the face of a pug-nosed dog. "Sit down, Antoine." Fabrice leaned in, his large belly looming over the judge. "So, what's going on?" Fabrice asked, half whispering. "The Bleys have asked for an inquest, eh?"

"Come off it, Fabrice!" Gaspard yelled, laughing, a bottle of champagne in his hand. Gaspard, just out of law school, and dressed in ripped jeans and handmade Italian shoes that he was still paying off, poured Verlaque some champagne. The young cigar aficionado grinned from ear to ear as he poured, thrilled to have been accepted into this group of bons vivants, most of them at least twenty years older than him.

Verlaque thanked Gaspard for the champagne and nodded, smiling, toward his good friend Jean-Marc, who was sitting in a matching armchair, smiling and smoking. "Fabrice, I smell something burning," Jean-Marc said, motioning toward the kitchen.

"Merde!" The club's president jumped up and ran toward the kitchen, followed closely by Loïc, a journalist and amateur chef.

Verlaque snipped off the end of his cigar and reached into his jacket pocket, realizing he had left his lighter in the car. He motioned with his thumb the act of igniting a lighter, and one was tossed across the room at him, the judge catching it in his right hand. Verlaque loved silent communications like this, especially with this group of friends, or with Marine, with whom they were as good as words. He was too tired to put on his glasses to look at the cigar band but was instantly impressed with the long, smooth taste that reminded him of freshly ground green peppercorns. "Petit Corona, Hoyo de Monterrey," a voice rang out from across the coffee table in perfect Spanish.

"Thanks, José," Verlaque answered. He then looked down at the coffee table and saw about fifteen lit scented candles and laughed.

"Fabrice's wife was hysterical before she left," Jean-Marc explained. "I got here early, and Fabrice was following her around the house, pleading with her not to open every window."

"Still, it's so much more pleasant meeting here, in a member's home, than getting stared down in a restaurant," José offered, in broken French. He knew, for one, that his wife would never have twelve cigar smokers in her home. He tried to make up for it by regularly supplying the club with cigars from Madrid, where they were cheaper.

"I was just in New York, and you can't smoke anywhere. It will soon happen here, mark my word," another accented voice suggested.

"No chance, Jacob. There would be a revolution in France before that!" Fabrice bellowed from the kitchen.

Jacob shrugged. "You think so? We tend to like following the Americans." Jacob, an Egyptian Jew, was a financial trader who commuted from Aix to London and had already heard his British colleagues talking of smoking bans that would soon hit the UK. "Anyway, meeting like this at a member's home is considerably cheaper than a restaurant, and the wine's better," he continued, motioning to the champagne. Jacob, a self-made millionaire, was extremely sensitive to the disparity of wealth amongst his fellow cigar club members. He knew that some—Pierre, for instance, whom he was fairly certain worked at one of the many Aix bookstores, and Loïc, a journalist for *La Provence*—made sacrifices to buy their cigars.

Swearing was then heard from the kitchen, and Verlaque got up and went in, where Fabrice, now sporting a flowered apron, was removing burnt pastries from a cookie sheet. "We salvaged quite a few," he said. "Loïc is now in charge of the oven. I quit!" Loïc and Verlaque exchanged smiles. Fabrice started for the living room, carrying the hot baking sheet with flowered oven mitts that matched his apron. "Fabrice!" Loïc called after him. "Put those on a serving dish!"

"Merde!" he said, turning around. "You're right." Verlaque chose an oval porcelain plate from on top of the refrigerator and helped Fabrice remove the savory pastries from the baking sheet, happy to be doing a simple task, instead of thinking about the Bremont death, as his club members assumed he was doing. He had, in fact, been thinking about Marine. "Are these *gougères*?" Verlaque asked, picking one up and tossing it into his mouth. Fabrice straightened his back and replied, "Of course! They're simple once you get the hang of it!" Fabrice took the platter and walked into the living room, where oohs and aahs could be heard. "One at a time!" Fabrice bellowed. "I saw that, Julien! Put one back!"

"What kind of cheese did you put in these?" Pierre asked the beaming chef.

"Cantal, with a bit of Parmesan."

"Cantal? And not Gruyère? Wow. What a good idea—it's salty and sharp. Perfect!" Pierre saluted Fabrice with his glass of champagne. He closed his eyes and sipped, as if he was enjoying every bubble, and in fact he was. Bookstores didn't—couldn't—pay well, and being in the cigar club was his sole luxury. He repeatedly told himself that he would happily eat beans and rice all week in order to smoke hand-rolled Cuban cigars once a month with his group of friends.

"Pierre, what's the latest trend in books?" Jacob asked, he himself the owner of an impressive library.

"Gardening," Pierre answered, leaning toward the coffee table and taking another *gougère*.

Jacob looked puzzled "Really?"

"It's April," Pierre replied. "Springtime."

Jacob smiled. "Ah, right! Fabrice, these are wonderful *gougères*, by the way."

Fabrice now shrugged, as if making *gougères* was child's play. "Just wait until you guys taste the T-bones. Hey, Loïc, is the barbecue ready?"

Loïc popped his head around the kitchen door. "Yes! The coals are perfect!"

"Okay! Who wants rare, medium, or blue?" Fabrice asked, looking at his friends. "Hands up for blue."

Pierre raised his hand. "You don't even have to heat it up that much for me."

"Okay. Now, rare?"

The majority of the club then raised its hands. "Good. José? You're the only one that didn't raise your hand. Do you want medium rare?"

José slumped down in his seat. "Actually, well done, please."

"That's not even an option!"

"Come on, Fabrice," Verlaque said. "Give our Castilian friend what he wants."

"Fine!" Fabrice huffed. "Excuse me, gentlemen, while I attend to the barbecue. Oh, sorry, Virginie!"

"It's all right, you made up for any faux pas with those *gougères!*" the club's sole female member said, laughing. A pharmacist, she had recently relocated to the Aix region after having sold her father's prosperous pharmacy near the Sorbonne in Paris.

"How's your pharmacy in Lambesc working out?" Julien asked, taking a *gougère* that he had hid in a paper napkin and putting it into his mouth.

"Great! Most of my clients are retired farmers, and half of them just come in to chat. I love it. Compared to Paris, it's zero stress." Virginie didn't have to add that with the proceeds from the sale of her two-bedroom apartment in the fifth arrondissement she had purchased a five-bedroom, 3,500-square-foot, seventeenth-century mansion in the village of Lambesc.

Jean-Marc, noticing Verlaque grow quiet, as he usually did when people spoke of Paris, left his coveted armchair, and in no time Julien had sprinted out of his hard-backed dining room chair and taken it over. Jean-Marc turned around and said, "I'm coming back, Julien. First come, first serve." He pulled a foot stool up beside Verlaque's chair and asked, whispering, "Did you see Marine at the château?"

Verlaque took a drag of his cigar, letting the aroma pass around his mouth before blowing out. "Yes, she came up this morning."

"How did it go?"

Verlaque looked at his friend, so silent when it came to his own love life, but somehow that had never bothered the judge. He trusted Jean-Marc with his life. "I was stunned, actually. Utterly unprepared."

"You had forgotten Marine's beauty?" Jean-Marc asked, smiling.

"Oh, her beauty I remembered. It was her grace and naturalness that I had forgotten." Verlaque looked up at the ceiling and turned to his friend. "I'm sure I pissed her off, as usual."

Jean-Marc easily imagined the scenario, and smiled. "Go easy on her, Antoine."

Verlaque put his hand on Jean-Marc's shoulder. "I'm determined to change my ways. Don't worry."

"To the table!" hollered Fabrice, arriving with a platter layered high with T-bone steaks. "Come on, Antoine and Jean-Marc! You can continue your lovers' symposium later!" He had guessed that they were talking of Marine Bonnet. Perhaps Jean-Marc was in love with her too, he thought to himself.

The club members almost ran to the table, as if they hadn't eaten in days. Verlaque looked at them and smiled, knowing that each and every one of them, despite where they were born or how much money they made, loved food and wine and cigars and laughter. He sometimes fantasized about bringing Philip Larkin with him to a meeting or Winston Churchill or JFK.

When they had finished eating their first course—a slice of foie gras made by Fabrice's wife and served on a bed of salad— Loïc came into the dining room with a baking dish of scalloped potatoes. "Cooked on low heat for four hours, with a tub of crème fraîche," he said, second-guessing the members' questions. "No cheese, lads, so it's low fat." The club members laughed, and Loïc, remembering his manners, served Virginie first, who happily scooped two ladles of steaming potatoes onto her plate. Fabrice walked the opposite way around the table, serving the steaks. "Julien!" he hollered. "Wait until everyone is served before diving in!"

"It will get cold!" Julien answered. "It's an insult to the chefs, eating your food cold."

"Nice excuse!" Verlaque shouted. Fabrice then sat down at the head of the table and raised his fork and knife in the air. "Bon appétit!"

Verlaque cut a bit of steak and was immediately struck by its tenderness. He put it into his mouth and chewed, staring at Fabrice. "This is amazing."

Fabrice beamed. "Tell them, Loïc."

Loïc leaned forward, as if sharing a national secret. "Since we already had the oven on, we put the steaks in there as soon as they came off the grill, for about fifteen minutes on super low heat," he explained.

"I've never heard of that," Jean-Marc said.

"A chef that I interviewed told me about it," Loïc replied, cutting his steak.

"How long were they on the grill for?" Julien asked, not looking up, his steak already half gone.

"For the rare ones," Fabrice said, glaring at José, "four minutes per side. They're pretty thick."

"It's like butter," Virginie added. She held up her glass, full of a Côte Rôtie red wine, and said, "To the chefs!"

After some discussion about the mayor's plans to change Aix, the dinner plates were whisked away by Gaspard and Jacob, Gaspard feeling that as the youngest member it was his duty to pitch in. Jacob, who had always had full-time staff at his home, enjoyed this kind of work and missed it.

"Should we take a pause before dessert?" Fabrice asked, folding his napkin and setting it on the table.

"You needn't ask that," Verlaque replied. "I think we're all anxious to smoke the Edmundos that are in that box on the coffee table."

"Great! Let's retire to the salon, shall we?" Fabrice suggested, with an exaggeratedly posh voice that barely hid the Marseillais accent he had grown up with.

"Julien! That's my chair!" Jean-Marc yelled as he left the table. Verlaque looked at his friend in surprise, and laughed. He had never heard Jean-Marc raise his voice before.

Chapter Eight

The mistral had stopped blowing and left a fine sunny morning, with a clear blue sky, in its wake. Verlaque loved it when the mistral blew for only one day—the bracing wind cleared the pollution from the air, and then quickly left; much like the housekeeper, Antonia, who had cleaned the Verlaque family apartment in Paris when he was small. Antonia made too much noise, sang to herself in Portuguese, and moved every bit of furniture around as she cleaned, causing total chaos; but she did her job in record time, always smiling, and left the 3,500-square-foot apartment sparkling.

The doors to the cathedral were open as Verlaque walked past it toward the parking garage where he kept his car. He stopped and turned around, watching the cathedral's caretaker as she unlocked the dirty green outer panels of the church's front doors with a huge antique key. A small group of excited French tourists surrounded her. He had seen only once before, also by chance, what lay underneath: an inner door that was hidden, and gloriously carved, protected from the harsh Provençal sun and wind. The caretaker had to be in a good mood to be persuaded to reveal the fifteenth-century wood sculptures, and a generous tip often helped. As she opened the green doors, a ray of sunlight lit up the exposed inner panels, more than three meters high, richly carved in dark wood. A group of six small female saints stood in miniature Gothic alcoves—each woman carved with incredible details in her jewelry, in the texture of her cloak and skirt and hair. They wore pointed slippers, hiding the toes that Verlaque craved to see. Delicately carved grapes, nuts, and leaves surrounded the figures—the bounty of Provence, as always. It was as if the sculptor had brought some of the vegetables from his garden and used them as models for his great work.

Verlaque's grandmother had never seen these doors, and he was sorry for that misfortune. She had died the previous autumn, and whenever they had walked into the cathedral, hoping to see the doors, the caretaker had been off duty. Verlaque had always loved to show her paintings or sculptures that he knew she'd like. He had craved her approval, and always received it. She had adored him. She, of all the members of his family, had visited Verlaque the most, taking the first-class car on the TGV down from Paris but choosing to stay in one of Aix's simple two-star hotels, when she should have been staying at the luxurious Villa Gallici. "I want to be downtown, near you," she would say. She had called Verlaque frequently—especially when he was dating Marine—and she liked to tease him about being involved in police work, often beginning her phone calls with "Hi, copper!"

Any bit of warmth that was left in Verlaque he attributed to her, to Emmeline. When they were young, she had read stories to Verlaque and his brother, in English, in the gardens of her Normandy villa. She loved Normandy—she used to say she could feel England's breezes from there: she had been born and raised in England and had met Verlaque's grandfather in Paris when she was studying painting in Montmartre for a year in the 1930s.

Emmeline had come from a poor but noble land-rich family, and in Paris she had been completely dedicated to studying art. She spent little time in the cafés and bars, like her fellow art students did, and she met her husband, a young, rich industrialist—the family money had come from flour mills—at one of the few parties she attended while in Paris.

The curves on la route de Cézanne were a delight in his dark green 1963 Porsche. He had bought the car just for roads like this— narrow, built for horse and carriage, and lined with olive trees. He was glad to have gone to the cigar club last night, he thought as he drove past the lane that lead to Fabrice's house—despite the slight headache this morning and the general fuzziness that came after smoking two cigars in the evening. And he was glad that Marine had called him, telling him of the suitcase. It at least gave him an excuse to call on Jean-Claude Auvieux again, and there would still be plenty of time for lunch, and then a drive to Cotignac.

Each time he drove by the estates in Le Tholonet he was tempted to call his realtor friend, Gilles, and ask if there was anything for sale. When she died, Emmeline had left Verlaque and his brother, Sébastien, a lofty inheritance, including her nineteenth-century home in a tiny village in Normandy, Saint-Germain-le-Vasson. It was in a part of Normandy little visited by tourists, about fifty kilometers south of Deauville. The surrounding terrain was rich green farmland, covered in orchards and pastures, and Verlaque shared Emmeline's love for the region's rolling hills and wooden barns. One could leave the front gate and just start walking, rarely coming across a car, more often just tractors. You couldn't do that in Provence—there were too many people, too many cars. If there were farm lanes good for walking in Provence, Verlaque had never found them. Upon receiving word of the inheritance, his brother had gone out and

immediately bought a chic apartment in Paris's sixth arrondissement. But Verlaque's money still sat in the bank, and he rarely
thought of it. Spending it never really occurred to him—it was
Emmeline's money.

One evening last year, Verlaque had come home late from
working on a complicated drug-trafficking case to find Marine
and Emmeline talking about the latter's younger days. The emo-
tion he felt when he saw the ease with which the pair got along
was not joy or happiness but, to his shame, jealousy. He wasn't interested in the family history—he only wanted to spend time with
Emmeline—the one woman in his childhood who had hugged
him unconditionally. It embarrassed him that he could have been
jealous of Marine: she was in fact the only girlfriend he had ever
introduced to Emmeline, for the very reason that he knew that
they would get along so well. He loved them both, he realized now,
his heart pounding.

In an attempt to stop thinking of them, he turned up the
music, taking the curves smoothly until he arrived at Saint-
Antonin.

He pulled into the drive of the Bremont house, and Jean-
Claude Auvieux was where Verlaque had expected to see him—
in the orchard. "Hello, Monsieur le Juge," Jean-Claude shouted
from the heights of an almond tree. "Would you like a fresh almond?" he asked.

"Yes, I would," answered the judge, and he cupped his hands
and caught an almond still in its thick, green, fuzzy skin. Verlaque
started to peel it away with his thumbnail, and he thought of the
green painted doors of the cathedral that revealed the delicious
sculptures hidden underneath. He ate the nut—it was incredibly
fresh and juicy.

"I'm sorry to take you away from your harvest, M. Auvieux,"

Verlaque said, "but I wanted to ask you something more about the attic." Auvieux shot the judge a worried look and got down off the ladder. When he got to the ground he still towered over Verlaque. "It's okay. The basket is full," Auvieux said, smiling at his bounty.

"Are you alone?" Verlaque asked.

"Yes, François has gone into town."

Auvieux went into the cottage to fetch the keys, which were kept in a kitchen drawer, and the two men then went into the château, up the three flights of stairs, to the attic. When the door was opened, the same mirror trick happened that had frightened Marine, only this time it was the judge and the caretaker side by side in the dreamy reflection. Verlaque quickly stepped aside so as not to remind himself of his dwarflike stature next to the giant caretaker. "Let's walk around, and please tell me if you see anything out of place," Verlaque said.

"But, Monsieur, I already did."

Auvieux turned the light on and Verlaque said, "Ah! You changed the lightbulb."

"Yes, your commissioner told me that the lightbulb was burnt out when he was here the other day. I usually come up here during the day, so I hadn't noticed."

Verlaque watched closely as Auvieux stooped to look at the contents of various boxes scattered around the attic. They made their way over to the window, and Verlaque asked if they could open it. Auvieux unlatched the window's wooden shutters and fastened each one to a metal clasp that was drilled into the outside wall. To do so he had to lean far out, but he held on the window frame with his free hand.

"Do you think that Count de Bremont could have fallen out of the window by doing what you're doing right now, fastening the shutters back against the wall?" Verlaque asked the caretaker.

"No, not likely," said Auvieux. "He's been doing this since he was ten years old, we all have." As he regained his balance, Verlaque noticed Auvieux's gaze fall on the Louis Vuitton case. "Here, let me move this suitcase out of your way," Verlaque said.

"Wait, I'll do it!" Auvieux exclaimed, taking the judge's arm. Auvieux bent down to lift the suitcase and, feeling that it was empty, immediately set it down again, almost dropping it. *"Mon Dieu!"* he said, looking at Verlaque and now rubbing his hands up and down his thighs. "It's never been empty. I was just up in the attic last week. Count François—" Auvieux abruptly stopped himself and stared down at the floor.

"What is it, M. Auvieux?" Verlaque asked. "What is normally in this suitcase?"

"I don't know, I don't know," Auvieux answered, his eyes still cast downward. Verlaque didn't reply, and so the caretaker continued, this time looking back at the judge. "François called me and asked me to find some of his grandfather's old polo trophies, so I had to come up here and get them for him. One of the bigger trophies was down on the floor, behind this suitcase, and I had to move the suitcase to get at it, that's all. The suitcase was heavy, full of . . . stuff . . . as it always has been."

Verlaque then asked the obvious, "Has anyone else been in the attic since then?"

"No," said Auvieux. "Except your policemen," he added.

"Don't worry, my policemen wouldn't take anything. Who else has keys to the attic?"

"Myself, Étienne had, and François. And I think Mme Bremont."

"Isabelle?"

"Yes."

"Do you know what was in the suitcase?" Verlaque pressed on.

"No, I don't."

Verlaque stared at Auvieux for a moment. "It belonged to Count Philippe de Bremont. Maybe it had old clothes in it? He was François and Étienne's grandfather." Auvieux then added, as if it were proof, "Look—here's his name on the tag."

Verlaque bent down and pretended to look at the tag. "Do you remember what day you were up here, getting the trophies?" asked Verlaque.

"Yes. It was Friday. I was in a hurry to get to my sister's for dinner. You remember me telling you. She was making a *blanquette de veau.*"

Verlaque nodded. "Yes, I remember." So that means that someone other than Étienne was in the attic on Saturday, or early Sunday, before the death was announced. Or perhaps Étienne had removed the contents of the suitcase himself, before his fall. "Let's look around the attic, one more time, for something that could have been in the suitcase. Please tell me if you see anything that shouldn't be here," Verlaque said.

"Okay," agreed Auvieux, shrugging. He then added, "I didn't take anything!" But Verlaque could see that they both knew that they would not find the contents of the suitcase.

Auvieux looked as if he felt like it was his fault—as if he had a personal responsibility for all things in the Bremont château—and although he had seemed surprised that the suitcase was empty, Verlaque was convinced that the caretaker knew more about its contents than he was letting on. They drank some coffee, the caretaker's hands trembling as he poured.

"Is everything all right?" Verlaque asked. "You seem upset, M. Auvieux."

Auvieux put his coffee down and said, "You see, Judge, the count's belongings are very important to me—that's why I clean the library myself—those are his books in there. Did you see how many there are? He was very kind to me when I was growing up."

"When M. Bremont gets back from Aix, could you ask him about the suitcase? I know that he just got here, so he couldn't have removed the contents, but he and his brother may have known what was in it."

The caretaker was now bustling around the kitchen, loudly rearranging the meager contents of the refrigerator. He looked at the judge as if his request had just registered. "Oui, oui," he mumbled, now frantically scrubbing the already spotless stone sink.

Verlaque stood up to leave, and then said, "Thank you, M. Auvieux. Maybe now you can get back to your almond harvest. I think I may have interrupted, and you certainly have a splendid crop."

The caretaker quickly nodded and, grabbing his hat and basket, said, "You're right! Those almonds won't wait all day!"

Everything of hers is sacred too, thought Verlaque as he got back into his car. He thought of the villa in Normandy, and all its contents under white sheets until he and his brother made up their minds as to what to do with the house. Her watercolors, which graced the old house's walls, mostly landscapes or flowers, all of them signed Emmeline, many with a dedication, "Pour Charles," Verlaque's French grandfather. He picked up his cell phone from the passenger seat, where he had intentionally left it. Two messages: one from Paulik and the other from Marine. He called Paulik. "My computer training has come in handy," Paulik said as soon as he picked up the phone.

"Oh yeah?"

"Yes, I'm a regular Bill Gates. Listen to what I found out. The girls . . . the ones that François de Bremont favors . . . and whom you sadly thought might be opera singers, sir. They are Russian, perhaps prostitutes, and definitely young."

"Here illegally?"

"No, they are here as models. Apparently everyone in Cannes knows about this except for the head of police. Or he does know and . . ." Paulik never finished his sentence.

"Did you find all this out on the Internet?" Verlaque asked.

"No, not all. The juicy stuff I got from my cousin Fréd, who owns a restaurant in Antibes."

"Ah! Restaurant owners should be on the police payroll. It always amazes me how much they know about a town and its goings-on," Verlaque replied, laughing. "What else did you learn?"

"Apparently François de Bremont has been causing some disturbances recently in Cannes."

"Maybe you should tell me about this in person," Verlaque replied. "I'll be right there. We can go out for lunch—I'm starving. And afterward we can drive out to the Var to see Jean-Claude Auvieux's sister, as promised. She finally returned my phone call this morning. On second thought, why don't you just meet me at one o'clock at Lotus."

"Lotus? The trendy new restaurant on the rue Frédéric Mistral?" Paulik sounded dubious. "I'm really more of a bistro kind of guy."

"You'll like it," Verlaque assured the commissioner. "I thought it was just a trendy minimalist restaurant when it first opened. But it's actually very good—simple Italian dishes, and they have a heavenly Corsican wine that's only available there. No one else in the south of France can get their hands on the stuff."

"Not Clos Canarelli?"

"That's the one."

"Hélène tasted it once, when she did a wine tour of Corsica

with some other winemakers. She's been raving about it. I'll have to tell her. Okay, I'll see you there. *À bientôt.*"

Verlaque drove quickly to Aix and parked his car illegally on the cours Mirabeau, putting his badge in the widow. A cigar was indispensable before he met with Paulik. As he was walking toward the *tabac*, he saw two people arguing on the opposite side of the *cours*. Couples in Aix were always either openly kissing or fighting. As he neared, he recognized Isabelle de Bremont and the back of the head of someone who looked exactly like Étienne de Bremont—he knew immediately that it must be François. Isabelle was running her hands through her red hair, and he was trying to talk to her, holding her by the elbow. A closer look was impossible, without being seen.

And then Verlaque saw him: the old man who sold nuts to all of the café clients up and down the cours Mirabeau. Verlaque had been buying from him for years, salted almonds usually, and Marine had always had a soft spot for the old, bald man who wore a blue apron and carried his nuts in an old-fashioned wicker basket. Verlaque regretted that he didn't know his name, but when he walked up to him, the nut seller instantly recognized him and gave him a hearty handshake.

"Could you do me a huge favor?" Verlaque asked him in a low voice. "It's police business, so you'll have to be discreet. Could you walk past that couple across the street—do you see them, the petite redhead and the man she's arguing with?"

"You mean Isabelle and François de Bremont?" the old man asked.

Verlaque smiled. "Is that who they are? Yes, well, could you walk past them and try to hear what they are arguing about?"

The old man nodded and slowly crossed the street. To Verlaque's amazement, the nut seller's car, a brand-new Clio, was parked beside the couple. Not bad, thought Verlaque, a new Clio for the nut seller. The old man fussed with the bags of nuts that he kept in the trunk and came back across the street after two or three minutes.

"He doesn't want to sell the château in Saint-Antonin," the old man reported. "She does."

"*She* does?"

The old man took his time replying as he put a cashew into his mouth. "Have we hired a deaf judge in Aix? Yes, *she*."

Chapter Nine

*P*aulik didn't like the look of the place. It was the kind of restaurant where everyone wears black, and they all look at you when you walk in. The food became secondary at these kinds of places—people weren't there to eat but to see and be seen. It surprised Paulik that Antoine Verlaque would like it here; he was well-known around the precinct to be a good cook and one who was fussy about food and wine. He walked up the four steps that led to the front door and looked around. Most of the tables were occupied: people in suits out for a business lunch; another table with three women who, judging by their clothes, worked at one of the fashionable boutiques in the quartier; and, next to him, two men wearing paint-splattered jeans and work boots, discussing their respective building sites and the problems with obtaining permits from the town hall. The music annoyed him. He didn't like music in restaurants.

A young woman in a top that ended about half a meter above her belly button saw Paulik and came up to him, carrying a stack of menus in her arms. She smiled a genuine smile at Paulik, who was not a beautiful man, and said, "Hi. Are you dining with someone?"

"Yes, I am," answered Paulik. "But he's late. We'll be two."

"Come this way. I'll give you this nice table under the open roof. Enjoy your lunch."

Paulik sat down in a blue velour armchair and looked up. He hadn't noticed it before—a large portion of the roof, about four meters square, was open to the bright blue, cloudless sky. Still, the restaurant wouldn't do well in summer, he thought. The Aixois need their terraces.

The mini-topped waitress returned with a glass of champagne and set it before Paulik. He opened his mouth to complain, and she walked away, calling over her shoulder, "*Cin-cin!* It's to celebrate your first time here!"

Watch, the champagne will be added to the bill, Paulik thought. I'll bet it's ten euros a glass.

Verlaque walked in after a few minutes and stopped to give the same waitress the *bises*. Paulik watched, not surprised that the judge knew her, for Verlaque had told him that he'd become a regular at Lotus since its opening a few months back. It did surprise the commissioner, however, when the *bises* took longer than usual and Verlaque put his hand on the girl's slender waist. Paulik buried his head in the menu, and Verlaque came and sat down, smiling when he saw the commissioner's flute of champagne.

"Have you ordered?"

"No, but I glanced at the menu."

Magically the waitress appeared, explaining the daily specials and adding, "There are a number of vegetarian dishes as well."

Verlaque looked at Paulik, and then looked up at the waitress, smiling. "Do we *look* like vegetarians?"

"I'm going to have the *jambon de Bayonne* to start with, and then the risotto with three meats," Paulik ordered, grinning.

Verlaque looked over the menu. He could still feel his stomach pushing against his belt in a way he wasn't used to. He would stick with fish today: shrimp wrapped in bacon with salad, and then a grilled trout. At least there was bacon. The waitress took their orders and left.

The judge glanced around him and noted, happily, two construction workers sitting at the table next to theirs: good food knows no class boundaries.

Paulik began to speak, ripping off a piece of warm bread. "I made some calls to Cannes, to the police station and to my cousin Fréd. François de Bremont owns a bunch of studios in Cannes and Nice—he rents them out to a modeling agency, and the apartments are used by the models. The girls are legally here with six-month visas. They often come and go on his sailboats, so it's hard for the cops to keep track of who is who."

"And now for the obvious question," Verlaque said. He sipped some of the champagne that had just arrived and continued, "Are the girls models or prostitutes? Do you remember that case in Paris, with the fourteen- and fifteen-year-old Romanian girls?"

"Yeah. The photo shoots were done in the nude, to train them into prostitution. One of them got out, didn't she, by asking to go outside for a smoke? A social worker had arranged to help her and was waiting for her in her car and whisked her to safety. The others . . ." Paulik's voice trailed off when the waitress came to refill their glasses with wine. "Anyway, this is where it gets gray," he continued. "The guys in Cannes haven't been able to determine that. They *are* models, definitely very jet set, and they go to parties with wealthy, often older, Russian businessmen. The modeling agency is legit, apparently—it's been around for years."

"So we don't know how much entertaining the girls do," Verlaque said.

"Right. The agency is owned by a rich, influential Russian. They're sending me his dossier later in the day."

Verlaque tried not to associate Russians with mafia, but he was always surprised when Nice's Russian criminal element came to light: the cold war ended and the villains moved to a sunnier location.

"There's more," Paulik continued, diving into his smoked ham, sliced paper thin and served over a bed of arugula, which the young waitress had discreetly placed in front of him. "Pellegrino called me this morning. He's the cop who plays polo in Cannes."

"Go on," Verlaque said.

"François de Bremont has had his hand slapped a few too many times recently. He's big into gambling at the casino, but recently he's been accused of betting on polo, possibly even trying to throw his own games."

"Nice guy. A cheat at sports and maybe a pimp. Then it doesn't make sense what I just witnessed on the *cours* ten minutes ago." Verlaque saw Paulik's look of curiosity and continued, "François and Isabelle de Bremont were arguing. But here's the interesting thing—Isabelle wants to sell the château and he doesn't."

"Really? I figured he would want the cash," Paulik replied. "Does he inherit the title now?"

"No," Verlaque answered. "Étienne's son will become *le comte*. But François gets the château, I would imagine."

The two men fell silent, both thinking over the case, knowing that, if the play was dirty, they didn't have much to go on: Someone sure-footed, a mountain climber, falls out of a window. An empty suitcase that is somehow important to the family, and no hint as to what was in it. A receipt for two brioches from 1954. The brother—a cheat—argues with the deceased's wife the day before his brother's funeral.

Paulik looked up and saw the judge watching a waitress in an impossibly short skirt put candles on the tables for the dinner service. "The waitresses sure are cute here. They must screw up the orders all the time," Paulik said. He shrugged and mopped the rest of his sauce with a piece of bread, and then wiped his mouth with his linen napkin and sat back, his arms folded across his chest.

"Though I am sure the waitresses are not half as interesting as your *belle* Hélène—I remember meeting her briefly at that wine-makers' dinner. What's she up to?" Verlaque asked.

"She's knee-deep in clearing up the vineyard—there are new cuttings to be planted," answered Paulik.

Their main dishes arrived, and Paulik looked at his doubtfully. His risotto was stacked high and artfully with different kinds of fried meats and shoots of asparagus pointed up toward the sky. "Tall," was all he said before he dug in. Paulik didn't like food that looked more like a sculpture than a meal. Verlaque's trout was perfectly cooked, served with new potatoes and sautéed fennel.

Paulik tackled his dish by eating the asparagus first, which was in season in Provence at the moment. It had been roasted in the oven with olive oil, garlic, and lots of salt and pepper, just the way Hélène made it at home. "Taste this," Paulik said, putting a forkful of risotto and meat on Verlaque's plate. "The meat juice has been reduced, and they've used all different kinds of meat. I think that's *figatelli* from Corsica that they've fried."

"It's *figatelli*, all right, and a good one. How do you like the wine?"

"Outstanding."

"And the restaurant?"

"Fine for a late lunch, but the true test is always a busy Saturday night," Paulik answered.

They continued eating and talked about another case—a series of break-ins that had been going on in downtown Aix and whose culprits had just been caught. They both declined dessert and had two espressos each. Verlaque got up to pay the bill—he was usually too impatient to wait for the debit card machine to be brought to the table. Paulik looked around the room; he had to admit that the big velour armchairs were quite comfortable. He could see Verlaque and the waitress talking and laughing. Verlaque gave the waitress his credit card, punched in his code, and then she handed him back the receipt, but first quickly jotted something down on it. The judge smiled and put the slip of paper in his pocket. The men walked through the restaurant, and Paulik looked around the room nodding his head up and down, as if rating the restaurant. "Thank you," he said. "Next time I'm paying."

The drive to Cotignac was beautiful. Neither man spoke, for each was looking out of the window at the springtime that had just arrived, almost magically, after one of the coldest winters in years—snow had stayed on the ground for three full days in December. Fields of fluttering red poppies were everywhere, and the vineyards were sprouting up young shoots of bright green leaves. This trip wasn't completely necessary, but Verlaque wanted to talk to Auvieux's sister to check up on his alibi and to tie up all the loose ends connected with Étienne de Bremont and the château.

Étienne, the earnest man behind the camera, deserved at least that. Yes, Verlaque thought to himself as he drove, even if the nobleman did die by accident, or suicide, he deserved a proper inquiry. Verlaque added up in his head what they had to go on: everyone had an alibi, although he still hadn't heard from Flamant about the train tickets. People had doubts, like Marine, or were enraged, as the Bley brothers seemed to be; but still they had nothing, no proof that Étienne de Bremont hadn't just lost his balance.

Mlle Cosette Auvieux hadn't returned his Sunday call until that morning. Since she had said that she wouldn't be coming to the funeral, Verlaque had arranged the meeting at her place in the Var. He preferred to interview people where they lived, so they'd be more comfortable, but also so he could see their surroundings. Cosette sounded surprised that the judge was willing to drive an hour and a half to meet with her.

Just outside of Cotignac, Verlaque remembered that he had forgotten to call Marine. While driving with his left hand, he dialed her number with his right. She answered on the second ring. "Hi," he said. "Sorry I didn't call you back right away." Be polite, he reminded himself.

"Hello," Marine replied, slightly annoyed but also curious. "Can I help you, Antoine?" she asked, trying to sound detached.

It was obvious to Verlaque that Marine was upset with him. He should have invited her over last night, after she left the church. "I went up to Saint-Antonin this morning and toured the attic with Jean-Claude Auvieux. He was shocked to see that the suitcase was empty. He said it had been full and locked last Friday, before he went up to his sister's in the Var. I'm on my way to her place right now."

"So someone, either Jean-Claude or possibly even Étienne, took the contents out of the suitcase after Friday and before Sunday," Marine answered.

"Yes. And I really don't think it was Auvieux—he was genuinely shocked and upset to find the suitcase empty."

"I agree," said Marine, pausing. "I believe that Jean-Claude is trustworthy, even if it's been fifteen years or so since I last saw him. He's always been so respectful when it comes to that place." Verlaque also filled in Marine on Paulik's recent discoveries. François de Bremont wasn't looking too good. "Why don't you come around for a drink tomorrow night?" Verlaque asked.

Marine hesitated. She hadn't been to Verlaque's apartment since they had split up—it might do her some good to see his flat again. Arthur had just left for California, so she was free to go. Even if Arthur had been in Aix, she could still go if she wanted to: she was thirty-five years old after all.

"Sure, but I won't stay late," Marine said. "I have papers to mark," she added, lying. They agreed on a time, and Paulik motioned to Verlaque to say hello to Marine for him. Hélène and Marine had got on well the one time they had met at Hélène's boss Olivier Bonnard's party. When they heard about the break-up, Paulik, but especially Hélène, thought that Marine was better off without Antoine Verlaque. During that dinner party at the Bonnard's, Verlaque had openly criticized Marine in front of the other guests because she had called some Roquefort simply "blue cheese." "If you ever do that to me, I'll kill you," Hélène had told Paulik on the drive home. Hélène had a theory that Antoine Verlaque wanted a perfect girlfriend at his side—one who spoke several languages, was well traveled, said the right things at social gatherings, was an experienced sportswoman, and was, of course, beautiful. But he would never be satisfied, for Marine was, from what Hélène's saw, a wonderful and near-perfect woman. And if he did find his perfect woman, on Mars or in Geneva or Monte Carlo, she knew he could never get close to her.

"Ah come on," Paulik had said to his wife, "everyone becomes intimate with someone when they're in love."

"Not Verlaque," Hélène insisted. "He can't get close to any woman. He can flirt. He can seduce. He can go through the motions. But he can't show his true self to a woman."

Paulik shook his head. He finally said, "Nobody's perfect. Besides, we don't know what's going on inside other people's heads. With the judge there could be some real messy stuff—his rich, uptight family—half-English too. They say that the English keep everything inside, right?"

"Ha! And the French don't? Look at your family," Hélène argued. Paulik looked at her, surprised. "Sorry, honey," she continued, "I don't mean it like that. I love your family, but they are weird, *non*? We can't, as adults, keep blaming our childhoods in order to justify our improper adult behavior."

Paulik let it drop at that—he had enjoyed the few times he had worked with the judge and felt uneasy speaking about him behind his back. Besides, they didn't really know Verlaque, or the professor, that well.

Verlaque pulled the car up to the address he had written down on the back of a receipt from the *tabac*. It was a cheap-looking house, with thin stucco coating hiding cement block, as in all new Provençal houses, and the neighbors' houses were identical. No attempt was made at a front lawn—weeds surrounded a beat-up Citroën AX that was parked in front of the house. A small, thin woman stood erect at the front door, and she watched the two men climb out of Verlaque's tiny Porsche. Verlaque tried not to frown as he got out of the car. Why live in the country if you're going to live in such a place? he asked himself. She would be better off in the village, where at least she could buy a baguette on foot, instead of this half country, without charm or even many trees.

"Mme Auvieux?" Verlaque asked. She was well into her fifties, he thought. It was hard to imagine that this small woman was the sister of Auvieux the Giant.

"Yes," she replied. Her face had seen too much Provençal sun over the years; her hair was spiked and cut short around her ears and dyed a burgundy color that many woman in the south seemed to think chic. Verlaque only liked long hair on women.

"I'm the examining magistrate in Aix-en-Provence, Antoine Verlaque, and this is my colleague, Commissaire Paulik."

Still in the doorway, she shook their hands without a word and then told them to come inside. Her house was as clean and sparse as her brother's cottage. They sat in the kitchen, around a table that was covered with the kind of waxy cloth that Verlaque detested—you never wanted to touch it for fear you'd stick to it.

"Thank you for letting us visit, Mme Auvieux. It is Auvieux, right?"

"Yes, I never married," she replied.

Verlaque stayed with *Madame*, for she was well over the age where one is addressed as *Mademoiselle*, even if unmarried. "We are investigating the death of Comte Étienne de Bremont, and from what I understand, you've had relations with the Bremont family, going a while back."

"Going back to my birth, Judge. I was born at Saint-Antonin, as was my brother, nine years after me."

"Your brother told us that he was with you throughout the entire weekend when Étienne died."

"Yes."

"What time did he arrive here?"

"He got here just in time for dinner on Friday, around 7:00 p.m. He would have been earlier, but he was sent on a treasure hunt by François de Bremont," she said. Both Verlaque and Paulik made mental notes of the sarcasm in her voice. "When François de Bremont wants something, it's always an emergency."

"What did he want?"

"Some stupid polo trophy," she replied.

"When did your brother leave here?"

"He went back to Aix on Sunday morning, ten o'clock or so."

"Did you both stay here all weekend?"

"Yes. We did a little shopping in Cotignac on Saturday afternoon, and we had a coffee on the square, at the Bar Centrale." She then added, "They can confirm that. I know the barman."

"And Saturday night?"

"We watched a movie at home." Jean-Claude Auvieux had also mentioned it to Verlaque.

"What movie?"

Mme Auvieux looked annoyed. "*The Matrix*, but don't ask me which one. They're all the same to me."

Verlaque didn't acknowledge her answer, but it corresponded to the caretaker's story. It was in fact the first *Matrix*, as Auvieux had tried to explain the movie in detail but was thankfully cut off by a call on Verlaque's cell phone.

"Were you close to Étienne de Bremont?"

"No, of course not," she said, looking away from Verlaque and out the window. Normally it would have been impossible for the daughter of the Bremont's servants to be friends with the young count, but Verlaque had asked the question anyway, especially since her brother seemed to have been so close to the family. "But I liked him very much," she continued, unprompted, with sadness in her voice. "He was a nice child, and he grew into a nice man.

It works like that, doesn't it? Children who are pleasant grow into pleasant adults."

"It should work like that, Madame, but it doesn't always," Paulik replied. "And how well do you know François de Bremont?"

"Not very well. He lives in Cannes. He only associates with fancy businessmen and fashion models." Her voice was edged with a bit of resentment.

"Why aren't you going to the funeral tomorrow?" Paulik asked bluntly. He thought it strange that someone who had grown up with Étienne de Bremont, removed as perhaps she was, would not want to pay her respects. In the Luberon, funerals were every bit as important, as sacred, as weddings.

"I have too much work. I co-own a hair salon in Cotignac, my partner is off sick, and we have a full day tomorrow," she replied. He was surprised to hear that she was a hairdresser, given the state of her own hair.

"All right, then, thank you for allowing us to visit," Verlaque said, as he got up to leave. "One last thing—your brother noticed that sometime between Friday and Sunday, while he was here, a Louis Vuitton suitcase in the Bremont attic was broken into and its contents removed. Do you remember such a suitcase?"

"No," she replied, again, coldly. "I didn't go into the attic very much when I lived on the estate." Again the resentment, Verlaque noted.

Both men got to their feet, and Paulik said, "Thank you, Mme Auvieux. We'll see ourselves out." She remained seated at the kitchen table, looking out of the window onto a treeless backyard, and then took a pinch of tobacco out of a pouch and began to expertly roll a cigarette.

Chapter Ten

≽

*P*aulik sighed and said, "She's very sad, *non*? She doesn't seem at all interested in the Bremont family, which is odd given that she grew up there and her brother still works for them."

"No, she doesn't," Verlaque agreed, staring straight ahead at the road. "Although she did perk up a bit each time we asked about François de Bremont."

"Yes! And she seemed genuinely saddened by the death of Étienne, even if she can't be bothered to go to the funeral."

"Well, it wasn't an entirely wasted trip—she confirmed Auvieux's alibi," Verlaque said, looking at Paulik. "Plus, Domaine Margui Romanis is about fifteen kilometers from here."

"So it is! I had forgotten," said Paulik, rubbing his hands together with childlike excitement. Margui Romanis was one of the Var's best kept secrets—a winery on par with the best southern Rhône wines but whose prices had stayed moderate due to the underrated appellation Côtes de Provence.

"Would you mind driving? I'd like to sit back and enjoy a cigar."

"I'd love to, sir," Paulik exclaimed, already undoing his seat belt as Verlaque slowed down the car and pulled over by the side of the road. They drove past signs for l'abbaye du Thoronet, a twelfth-century Cistercian abbey surrounded by a verdant pine forest. Verlaque suggested that they make a quick detour to visit the abbey but was met with a big smile from Paulik, now at the wheel, who answered dryly, "No thanks."

The last time Verlaque had been at l'abbaye du Thoronet was with his grandmother, Marine, and Sylvie. He remembered seeing his grandmother, Emmeline, in a ray of light turned golden by the honey-colored stone, standing alone in the middle of the long nave and looking up at the carved capitals atop the columns, the only decoration in the abbey's simple but majestic church. She was wearing a long, white linen tunic over wide linen pants that made her look a bit like a ghost, floating, rather than walking, through the dark, cool church.

Minutes after they passed the signs for the abbey, the judge and commissioner pulled into the winery's pristine drive, lined on either side with century-old olive trees. Marc Nagel, the winemaker, came out of the restored stables when he saw the dark green Porsche. "Monsieur le Juge," he said, putting the two cases of wine he had been carrying next to a stone fountain. "It's been a long time!" Nagel had perfect big white teeth and a golden tan, the kind of look that Verlaque usually associated with Californians. His smile was, in fact, the work of a dentist-uncle in Marseille—a trade for cases of wine—and the tan came naturally from hours spent in among vines. There was a certain irony in Verlaque's prejudice: Marc Nagel had spent a very satisfying year studying enology at the University of California, Davis. He hosted, yearly, a visit of American winemakers to the south of France, and made the same kind of trip to the States and other wine-making countries once a year.

"Yes, too long," Verlaque said as he got out of the car. "I've run out of white and only have two reds left."

Verlaque introduced Paulik and within seconds it was understood that Marc knew Hélène Paulik and greatly respected her. "Hélène is your wife? Well, I'll be damned! She's done a lot for the Côteaux d'Aix-en-Provence appellation," he said. "Her 1998 old-vine red was sublime. We've met at some wine fairs, but I didn't realize that her husband was a policeman. Sorry—a commissioner."

Paulik smiled. "Yes, she tends not to talk about my job. I'll pass on your greetings. And I agree about the red. It was so good she sold out."

The three men made their way into the cool recesses of the renovated stables, where they would taste the château's wines. Towering above them were giant stainless steel vats where this year's rosé was being aged. The floor was wet with water and wine, and Verlaque tried to stand in a dry spot to protect his Westons. Paulik noticed his boss's sidestepping jig and turned away to hide his grin.

"What brings you to the Var?" Marc asked as he took three glasses down from a shelf.

"We're investigating the death of an Aixois," Verlaque replied. It was very unlikely that Marc knew Étienne de Bremont. Marc's winery was a good hour and a half east of Aix, and in a different department, but Verlaque saw that Marc's curiosity had been aroused and so he continued, "Étienne de Bremont. Did you know his films?"

"Bremont, Bremont . . . any relation to François de Bremont from Cannes?" Marc asked as he opened the door to a mini refrigerator and took out a bottle of white.

"His brother," replied Verlaque.

"Small world, then. François comes here every other weekend and stays in my bed-and-breakfast." Immediately after he said this, Marc seemed to realize that perhaps he had revealed too much—Verlaque and Paulik both saw the winemaker grimace for a split second.

"Alone?" Verlaque and Paulik demanded in unison.

Marc kicked aside a rubber hose that stood at his feet. "Will this information help, I mean, with your investigation?"

"Yes," answered Verlaque. "And we won't make your information public knowledge unless absolutely necessary."

Marc took a breath, and then he began: "François de Bremont drives up from Cannes every other Friday or so. At least I think he said Cannes—anyway his car has 06 plates. A woman arrives in a separate car, a white BMW, with Bouches-du-Rhône license plates. They usually stay just the night and leave early in the morning, after they've finished breakfast in their room." He then added, "They are very discreet," as if wanting to protect them.

"What make of car does François de Bremont drive?" Verlaque asked. Marc Nagel looked up at the ceiling, thinking. "A small VW, I seem to remember." He poured out three glasses of white wine and passed two to Verlaque and Paulik. The three men held the glasses in the air, looked at the wine's pale golden color. Not at all cloudy, thought Verlaque. They then smelt the wine, which Verlaque thought had a peach bouquet, and tasted. Both Nagel and Paulik made a lot of noise swirling the wine around in their mouths and then spitting in the spittoon. Verlaque winced—he knew that the loud smacking noises were what wine professionals did, but it embarrassed him all the same. He didn't spit either—he drank. Verlaque opened his mouth to compliment Nagel on the wine but was interrupted.

"It's a soft top, maybe a Golf?" Nagel said. Verlaque and Paulik exchanged looks and were both perplexed by the same thing—the car that was parked right outside the Bremont château was a VW Golf convertible with 06 plates. Why would François de Bremont drive all the way to Aix to pick up the car and then drive an hour and a half back east to the Nagels' B and B?

"What does the lady look like?" Paulik demanded, beating Verlaque to the question.

"Very preppy, very thin. The jacket with the gold buttons, the Tod's leather loafers—she doesn't like wine. In her late thirties, I'd guess."

"Not blonde and tall with an eastern European accent?" asked Paulik, with more than a bit of voyeurism in his voice. Marc looked at him and smiled. "Oh, no. Very French."

Verlaque and Paulik exchanged surprised looks. "Do you know her name?" Verlaque asked.

"Sorry. They always sign in under his name. He pays in cash. No, wait, once she had to pay. He had forgotten his wallet, and she had to put the room on her card. After we taste the red we can go and check the records. My wife, Véronique, is inside."

Verlaque finished drinking his white and Paulik, on his best behavior, poured the remainder of his out into the silver spittoon. Nagel opened a red wine with a very simple label that looked as if it might have been handwritten, with no imagery, no color. And no pencil drawing of a château behind wrought-iron gates, like so many Bordeaux winemakers fancied. Verlaque nodded in approval.

Nagel slowly poured the red into the rinsed-out glasses. "It's 100 percent Syrah, so I'm not allowed to give it the Côtes de Provence appellation. We're far from the Rhône valley here." A waft of raspberries hit Verlaque in the face as he stuck his nose in the glass, closed his eyes, and breathed in further. He held the wine in his mouth for some time before swallowing. It had a peppery taste with a smooth, long finish. "I'll take two cases," Verlaque said. He was already thinking of having the wine with the local lamb he bought at his butcher shop. "I'll take two as well," Paulik added. "But we'll have to jiggle them around to fit four cases in the Porsche," he added, looking at Verlaque.

"I've seen worse. One guy came up on a motorcycle and drove away with a case. He divided up the bottles between his saddle bags and knapsack," Marc said.

They finished their tasting—this time no one used the spittoon—then made their way toward the farmhouse, its red shutters partly closed to keep out the afternoon sun. Véronique was at her desk inside, doing paperwork. Introductions were made, and Marc explained to his wife about the death of Étienne de Bremont. She opened a drawer and paused for a minute. "Let's see, they argued out on the driveway after she had paid the bill, and it was cold. Yes, it was cold, because I kept thinking, why don't they argue in the car where it's warm? I suppose it's because they came in two cars. So it was winter, and we're closed December and January. I'll start with February." She picked out a red folder and started shuffling through the names. "Many of the names are foreign, so it should be easy to spot the French names." After less than a minute's search she said, "Voilà! Friday, February 21." Véronique looked slowly at each of the three men, proud to be the bearer of news, but at the same time she whispered, as if the walls could hear her: "Mme Sophie Valoie de Saint-André. Does that help?"

"Yes, thank you," said Verlaque, nonplussed. "I'll make a note of the name just in case I need it later on. In the meantime this information won't go beyond these walls." Verlaque then reassured Marc and his wife that they had broken no rules by telling

Verlaque about the Friday nights François de Bremont spent at their bed-and-breakfast. He gave Paulik a look that said I'll fill you in later.

Nagel walked the two men out to their car and helped them load the wine into the Porsche's minuscule trunk.

The judge and commissioner said their good-byes and got into the car slowly, as if leaving too quickly would look like they wanted to get away from the bad news that seemed to be lurking at the Nagel household.

Paulik was impatient. "What gives? Do you know something about the mysterious Friday-night guest?" he asked, as soon as they had rolled up the car's windows and waved good-bye to Marc and Véronique.

"She is Isabelle de Bremont's sister," Verlaque answered, now at the wheel.

"No kidding? I guess it pays to buy wine on workdays."

"It sure does."

"From Marc's description, she doesn't sound like François de Bremont's cup of tea, though."

"No, she isn't what François would call a babe, but you know, *le goût des autres*," Verlaque said, shrugging. *Other People's Tastes* was a popular intellectual movie that had been released a few years before. Verlaque remembered that it was one of Marine's favorite films.

"That's true," Paulik said, laughing. He was not thinking of the film but of the strange assortment of girlfriends his divorced brother brought home for Christmas over the years.

"If Monica Bellucci sat down beside me in some dark bar in Paris and started flirting with me, and then went on to tell me that she wasn't really into food and she didn't drink wine, I'd be turned off immediately," said Verlaque out of the blue. He thought of Marine and realized that although she was an inexperienced cook, and could never remember that red burgundy was only pinot noir, she really did love good food and wine, and it had been a pleasure to cook for her. "I could support the Tod's loafers, *maybe*, but no wine?"

"Even Monica Bellucci?" Paulik asked.

"Sure, even Monica. Wouldn't you be turned off, I mean, if you weren't married?"

"Yes, I suppose you're right," Paulik said, looking out of the car window. "But, you know," he continued, turning to look at the judge, "Monica Bellucci is Italian, so there's a good chance she drinks wine."

"I know, Bruno. She was just my example," said Verlaque, laughing.

"In fact, I'll bet she drinks wine at lunch and at dinner," Paulik continued. "She probably even likes grappa."

"Stop it, or I'm going to drive off the road thinking of Monica drinking grappa in my apartment."

"Sorry, Judge. I'll get you back to reality and this Sophie Valoie de Saint-André. It's quite a scoop. She's married, I take it."

"Yes," Verlaque said.

"Do you know who her husband is? Is that why you gave me that look back there? Her last name rings a bell."

Verlaque nodded. "It should!"

"Okay, okay. Where does he work?" Paulik demanded.

"With me. He's a judge in Marseille," Verlaque said, looking over at Paulik.

"Henri Valoie de Saint-André? *Mon Dieu!*" Paulik exclaimed, whistling through his teeth. "*Mon Dieu!*"

Chapter Eleven

꙳

Wednesday morning, Marine stood under the hot shower unable to move. She didn't want to see Verlaque at the funeral. She would do her best to avoid him, which she hoped would be easy, as she expected Saint-Jean-de-Malte to be full to capacity. She lingered under the shower, watching the hot water roll over her tummy, which was beginning to protrude a bit, down to her toes. She got out and dressed in black pants and a white blouse, both from Agnès b. across the street. She applied her various face creams—she didn't buy much makeup but loved face creams—and she put on an extra helping of foundation powder. The buzzer at her door rang—it would be Sylvie coming to pick her up. She quickly put on her black high-heeled boots—the weather had turned cloudy and cold—and ran down the hall to buzz Sylvie up.

"Thanks for taking such good care of me last night," Marine said, as they stood in the kitchen while she made them both coffee. Sylvie had invited Marine over for dinner, and they had watched, after Charlotte went to bed, reruns of *ER*.

"Hey, you would do the same for me," Sylvie answered. They both started laughing, and Sylvie answered, "Okay, okay, you have done the same for me, time and time again!" Sylvie sipped her coffee and added, "It's normal to be upset. You haven't seen Verlaque in months, and now you see him while he's investigating the death of your old friend." Sylvie started rummaging around in her oversized purse. "Hey, do you have Kleenex?"

"Yeah, I emptied almost a whole box into my purse," Marine answered.

The church bells started, not their melodic ringing for morning mass, but a slow, forlorn pealing, each strike about five seconds apart, which seemed an eternity to Marine.

Although it wasn't yet nine o'clock, when Sylvie and Marine went down to the rue Cardinale it was full of people slowly making their way to the funeral. The small square in front of the church, with one lone chestnut tree beginning to flower, was bursting with mourners, some of whom looked at the dozens of bouquets of flowers that had been set out in front of the church doors. Others had formed a long queue, waiting to sign the family's guest book. The bells continued their sorrowful dirge. Marine saw her parents through the crowd and immediately burst into tears at her father's embrace.

"I'm so sorry, *mon coeur*," her father whispered, stroking Marine's hair.

"Do you want to sit with us, *chérie*?" asked her mother. "We've promised to sit with Étienne's aunt. She's taking this whole thing very badly."

Marine couldn't stand Étienne's *tante*, Mathilde, an old busybody who talked in clichés or gossip, nonstop. "No thanks," answered Marine. "Sylvie has promised to hold my hand."

"Good old Sylvie," said her father, smiling as he saw her across the crowd, looking at the flowers. He hugged Marine once more and shrugged when his wife nudged him to move along, his way of telling Marine that he too would rather not sit with Mathilde Bley.

The bells stopped their ringing, and the crowd became hushed as the guests filtered into the church. It took Marine a while to walk through the crowd to reach Sylvie. Sylvie passed her arm though Marine's, and they walked up the stairs together. Marine began to feel a sudden twinge of panic, a feeling of too many people in one place, all of them wanting to be near the front. She felt like she was in an airport, late for her flight. She began to sweat and breathe deeply, when someone tugged on her sleeve and whispered in her ear, "Marine." Marine swung around, half relieved and half anxious. It was Verlaque. Sylvie gave him a cold stare and said nothing. He moved forward, about to take Marine by the arm, but the throng of mourners pushed Marine forward. Sylvie pulled her quickly, and she turned around only to see Verlaque walking toward the back of the church, against the flow. She moved on, glad to have Sylvie's lead. The nave was filling up fast, so Sylvie ushered Marine toward a chapel on the south side, where they found two empty cane-seated wooden chairs side by side. They were on the edge of the chapel, so they could see Étienne's coffin, the choir on the left side of the altar, and a group of schoolchildren sitting on short stools in front, just to the right of the altar and the casket.

"They must be the classmates of Étienne's son," Marine whispered.

"They're adorable," Sylvie answered. The kids were silent, most of them looking straight at the coffin or trying to look at Étienne's son, who was in the first pew with his mother and siblings. Marine didn't want to look at Isabelle de Bremont, for fear of feeling like a voyeur. She felt eyes on her, and she slowly looked behind her toward the back of the church. Verlaque was leaning against a stone pillar, staring at her.

Toward the front of the nave, on the north side, opposite the chapel, were thirty or so lawyers dressed in their black robes. Marine saw Jean-Marc, who nodded and raised his palm. Marine did the same and smiled. She noticed Yves Roussel sitting with the mayor and her husband a few pews behind the immediate family. Roussel took out his phone, looking at a text message. Such bad taste, Marine thought. Verlaque was pacing up and down the side aisle, looking into the crowd as if searching for someone. He stopped and said something to Jean-Marc, who looked into the crowd as well. Jean-Marc obviously didn't find what, or who, they were looking for, and shrugged to Verlaque. Verlaque then reached into his suit pocket and took out his cell phone and walked toward the doors, followed by Roussel, who noisily left his seat and almost ran out of the church.

Père Jean-Luc, the eldest of the Dominican priests at Saint-Jean-de-Malte, walked across the altar toward Étienne's casket and addressed the congregation. "On behalf of Isabelle de Bremont and the Bremont family, I'd like to thank you all for coming today," he said. The priest then looked at the children and continued, "We are going to begin this ceremony with something a little out of the ordinary. The classmates of Raphaël, who are seated here beside me, have each written a letter or drawn a picture of heaven for the Bremont family. I would like to ask the children to come up now and place your offerings around the casket." The children slowly got up and one by one knelt down and placed their drawings and letters in a circle around the box that held Étienne's body. Marine's eyes welled up with tears, and Sylvie was openly crying, as she did at every wedding and funeral.

They were too far away to see the drawings, but from where

she sat, Marine could see that most of them were awash with bright greens and blues: trees, grass, and sea, she imagined. Marine's drawing would have been much the same, but she would have added splashes of dazzling pink to represent the bougainvillea that climbed up the yellow stone walls of Paradiso, her nickname for the Ligurian medieval village where she and Verlaque had once spent a two-week holiday. They fell into each other's arms and laughed when they stood on their vacation apartment's rooftop terrace that first night—there were views of the Mediterranean on three sides, and behind them sat the pink and yellow Baroque church, paid for by proud villagers in the seventeenth century. Mornings were spent swimming in the crystal clear sea, reached by a series of stone steps that led down from the village. They would climb back up to the apartment for lunch, delicious pastas that Verlaque would cook, sweet plump peaches for dessert, followed by a nap, the sea air gently blowing the bedroom's white linen curtains. They would wake near three o'clock, ready for strong Italian coffee, and would work or read until six, and then walk back down to the sea for a last swim, sometimes chatting with the other villagers who kept to the same routine. Dinner was eaten on their terrace, or in the restaurant in the village, also with sea views, and run by an eccentric man from Genoa who had fallen in love with a village girl in 1959 and had never left. They vowed to keep the village's identity a secret, even to close friends, and although Marine knew this Italian coast well— she had been coming here with her parents since she could walk—she had never stayed in that particular village and couldn't imagine how her parents had missed it.

She looked over at her parents now, sitting with Mathilde Bley, and she realized that it was entirely possible that they had never set foot in Paradiso—their vacations were much different from hers. M. and Mme Bonnet came from a generation of French civil servants who walked—no, hiked—on holiday, traveling yearly to the same spot, their sandwiches made up that morning and carried in a backpack, many of their foodstuffs having been purchased in France. Marine never knew if this was because they thought the Italian products more expensive or not as good. Probably a bit of both. No visits to local restaurants, no hedonistic activities at all, save for a glass of French rosé in the evening. Luckily they brought with them, on each August holiday, an older cousin of Marine's, who would take Marine to the sea during the day, both of them happy not to be walking in the hot, dusty olive groves.

Marine faded in and out through the rest of the service. Eric Bley and a filmmaker at Souleiado Films gave excellent eulogies, concentrating on Étienne's life and his dedication to his family and his art. Marine thought it strange that François, Étienne's closest living relative, didn't speak. She looked at the people in the first few pews and realized that she hadn't seen François that morning. She leaned over to Sylvie and whispered, "Étienne's brother isn't here."

"That's weird. Maybe he's stuck in the back," Sylvie said. "The church is packed to the gills."

Once the ceremony was over, the bells began their slow ringing, and about half of the congregation started walking up the rue du Maréchal Joffre, toward Aix's cemetery. It was warmer outside than it had been in the church, and the sky was less gray than earlier.

At the graveside a large group of friends and family gathered around, most of them donning designer sunglasses because of the sharp sunlight. Marine thought it strange to see mourners wearing Ray-Bans. She could hear the military academy students running around the track next door, some of them laughing and talking. Life goes on. Père Jean-Luc said another prayer, and Isabelle de Bremont walked up to the hole in the ground, picked up a fistful of earth, and threw it onto the casket. The rest of the guests formed a line and followed her example. Isabelle's sister Sophie, whom Marine knew but had never spoken to, stood by herself and was weeping uncontrollably.

As Marine waited in line to toss in her dirt, she felt her cell phone moving around in her coat pocket. On the walk over Marine had turned her phone on to vibrate mode, in case someone called from the university—she had canceled two classes to come to the funeral. She jumped out of the line and picked it up.

"Are you at the cemetery?"

It was Verlaque. No introduction as usual.

"Yes, of course," Marine replied curtly.

"I need your help. Are you still coming over tonight?"

Marine considered canceling. "Tonight?" she asked, hesitating.

"Yes, remember?"

"I don't know if I can make it, Antoine."

"Marine, François is dead."

"What?" Marine said, cupping her hand over around her phone.

"Didn't you notice that he wasn't at the funeral?" asked Verlaque, not waiting for a reply. "He was found dead in the pool at the château this morning. The caretaker has been taken in for questioning. This time it's clear that the death wasn't an accident. That's two deaths now, both in Saint-Antonin, and I think the deaths are now linked to that place or the past. I need to quickly understand the history of that family, and since you were connected with them, I may even need you to come to the Var and question Auvieux's sister with me. She's a cold fish, but since you knew her when she was younger—"

Marine cut him off and asked, "Jean-Claude? Why is he being questioned? Did he see anything?"

"No, he claims he was in the olive grove when it happened."

"Claims?" Marine asked. "Antoine, you trust Jean-Claude, don't you?"

"I want to, believe me." Verlaque paused and then quickly added, "Can we forget about our past for a moment, and I'll explain everything tonight?"

Chapter Twelve

꙳

The rue d'Italie was Marine's neighborhood shopping district and a street that still had everything one needed for decent living—two *boulangeries*, three butcher shops, a pharmacy, two flower shops, a wine store, a cheese shop, a hardware shop, one travel agent and two realtors, a health food store she had never set foot in, and a handful of cafés. Marine had gone out of her way to support these small shops ever since her friend André's cheese shop had had to close due to the ridiculous rise in Aix's rents and fewer people buying good cheese. Since André had moved to Marseille, where business was even worse, his former shop had been turned into three different clothing stores, each lasting less than a year. André told her that his profession was a dying one—young people are no longer interested in traditional métiers. Cheese sellers get up with the dawn to receive their deliveries and butchers drive to the abattoir at 4:00 a.m. It is easier to work at the Gap. She reminded herself to call André to see how he was doing.

A teenager bumped into her, saying *pardon*, and Marine realized that she had been looking at stainless steel Italian garbage cans, displayed in the window of the hardware store, for over five minutes. She couldn't believe what was happening: that Antoine Verlaque was back in her life, Étienne was dead, and François had been killed. "Murdered," she mumbled aloud. She shuddered, and then quickly walked down a side street to a clothing boutique owned by one of her best friends, Vincent. Vincent sold men's clothing, very traditional suits that were exquisitely cut, although he was beginning to branch out into designer items and held the sole rights in Aix for the new, exclusive line of Levi's women's and men's high-end jeans. Perhaps some shopping was what she needed.

Marine opened the glass door to his shop and was met with a blast of air-conditioning. "Do you really need the air-conditioning in April?" she asked, when she saw Vincent.

"*Chèrie!* You look great!" Vincent said as he embraced Marine and gave her not two but four *bises*. "My clients get hot in the changing rooms," he answered. "If they're comfortable trying on clothes, they'll buy more." The two old friends exchanged pleasantries—their families had been close for years, and Marine had been in the same class as Vincent's older sister, Josie. Vincent then turned serious and said in a high-pitched whisper, "It's terrible about Étienne de Bremont, isn't it? I saw you at the funeral, but you were miles away."

Marine smiled at Vincent's comment, not sure if he intended the pun—she may have been far from Vincent in the church, but she had also been miles away in thought. "Yes, I was."

"Josie couldn't come down for it from Paris, but she's coming this weekend. Maybe we can all get together for a drink."

"Sure. It will be nice to see her again. It's been years," Marine said.

"It was beautiful, wasn't it?"

"Uh?"

Vincent reached out and grabbed Marine's shoulders. "*Cou-cou!* Marine! Earth to Marine! The funeral!"

"Oh! Yes. Yes, it was beautiful. Those children . . ."

Vincent stood on the balls of his toes and made quick flapping motions with his hands. "And those lawyers! In their black robes!"

Marine laughed out loud. Wanting to change the conversation, not because she didn't want to speak of the funeral, but because she couldn't tell Vincent that François was also dead, she said, "I need to get a pair of those cool jeans." She adored Vincent, but there was no way she could tell him that François had been murdered, not unless they wanted all of Provence to know about it, and half of Paris. She still couldn't believe it herself.

"Let's see," Vincent said, as he held on to her waist and hummed a bit. "You're a thirty."

"I was a twenty-nine last time," Marine said. She had gained weight over the winter, a combination of both she and Sylvie breaking up with their boyfriends at roughly the same time and her preference for winter foods—she was a meat-and-potatoes, cheese-and-red-wine kind of person. Her current boyfriend, Arthur, was a vegetarian, and she realized now, remembering him eat, that he didn't seem to enjoy food, or at least it wasn't something they talked about.

"I thought so, but I didn't want to say anything. Besides, you're so pretty that it doesn't matter.

"I want you to try on these," he said, pulling out a size 30 with bleached-out legs and rear pockets that looked as if packs of cigarettes had been burned into them. Marine liked them, despite the gimmicky bleach. She took them into the fitting room and continued talking to Vincent, every now and then poking her head out from behind the velvet curtain.

She came out of the stall and turned around in front of the mirror. "These are great," she exclaimed. Marine looked at herself in the mirror, coming to terms, at thirty-five years of age, with the curly auburn hair that she could never seem to do anything with, her hawkish nose, and full reddish lips. Despite her faults, she still managed to turn some heads, a feat in a town like Aix, full of gorgeous, tiny twentysomethings.

"Perfect fit, they make your legs look longer," Vincent said. "You have short legs for a tall woman. You're all torso, which is a look I happen to like. Your inseam is about thirty-two, in American measurements, but I gave you a thirty-four so you could wear boots with heels."

"You're an expert, Vincent," Marine said, rubbing his arm. "Why don't you open a women's boutique?"

"I'm thinking of it, *chèrie*," he answered. "You know I prefer dressing women—they are so much more sensitive and daring than men when it comes to clothing. I just need to find the right space—there's nothing interesting for rent or for sale at the moment in Aix. Almost every day I get realtors coming in here asking me if I want to sell. Times have changed since we were kids, *non*?" Vincent took ahold of Marine's shoulders and looked at her. "And since we've known each other for so long, I can see that something is bothering you. What's going on, kiddo? I can see it in your big green eyes."

She lowered her voice and said, "Antoine Verlaque is investigating Étienne's death."

"Ah, that's it. I knew there was something. I saw him at the funeral, but he left early. Why should he investigate it?" Vincent asked.

"Charles and Eric Bley asked for an inquest."

Vincent nodded, not quite sure what an inquest was, but he

did like dressing Eric Bley. The man had lovely wide shoulders and quite daring taste when it came to jackets and accessories. Vincent pointed a finger at Marine and said, "I hope you're over that big Verlaque ape."

"Getting there," Marine replied, smiling.

"I feel so sorry for the Bremont family, especially Isabelle. At least François and Étienne got to see each other last week."

"How so?" Marine asked, her voice cracking at sound of François's name.

"François came into the shop last week and bought this fantastic blue-velvet Pierre Cardin suit. It was gorgeous on him! He looked like he walked out of a painting!"

"Last week he was in Aix?" Marine asked, surprised. "When?"

"Let me think." Vincent continued, "Near the beginning of the week, Monday or Tuesday, if I had to guess. Yes, because I took Wednesday off and left the girls in charge of the store, and I went to Saint-Tropez to work on my tan. Do you want to know what he talked about?"

"Sure," Marine said, pretending to be only casually interested.

"He was telling me about the beautiful blonde models he has on his boat. He must think I'm straight." Vincent paused and looked at himself in the mirror—he was *petit* in size and was wearing a flowered women's blouse and had sandy colored hair with long bangs that he was constantly tossing out of his face. "No," he answered his own question, "he can't think I'm straight." Vincent leaned in and whispered, "Everyone knows the girls are Russian prostitutes. The Russian mafia is everywhere on the Côte these days."

"How do you know that?"

"I just know," Vincent said, rocking back and forth on the back of his heels and smiling an impish grin. "Also, Étienne and

Isabelle de Bremont were in here about a month ago, and I overheard them arguing about François and the château."

"That doesn't sound very discreet of them," Marine said. "To be talking out loud of such affairs."

"They couldn't help it. Étienne was in the changing room, trying something on. He couldn't come out to talk because he was half naked, and Isabelle kept tucking her head into the dressing room, you know, as wives tend to do. They probably thought no one could hear because of the thick curtains, and we had some music on, but I was in my back room, my office and the space where we do the alterations. The wall in the changing room doesn't go all the way to the top, so I could hear everything," Vincent continued. "Anyway, they were arguing about the château." He gave Marine a quick, worried look and continued. "Don't tell anyone. It isn't good to be speaking of the dead this way. So, Isabelle said that she wanted to sell it, that she was tired of being penniless, and what good was the château if no one in the family used it? And she didn't want him to waste money on a suit."

"It surprises me that Isabelle would say that."

"I know. That suit looked gorgeous on Étienne."

Marine hit Vincent over the head with her newspaper. "You rat! You know that I was talking about the château."

Vincent laughed. "I know. It sounds terrible, but maybe now she can sell it after all. I'm sure François isn't interested in keeping it." Marine nodded and walked to the cash register, anxious to be gone before she blurted out everything. She wished she had someone to talk to, someone whose shoulder she could cry on. There was only Verlaque.

"Well, I have to get to class," she said, getting her wallet out of her purse. "Great jeans, Vincent. I'll leave them on. Just rip off the tag so I can buy them."

"At your service," Vincent answered. "And I'll give you my student discount, since you're sort of a permanent student." They walked to the front door together, and Vincent then asked, "Do you want to know what I know about the judge?"

Marine frowned, and thought for about three seconds. "No," she said.

"Good girl," Vincent answered, and he gave her a loud *bise* as she left the shop. Vincent stood in the doorway, remembering his sighting of the judge and an English model the week before. Lotus had been packed, and so Vincent had found himself standing next to the couple at the bar, waiting for tables. This had annoyed Vincent, for up to that point he had been making much progress with Dario, the Italian barman. Vincent and Verlaque had said hello and chatted briefly, and then the judge had turned his attentions to his companion, who seemed to Vincent to be one of those women who demanded a lot of attention. And although he didn't understand their English, he understood well enough their unspoken words: the affectionate gestures and cooing noises that couples always make, whatever their sexual preference or nationality. He was fairly sure that Marine had been hiding something from him. Well, he had his secrets too.

Marine walked up the rue d'Italie, to a café that she didn't like, but it received the afternoon sun. She took a seat at a round marble table and ordered a coffee, thankful to be sitting. She was exhausted. She put on her sunglasses and watched people walking by, most of them unaware that a young man, father of four, had just had his funeral. She watched as a tall, wide-shouldered man approached her. She shuddered at first, thinking it was Verlaque, but this man was too tall, and she relaxed her shoulders. She then sat up straight, embarrassed—it was in fact Arthur. In the past few days she had forgotten all about him. Was that normal? She now realized how much Arthur resembled Verlaque. One of Sylvie's theories was that women always go after the same physical type. And like many of her friend's theories, it was right.

"Hello, sweetie," Arthur said. "Are you watching the world go by?"

"Yes. Funny how life goes on."

Arthur Vassan took Marine's hand and kissed it. "How was the funeral?"

"Beautiful," Marine answered. "Does that sound horrible? Can a funeral be beautiful?"

"I would imagine so, yes. I've never been to one, though."

"You're kidding. Not even your grandparents'?"

"All still living," he said. Marine reminded herself that Arthur was still in his twenties. He continued, "Some of my great uncles and aunts have passed away, but my parents thought it best that the children stay away from the funeral." Marine thought it odd that a doctor would use the term "passed away."

"Oh, I totally disagree. At the funeral you come to terms with the death. And you are there, in spirit, with the deceased. They know you are, of that I'm sure. They can feel it."

Arthur shrugged his shoulders and smiled. Marine would have liked to carry on with this discussion—she would have done so with Verlaque.

"Let's not talk about funerals," Arthur suggested, putting his arm around Marine and leaning in to kiss her.

"So, when do you leave for Palo whatever?" Marine said as she pulled away from him.

"Palo Alto. Tonight. Marseille to Frankfurt, Frankfurt to San Francisco."

Marine finished her coffee and left some coins on the table. She was desperate to get home, but to get away form Arthur too.

She couldn't stop thinking of Verlaque and their meeting that night.

"Do you have to go?" Arthur asked. "I thought you might be able to help me pack," he said, winking.

"I have to go to the university." At least that wasn't a lie, Marine thought. She really did have a meeting with the head of the law faculty. "Have a great time in California, and wow them at the conference!"

"Thanks! I'll call you when I get back."

Marine smiled and waved and yelled, "Righto! Ciao!" over her shoulder as she walked down the street in the direction of the university. Why not just say "died"? she thought as she wove her way through the throng of shoppers. She then realized that it was one of Verlaque's pet peeves: why use an incorrect, long word when a short, true one will do?

Chapter Thirteen

꩜

Marine walked up the rue du 4 Septembre, from the university, as if in a daze. The thought of going to Antoine's apartment—however much she wanted to be involved in the investigation and help to determine how Étienne de Bremont, and now François, died—gave her butterflies. As much as she tried to deny it, Marine had never been as physically attracted to anyone as she had to Verlaque. She couldn't explain it. Sex with Arthur was sweet and tender, but Arthur did not have the same effect on her as Antoine did. Just thinking of his hands on her body caused her to blush, as she had done while reading *Paris Match* in the dentist's office.

She passed some of her third-year students trying to splash each other in the fountain on the place des Quatre Dauphins. "Salut, Professeur Bonnet!" they shouted. She waved and kept walking. She remembered fountain fighting when she was younger—in high school perhaps. It was certainly in high school, she thought. Junior high, even.

Her students this year seemed so young and apathetic. She had just given a lecture on French legal history to her first-year students, a class that she herself had loved when she started law school. But today she struggled to keep their attention, trying to incite some kind of debate. It was as if they only wanted to be spoon-fed, to take notes and then strut off and throw each other into fountains. Each year she noticed that her students were just as intelligent as the previous year but less cultured, not interested in the world around them. Verlaque blamed it on the Internet and MTV, but Marine remembered her mother making the same complaint over thirty years ago.

She turned right, onto her street, past a third-story apartment from which classical piano music poured out onto the street through the open windows. Aix-en-Provence touted itself as a *ville de musique* and was certainly right to do so. One could walk down any street in the quartier Mazarin and hear live opera singing or cello or piano. "Love is the voice of music; love is the voice of music"—she couldn't figure out where those lyrics came from. Some house music CD Sylvie had burned for her, she was almost sure. Marine scolded herself. Now is not the time for such whimsies. Two brothers dead, one murdered. She thought of Jean-Claude and what it must have felt like to discover the bodies—bodies of your employers and your former playmates. What did he do? Did he yell for help? Or was he speechless?

The guy who owned the computer store on her street was walking the opposite way. Marine stopped and gave him *bises*. Normally she would have taken a moment to talk, but she wanted to have a glass of white wine on her terrace before heading off to Antoine's. There were times when she needed to see the spire of Saint-Jean-de-Malte, and today was one of them: she needed to feel grounded, and the church's steeple always did that for her. She also wanted to check on her climbing rose bushes, which had started to bloom. Marine liked to fuss over her plants—it made her feel as if she were one of those cultured English women who spent all day untangling rose bushes in their immense gardens in Somerset or Devonshire and at night ate simple dinners of tinned tuna and fresh tomatoes, and then wrote poetry in the fading twilight, looking out onto their dewy gardens or the rough English sea. Antoine and his grandmother had introduced Marine to English literature, which, unlike them, she read in translation.

Marine punched in the code for her building's heavy green door, and walked quickly up the stairs to her third-floor flat. She dropped her purse and keys in an old Quimper faience dish that sat on a black glass console she had bought on sale at Habitat, and walked into the kitchen. She opened her fridge and poured herself a glass of white wine. Not wanting to go to Verlaque's on an empty stomach—for fear of getting drunk too quickly, or for fear of repeating the olive scene from Monday's lunch—she forced herself to nibble on some cheese while she looked out the patio door at the church's spire. The wine was excellent with the cheese, even she could tell. The cheese was an old Comté— hard and dry on the outside yet the inside still very moist, almost fatty on the tongue. She opened the patio door and walked out onto the terrace.

The church's spire was the pale yellow of an early evening in April. By eight o'clock it would be a brilliant orange, lasting only for a few minutes, and then, with the blink of an eye, it would turn to gray, the gray of Paris and of other northern French cities. Marine sipped her wine—and thought, once again, of Étienne de Bremont falling from the window. The hollowness she had felt earlier returned. Her head felt heavy: Étienne was her past—her easy, comfortable childhood. He was dead, and she suddenly felt old. She couldn't bring herself around to the idea that François de Bremont could have pushed his brother to his death, even if

François was in debt and possibly in trouble with the law. And if their hunch was right, and Étienne was killed, the same person must have killed François. She had never liked François as a child—he had had a sinister side to him that had frightened her. Marine once overheard her mother say to her father, when she thought Marine was out of earshot, "It's as if one brother received all the good and the other all the bad."

The plants were looking green and healthy, she was pleased to note. The snowball plant was always the first to bloom in spring— Marine ran her fingers over the snowballs—each one was made up of forty or fifty tiny delicate five-petaled, ivory-colored flowers. Her two climbing rose bushes, one on either side of the kitchen door, were full of fat buds waiting to burst into flowers. On the other hand, her raspberry bush, which she had planted for Sylvie's daughter, Charlotte, looked half dead. Marine would call her parents to get advice about the plant —she liked to have a reason to call them, they were so busy that at times she felt like she was bothering them if she called out of the blue.

And the lavender—always the last plant to bloom—it waited until the deathly heat of July, a time of year so hot that Marine couldn't stand to be out on the terrace during the day. But at night, while she ate dinner by candlelight, the lavender's scent would linger. She knelt down and shook the leaves a bit, the scent reminding her of afternoons driving around Haute-Provence with Verlaque: the top of the Porsche down, and the scent of wild lavender surrounding them. Verlaque didn't like the topography of Provence. He was always complaining of the lack of green grass and cows. The real Antoine, she reminded herself, is lurking somewhere around a villa in Normandy. But he had grown to love Provence, she was sure, and he now had read more Jean Giono stories than she had. Once when she was sick in bed with the flu, he picked up Giono's *Man Who Planted Trees* and read it to her, sitting on the edge of her bed.

Marine walked back into the kitchen and put her empty glass in the sink and picked up her purse. Merde, she mumbled, looking at the clock on the oven. She would be a few minutes late meeting Verlaque. She opened the front door and ran back to get her cell phone, which lay on the kitchen counter. Out on the street her telephone vibrated, telling her she had a text message. It was Verlaque: "I'm leaving the Palais de Justice now. Could you pick me up a cigar?"

Half of Verlaque's cigar club was sitting on Le Mazarin's terrace when she crossed the cours Mirabeau. *Bises* were exchanged and numerous iterations of *tout va bien?* and *ca va?* Jean-Marc jumped up and pulled Marine aside, kissing her on the cheek. "That was a beautiful funeral, wasn't it?"

"Yes, exactly what I thought. Beautiful." Marine was calm now, a serenity she always felt in Jean-Marc's presence. "Jean-Marc, when somebody dies, what do you say?"

"I don't get it."

"You know . . . do you say he 'passed away' or 'moved on' or something of that nature?"

Jean-Marc laughed. "No, I just say that he died. Simple, straightforward talk for a lawyer, *non*? Did I give you the right answer, professor? I have a feeling I was being quizzed."

"Yes, good answer." The butterflies in her stomach disappeared. "Now, what kind of cigar should I buy Antoine? I'm on my way over to his place for a drink." Two of the other men overheard and a series of whoops and "na-na-nana-na's" began. "Business," replied Marine, which only got the men teasing her even more. She turned back to Jean-Marc. "Any suggestions?"

"An Upmann. Definitely a Cuban," said Fabrice, president of the club and a permanent fixture at the café. "An Upmann 46. Just ask Carole to get it for you," he said, referring to the olive-skinned beauty who ran her parents' *tabac*. More laughs from the guys. Marine excused herself, bought Verlaque's cigar, and walked up the rue Clémenceau, glancing in the store windows as she walked. She passed two lingerie shops on the tiny street—Aix had recently been voted by some magazine "the sexiest town in France." It seems that women in Aix—les Aixoises—buy, per capita, more lingerie than even Parisiennes. Well, it was certainly true of herself and Sylvie, and probably Carole.

She turned left onto the rue Espariat and stood to look at the place d'Albertas, where two young men were busy placing a piano on the cobbled square. "Concert tonight?" she asked them. "Yes, ragtime jazz," the more disheveled of the two answered.

"At what time?" Marine asked.

"Whenever we get our shit together," the other answered, laughing as he struggled with the piano.

"Seriously, Madame, around nine p.m.," said the first. Marine walked away laughing, and then stopped. They had called her "Madame." Merde! I must look like I'm forty, she thought. Her cell phone rang with a message from Sylvie, who knew that Marine was on her way to Verlaque's. The message was Sylvie, attempting to sing the words to Gloria Gaynor's hit "I Will Survive" in very bad English. At the end of the song Sylvie said, "Be careful— remember that you are just as strong as he is, and sexier, to boot. And can you babysit Charlotte on Saturday night? *Bises*, ciao *chèrie*." After another five-minute walk she reached Verlaque's street and turned right. She pressed the only button that had no name posted on it. The door buzzed open without words exchanged on the intercom, and she began climbing up the four flights of stairs.

Will Verlaque be there to greet me? she wondered. He'd usually left the door ajar a bit, and she had to walk into his apartment and find him. She had never been easy with the fact that he wouldn't greet her at the door when she arrived. Rude man, she thought, especially after she had just killed herself walking up the four steep flights in heels. She got to the top of the stairs and took a deep breath, not wanting Verlaque to know she was a bit out of shape. He wasn't at the door, and so she walked in. "*Coucou?* Where are you?" she called out. "Typical, Verlaque, that you're not at the door to greet me," she muttered. She might regret saying that later, but the words had fallen out of her mouth naturally.

"I'm on the terrace," Verlaque yelled. She followed a trail of wet footprints through the glass doors that opened onto the patio, where Verlaque stood, drying himself off. "Oh," said Marine, turning half away. "You're not shy."

"Sorry," Verlaque, who was wearing only boxer shorts, replied. He had installed a teak shower on his deck and preferred to shower out there when the weather was warm enough. He quickly grabbed a clean polo shirt and put it on. She was looking absolutely beautiful, but then she always did on his terrace.

The pink light of dusk shone on her freckled face; the birds chirped and circled quickly above their heads; kids kicked a soccer ball in the square below. She stood there with her hands on her slender hips and stared at him, smirking; her confidence was palpable and Verlaque had to hide his sudden desire for her. "I didn't think you'd get here so fast," he stammered. "I have the champagne chilling here in a bucket." Verlaque pointed with his bare foot to an antique silver bucket on the teak deck. "Would you mind getting two glasses from the kitchen?"

"No problem," Marine answered, glad not to have to watch Verlaque finish getting dressed. She walked into the kitchen and opened the cupboard to the left of the sink, only to find it full of plates and bowls but no glasses. Antoine's done some rearranging, she thought, and she finally found the glasses on the right-hand side of the sink. She ran back up the steps, anxious to hear the news about François.

She walked back out onto the deck, and Verlaque opened the champagne, not taking his eyes off her.

"So what happened to François?" Marine asked, panting. "Tell me everything."

"Murder, it's certain. Strangled."

"My God," Marine murmured, feeling sick. They sat down at Verlaque's teak table, and Marine sighed and put het head in her hands. François de Bremont may not have been a trustworthy character, but Marine now felt incredibly sad.

"Poor Jean-Claude," she said, sighing. She looked up through her curls at Verlaque and saw his stern expression. "Antoine, you don't think he did it? He couldn't hurt a fly."

Verlaque answered, "We questioned him at the police station but let him go home after a few hours. He was in a bad state but nervous too. We'd all like to think he didn't do it, but the fact is that we have a dead body in the morgue right now. Bruno thinks that François was killed by someone he knew—there was no sign of a disturbance—and I agree with Bruno. Anyway, I went out to Saint-Antonin as soon as we got the call. The firemen and the medical examiner arrived just as I did. Poor François was floating facedown in that ornamental pool in front of the château. He had been dead less than an hour. I questioned Auvieux on the spot. He said that he woke up at six, as usual, and around seven thirty put on the coffee for François—they were planning on going to the funeral together. Around seven forty-five, Auvieux said, he took a walk in the olive orchard."

Marine interrupted, "On the morning of the funeral?"

Verlaque nodded. "I asked Auvieux the same thing, but he said that he walks in the olive orchard every morning. He told me it was like coffee for some people." He continued, "As Auvieux was coming back through the orchard, he heard a car and ran out to the drive. A black Mercedes was pulling quickly out of the gates. The license plate had mud smeared on it—something that could have happened on la route de Cézanne, since it rained last night. But Auvieux could vaguely make out that the license ended in 06. He told me that, quite rightly, he didn't like the look of the car, and ran over to the château as quickly as he could. He said that he went inside and called François's name from the bottom of the stairs, but the house was silent. He went back outside, and it was from the steps of the château's entryway that he saw the body floating in the pool. He ran and pulled up François's head, but he was dead. The medical examiner says that Bremont was strangled first, with bare hands it seems. It could have taken less than five minutes, and Auvieux said that he was in the orchard at least fifteen minutes."

"Bare hands?" Marine asked. "François wasn't big but he was strong, as I remember."

"He was in good shape," Verlaque agreed. "But someone bigger and stronger than him could have murdered him. Someone of Auvieux's size, for example."

Marine winced. "Or there could have been more than one of them?"

"It's possible," Verlaque answered. "It's also thanks to his daily tour of the olive orchard that Auvieux was spared. The murderer probably checked the house but didn't think of walking behind it or didn't have time."

"I have some information for you," Marine said. "I'm not sure if it's important."

"Go on."

"It happened by accident, or sort of. I went to see Vincent, you know, my friend with the boutique on the rue d'Italie. I wanted to buy some new jeans, but also I think I went in subconsciously knowing that Vincent knows everyone in Aix."

Marine noticed Verlaque flinch. "Yes. He has my suit and shirt size memorized," he said.

"Exactly," Marine said. She went on to tell Verlaque about her conversation with Vincent and the argument the Bremonts had had. Verlaque in turn told Marine of the argument on the *cours* between François and Isabelle.

"Do you trust Isabelle de Bremont's word?" Marine asked, finally able to look at Verlaque.

"No. She's hiding something, as is her sister. In fact, everyone is hiding something—Jean-Claude is as well. It's turning into one of those old-fashioned plays in which everyone has a secret, all the characters casting sideways glances whenever someone moves an inch in the elegant living room."

"Ah, yes. The flower-filled salon. The women wearing dark velvet, and the men handsome tweeds, and everyone smokes from long ivory cigarette holders."

Verlaque laughed. "Exactly." He stared at Marine, unable to take his eyes off her. He had a lump in his throat, and Marine broke the silence by asking, "So . . . what happens next?"

"Right. I spoke with Bruno about it this afternoon. I'd like you to talk to Auvieux's sister, first to explain to her what happened, and then try to get whatever information you can from her—I'd like to know if the caretaker liked François, or hated him, or had some kind of grudge against him. As I told you on the phone, you knew each other growing up."

"If she remembers me. Here," Marine said, handing him his cigar while he handed her a glass of champagne.

"Wow. A 46. What a treat. Thank you," he said, kissing her on the cheek. Marine's cell phone rang, and she reached into the depths of her purse to see who was calling. "It's probably Sylvie," she said to Verlaque, who was staring at her. "She wants me to babysit on Saturday." Marine looked at the caller's name; it was her friend Marie-Pierre from the bank. "Hello, Marie-Pierre," she said.

"Listen, I don't have much time because we're off to a movie," Marie-Pierre said. "But I looked into the accounts of Étienne and Isabelle de Bremont. I could lose my job for telling you this."

"Don't worry," Marine said. "It's in the name of the law."

"I know, I know. Well, here it is. The Bremonts aren't poor."

"What?"

"Well, there's not much money in their joint account, but lots in a separate account that Étienne seemed to use. I almost didn't spot that second account because the address is different—the statements get sent to Saint-Antonin."

Marine was dumbfounded, and then realized that she hadn't thanked her friend. "Thanks, Marie-Pierre. Have fun at the cinema."

"I doubt it. It's a Harry Potter—I'm taking the kids. *Bises*, ciao!"

Marine hung up the phone and told Verlaque what her friend had said. "That's so typical of the nobility," Verlaque said.

"What do you mean?" Marine asked, helping herself to a handful of cashews.

"To pretend you don't have money when you really do. What's the shame in having a nice car? Why are the nobility so proud that they have to hide their money?"

They had had this argument a thousand times. "They see it as being discreet, I think." But she thought of the rickety baby buggy and had to agree a bit with Verlaque. "Wait a minute . . . Vincent said that they argued about money in his shop, and that Isabelle said that she was tired of being poor."

"So she didn't know about the second account." Verlaque poured them both some more champagne. Marine was having a hard time figuring out why she was there—Verlaque was doing a good deal of staring but not much more. They could have said any of this by telephone. But the champagne worked its magic, and Marine saw that Verlaque was smiling and leaning back and rubbing his tummy, something he always did when he was completely comfortable. He said, "That was very moving this morning, the little I saw of it. The lawyers in their robes, the school kids . . . What did you think?"

"I agree. It was somehow magical. After you left, the children offered drawings they had done of heaven. They made me think of Paradiso, our Italian hideaway."

"That was heaven, wasn't it?" Verlaque closed his eyes and drew on his cigar, and then suddenly asked, "How's your new boyfriend?" leaning toward Marine with mock sincerity.

Marine looked back in pretended shock. She refrained from telling Verlaque that she and Arthur were definitely not yet boyfriend and girlfriend. It wasn't any of his business. "How do you know about him? He just left for California anyway."

"I know. Stanford University." Verlaque saw the look of surprise on Marine's face. "Do I always have to remind you, darling, that Aix is small? Word gets around. We have some of the same friends, remember. So, what's going on between the two of you? What do you do for fun?"

"Shut up!" Marine tried hard not to laugh. She felt almost delirious being on the terrace with Antoine, and she wanted time to stand still. No—she wanted to reverse the clocks and have Étienne still be alive. And François.

"Where *does* a vegan go out for dinner?"

Marine laughed aloud. "He's a vegetarian, not a vegan, and I'm going to *kill* Jean-Marc!"

"Don't be too hard on Jean-Marc. He was looking out for your best interest. I forced him to tell me all about the good doctor."

"And why would Jean-Marc do that?"

Verlaque's smile faded slightly but still played on his charming, wide mouth. He stared at Marine. He paused, and in a quiet voice said, "Because, my silly, beautiful girl, he knows how much I still care for you." Marine looked at him, stunned, unable to answer. The silence stretched for minutes as they stared at one another, neither daring to move or to breathe. Verlaque broke the ice by standing up, leaning his back against the terrace's wrought-iron balcony.

"Hey," Verlaque said, looking down at his stomach. "Do you think I've lost weight?"

Marine laughed out loud and reached over and patted his middle. She looked up at Antoine, keeping her hand on his stomach.

"You always did have a soft spot for my big tummy, didn't you?"

Verlaque's cell phone then rang, and, seeing that it was Paulik, he excused himself, mussing Marine's hair as he walked by her to take the call in the kitchen. "I called my cousin Fréd and asked him what kind of vehicle François de Bremont drives on the Côte," Paulik told Verlaque. "A black Range Rover. And in the summer he zips around on a Vespa," Paulik continued.

"So he doesn't have a fetish for VW Golfs?" Verlaque asked, looking at Marine through the glass doors.

"Apparently not," Paulik replied. "But why go to all that trouble to get the Golf from Saint-Antonin?"

"I have no idea. It's really beginning to bother me." Verlaque thanked Paulik for the call, and they wished each other a good evening and hung up.

Marine noticed with surprise that they had very quickly drunk a bottle of champagne, and now Verlaque was opening a bottle of red. She looked at the label and saw that it was a Gigondas; the name rang a bell: she was fairly certain that it was a small town in the Rhône. Sylvie had a theory that one should always check the alcohol level of a wine, especially when one was alone with an attractive man whom one wasn't dating—if the alcohol was above 12.5 percent, the evening could become dangerous. Verlaque turned away to put some lamb chops on the grill— there was also some tiny, thin asparagus in the oven, with loads of olive oil and garlic—and Marine grabbed the bottle and saw that the alcohol was 14 percent. But she had already drunk enough champagne that her ability to reason was, well, beyond reason.

They ate their dinner, laughing and talking of a trip to Piedmont they had taken while still together, a trip on which Marine must have gained five kilos. She didn't have a scale in her house, but she could not fit into her favorite jeans after the trip. They teased each other, and Verlaque began to caress her leg while he ate. It didn't seem unnatural for him to do this, despite their recent months apart. She let him continue. He caressed her throughout the dinner, and through the cheese and more wine, and during the fresh strawberries.

"We're just like an old couple," he finally said.

"No, Antoine, we're not a couple," said Marine. "Are you happy?" she asked gently, after a pause.

"So-so," he answered, looking at his wineglass.

Marine began to feel panicked. "Vincent hinted today that you've been up to something lately. Is there someone else in your life?"

"No," replied Verlaque, not looking at Marine.

She shivered and wanted to be home, alone. "I have to go," she said, folding her napkin and setting it beside her plate.

"Wait. Please. Don't go yet," he said, this time looking at her.

"All right. Wait two seconds," Marine answered, and she walked quickly toward the bathroom. As usual, she had to go pee at a crucial moment in the evening. Was he going to ask her to sleep over? And what if she did? Who would care? Except Sylvie, and she needn't find out about it. Marine maneuvered her way down the hallway and up the two stairs that led to his bathroom. She locked herself in and breathed deeply, leaning against the wood door.

She sat down on the toilet and Sylvie's musical message came into her head. Be careful, she thought. She began flipping through the magazines on the tiled floor—Verlaque's usual assortment: sailing magazines; two *Cigar Aficionado*s; an *Economist*, in English. And, then, at the bottom of the pile, a French *Vogue*. Verlaque hates fashion magazines, she thought. She picked it up and flipped it over to the front cover—it was this month's *Vogue*. It had an address label still attached—Lady Emily Watford, 76 rue d'Assas, 75006, Paris. Marine knew the street well. She had spent a year researching law at the Université Panthéon-Assas, located on that same street, across from the Jardin du Luxembourg. Even small apartments cost a fortune in the sixth arrondissement. She felt sick to her stomach. Someone with a posh name and address had been visiting Verlaque very recently. Stupid Lady Emily had probably read the magazine on the TGV on the way to Aix. Marine imagined a blonde sitting in first class, her Prada miniskirt showing off her thin, long legs. Tanned, long legs. That's who rearranged the fucking kitchen! That's what Vincent was referring to! He must have seen them around town. Aix is small, indeed.

Marine walked back out onto the terrace and picked up her purse. "Are you leaving?" Verlaque asked, looking up at her. "Don't you want to stay and hear what I want to tell you?"

"No, I can't. I mean, I don't have time. I have papers to mark, and I'm exhausted." She heard Verlaque speaking behind her, but she couldn't make out his words—she was at his front door in seconds, ran down the stairs out into the street, not stopping until she had turned into the place de l'Archevêché. She spotted a garbage can in front of her and discreetly, she hoped, threw up the contents of her dinner. As Sylvie said later, it wasn't the champagne or the wine that caused her to be sick, but her heart and her stomach were so full of love that something had to give, something had to escape. Maybe it was Verlaque finally leaving her system? "That's our worst nightmare," Sylvie added, placing a warm washcloth on Marine's forehead. "To discover that the man we love is screwing somebody else."

"Do you have to be so blunt? What are you saying? That Verlaque loves this Emily?"

Sylvie put the washcloth down and had a sip of green tea. "Maybe you should consider that possibility."

"Thanks a lot, Sylvie," Marine moaned. "So why am I so upset? I'm seeing someone too!"

"Are *you* in love with Arthur Vassan?" Sylvie asked. She then snorted.

"What's so funny?"

"Arthur Vassan. Antoine Verlaque. Same initials."

Marine paused before snapping, "That doesn't mean anything."

Sylvie put her hand on Marine's shoulder. "Yeah, you're right. But . . . you *could* get an 'AV' with a heart tattooed on your butt." They both burst out laughing.

Chapter Fourteen

۶

*H*is cell phone rang, forcing him to move away from the doorway of the terrace where Marine had left him standing, perplexed, for some minutes. She was so frustrating, so unbelievably stubborn, so intoxicating.

"*Oui*, Verlaque here."

"This is Olivier Madani, president of Souleiado Films in Marseille. I'm sorry to call you at this hour, Judge Verlaque, but we were editing until late this evening. One of your officers visited me on Monday, and we were so busy that I couldn't spend much time with him."

"Thank you for calling," Verlaque answered. He was a little surprised that Madani would call him personally. He closed the front door to his apartment, left open by Marine, and walked across the living room to close the windows. It was cooler now.

"Morale here is pretty low, Judge. Étienne was well liked—he kind of held this place together. Artists are difficult at times, but he wasn't," Madani said.

Verlaque answered sincerely, "It doesn't surprise me—I was very impressed with Étienne de Bremont when he filmed me for your crime documentary."

"Well, that's why I'm calling. The crime documentary . . . I should have told the sergeant about it, but we were so busy, and I'd been sitting in a dark room too long, so I was a little foggy. That documentary was released nine months ago, but while Étienne was filming we received a call from, um," Madani hesitated, "them."

Verlaque understood but carefully asked, "Who?"

Madani paused. There was a silence on the phone. Madani cleared his throat. "I think we both know whom we're talking about here."

Of course, thought Verlaque, the mafia, with ties to Ajaccio in Corsica. While tourists slept, after a day of taking pictures of Aix's seventeenth-century mansions and fountains, the Corsican mafia was setting off bombs in nightclubs or bars that refused to pay protection money. In February an English pub that poured, in Verlaque's opinion, a fine Guinness, was bombed. Nobody was hurt, as the bomb went off at 4:00 a.m., but the owner packed his bags and moved back to Manchester.

"Judge? Are you there?"

"Yes, go on."

Madani continued, "During the filmmaking, after Étienne had finished his first few interviews, I was invited—*told*—to come to lunch. Lunch with"—here Madani lowered his voice—"Fabrizio Orsani."

"Ah," Verlaque answered. He knew the name well. Orsani was the godfather for the Marseille region.

Madani, relieved of this weight, continued quickly, unprompted by the judge: "He came with about four young guys, huge guys. They were all Corsican—I know because my parents both grew up in Cargèse. He was very pleasant. I must admit, I kind of liked him. He just told me to be careful, careful with what we chose to put in the film, careful with what we chose not to put in. He wanted to meet Étienne, but I told him that Étienne was my best director, and I had full confidence in him. It's funny, because Orsani then laughed and said, 'I hope he's nothing like his idiot brother.'"

"And since then, nothing?" Verlaque asked.

"Nothing. They couldn't have been displeased with the film—it was fairly neutral, I thought. I later heard, after we won the award, that Orsani was even a bit flattered at the references made to him."

"I found it curious that Étienne didn't cover the Russian mafia in his film," Verlaque said, taking some dark chocolate out of the cupboard and snapping off a piece, while cradling his cell phone between his shoulder and ear.

"I did too, and I asked Étienne about that before he even began filming," Madani answered. "But Étienne felt the film would be stronger if he concentrated on one city and its mafia. As you know, the Corsican mafia has always been based in Marseille, while the Russians are on the Côte d'Azur. Étienne loved Marseille.

"Another thing," Madani continued. "It was almost as if, and I don't think it came across strongly in the film, Étienne had a love—*non*, that's not the word—a respect for, or a weird curiosity about, the Corsican mafia. That's something I picked up from talking to him and seeing the footage before it was edited."

"And you're sure Étienne never met Fabrizio Orsani?" Verlaque asked.

"Fairly sure," Madani said, "but, you never know. Étienne was easygoing and very pleasant, but he could also be secretive. Sometimes I felt as if I didn't really know him, despite our working ridiculous hours side by side for over five years. But that's maybe just human nature. Don't you think so, Judge? We all have our secrets."

Verlaque lit his cigar and took a few puffs before grunting his agreement. He thought of Paris, his parents, her eyes, orange-flowered sheets, tangled limbs, and betrayal. He thought of Marine running down the stairs before he had a chance to tell her his story. Surely what happened all those years ago hadn't been his fault? He opened his eyes and stared at the Venetian painting in his dining room, gathering strength from it. He continued, now focused, "What was Étienne working on recently, before he died?"

"Part two."

"Part two?" Verlaque asked.

"Part two is a sort of behind-the-scenes look at the filming of the first one. He was getting ready to go to Corsica but then . . . then he died. I got a call from your commissioner, who is going to come watch the cuts. You can come too, naturally."

"Yes, perhaps I will. I really like Marseille," Verlaque answered.

"Great," Madani answered, his voice getting louder with Marseillais pride. "I feel so sorry for you Aixois. What a dull place to live."

"It's quiet, that's for sure," Verlaque agreed. "By the way, Mme Bremont told me her husband was hoping to make a commercial film and that his funding was turned down. Did you know about the film?"

"Yes, and, to be honest, I wasn't too pleased about it. I mean, I was happy for Étienne that he had a screenplay, and possibly some funding, but a feature-length film would mean that he would have to leave us. When it fell through, I was somewhat relieved. Terrible, *non*?"

"*Normal*, Monsieur. I understand. And as far as you know, he never got the funding?"

"No, I don't think he did," Madani answered. "He was quite glum for a few weeks, but recently he was in better form. You know—happier."

"Thank you for this call, M. Madani," Verlaque said before hanging up.

Verlaque turned on the espresso machine that he had permanently set to make short, strong espressos. He could drink coffee anytime and still sleep like a baby, and he thought that people who claimed that they couldn't drink coffee after three o'clock in the afternoon were hypochondriacs or at least very messed up. He dropped a sugar cube in the coffee and turned it about with a silver spoon, and then he did what he always did: he slowly licked the spoon, relishing the heavy, thick coffee sweetened with sugar. "Un bonbon," he muttered. This single pleasure may have been the principal motivation behind his coffee consumption. He drank the coffee in two sips and set the demitasse in the dishwasher.

The mohair plaid blanket that Emmeline always used to lay on her knees in the evenings had fallen off the sofa onto the floor. As he bent down to pick it up, he saw, on a bottom bookshelf, the photo album she had made—she had given one to each brother. He picked up the album and started flipping through the pages while still squatting. The photos were in color but many had faded. There were even a few Polaroids—Charles had bought Emmeline one of the first Polaroids on the market so that she could use it to keep track of her garden and her paintings. Verlaque remembered this photo—the old, bent-over gardener had taken it. It was of Emmeline and the two boys, Antoine and Sébastien, in her garden. This part of the garden, by the south wall, Emmeline had designed using dozens of varieties of flowers—all of them white. Verlaque had forgotten that. The garden faced south, on an acre of flat land, and it always seemed sunny to Verlaque, although he realized that they only went into the garden when it was sunny. When it rained, which was often, they stayed in the house, playing board games. The red brick wall that surrounded the property looked small and weather-beaten. It had seemed so tall and mighty when Verlaque was young. The wall ran around the entire property. The north side of the house was always damp and in shadow and it backed up against a hill, a sort of no-man's-land. One only went behind the house to fetch wood or to walk up into the village. Set into the brick wall was a green wooden door through which one could head up a flight of stone steps and onto the main street of the village of Saint-Germain-le-Vasson that housed the *boucher*, pâtissier, *boulanger*, and the tiny school that Verlaque had attended for one year when Emmeline had taken him—saved him—from Paris.

He turned the pages and came to another photograph—one of him with his parents on either side. He couldn't remember how Sébastien had wormed his way out of being in that picture. His father's face was strained, as if the sun was in his eyes, but it wasn't sunny. His mother's smile was faked, and her body straight, poised, and thin, as it still was. She was a beauty, but she had married for money, the money of Charles and Emmeline, and everyone, even the boys, knew it. Verlaque's father, shortly after the wedding, began having a string of mistresses; some of them Antoine and Sébastien met. The boys would regularly have lunch with their father at Café de Flore in Paris, and one of the girl-friends would often show up, supposedly out of the blue, but it was obvious to the boys that the encounter had been planned beforehand. It never bothered Verlaque—the women were always fantastic looking, and, unlike his mother, they doted on him and Sébastien. He sat on the floor, his legs stretched out before him, puffed on his cigar, and recited aloud, in English: "They fuck you up, your mum and dad. / They may not mean to, but they do. / They fill you with the faults they had / And add some extra, just for you." It wasn't his favorite Larkin poem, but it suited the moment, and his parents. Parents, thought Verlaque. Nobody has said anything about the parents of Étienne and François. It was as if they never existed.

He closed the album and thought of his father, who was approaching seventy—Verlaque assumed that the girlfriends had stopped. His parents were somehow still together, but they lived very separate lives in Paris. His father had always seemed happier in Normandy, and Verlaque kicked himself for not suggesting that they go to Emmeline's house together more often. At first Verlaque hadn't mentioned it, because he knew it would be emotionally too difficult for his father, but Emmeline had been dead for over six months now, and the house was still sitting empty. He looked at his watch—it was after eleven, too late to call his father in Paris.

He got up and called Marine's cell phone, but she wasn't answering. His bewilderment at her abrupt departure was slowly turning into anger. Why hadn't she told him the truth about why she was leaving? He knew, after being with her for over a year, that she was extremely organized, and it was unlikely that she had papers to grade so late in the evening. She had run down the stairs so fast—as if she were fleeing something terrible. He had said nothing out of place; he had done nothing wrong. He poured himself a large glass of Vichy sparkling water. Vichy wasn't his favorite brand, but one of the funnier detectives in Aix, Pierre

Minard, had studied all the different sparkling waters and come to the conclusion that Vichy, with its high level of bicarbonates, was the best to ward off a hangover. He laughed out loud when he thought of Minard, leaning drunkenly over the bar at a policemen's party and, while the other officers yelled out brand names, replying with each water's level of bicarbonates, which he had memorized. Verlaque poured himself a second glass, forcing himself to drink it—he hated water—when his cell phone rang. He ran to it.

"Antoine Verlaque," he said, not recognizing the number.

"*Coucou, chèri,*" said a voice with a thick English accent.

"Hey, I was just thinking of you," Verlaque said, lying.

"You were not, you liar," she answered in English. "Did you already forget about me? We spent the night together only last week. I usually don't travel around to see lovers—they come and see me. You're a very lucky judge, Judge."

Verlaque remembered their night; it had taken him two days to recover. Emily was, Verlaque thought, at least *un bon coup*.

"Listen, I'm on my friend's cell phone, she doesn't have much battery left," Emily said, not waiting for Verlaque's reply. "When can you come up to Paris?"

She was obviously in a restaurant—it was noisy in the background. Verlaque could hear plates and glasses rattling. He missed Paris. "I don't know when I can come up to Paris," he answered, "I'm in the middle of something right now. But I have another idea. How about Normandy sometime soon?"

"Where? Did you say Normandy? On the coast, at least? Deauville?"

"No, inland, a little village called Saint-Germain-le-Vasson. I think you'd like it. I can't hear you very well. Where are you?"

"Georges," she answered. Verlaque loved Georges—it was the

best thing going in the Centre Pompidou. He could eat a great meal at the top-floor restaurant and not feel obligated to look at the modern art. He liked few contemporary painters, with the exception of Pierre Soulages.

"Well, listen, I'm sure your Saint-Germain in Normandy is lovely," she said. He could hear laughter in the near background. "But I have to stay in Paris for the next few weeks. I'm writing an article on luxurious French hotels. Call me! Promise to call me! Ciao!"

"Bye, Emily," he said, hanging up his cell phone. He tried Marine's number again—no answer. While plugging his cell phone in to charge overnight, he saw the pile of what had been the contents of his pockets: various keys, coins, cigar bands, and the receipt from lunch at Lotus. He turned the receipt over and saw Caroline's cell phone number, and then walked over to the garbage can. He looked at the number again, walked back, picked up his cell phone, and entered her number in his directory.

He turned off the living room lights and walked down the hall toward his bedroom, stopping in the bathroom to brush his teeth. He grabbed his toothbrush and looked around for the toothpaste. He couldn't find it. Voilà, he said to himself. He saw a *Vogue* that he didn't remember seeing before—it must have been buried in the basket beside the toilet with the other magazines and he moved it and found the toothpaste. As he was brushing his teeth he looked at the *Vogue*, and then he saw the address label. He closed his eyes, now understanding why Marine had left so hastily. "Too complicated," he said aloud. Exhausted, he walked into his bedroom and took off his clothes, leaving them uncharacteristically in a pile on the floor, and fell into bed.

Chapter Fifteen

❧

*V*erlaque saw Marine by the roundabout, straining to see into each car that passed. The sun was shining on the windshields, making it difficult to see the drivers. He was driving an unmarked police car, so he slowed down, flashed the light blue Clio's lights once, and pulled up to the roundabout. He watched Marine walk toward the car. Two university-aged boys, smiling, also watched her. Verlaque grinned—he liked to see men staring at Marine. She's beautiful, he thought, almost saying it out loud. Marine's black crepe de chine dress clung to her in an unconscious way, making her beauty all the more irresistible.

Paulik got out of the passenger side and squeezed his large frame into the backseat. Marine quickly got into the front. Verlaque saw that her eyes were puffy. He put his hand on her shoulder and asked, "Are you okay?"

"Yes, yes. I'm fine." She and Sylvie had stayed up late, Sylvie forcing Marine to drink gallons of water while the two of them goofed around on the Internet, looking up Lady What's-Her-Name. Thanks to Sylvie, Marine didn't feel ill this morning—at least from the alcohol. Her stomach was turning at the thought of seeing Lady Emily's photograph in *British Vogue* online, wearing a tiny bikini in Saint-Tropez. What were the chances that Verlaque would find one of the few thin English women? Or perhaps they were thinner in general than their American cousins. Judging by the tourists who walked around Aix, American women were almost invariably large, clutching liter-sized bottles of water to their breasts. Why didn't they just order a coffee and a carafe of water in a café? But then Marine remembered one of Sylvie's many theories about Americans: they were extremists, either overweight or thin and muscular, beer drinkers or teetotalers, overeaters or obsessed with eating only foods that contained no fat. Perhaps the English were the same way.

"So, what do you remember about Cosette Auvieux?" Verlaque asked, looking over at Marine.

"Not much," Marine answered. "I should remember her better, considering how much time I spent up at the château. She always seemed to be lurking in the corner or off with François. Do you really think I can help? What if she doesn't remember me?"

"It might not matter. I somehow think she'd prefer to be questioned by a woman," Paulik offered.

"I agree," Verlaque said. "Plus, you make people feel good." Verlaque looked quickly over at Marine, and then back at the road. "Most of the time," he whispered.

Marine's heart sank. She began doubting herself and her stupid compulsive behavior. Maybe there was a reasonable explanation for the *Vogue* magazine. A cousin from England, perhaps? She didn't respond—she didn't want to argue in front of Bruno.

Marine frowned and asked, "Does Cosette have an alibi for yesterday morning?"

"Yes," replied Paulik. "She was in the Bar Centrale in Cotignac at eight, having a coffee. She had to open the salon early because her partner is off sick. The first client arrived just before nine."

Verlaque said, "Before we visit Mme Auvieux, we are going to visit my friend Marc, who owns a winery near Cotignac. Paulik and I discovered, on our last visit there, that François de Bremont is having an affair—was having an affair—with Sophie Valoie de Saint-André."

"Are you nuts?" Marine asked in amazement.

"Strange couple, I agree. But they had been spending every other Friday night at Marc's B and B since January."

"This is going to be a strange afternoon," Marine said. "Should I be taking notes?"

"I'll take notes," Paulik answered.

"Bruno," Verlaque asked, "can you tell us now what's going on in Cannes?"

"François de Bremont has been suspiciously friendly with a man called Lever Pogorovski," Paulik said, pronouncing the Russian name slowly while looking at Verlaque and Marine.

"I'm afraid I've never heard of your Pogorovski," Verlaque said.

Paulik rolled up his sleeves and leaned even farther forward between the two front seats, excited to be the bearer of information. He took out a small notepad and began reading: "Lever Pogorovski, Georgian, born 1952. Holds Canadian citizenship, as does his wife, Maria. In 2001 they bought the famous Villa Nina in Saint-Jean-Cap-Ferrat, on the Côte d'Azur, for one hundred million euros." The commissioner paused here, waiting for, and getting, the appropriate gasps from his audience. He continued: "Two months after, they bought a chalet in Megève for 3.2 million. The following year, they purchased a ski resort in the mountains behind Nice—13.7 million. For his wife's fiftieth birthday he had a miniature Taj Mahal built on their terrace." Verlaque snorted and Marine laughed out loud. Paulik continued, a little perturbed at the interruption: "They spent sixty-eight thousand euros that night for the fireworks and ten thousand euros for the flowers. He has a Swiss lawyer in Zurich and a company called Astro Holding, located in Luxembourg, which in turns owns his oil company, Comgaz."

"Has he ever been arrested?" asked Verlaque.

"No," answered Paulik, "he's clean—in fact Boris Yeltsin's daughter Tatyana is a frequent guest at Villa Nina. But my cousin Fréd confirmed for me this morning that he is high up in the Russian—in this case Georgian—mafia. Plus," Paulik continued, "Pogorovski's wife owns a modeling agency in Nice. And guess who works there from time to time?"

"François de Bremont," said Verlaque.

Marine threw up her hands in disgust. "That's incredible. How did we let that happen? How could a bunch of Russian crooks be running the Côte?" Marine asked.

"It's been happening since the late nineteenth century," said Verlaque. "Czar Nicholas's widow, Alexandra, was among the first wave of Russians to discover the Côte d'Azur."

"True," Marine answered, annoyed. It was so irritating when Verlaque pretended to know more about history than she did. "But she wasn't selling heroin."

"No," said Verlaque, "but she did throw some really good parties." The three laughed. "Go on, Paulik—how is François de Bremont involved?"

"The Cannes police told me that for the moment he's only involved, or was only involved, in booking dates for the Russian girls. Whether they were just escorts, or high-end prostitutes, isn't yet clear. Their clients were Russian and French. Both my cousin Fréd and Pellegrino—the cop who plays polo—confirmed that whenever François de Bremont's name is mentioned among the mafia or even between policemen, it's always with a sigh and some foul words. Fréd said it best: 'François is more of a pest than anything else, but a pest with good connections.'"

"Which equals power," Marine said.

"Exactly," Paulik answered.

Verlaque stared out the window and continued driving. He thought of what Madani, Étienne's boss, had repeated: the godfather of Marseille, Fabrizio Orsani, had said that François was the "idiot brother." The comment made Verlaque think of the film *The Godfather*. One has all the good and the other all the bad, as Marine had said of the two Bremont brothers. One brother: calm and intelligent. The other: wild and irrational. Verlaque thought of the faces of the two actors, and then said, "Bruno, I'll buy you a magnum of Marc's wine if you can tell me the name of the actor who played Sonny in *The Godfather*."

"James Caan," Paulik replied, smiling.

"Merde."

Chapter Sixteen

❧

*G*reetings were exchanged and Verlaque introduced Marine as a professor of law at the university in Aix. Marine tried not to let it bother her—and even if they had been still a couple that's how he would have introduced her. They were here on police business, investigating two deaths, one of which was definitely murder.

Nagel seemed a little surprised that they declined the invitation to taste wine, but Verlaque assured him, "I will be buying a magnum of your Syrah." He shot a nasty glance at Paulik, who in turn grinned from ear to ear. When they got inside, Marc's wife, Véronique, was once again sitting at the desk. Verlaque explained the case so far and the discovery of François's death early that morning.

"How awful . . . He was so pleasant," said Véronique, visibly distressed.

"Really?" asked Marine, unable to hide her surprise.

"Oh yes, he always behaved very politely," Véronique replied. She paused. "But I did overhear him yelling at his mistress once. It made me uneasy."

"Really? You didn't tell me about that," said Marc. "But I

agree—he was refreshingly curious. He wanted to know about the wine, how it is made, and especially about the life of the vineyard—the seasons and so on. He was quite intelligent. He kept the conversation limited to the weather and wine-making, though. I assumed because it was pretty clear that he was having an affair."

Marine thought for a moment, trying to remember François. Something was not quite right. She held up her finger and said, "The François I remember didn't like wine, didn't drink alcohol at all. Although people change."

"Oh, this one did!" exclaimed Véronique. "Not too much, mind you, but he really loved it. You could tell." Marc nodded in agreement.

Verlaque said nothing. Paulik reached into a file and slid a photo of François de Bremont, on his boat, across the wood desk to Marc and Véronique. "This is a recent photograph of him, just so we're certain that we are speaking about the same man."

"Well . . ." Marc hesitated, picking up the photograph so that he and Véronique could get a closer look. "The sun is shining on him . . . I guess it could be. But his hair isn't dark enough."

"I'm not sure that's him. His shoulders weren't that big," Véronique said, biting her bottom lip. "That guy's buff," she added, whistling under her breath and grabbing the photograph to get a better look.

"Are you sure?" asked Paulik. "You said he signed himself in as François de Bremont."

"That's true, although come to think of it we never asked for an ID," Marc replied.

Verlaque said nothing and took another photo out of his file folder and gave it to the wine-making couple.

"That's him!" Marc exclaimed.

"Yes, that's more like it," his wife agreed, smiling now.

"Now I understand why you thought him interesting and intelligent," Verlaque said.

Marine shot Verlaque a puzzled look and reached for the photograph. Paulik leaned in toward Marine so that he too could see the photograph. It was a large black-and-white photo of Étienne de Bremont receiving his documentary film award in Paris.

"Well, I'll be damned," Paulik said when they were out on the drive.

"I still can't believe it," Marine added. She felt her heart give a hollow shudder. It had been years since she had spent much time with Étienne, but how could he have changed that much? An affair with Sophie Valoie de Saint-André? His wife's sister, of all people! Marine thought of Isabelle de Bremont's beautiful, fragile, newly widowed face that morning. It was almost too much to bear.

"Nor can I," said Verlaque. "Sophie Valoie de Saint-André is the last woman I'd want to sleep with." He then added, causing Paulik and Marine to look at him in mild shock, "What a thin, uptight bitch." He knew immediately that he had been too harsh, but he had someone else in his head, not Mme Valoie.

"That solves the mystery of the VW Golf. Étienne obviously went and picked it up from Saint-Antonin before heading here on those Friday nights," Paulik offered.

The five of them were standing by the car, having stayed an extra hour to talk further with Marc and Véronique and to explain the secrecy and new urgency of this case. They had also made photocopies of receipts from all the nights Étienne and

Sophie had spent at the Nagels' B and B. "Étienne de Bremont may have died accidently," Verlaque told the Nagels. "But his brother was murdered, so if you remember anything unusual about Étienne, could you please call us?"

"Certainly," the Nagels said in unison, Mme Nagel linking her arm around her husband's and leaning in closer to him.

"Come to think of it," Marine said, "at the cemetery I noticed that Mme Valoie was taking it particularly hard. Some people cry more than others at funerals, but she was really in a state."

"How was Isabelle de Bremont?" Verlaque asked.

"Stoic," Marine replied.

Paulik's cell phone rang. As Paulik moved away to take the call, Antoine and Marine tried not to acknowledge the fact that they were standing within a foot of each other but with nothing to say. Verlaque finally got out his cell phone to check for messages, while Marine walked over to the vineyard.

She looked at gnarled vines, marked by small, bright green leaves just beginning to grow. So much pleasure given to the world from such a small plant, Marine mused. "They're old vines, these," said Marc, who had come outside and was now standing beside her, smiling. Marine looked up at him. He had the tanned, weathered face and clear blue eyes of many the other vignerons she knew. "My grandfather planted these Syrah grapes in the late forties," he continued. He had been looking at Marine, but now glanced across at the rows of vines. And Marine did too, thinking that vines often resemble the sea—row upon row of green.

"You seemed upset when you saw the second photograph," Marc said.

"Yes," replied Marine, not sure what to say. She paused for a moment and then added: "Life is so unclear at times. What you think you know, you don't. You see, I knew Étienne very well, when we were young. We live in different social circles now, but I was still quite shocked to hear that he was having an affair with his sister-in-law. I guess I'm very prudish!"

Marc continued looking at her, and then said, "I stopped a long time ago trying to second-guess people and their actions and motives." He laughed and added, "It makes life easier, *non?*"

Marine smiled and said, "Yes, I suppose so."

"And if this man, Étienne, was the honorable man that everyone says he was, this woman, Mme Valoie, must be more complicated than meets the eye," Marc said.

"Are all winemakers this wise?" Marine asked, laughing.

"We spend a lot of time outside, thinking. I sometimes wonder if I don't talk to the vines."

"I'm sure I talk to myself. It's a teacher's habit. You imagine that there is a roomful of students, listening." The two laughed.

"Am I interrupting something?" asked Verlaque, who had just arrived and was looking back and forth between Marine and Marc.

"We were talking about vines, and about people," Marine said. "I suppose you'll be interviewing Sophie Valoie now."

"Yes, as soon as we get back to Aix. Listen, I'm sure Marc doesn't want us to talk shop. Marc—I'd like to buy that magnum now."

Marc hit his forehead and apologized. "Of course! Let's go into the stables."

"I'll wait here," Marine said. Neither man acknowledged her comment, and so she turned and stared off into the vineyard again. The view of the hills was mesmerizing, and she vowed never to live in a landscape that was flat. She found herself thinking of Étienne, and it made her unhappy to have to replace the picture of Isabelle de Bremont in her head with that of her sister

Sophie. What was he doing with her? And what was he doing in the attic that night? A knot formed in her stomach and she turned around to face the parking lot, the vineyards no longer able to calm her. She was anxious to get going to Cotignac, anxious to unravel the mysteries behind the two deaths. She started walking to the car, where Paulik was waiting, and Verlaque and Marc Nagel soon rejoined them.

"Let's get going," Verlaque said, taking Marine's arm and putting himself, Marine thought, purposely between her and the winemaker. Marc followed them to the car. They said their goodbyes and thanked the Nagels for their help, and Marine turned to Verlaque, who was staring at her.

Once in the car, Paulik leaned forward and spoke. "That was Flamant on the line. He's heard back from the SNCF." Marine turned to look at the commissioner, and Verlaque looked at him in the rearview mirror. "And?" he asked.

"Isabelle de Bremont went to Paris on Saturday morning on the 10:42. She came back on Sunday morning."

"Why would she lie about that?" Marine asked.

"She must be protecting the person in Paris who would provide her alibi. She told me that she was in Aix, with her sister, the night Étienne died," Verlaque answered.

"I still don't understand," Marine said, looking at both men. She then sighed and said, "Ah. An affair. But why not just say so? Is he married? Is he famous? He would at least give her a truthful alibi. Surely that would be more important?"

"You would think so," Verlaque answered. He thought of the crucifix and the Madonna in Isabelle de Bremont's salon. The three remained silent for some time. The continuous fields of olive trees and vineyards finally made Marine restless, and so she began to speak. "Has Jean-Claude Auvieux's sister been told about what happened this morning?"

"Yes and no," replied Bruno. Marine turned around to see him still cradling the magnum in his arms. "A local cop called in at her salon this morning and told her to go home, and that we would be visiting, but that's all she knows. I'm not even sure how well she knew François de Bremont."

"Oh, she knew him all right. At least when we were young. They were thick as thieves," Marine answered.

Verlaque looked at Bruno in the rearview mirror. "You can put the bottle down on the seat beside you," he told his officer.

"It's fine like this," Bruno replied. "Ask me more movie trivia."

"No, thanks," said Verlaque, smiling.

Verlaque slowed the car down as they approached Cosette Auvieux's *lotissement*.

"Depressing," mumbled Marine.

"No kidding," replied Verlaque. "It would be bad enough to have to live in the Var, but to live in a place like this . . ." Verlaque's voice trailed off as they stopped the car in front of the house. There was a small front lawn where Mme Auvieux chose to park her car instead of plant trees or flowers. She opened the front door before they had a chance to ring, and without words, Mme Auvieux motioned them into the house and closed the door behind them.

"I hope you have a good reason for this visit," she said, looking straight at Verlaque. "This is costing me good money at the hair salon."

"We have a good reason, Madame," Verlaque answered. "You remember the commissioner, I believe. And I think you may remember Professor Bonnet, Marine Bonnet, from Aix-en-Provence."

Cosette Auvieux squinted and looked Marine up and down. Without a smile, she offered Marine her hand and said, "I do remember you. You were always up at the château, playing with Étienne."

"Yes," Marine answered. "I played with your brother too. I saw Jean-Claude a few days ago, and he reminded me of the time François broke the window in the salon."

Mme Auvieux smirked and rolled her eyes. "Étienne broke the window, and François took the blame. It always happened like that."

Marine remembered what Jean-Claude had said, "And it wasn't even François who broke the window! It was Étienne!" She was confused about this—in her memory it was clearly François.

"Your brother, Mme Auvieux, is being questioned about a murder," Verlaque said.

"Who says Étienne de Bremont's death was a murder? I thought he fell. Besides, any nitwit can tell that my brother wouldn't hurt a fly, and he has an alibi—he was here with me."

"Jean-Claude has the bad luck to keep ending up in the wrong place at the wrong time." Verlaque looked at Marine, as if to give her her cue.

"Cosette," Marine said, "There's been a second death at the château."

"Impossible!" Cosette Auvieux cried.

Paulik and Verlaque exchanged looks.

Marine continued, "François de Bremont is dead, found yesterday morning in the *bassin* in front of the château."

Cosette Auvieux's face turned white, and she sat down at the kitchen table. Only then did Marine realize that they had been standing the whole time, waiting for an invitation to sit down that had not been offered. Mme Auvieux began suddenly to cry, covering her face with her hands.

"Can we get you something?" Verlaque asked.

Auvieux motioned to a bottle of marc on the kitchen counter. Verlaque caught Paulik's wide-eyed expression at the choice of beverage. Marc, a distilled alcohol made from grape skins—much like grappa—was extremely high in alcohol, strong even for someone as big as Paulik.

Marine sat down beside Mme Auvieux. "Cosette? Are you all right?" She wanted to put her hand on Cosette's but hesitated. Cosette had begun to cry again.

"I was very close to him when we were kids," she said.

"I remember," Marine said. "Did you stay in contact over the years?" she asked.

Cosette Auvieux looked at Marine as if she were crazy. "Of course not!" she snapped. "We lived in totally different circles."

"Professor Bonnet is right to ask these questions," Verlaque said, suddenly protective of Marine. "François de Bremont's death was a murder. That was confirmed this morning by the on-duty coroner. We need to question everyone who knew him—and you knew him, and your brother was present at the scene of the murder."

"All I know is that François lived on the Côte," Cosette replied. "Did my brother see anything? Did anyone?"

"No," replied Verlaque. He did not tell her about the Mercedes with Côte d'Azur plates. "Your brother claims that he was in the olive grove at the time of the death. The two of them were going to go together to Étienne de Bremont's funeral."

Marine leaned across the table and gently asked, "Cosette, would Jean-Claude have any reason to hurt the Bremonts?"

"What? Are you insane?" Cosette Auvieux shrieked.

Marine looked at Paulik and Verlaque.

"Mme Auvieux," Paulik said. "Your brother discovered both bodies. You must see why we have to ask you this."

"Will he be safe?" Cosette asked.

"Yes," Paulik answered. "We'll have the château watched. Now, can you answer Professor Bonnet's question?"

Cosette leaned forward on the table and looked at the commissioner for a good five seconds before answering. "No, he had no reason to hurt them. He *didn't* hurt them."

"Thank you," Paulik said. Cosette stood up for a moment, holding on to the table for support, but quickly sat down again, burying her head in her hands once more. "The two brothers . . . dead now." She sobbed and then added, "You can see yourselves out," as if it were an order.

"She was more upset than I expected," Verlaque said, looking over at Marine as they drove away. "She definitely didn't seem this broken up about Étienne's death."

"Cosette and François always did seem to have a special connection when we were growing up. I had forgotten how close they were. I suppose she hasn't had an easy life, either. Her mother died of cancer when she was about sixteen. She immediately left the château after that, and came here to the Var to live with an aunt and go to hairdressing school. Jean-Claude was younger, so he finished high school and stayed on at the château. Their mother was lovely. I adored her. Beautiful and soft-spoken, and kind."

"The father?" asked Verlaque.

"He left her, and the children, when Jean-Claude was a baby. Mme Auvieux was much loved by the Bremont family, so was invited to stay on. She ran the household and the kitchen."

"I take it her daughter doesn't resemble her much," Paulik said.

"No, you're right. But then she never did. Jean-Claude was more like his mother and was more attached to the Bremont family and the estate."

Paulik's telephone rang and he answered with a "Salut, Fréd!" Marine was thinking of her childhood and of the people she had known and somehow forgotten. Verlaque startled her by asking, "Can you cancel your classes tomorrow? We're halfway to the Côte. We could just drive straight there and question Bremont's Cannes friends. It's a little unorthodox taking a nonpoliceman with us, but tough. I can make up some reason."

"No need. Classes are canceled, starting tomorrow, for the rest of the week," Marine answered, not sure what she was getting into.

"Classes are canceled?" Verlaque asked. "Don't tell me," he continued. "A strike?"

"Yes," Marine answered, smiling. The great number of strikes at the university angered Verlaque, and strikes in general were one of his pet peeves—he had absolutely no patience for them. Nor did Marine, for that matter, and during strikes she usually stayed in contact with her students via the Internet, and she often held class off campus, in the English-language bookstore, which was the only bookstore in Aix that had a café and comfortable chairs and tables.

Paulik hung up and said, "Fréd can meet me this afternoon. Why don't we go straight to Cannes?"

"That's what we were just thinking," Verlaque answered. "If I speed a bit, we might just make it to the Côte in time for a late lunch."

"Great. You're both invited to lunch with me at Fréd's," Paulik said.

"That's really nice of you, Bruno, but I think I'd like to take Marine out in Cannes." Before Marine could protest, Verlaque said, "Bruno, can you call ahead to the police station and let them know that we are coming? See if they can book us an interview with Lever Pogorovski later this afternoon. We'll need a car and a driver too. I can't stand the traffic on the Côte."

Paulik started dialing. Verlaque looked over at Marine and asked, "Do you think you could do some research for us while Bruno and I are at Pogorovski's? Find out anything you can about Pogorovski and his wife. You can use the computers at the Carlton—I know the manager. I'll let him know that you're coming."

Marine looked out the window, thinking of the teenage Bremont brothers. "When they were young, people used to get them mixed up," she mused.

Verlaque looked at her. "The Bremont brothers?"

"Yes," Marine answered. "Even the Nagels had to look closely at the photographs to figure out who was who." She then turned to him and said, "Think about it. In a dark attic . . ."

Paulik then leaned forward. "Maybe the killer thought Étienne was François?"

"They killed the wrong guy. And yesterday morning they went back to do it correctly," Verlaque suggested.

He then looked straight ahead at the road, and after a few seconds shot Marine a piercing gaze, what Sylvie used to refer as the "Antoine stare." Marine looked at him and, much to her amazement, saw a slight smile form at the corner of his mouth.

Chapter Seventeen

※

"*Y*ou *what*?" yelled Sylvie into her cell phone.

"You heard me," Marine whispered back, looking through the large windows of the Villa des Lys, out to the Croisette, and beyond that, the sea. It was a warm, clear day. The sky was its constant bright blue, and the fronds of the tall, straight palm trees swayed as if to music. She was waiting for Verlaque, who was parking the car—something that's always a challenge in Cannes. She glanced around at the diners, who were what she expected at a three-star restaurant: elderly and rich. A white-haired woman, sitting alone at the next table, was enjoying her oysters with gusto. She smiled at Marine, and Marine reciprocated. She loved to see people who ate alone without embarrassment or shame.

"Are you looking for punishment?" Sylvie continued. "You threw up into a garbage can in the middle of Aix, remember?"

"I'm here for Étienne de Bremont. The university is closed, and it was easy for me to decide to come," Marine said, still looking out the window. As soon as she had uttered these words, Marine realized that she hadn't a leg to stand on. She simply had no excuse for this last-minute trip to Cannes, except for the obvious one. She added, honestly, "I guess I'm not sure why I came."

"Wait a second . . . He gave you the Antoine stare, didn't he?"

"I'm hanging up, Sylvie!"

"No! Wait! Antoine always does that when he feels threatened, or jealous. I remember. Did you talk about another man?" Sylvie sputtered, afraid that Marine would hang up. "Did you talk about Arthur?"

"Arthur's at a medical conference in California."

"You didn't answer my question. What about that other policeman you're with?"

Marine laughed. "No chance." She paused, and then said, "There was a winemaker we spoke to, who was very handsome . . ."

"Aha! I knew it! Was the winemaker charmed by you?"

Marine paused a little too long before she said, unconvincingly, "I don't think so."

"Yes, I think so too," Sylvie replied. "When you get back to Aix and want to cry on my shoulder, I'll be here for you. It's become a big part of my life, you showing up on my doorstep and using all my Kleenex."

Marine laughed, and the white-haired woman once again cast a smile her way. She hung up the telephone just as Verlaque was being directed to the table by the maître d'. The two men had been talking on the way in, and Marine heard Verlaque address the waiter by his first name.

Antoine looked around and said, under his breath, "They really need to change the decor in here. Why do so many good restaurants in the south have such outdated furniture?" Marine agreed, and they laughed at the bright orange banquettes and red velour chairs. "Even my old aunts wouldn't like this porcelain," she said, tilting a plate painted with jungle scenes up so that it faced Verlaque. "You're right, but it's probably Hermès," Verlaque said. Marine took a quick peek underneath and added, "Well done—it is."

Two glasses of champagne arrived. Marine wasn't sure if they were compliments of the house or if they had been ordered by Verlaque on his way in, but she knew better than to ask. Questions like that irritated Verlaque. Taking too long to order also bothered him, so Marine quickly closed her menu as a sign that she was ready. A waiter appeared and took their orders, and then disappeared. She reached into her purse and dug out a pen and a small notepad and put them on the table.

"Two brothers dead," Marine said, writing at the same time. "One brother was more of a mystery than we thought—he was having an affair with his sister-in-law, whose husband is a judge in Marseille. Coincidence?"

"Perhaps," Verlaque said, puffing on his Cohiba. "Étienne's boss told me that Étienne could be mysterious at times. I thought he was referring to Étienne's work, but it sounds like it applies to his personal life as well."

Marine sipped some champagne; the delicate bubbles immediately refreshed her. She continued, "François seems to be less complicated—a gambler, a cheat, and somehow involved with the Russian mafia. Dirty, but more straightforward than Étienne."

"And we have two mafia organizations potentially involved— Russian and Corsican," added Verlaque.

"Or not involved," suggested Marine.

"No way—one of them has got to have a hand in all this," Verlaque said as he let his cigar burn out in the ashtray. Marine knew that Antoine always saved his unfinished cigars and smoked them when he had a chance later in the day. Sylvie, who hated this habit, used to tease him when she saw Verlaque putting a half-smoked cigar in its leather holder, by saying, "Better save it! There's a least six euros of cigar left there!" Verlaque's response to this was, as with most of Sylvie's jabs at his expensive tastes, silence.

A waiter appeared with their first course. "Monsieur has the oysters," the waiter said, and he began to set the oysters down before Verlaque. Verlaque quickly put out his thick hand to stop the plate.

The waiter froze, and said, "I am sure that it is Monsieur who ordered the oysters."

"He's right, Antoine. You know I can't stand them," Marine said, smiling up at the waiter.

"Neither of you understand," Verlaque said, with impatience. He glared at the waiter. "Since when is the man served before the woman?"

The waiter blushed, immediately realizing his mistake. "*Excusez-moi*," he stammered. He set down Marine's seafood risotto, then Verlaque's oysters, and disappeared.

"Now, so that I can enjoy these oysters—and of course I remember that you hate oysters—I want you to explain what happened last night," Verlaque demanded, folding his arms across his chest.

"The *Vogue*," Marine whispered.

"I thought so," answered Verlaque. "A friend from Paris brought it to Aix with her. A *friend*. In fact, she called me right after you left."

"I don't need the details, Antoine!" Marine exclaimed, a little too loud.

"I want you to have the details," Verlaque continued, leaning across the table to get closer. "She invited herself to Aix—she hangs out with my brother Sébastien's trendy Parisian crowd."

"When did she come? This week?"

"No, last week."

"Did you sleep with her?" Marine asked. She then covered her mouth and said, "I'm sorry, it's none of my business."

Verlaque stared at her. "Yes, I did." He held his hand up to stop Marine from leaving. "But last week I hadn't yet seen you again. It's been months, remember?"

"Is it over with her?"

"As far as I'm concerned, yes. She was fun while I was in Paris. I needed some distraction. But she's as empty as a tin can. I read her some poetry to shut her up."

Marine laughed and covered her mouth. Antoine went on, "And so what I wanted to tell you that night on my terrace is this—that I remember everything about you, about our time together. I know that you hate oysters, that you take too long to order in restaurants, that you have no palate whatsoever for wine. But I don't care. I also know that some of your law lectures elicit genuine applause at the end of them."

Marine set down her fork and stared at Verlaque. "How do you know that?" she asked.

"Aix is a small place," Verlaque replied, smiling. He dropped an oyster in his mouth, swallowed it, and continued: "And you're beautiful and wise and funny, and I miss you." Verlaque took a sip of wine, as if he were putting a period at the end of his sentence, and then set his glass down. The two of them stared at each other without moving or speaking. Marine had been dreaming for six months that Verlaque would say this, but Sylvie's warning was ringing in her head. Verlaque knew she was seeing Arthur.

"I don't think I can eat my risotto," Marine said.

"*Non?* Let me get you some olives," Verlaque said, pretending to look around the room for the waiter. At that moment they both reached across the table and took each other's hands, laughing. Verlaque leaned back and rubbed his tummy.

A cough made them both look up, and Paulik stood above them, looking down at their untouched food. "I'm so sorry to interrupt," he said. Marine and Verlaque quickly let go of their hands and began speaking at once.

"What happened to your lunch at Fréd's?" Verlaque asked, looking up at the commissioner.

"Sit down, please," Marine added, pulling out a chair.

Paulik sat down and said, "Cut short. We had been talking for about ten minutes, Fréd doing most of it, when a group of twenty showed up, claiming that they had reserved his private room upstairs. It was 'all hands on deck.' I didn't feel like helping."

Marine interrupted, "Bruno, did you eat? Do you want to look at a menu?"

"I'm famished, thank you. We only had a beer and some peanuts."

Verlaque signaled for the waiter to come over, and within minutes Bruno had ordered and his place had been set. Verlaque poured some wine, and Paulik looked at the Loire valley sauvignon, commented on its rich golden color, rolled it around in his glass, sniffed the wine with his eyes closed, and then took a sip. He did all of this slowly but naturally, easily. It was clear that he had been tasting, and appreciating, wines for a long time. "Is this a 1998, by any chance?" he asked Verlaque.

Marine stared at Paulik and asked, "Bruno! How did you know?"

Verlaque leaned over and showed the label, confirming that

the *commissaire* had guessed correctly. Paulik said, "Its rich, dark color was my first clue. And then its strong, buttery taste, which is more like a Bourgogne chardonnay than a sauvignon from Anjou. But I was cheating, really, because 1998 was such a non-characteristic year."

"Nineteen ninety-eight?" Marine asked.

"Don't you remember?" Antoine said, looking at her. "That's the summer we took my grandmother to northern England."

Marine nodded, remembering the Larkin-inspired journey, driving up the coast to Hull, with Antoine and Emmeline, visiting country pubs and village churches along the way. She then exclaimed, smiling, "Nineteen ninety-eight! The year of the heat wave! We were so happy to be in northern England, and not in France. Bravo, Bruno!" she said, clinking glasses with Paulik.

Paulik, uneasy in his new role as wine expert, shifted in his chair and changed the subject. "When I left Fréd's, I placed a call to the Cannes police station and spoke with Officer Pellegrino. He told me that a complaint had been made to the Cannes police a few months ago, by a housekeeper, about an incident of domestic abuse at a party at Lever Pogorovski's."

Marine's stomach turned. Despite her experience as a lawyer, she always had trouble listening, or even reading, accounts of abuse of women or children. She asked, "Was the maid mistreated, Bruno?"

"No," replied Paulik, shaking his head back and forth. "She was more shocked and outraged, and it was Pellegrino's feeling that she just wanted someone to talk to. She went to the precinct the next day, and Pellegrino was on duty and spoke to her."

"What exactly did this maid witness?" Verlaque asked, moving in closer.

"It was after dinner. There had been a fair amount of dancing and drinking, and the guests, Russians, began, one after the other, to burn five-hundred-euro notes, throwing the flaming bills into the air, all the while splitting their sides with laughter."

Marine buried her head in her hands. "That's disgusting."

Paulik nodded and continued, "The really disgusting part is that after the party the domestic staff was told to collect the ashes."

"The maid, Inès, she's called by the police, doesn't need much encouraging to disclose what goes on at the Pogorovski's. She regularly contacts the police to complain about some new outrage. Anyway, François de Bremont was a frequent visitor, with a tall blonde Russian girl on his arm. Three days ago Inès overheard Pogorovski telling François that he was going to send him to Spain to work, that the Côte d'Azur was too dangerous a place for François de Bremont."

"Did Inès hear why?" asked Verlaque.

"Yes," answered Paulik. "It seems François had lost heavily at the casinos in both Cannes and Monaco, and he had tried, unsuccessfully, to throw one of the polo matches. Apparently it was obvious to everyone present at that match, and he was about to be kicked out of the French polo league."

"Anything else?" Marine asked.

"No, not yet. Our conversation was cut short because Pellegrino had a meeting. But I did manage to learn from Fréd that the Russian mob has shocked some of the local hoods, who normally aren't known to be squeamish. Besides the Onassis-style real estate wars these Russian guys are involved in, they also dabble in kidnapping, extortion, fraud, money laundering, drug trafficking, and contract killing."

Verlaque took a deep breath and said, "It sounds like after our visit with Lever Pogorovski we should see the managers of the casinos and the polo club."

"I'll start making some phone calls," Paulik answered, and he grabbed his cell phone and left the dining room.

"I'm sorry that our lunch was cut short," Verlaque told Marine.

"So am I. But be careful!"

Verlaque wiped his mouth with the linen napkin and smiled and said, "Don't worry, Bruno has a gun."

Chapter Eighteen

⁓

*E*ven though Verlaque had been to the Côte d'Azur many times, on each visit he was astounded by two things: how beautiful, and how different, the flora and fauna were compared to Aix; and how awful the traffic was. He sat back and tried to enjoy the drive and ignore the bumper-to-bumper lineup of cars that followed the coast, their wait only accentuated by the hundreds of scooters that whined in and out of the traffic. Verlaque was relieved that he had ordered a car and driver from Cannes police headquarters—he was suddenly very tired and wanted to put his thoughts together instead of having to concentrate on the road. It had been a good decision. He looked over at Paulik, who was staring out the window, with his chin resting in his hand. Verlaque wondered what the commissioner was thinking about.

The judge broke the silence by reading aloud from some reports that had been thrust into their hands before leaving the precinct. There were pages and pages of recent real estate acquisition listings—the Riviera luxury market was dominated, as it stated in one report, by about two hundred wealthy Russians. Pogorovski's name came up frequently. Verlaque passed the documents over to the commissioner and then made a quick telephone call to his brother, Sébastien, who, among many other things, dealt in high-end Parisian real estate. Sébastien had no trouble giving his brother the name of a colleague on the Côte who did the same thing. Verlaque dialed this Riviera realtor, Pierre Dupont, who picked up his cell phone on the second ring. Verlaque quickly explained who he was and what he was doing in Cannes. "Have you sold any houses to Russians?" he asked, after they had been chatting for a few minutes.

"Yes, about a dozen in the past few years. I didn't sell Pogorov-ski the Villa Nina, unfortunately for me, but I know who did."

"What's it like dealing with these people?" asked Verlaque.

"Not very pleasant. Real estate is like a game for them. They're always trying to outbid each other on pricier and pricier homes," Dupont said, confirming the information that Verlaque had read in the police reports. The estate agent continued: "If you don't have a house to show them that's at least fifty million euros, they throw you out. And not very nicely, either. I haven't dealt with them in a while because I haven't had anything available in that price range. Homes like that just don't appear on the market that often. I do have a yacht, though, designed by Philippe Starck, if you're interested."

Antoine laughed. He had a very poor opinion of realtors, his brother included, but M. Dupont was growing on him. "Philippe Starck? The designer?" Antoine asked.

"Yeah, it's the big thing now, to have a superstar designer or artist design your boat. Jeff Koons did one too."

Verlaque winced; he loved sailboats and couldn't imagine one designed by Jeff Koons. "How much for the Starck?" he asked.

"Forty-six million. The gas in one of those things costs about two thousand euros for a trip between Nice and Cannes."

Verlaque looked into his phone, stunned. "Nice and Cannes are about fifteen miles apart."

"That they are, Judge. Is there anything else you needed?"

"No, but thanks," Verlaque answered. "Unless you have any words of advice regarding Pogorovski."

"Just enjoy looking at the girls, if they're around," Dupont replied.

"Russian girls? Tall, young, and blonde?"

"Yeah, models."

Verlaque laughed again. "Models, my foot."

Verlaque hung up and looked over at Paulik. "Tell me what you learned while I was on the phone."

"Nothing," Paulik replied.

"What?"

"Nothing, sir. I can't read in a car. I get carsick."

"Seriously?" Verlaque asked, looking puzzled.

"Yes, seriously. Being a policeman doesn't make me immune to car sickness," Paulik said, his voice sounding a little bit on the defensive. He then added, "My wife and daughter get it too. We can't even read maps when we're in the car."

"That must make family vacations fun," Verlaque joked.

Paulik smiled, feeling less ill at ease, and said, "We have to look at the map and figure out our route before we get in the car."

Half an hour later their unmarked police car stopped, and they were facing a stone wall with a black solid-iron gate. Two guards, smaller than Verlaque had imagined Russians, or Georgians, wearing earphones and bulletproof vests, walked up to the car and peered in. Police badges and IDs were shown, and the guards stepped away from the car, spoke on their headsets for about fifteen seconds, and then the gate slowly opened. The driver put the car in gear, and they slowly began their ascent up a drive lined with cypress and olive trees as far as the eye could see.

"I couldn't place their accent," Verlaque said, speaking of the guards down at the gate. "It didn't sound Russian to me."

"Israeli, sir," the driver said, looking in his rearview mirror so that he could make eye contact with the judge. "It's fairly common around here," he added.

After an ascent that seemed to take forever, the grounds began to level and Verlaque sighed at the riot of colors before him—a hundred variations of green appeared in the plants, from the silvery green of olive trees to the dark green of rosemary. All of this was offset by the brilliant oranges and pinks of the bougainvillea flowers that seemed to drape every vertical surface in sight. Paulik had evidently been enjoying the same scene and said, "Too bad Aix is too cold for bougainvillea." Verlaque smiled to himself, thinking how amazing it was that he had been teamed up with a commissioner who could guess the dates of wines and who openly loved plant life. Verlaque nodded and said, "Yes, the climate in Aix would kill those flowers. When I moved to Aix from Paris, I bought a lemon tree for my terrace, but it didn't even make it into the winter."

A large stone house appeared, and Paulik leaned forward and said, "Here we are."

The driver coughed and said, "I believe that this is only a staff house, Commissioner."

Paulik leaned back and grunted.

They drove a few hundred more meters, past another stone house and various garages and outbuildings, all immaculate, until they arrived in front of Villa Nina, an immense multiturreted stone house, a small castle really—built sometime at the turn of the century, Verlaque guessed. Various aspects of it reminded him of his grandmother's now-empty house in Normandy, including the size, but he kept quiet. Besides, Normandy real estate was nothing like the outrageous prices paid in the south, or in Paris, he reasoned with himself.

Two more guards appeared and opened the rear doors of the car for Verlaque and Paulik. It was assumed by everyone that the driver would stay in the car, which he did, pulling the sporting newspaper *L'Equipe* from the glove box before the two men had even got out. Verlaque and Paulik were ushered into the front hall, the size of a ballroom, which was dominated by an immense crystal chandelier, about two meters in diameter. Both men naturally looked up at it, and were still doing so when a handsome man in his midfifties walked out of a room and came toward them, his hand outstretched.

"Gentlemen, welcome. Do you like it?" he asked, also looking up to the chandelier. The Russian spoke flawless French.

"Very much," Verlaque answered, shaking the Russian's hand and introducing himself and Paulik.

"It's Russian, not Venetian, as most of my visitors think. Come, let's talk in the living room. I hope the traffic wasn't too bad."

"It was, actually—as usual," Verlaque replied.

"Ah, a pity. I go everywhere now in a helicopter. It's the way to go. I'm so hooked that I bought the company."

Pogorovski opened a set of double doors that obviously led into the living room. Nothing could prepare Verlaque and Paulik for the view from its windows. The turquoise sea spread out before them, there was little else in view save for a bit of lawn. Still standing, the Russian turned to Verlaque and said, "So you would like to ask me questions about François de Bremont? Your offices called me this morning, telling me of Bremont's death."

"His murder," Verlaque replied coldly. "What exactly were your business dealings with the count?" Verlaque asked.

"He rented out flats to our models who come from Russia, showed them around town, got them settled in—that sort of thing," replied Pogorovski.

"You own a modeling agency?" asked Paulik, ready with his pen and notepad to write down the Russian's reply, although he already knew the answer.

"Yes, but you must have known that," the Russian replied, winking. "Actually, it's in my wife's name. My business is oil, Comgaz, but I am sure you know that too." Pogorovski smiled at the two men.

"Were you aware of Bremont's debts?" Verlaque asked.

"Yes, and I had encouraged him to start paying them off, but to do so he tried to gamble, each time sinking further and further into debt. And then I'm sure that you've heard about the polo game."

Verlaque nodded. "Had his life been threatened?"

Pogorovski grunted. "Many times, by everyone from casino owners to pissed-off fellow polo players. He annoyed everyone. Fine sailor and polo player, though."

"You don't seem to show any remorse, Mr. Pogorovski," Verlaque said.

The Russian shrugged. "Should I?"

Verlaque remained silent, looking at Pogorovski. When the Russian realized that the judge wasn't going to speak, he continued: "Listen. I deal with many, many people. I have seen people die, here and in Russia. My brother died of cancer when he was twenty-two years old. Life goes on."

"Are you a big polo fan?" Verlaque asked.

"Yes," answered Pogorovski. "I still play from time to time, but just for fun." As he said this, the Russian patted his flat stomach and grinned, and, ever so slightly, glanced down at the judge's bulging belly.

"Where is your wife's modeling agency located?" Paulik asked, changing the subject.

Pogorovski folded his arms and looked out the window, and then replied, still looking at the sea, "There are offices in Nice and Paris and Milan. You'll find it easily. Tribeca Models, Inc."

Verlaque, who had been looking out the window while Pogorovski spoke, now turned to him and asked, "Do you have an alibi for Wednesday morning, between six and nine?"

The Russian replied, "Of course. I was here, working in my office. You can ask any of the servants, or my wife, Maria, who is working right now at Tribeca's Nice office."

Verlaque didn't want to leave just yet and took a chance on giving away Inès's identity by saying, "Rumor has it that you were going to send François to Spain for work."

Pogorovski looked at Verlaque and narrowed his pale blue eyes. He wasted no time in saying, "Who told you that?"

"It doesn't matter," Verlaque replied. "Why Spain?" he continued.

"Comgaz has holdings in Gibraltar," Pogorovski said. "François was in trouble here, and he wasn't managing to sort himself out. I thought I could help him by sending him to Spain—a fresh start, you know?"

Verlaque highly doubted that the Russian would care about helping anybody, especially François. He also knew that in Gibraltar legal companies were easily created by anonymous owners, who then bought luxury real estate on the peninsula in the name of their company. All of this information came from a recent dinner with his brother, Sébastien, who had also told Verlaque that Spain was becoming the new Côte d'Azur for money laundering—helped by five flights a week between Moscow and Málaga on Aeroflot. An Air France pilot-friend of Sébastien's had reported that Russians disembark from the planes with plastic shopping bags full of cash, which they openly present to the Spanish customs officials along with a certificate from the Russian government authorizing the departure of this capital from Russia. The more discreet ones, Sébastien had said, opened businesses in Gibraltar. While listening to this story, Verlaque had eaten a five-course meal and Sébastien had merely played with his food and drunk a bottle of red burgundy on his own. What disgusted Sébastien most about the story, it seemed to Verlaque, was not the dirty money but the plastic bags. Paper bags from Le Bon Marché would have better suited his brother. Better yet, leather from Louis Vuitton.

"Could you please tell your wife to be at the agency tomorrow morning at ten o'clock?" Verlaque half asked, half demanded.

"Yes, of course," Pogorovski said. Verlaque turned to leave, and Paulik followed, after shaking hands with Pogorovski. The Russian accompanied them to the massive front doors, and as they walked to the car he said, still standing in the entrance, "You'll let me know as soon as you find out who did this to François, *non?*"

Verlaque said nothing, but nodded and got into the car. The driver threw his *L'Equipe* on the passenger seat, and Verlaque told him to take them to the Cannes polo grounds. "We're lucky that all the players are there this evening," he said, looking at Paulik.

"Yeah. They just had their annual meeting, and the gala dinner is this evening. The president of the club has warned them that we are coming, and has told them that we will be as discreet as possible. Their wives will be present, and he didn't want to upset them, but, the sponsors will also be there."

"The sponsorship of a polo club is a big deal, I take it."

Paulik nodded. "Fréd told me that the polo club in Cannes has some amazing sponsors—private jet companies, movie studios—the big players."

They began their descent down through the olive groves and gardens.

Paulik turned to Verlaque and said, "That guy's as honest as a donkey walking backwards."

"I agree, but we can't do anything unless we can prove that he hired a contract killer, and that will be very difficult to do," Verlaque replied. He then smirked and said, "A donkey walking backwards? Where did you come up with that expression?"

"It's an old saying from the Luberon," Paulik replied. The mention of the Luberon reminded Verlaque that Paulik hadn't always been a commissioner, or a wine connoisseur, or an opera buff. "In the Luberon," Verlaque asked, "did you have opera? How did you become such an opera fan, if you don't mind my asking?"

"It was a school trip, when I was ten," Paulik replied, leaning back. "We had a teacher who organized a field trip for us to see a matinee at the Aix opera festival. Funded by the government. You know—invite the country kids to get some refinement. I loved it. I was speechless. When I got back to the house, I would hum some of the bits I had memorized, and my older brothers teased me that I was in love. I guess I was. After that, any pocket money I made working on neighbors' farms I spent on opera records or for the festival. Plus on my moped, naturally," he added, smiling.

"You're an amazing person," Verlaque said, looking at Paulik's big, burly body; his face with its pug nose and soft brown eyes; and his scarred bald head. Paulik shrugged. "We all are," he replied.

Chapter Nineteen

✗

*H*er pencil moved quickly across the paper, hatching, in small straight lines, to form a high-pitched roof. Almost never leaving the paper, the pencil began to work on the other side of the old house, where there stood rows of vines. Marine added three tall, straight cypress trees and then sat back and studied her drawing. She had been sketching old stone buildings for years and now could do a fair job by memory. It was a habit she had started in high school, when her mind drifted away from the pages of her textbook. But what had begun, in her head, as Château Bremont in Saint-Antonin, was now, on paper, Marc Nagel's winery.

Marine had been working in the staff room of the Cannes police headquarters for two hours, and doodled while waiting for the dinosaur computer to download the web pages she'd requested. The Internet at the Carlton hotel was temporarily down, and since Verlaque and Paulik had to go to the police station to pick up their car and driver, Verlaque had called to ask if Marine could work there. "She definitely can't work on one of the staff computers—there's too much sensitive information on those," Inspector Boutard told Verlaque over the phone. They had worked together on a drug bust the previous year, and Boutard was, Verlaque thought, an idiot. "Yes, of course," Verlaque agreed, yawning.

"But there is an old computer in the staff room. It's only hooked up to the Internet—it's not on the police station's network," Boutard continued, wanting to be helpful. In the early days of computers, French employers were worried that employees would, if given the chance, surf the Internet while at work, and so many of the staff workstations in public institutions had no Internet connection: one or two computers would be set aside, often in a staff room or an empty office, for searching the Internet. The employers claimed that it was a security issue.

Marine had made space for herself in front of the dusty computer, and had been taking notes on a pad she always carried. The printer was ancient; besides it had no paper, nor ink. It looked like one of the first printers that appeared on the market, like the one she had when she was doing her law degree, whose carriage loudly banged back and forth, back and forth, while printing.

She had found some newspaper articles on the web confirming what she had heard about Russians in the Côte d'Azur and their real estate acquisitions. She was about to look into Mme Pogorovski's modeling agency when she stretched, realizing that since Étienne's funeral the day before she had been moving nonstop. She had buried a childhood friend, whose brother had since been killed; she had spoken to another whom she hadn't seen in years; had received a thrashing—much deserved—from Sylvie; and had heard the words she so longed for from Antoine. She got up and walked to where the staff vending machines were kept, in search of a much-needed coffee. She came quickly around the corner only to stop in her tracks as she saw a young uniformed officer at one of the machines. He seemed surprised to see someone he didn't know in the staff room, but politely smiled and said hello. Marine returned his greeting. When he reached down for his change, she couldn't help admiring his tanned, muscular arms and wide shoulders. As he was taking his espresso out of the machine another policeman came into the room and bellowed, "Hey, Pellegrino! You're going to be late for your chichi party!" The young officer turned around and replied, "I was on the beat all day. I need some caffeine before I hit the champagne!"

"Ah, you poor devil!" his friend yelled back.

Pellegrino, Pellegrino, Marine tried to remember. Paulik had been just talking to him.

Marine smiled and said, "Excuse me. Are you the officer who plays . . . or played . . . polo with François de Bremont? You'll have to excuse me . . . I overheard that other officer call you Pellegrino. You see, I'm a law professor from Aix-en-Provence, and I grew up with François and Étienne."

"You're kidding?" He stared at her, and then asked suspiciously, "What are you doing here?"

"It's a long story, but I'm in Cannes with Aix's examining magistrate . . . on . . . er, other business."

"Antoine Verlaque?"

"You know him?" Marine asked.

Pellegrino shook his head back and forth. "Only by reputation."

"Would you mind if we spoke for a few minutes about François?"

"I guess not, if you say that you're here with Judge Verlaque. I'm still in shock at the news, as are all the polo players." Marine thought he sounded as sincere as her students who tried to make excuses for late papers. The polo player then added, as if it were an afterthought, "You must be too, if you were friends with him."

"Yes, I am. But we were childhood friends. I hadn't seen him in years," Marine replied. They began walking toward the tables that were set up in the staff room when Pellegrino said, "I just finished my shift and I have to go to the polo club for a gala dinner. I hope this won't take long—I already missed the annual meeting this afternoon because I had to work."

Marine noted the resentment in his voice at not being able to change his shift. But she imagined that it must be difficult for a young police officer to play polo with millionaires whose schedules are more flexible.

Marine sat down and motioned for Pellegrino to do the same. As he sat she marveled, once again, at his thin but muscular thighs and arms, and she quickly turned her attention to his blonde hair and tanned face. He seemed quite pleased with his good looks as well. "I've been doing some research, on the Internet," Marine said, trying to sound vague. "You probably heard that François's brother died last weekend. Could you fill me in a bit about François's life in Cannes?"

"I played with François for three years. He was a really gifted player, rated a six." Marine noted that he didn't seem to care that the two brothers had died during the same week. Pellegrino hadn't asked anything about Étienne de Bremont and didn't seem the least bit curious about it. The young officer then said, "I am a seven." Marine looked puzzled, and then realized that Pellegrino was talking about his polo rating. She liked him less now. She raised her eyebrows and asked, "Is that good?" trying to hide her mocking tone.

Pellegrino nodded and answered, "The best polo rating is a ten, but not many players in France have that." He waited for Marine to ask more questions, but since she didn't, he continued, "The best players in the world are in Spain and in South America. They very often have handicaps higher than five."

Marine nodded, a bit bored. "Were you surprised to hear about François's death?" she asked.

"Yes, of course," he answered, his eyes widening. "Even if François had a lot of enemies, he didn't deserve to die. He could be a dirty player, as I told Commissioner Paulik on the phone, but he never did anything wrong to me. He had everything—good looks, good humor, and a noble name. He impressed a lot of people in Cannes, especially the Russians. They seem to go in for that sort of thing—nobility, that is. Up until recently, I would have said that he was well liked. But since this winter he's . . . he had been really edgy, and he tried to rig a polo match last week. Some of the other players say that he had gambling debts."

"I heard about that game. Do you think he could have been killed over it?" Marine asked.

Pellegrino tilted his head back and laughed. "No, I doubt it. In Argentina maybe, where polo is king, but not in France. Sure, the other players and the management were royally pissed off, but François has been in such a state lately, all nervous and jittery, that the whole thing seemed kind of pathetic. The match was canceled halfway through, and a bunch of us went to the club-house bar, but François was told to leave. That was the last time I saw him."

"And his work with the Russian, Lever Pogorovski? Had the local police been monitoring that?" Marine knew from Paulik that they had been, but she wanted to hear Pellegrino's version.

"Yes," replied Pellegrino. "François worked for Pogorovski's wife, Maria, at her modeling agency, Tribeca. Despite the Russian connection, and her husband's massive wealth, the agency seems clean. We've had them checked out a number of times by undercover agents."

"You mean that these young Russian girls—"

"And African," Pellegrino interrupted.

"They really are models?" Marine continued.

"Yes, some are even supermodels. They have their own web-sites and all that. Legitimate work as far as we can tell—magazine work for *Elle* and *Vogue*, here and in New York and Milan. And they do runway jobs for top designers."

Pellegrino saw the look of disbelief on Marine's face, and he continued: "Believe me, we tried to make the connection between the models and prostitution, especially when Pogorovski's oil associates visit the Côte. The models usually accompany the men to dinner, and they all go to the same parties, but we can't arrest Lever Pogorovski for that. These girls can go to parties if they want to. When we questioned the models, or their dinner partners, it was silence all round."

Marine frowned and asked, "What's the name of Pogorovski's company?"

"Comgaz," Pellegrino replied matter-of-factly, sliding his chair back a few inches, as if to signal the end of their talk. The policeman's ambivalence bothered Marine, and so she felt no pangs in asking, "Isn't it really expensive, playing polo?"

"Yes, it costs a fortune, especially if you keep your own horses, which many of the players do. As you know, I have a civil servant's salary, so a horse is loaned to me, and I'm paid to play, thanks to my rating. It happens frequently in polo," Pellegrino replied, starting to walk down the hall. "We also have company sponsorship, naturally," he added, and he waved good-bye.

With the muscular policeman/polo player gone, Marine went back to the computer and stared at the screen. She thought about what Pellegrino had said and was still surprised that the Russian women really were, from what the Cannes police could tell, models. Perhaps we are too quick to assume that the Mafia is behind every business that makes money or involves glamour, Marine thought. Too many Hollywood movies. One last try, she told herself, as she clicked on Google and typed in "Russian Mafia Côte d'Azur," this time in English. Various articles came up, many of them involving Russian-bought luxury real estate, and then, finally, on page three of an American web magazine that she hadn't heard of, she saw a color photograph of a beautiful girl, with long blonde hair, blue eyes, and abnormally perfect features, hugging herself, staring straight at the camera. Natassja Duvanov was from Kazakhstan, the article said, but worked as a supermodel in New York. In addition to the photograph of the shockingly beautiful girl, two things caught Marine's eye: that she was represented by Tribeca Models, Inc., and that in January she had flung herself from of the balcony of her high-rise Manhattan apartment and committed suicide.

Marine was staring at the article, mesmerized by Duvanov's photo, when her cell phone rang. Seeing that is was Verlaque's number, she answered. "Yes, Antoine."

"Hi. We're leaving Pogorovski's estate now, and we're driving up into the hills to the polo club. We won't be back in Cannes until late, around nine p.m. Can you meet us then, in the bar at the Carlton hotel? It's only about a ten-minute walk from where you are. Or do you want us to pick you up?" he asked.

"No, a short walk would clear my head," Marine answered. "I've found some interesting articles on the web. I'll just stay here for a few more hours until you're through questioning the players." She'd need that walk to stop thinking about Natassja Duvanov. She hung up and quickly ran upstairs in hopes of finding

Pellegrino still in the building. She found him easily—he had obviously showered and changed in the officers' changing room and was just putting on a navy blue velvet jacket and walking toward the exit. Running down the hall, she got to Pellegrino as he put his hand on the door handle. She placed her hand on his shoulder, saying, "One last question. Can you come and look at something on the computer in the staff room?"

"I really don't have time."

Marine used her charm, smiling and taking the officer by his big, velvety shoulder. "It will take just a minute, I promise!"

He shrugged, and she led him quickly to the staff room. He followed her, checking messages on his cell phone. She leaned over the computer, whispering, "Did François de Bremont ever talk about a Russian model named Natassja who lives in New York?"

Pellegrino bit his bottom lip, thought for a few seconds, and said, "He did have a model friend who moved to New York, but I can't remember her name. To be honest, I used to get the Irinas and Natassjas and Anastasias mixed up."

Marine showed Pellegrino the photo. "Oh yes, I recognize her. She came to some of the matches, and she accompanied François to some of the executives to dinners and parties."

"Were she and François dating?" Marine asked.

"Hard to tell. François would brag about a lot of things, but never about women."

"Or girls," Marine suggested, tapping the photograph with her finger. "She committed suicide in January. She was twenty."

Pellegrino looked stunned. "I had heard that one of their models died in New York, but I didn't know which one or how. That could have put him in that edgy state, that's for sure."

"But you're not sure if they were dating."

To Marine's amazement Pellegrino actually stifled a yawn. "I couldn't care less."

"Thanks," Marine said, adding, "have fun at the party." Pellegrino mumbled a good-bye and walked quickly out of the staff room, checking his watch.

Chapter Twenty

ぞ

Marine walked over to the coffee machine and bought an espresso and a chocolate bar, which she had meant to do before running into Pellegrino. Her fatigue was catching up with her. She got back to her makeshift desk and looked again at Natassja's photo. She saved it and then spent an hour looking up articles on the Internet about Russians in the Côte d'Azur. She came across an article in *Le Monde* on the purchase of the Villa Nina by Pogorovski and a half dozen other articles on his business dealings and property purchases. What she couldn't find were articles featuring Pogorovski at social events—that was something Marine assumed billionaires did, something that went along with the "job"—black-tie parties and the almost-weekly obligatory fundraiser. She spent the second hour looking at the Cannes polo club's website, which was surprisingly detailed and obviously professionally done in both French and English. She immediately looked up the players and their ratings—both François and Officer Pellegrino were there, as were their handicaps, just as the officer had said: six and seven. The club's website also mentioned that Eric Pellegrino was a polo teacher at the club, something he hadn't told Marine. Perhaps he thought it wasn't relevant. She clicked on Pellegrino's photograph and admitted to herself that he really was quite handsome.

At a little before nine she worked her way, after about five minutes of walking down hallways, out of the building and into the balmy Cannes evening. She couldn't stop thinking of the young beautiful Russian committing suicide. Wasn't that the dream job of millions of girls around the world, regardless of their nationality, religion, or education? Something had bothered Marine about Pellegrino too. It might have been the self-confidence that athletes, especially young, handsome ones, always seem to have. But why did she get the feeling that he answered only the bare minimum of questions? He hadn't seemed too interested in the Russian models, either. What kind of southern male was he? She thought of Antoine's cigar friends at Le Mazarin and how they would fawn over pretty girls, let alone a top model. She laughed out loud, then thought herself a little foolish—she was already missing Aix after less than ten hours away from it. But it always happened like that, even when she visited Paris. The cours Mirabeau and the voices and faces she knew would stay with her, like part of her baggage, for at least a day.

Up ahead Marine could see the dark silhouettes of palm trees and colored lights on the sleek turn-of-the-century white walls of the Carlton hotel, and she began to feel happy to be away, away from the university and her parents, and even Sylvie. She knew she needed Sylvie, and yet often needed a break from her too. Marine skipped up the steps, saying *bonsoir* to the doorman as she passed through the heavy glass doors of the hotel. Live piano music wafted through the lobby, and Marine followed it to the wood-paneled, dimly lit bar. There she saw the huge bulk of Paulik, and the back of his bald head, and, facing him, Antoine, who winked when he saw her, causing her heart to race. Paulik got up and pulled out a chair for Marine, and the three quickly began talking of their impressions of that long day. "Where are we sleeping tonight?" Marine suddenly asked, causing Paulik to laugh and add, "Yes, where?" They both looked at Verlaque, who was in the middle of taking a long puff on his Partagas corona. "Here," he answered, slightly closing his eyes to the cigar smoke that enveloped him.

"The Carlton?" Marine shrieked. "Are you nuts?"

"I showed my badge to the front desk, and told them we were working with the Cannes police on a homicide, and they gave us a cut rate, three rooms, in the back. No view, I'm afraid," Verlaque said.

"I'm too tired for a view," Paulik said, and Marine nodded in agreement. She had also heard, very distinctly, three rooms, not two. As it should be, she mused. Verlaque gestured for the waiter and then looked at Paulik and Marine and said, "Why don't we just order bar food for dinner? This is the Carlton—I imagine their bar food is quite good."

"Fine with me," Paulik replied, then turned his head toward Marine to get her opinion.

"Yes, fine, fine," she answered, forcing a smile. She would have preferred to have eaten in the dining room, but as usual Verlaque had decided for everyone. Realizing that she hadn't told the two men about Natassja Duvanov, she mentioned what she had learned on the Internet and by talking with Officer Pellegrino. Almost immediately Paulik asked how the girl had committed suicide, and both men winced when she told them of the Manhattan high-rise.

"So they were friends, this Natassja and François de Bremont?" Verlaque asked.

"Yes, and Officer Pellegrino said that François had been out of sorts for a few months. It could have been because of his debts or that combined with Natassja's death," Marine offered.

"Were they a couple?" asked Paulik. Marine looked up from her drink and saw Verlaque staring at her over his reading glasses.

"Pellegrino didn't know," she said. "Apparently François was quiet about his lovers."

"Weird," Paulik said.

Verlaque rolled the tip of his cigar around in the ashtray, letting the ashes slowly break off. Marine and Paulik watched, as if mesmerized. Verlaque then said, "Maybe François wasn't permitted to date any of the models. I can see Pogorovski setting a rule like that. Perhaps their relationship was hidden. Who would know if they were romantically involved?"

Marine thought immediately of her friendship with Sylvie and said, "Her best friend." She paused and then added, "Or her mother, but her mother lives in Kazakhstan."

"We'll go to the modeling agency tomorrow morning," Verlaque said. "Perhaps there you can find out who she was close with. How did you find Officer Pellegrino?"

"Next to the coffee machine," Marine replied.

Verlaque sighed. "No, I meant how did you find his mood, his character?"

"Oh, sorry," Marine replied, putting her fork down. "He's an egomaniac, for one thing, and was more worried about getting to the polo club on time than interested in talking about François's death. And, come to think of it, he didn't even make a remark when I reminded him that Étienne also died this week. He's cold, I'd say. Or maybe just a bit thick."

"That's the way I found him, when I talked to him at the club."

"How can he afford to play?" Paulik asked.

"He's actually paid to play, because of his high rating," Marine offered. "Plus they have company sponsorships."

"When I spoke to him at the club, I noticed a fair amount of . . . how can I describe it? Jealousy? He had a chip on his shoulder because of his civil servant's status among all those high rollers at the polo club," Verlaque said.

"I noticed the same thing," Marine replied. "And when I asked him if he thought François had been dating Natassja, he said that he couldn't care less."

"He's frank at least," Verlaque said.

The three sat in silence for some time. "This wine is delicious," Marine said to Paulik, aware of an awkward silence in the conversation. But she *had* noticed that the wine was unusually good, and she swirled the last of it around in her glass.

Paulik smiled. "It's Marc's."

"How cool is that!" Marine said, proud of her newly acquired taste buds.

"Pellegrino gave me his alibi," Verlaque said. Turning to Marine, he asked, "What did he tell you about the morning of François's death?"

"He mentioned that he was on day shift that day. That would have made it impossible to get from Cannes to Saint-Antonin," Marine offered.

"Shift?" Verlaque asked. "Did he use that exact word?"

"Yes, I'm sure of it. I remember because I imagined, for some reason, policemen walking up and down the Croisette, in their uniforms, under the palm trees."

Paulik swirled the wine in his glass and asked Verlaque, "What did he tell you?"

"He said that he was working, and it was clear that he wanted to leave. When I pressed him about it, he admitted that he wasn't patrolling but attending a computer-training session," Verlaque said. "So he wasn't entirely up front with Marine. You've taken those classes, haven't you, Bruno? Do they take attendance?"

Paulik thought. "Sometimes."

"François was killed by someone he knew," Marine whispered. Both men turned to look at her. "That's what both of you said."

"Bruno, let's call the Cannes police tomorrow and find out who was running the computer session that day," Verlaque replied. Was jealousy or envy a motive for murder? Verlaque thought to himself. He remembered Pellegrino's words when they had stood on the terrace of the polo club, surrounded by tanned men and women draped in jewels: "I'm paid to play. Did you see the cars in the parking lot?"

The bill came and was paid, and the three got up and headed toward the elevators. In the elevator Verlaque handed Marine and Paulik their keys, and Marine leaned against the elevator wall, suddenly exhausted. She closed her eyes and thought of Natassja and of the young woman's long, perfect body hitting the New York pavement. She shuddered and then opened her eyes. Verlaque put his hand on her shoulder and said, "Are you all right?"

"Yes, I'm fine, just tired." Marine then looked at Paulik and said, "You asked right away how Natassja Duvanov killed herself."

Paulik looked surprised and said, "Yes. Is that morbid?"

"No, not at all," Marine answered.

"It was the first thing I thought of as well," Verlaque added.

Marine shook her head back and forth and pointed her index finger in the air, at nothing, but as if to signal a sudden understanding. "Pellegrino didn't ask."

"Maybe he already knew?" Paulik suggested.

"No, no," Marine answered, "he didn't even know her name. He only recognized her when he saw the photograph."

"There *are* people who have very limited imaginations or curiosity," Verlaque said. He was thinking of Lady Emily and his mother.

"I guess so," Marine said, not entirely convinced. And then she found herself thinking that a policeman, at any rate, is normally curious.

The elevator doors opened, and they walked down the hall to their respective rooms, opening their doors with the key cards almost at the same time, and said their good nights. Marine took a hot shower and wore the hotel bathrobe to bed.

She was just about to turn off the bedside light when she heard a knock on the door. She got out of bed and walked over to the heavy door and opened it slightly. It was Verlaque.

"May I come in?" he asked. He then added, grumbling, "It's not to sleep with you."

Marine stared at Verlaque and then looked down at her bare feet. "Come in," she whispered, if only not to have this awkward moment occur in the hallway of the Carlton. She opened the door, allowing Verlaque to pass. He walked over and sat in one of the armchairs, and then quickly got up and stood in front of the minibar.

"Would you like a whiskey?" Marine ventured.

Verlaque quickly opened the refrigerator door. "Don't mind if I do," he replied in English. Marine shrugged, not perfectly understanding the English but getting the gist. "Help yourself," she muttered. Inside was the usual assortment of sodas and miniature bottles of alcohol and wine. Verlaque selected a Johnnie

Walker, looked at the red label and winced, and unscrewed the cap, pouring the entire contents into a glass. He looked at Marine and said, "I'm so sorry. Would you like some?"

"No, thanks. You taught me well," she replied. "Even *I* know that stuff is crap. What's up? Would you like to tell me something about the case? Or should we talk about it in the morning?"

Verlaque drank half of it in one exaggerated gulp, pretending to have enjoyed the industrial liquor. He took a step toward Marine and ran his fingers through her hair. "I couldn't resist you in the elevator," he whispered.

"What are you doing, Antoine?"

He drank the rest of the whiskey and sat down on the bed. "I wanted to talk to you that night on my terrace, but you left." Marine tried to speak, but Verlaque held up his hand, stopping her. "*You left*. But maybe you were right—it wasn't the right moment that night. It was too bright. The birds were making too much noise. It was too beautiful out."

He patted the bed beside him. Marine walked over but did not sit down. She stood, one hand on her hip, looking down at Verlaque. "And so now you expect me to drop everything, stop seeing Arthur—wipe that smirk off your face!—and run into your arms?"

"I know I should have called you when I was in Luxembourg and England or Paris."

"That would have been nice," Marine whispered. "But you were busy with Lady Emily."

Verlaque ignored the reference. "I seem to be good at only one thing—my job. My relations with my family are horrible. I messed up what we had. I find too much solace in being by myself with a cigar in one hand and a whiskey in the other."

"Don't say that. You had a wonderful relationship with Emmeline, for one thing."

"Ah yes, my savior."

Marine paused. Emmeline always came before everyone else. Couldn't Marine have been Verlaque's savior too? "What did she save you from, Antoine?"

Verlaque slightly winced, as though now that he had been given the permission to speak, it disgusted him. His phone rang and swearing he took it out of his pocket and looked at the caller's name. "Merde! It's Roussel! Listen, Marine, I'm going to have to take this call and calm him down. He's probably furious that I still haven't closed Étienne de Bremont's case."

Marine nodded and walked Verlaque to the door, and he answered the phone on the way to his room. She closed the door, sighing and leaning her body against the cold wood. Whatever it was that Verlaque had wanted to say, he had needed a tumbler full of mediocre whiskey just to do it, and then had been easily dissuaded from doing so by a call from someone he couldn't stand. Perhaps a simple, kind—if dull—man like Arthur was better. She was getting too old for this.

"*Putain!* What in Christ's name is going on in Cannes?" Roussel yelled into the phone.

"We're investigating a murder," Verlaque replied, perplexed.

"Why are you there with your girlfriend? Oh, sorry . . . Your *ex*."

Verlaque took a deep breath and tried to stay calm. "Who told you that Marine is here?"

"Eric Pellegrino, who else? He just called to complain that he was questioned twice! Once by you and once by a teacher!"

"Professor," Verlaque corrected.

"Whatever! Pellegrino is an officer of the law, and Mlle Bonnet isn't! She has no right to be there, and she certainly shouldn't be hanging around the police station, talking to the officers! All I need is for the *commissaire* in Cannes to complain too! Can you imagine the shit we'd be in?"

Verlaque closed his eyes, knowing that Roussel was right.

"Do you have any developments on Étienne's case? The Bleys have been calling me, and I'm still on vacation!"

Verlaque cringed when Roussel referred to the deceased by his Christian name. That Roussel had known the father probably meant nothing more that they had sat beside each other once at an official dinner or meeting.

"Only the fact that his brother has just been murdered, also in Saint-Antonin," Verlaque calmly replied.

"The two deaths are not related! One brother was a good, Catholic citizen of Aix. The other, a highflier playboy on the Riviera!"

"Yes, a highflier with Russian mafia connections!" Verlaque said, his voice, too, now rising. He told Roussel of the close physical resemblance between the two brothers and his feeling that Étienne might have been mistaken for François that night in the attic.

"Listen, Judge. You're acting on a hunch, if you don't mind me saying so. How many hit men do you know who just push a guy out of a window? That's a pretty clumsy way of killing someone. He could have survived the fall!"

Verlaque said nothing, but his silence confirmed Roussel's point. It was, he knew, not a professional killer's method. It was more like an act of passion. He thought of those who seemed capable of such an act: Isabelle, who didn't know about the second bank account and couldn't be bothered to read her husband's script; and the cold mistress, Isabelle's own sister. Love and money were the prime reasons for homicide, and either woman could have, during a passionate argument, pushed the young nobleman.

"You'll be back tomorrow?" Roussel asked.

"Yes." Verlaque didn't tell Roussel that Pellegrino could have easily not shown up at the computer-training session. As if reading his mind, Roussel said, "And stay away from Officer Pellegrino!"

Verlaque hung up and turned off his phone. He undressed and took a long hot shower and thought of his past loves: those he chose not to think about, and others whose faces always brought him a smile, like Agnès, his first big love at university. He and Agnès had shared a tiny Parisian garret-apartment and had split up after two years on good terms, both acknowledging the fact that they were too young for the relationship to go any further. There had been dozens of girlfriends after Agnès, but none had got under his skin the way Marine had. He thought of going back to her room but knew that it was a bad idea. Besides, Marine was probably fast asleep. He used to watch her as she fell asleep, and as he got into bed he thought of those glorious afternoon naps in Paradiso, the white linen curtains blowing in the breeze and the sound of Italian children, playing on the beach, floating into their bedroom.

That night Marine dreamed of long, tanned bodies floating past gray skyscrapers. Verlaque dreamed of Emmeline in Normandy, only it wasn't her house in the dream but Pogorovski's. And somewhere down the hall Commissioner Paulik fell asleep with the celebrated aria from *La Wally* in his head, and he saw in his dream the opera's heroine, who flings herself into an oncoming avalanche in the Austrian Alps, desperate in love.

Chapter Twenty-one

꼭

*T*ribeca Models was located on a backstreet in old Nice, but the building stood out from its medieval neighbors thanks to a polished white marble facade, automatic smoked-glass doors, and brass light fixtures—universal 1980s design. Inside, large, framed photographs showcased the agency's wares—models, mostly women—clothed or partially clothed. Bruno Paulik slowly made his way around the foyer, looking at each photograph and tilting his head as if he were in an art gallery. Marine didn't know if he was mocking the photographs or not; in either case, she had to turn away to hide her grin. Verlaque was speaking to the receptionist, who could have been a model herself, and then walked over to Marine and slipped his arm through hers, giving it a gentle but firm squeeze. The stainless steel elevator doors opened, and Verlaque immediately withdrew his arm, as if by instinct. A white-haired woman stepped out of the elevator and introduced herself to the trio as Maria Pogorovski. She was a handsome, tall, and big-boned woman, a good ten to fifteen years older than her husband. She was bedecked in chunky and expensive-looking jewelry and was wearing a bright pink tailored pantsuit. The color of her lipstick and nail polish perfectly matched her attire, something Marine always associated with women of a certain age on the Côte d'Azur.

Mme Pogorovski led them into the elevator, and they rode it four flights up to the top floor. Evidently she had thought their visit merited a formal greeting in the lobby, and if she was surprised to see a law professor in company with a judge and a policeman, she didn't let on. The elevator doors opened directly into her office, a large room with floor-to-ceiling plateglass windows that looked over the roofs of Nice and, to the south, the sea. Seeing the expression on Marine's face, she warmly said, "Nice may not be the center of fashion, but as you can see, I must have a sea view where I live and work." She made a sweeping circular motion with her hand that included the large windows and then the whole room, as if inviting the Aixois to take in the beauty, and luxury, of the office. Her French was very good, but a strong Russian accent gave her words a heavier sound than her husband's more fluent, more songlike voice.

The furniture and artwork were surprisingly contemporary given the Russian woman's conservative clothing. The four sat down at a round table designed by Eero Saarinen in the 1950s; Verlaque had recognized the white pedestal base and marble top immediately. "My husband told me that you are here investigating the death of François de Bremont," Mme Pogorovski said, looking mostly at Verlaque, having assumed that he was in charge of the investigation.

"That's right," he replied. "François de Bremont worked for your agency, *non?*"

"Worked," Mme Pogorovski repeated, sounding out the word "worked" with a long drawl. "If you can call it work. Nice work if you can get it—isn't that the song? Yes, he arranged apartments for our girls and showed them around Nice, helped them with paperwork, that sort of thing."

"Didn't he work well?" Verlaque asked, hearing the sarcasm in the Russian's voice.

"He was difficult to tie down," she went on. "When you needed him, he was never around. The girls loved him, though. He was good to them, and, don't get me wrong, we at Tribeca were all very sorry to hear of his death."

Marine looked at Mme Pogorovski and asked, "What exactly was M. de Bremont's relationship with Natassja Dubanov?"

Mme Pogorovski's tanned face lost its elegant composure for a second, and then tightened again. "Why do you want to know about Natassja?" she asked suspiciously.

"I know that she committed suicide, and that she and François were friends," Marine replied. Feeling the Russian's stare pierce her skin, Marine then added, "A suicide and a murder—they are both violent deaths, even if one is chosen, and the other not. We'd just like to know if there is a connection between the two."

"How could there be?" Mme Pogorovski answered, her voice strained but softer. "Natassja committed suicide, as you know, in New York. Yes, I think they were friends, but we are all friends here, at Tribeca." Again, she made a sweeping motion with her arm to include the whole room.

"Do you know why Natassja killed herself?"

Mme Pogorovski looked down at her hands, and then looked up at Marine, with, Marine thought, a true sadness in her eyes. "No, I don't. I know that Natassja was homesick for Russia—Kazakhstan in her case—she had called me the day before she died, crying. But I thought it was a temporary homesickness, that's all. All of the girls get it, after the glamour of modeling wears off and the hard work becomes a reality." She looked down at her hands again and, twirling the diamond bracelet on her wrist around and around, added, "I still cannot forgive myself." The Russian's dark eyes were watery.

"Was Natassja particularly close to any of the other models?" Verlaque cut in, wanting to give Mme Pogorovski some relief from her guilt, a guilt that to him seemed entirely real.

"No, she didn't have any particular friends that I knew of, at least here in France," Mme Pogorovski answered quickly.

Marine opened her mouth to protest, but Verlaque had already got to his feet and, outstretching his hand, said, "Thank you, Madame, for your time. We'll let ourselves out."

Once in the elevator, Marine demanded, "How could a twenty-year-old girl not have a best friend?"

"Do you think that's weird?" Verlaque asked, reminding Marine that Verlaque, at twenty, probably hadn't had a best friend, either. Not waiting for an answer, Verlaque turned to Paulik and asked the commissioner if he had had a best friend at that age.

"Sure," Paulik replied. "*Ma moto.*"

Marine and Verlaque looked at each other and laughed. Paulik then added, "Just kidding. I loved my motorcycle, but I also did have a great buddy named Lili."

"Lili?" Verlaque asked. "What an old Provençal name. Where is this guy now?"

"Runs a bistro in Paris. I haven't been there in years, but the last time we ate there the food was delicious and the place was packed." Paulik gave Verlaque the bistro's name and address, which Verlaque immediately entered into his phone.

The elevator doors opened and Marine walked on ahead, stopping at the receptionist's desk. Marine leaned over and the two women spoke, in hushed tones, for a few minutes. The young receptionist then passed Marine a small piece of paper. Once outside, Marine showed Paulik and Verlaque what was written on the paper: a telephone number. Verlaque looked at it and asked, "The best friend?"

"Yes," Marine said. "She's a model here in Nice, with Tribeca."

"Well done."

"So Mme Pogorovski obviously didn't want to give us another model's name," Paulik said.

Verlaque nodded and said, "Apparently. But I do think she seemed sincerely upset at the girl's death."

"I agree," said Marine. "Maybe she is. But maybe at the same time she doesn't want us to know more about the reasons why Natassja killed herself. Perhaps she feels that she might be at fault somehow."

The three walked on in silence until they got back to the car. Verlaque looked at Marine as he was unlocking the car doors and asked, "Can you give the best friend a call and try to visit her, while Bruno and I go to the casino in Cannes?"

"Sure," Marine said, and once they were in the car she dialed the model's phone number. The girl was very reluctant to see Marine, and only once Marine promised to show her identification did she agree to meet. Verlaque dropped Marine off on the promenade des Anglais, and they arranged to meet in two hours at the same spot.

Marine walked along the boardwalk, looking out at the sea and at some brave bathers—mostly elderly—and thought about what she wanted to ask the best friend, whose name was Tatiana. They had agreed to meet, at Tatiana's suggestion, on a bench directly across from the Hôtel Negresco. When Marine saw the hotel, she looked across the street to the benches that lined the promenade. She saw, sitting on one of the benches, a girl dressed in loose-fitting sweatpants, listening to her iPod. Marine sat down beside the girl, and after a few seconds the girl slid her earphones off and demanded, "Are you the professor?"

Marine nodded. "Yes. My name is Marine Bonnet," she said, turning and shaking the girl's hand. "I teach law at the university in Aix-en-Provence. Here's my card." The girl took the card and looked at it, and handed it back to Marine, saying nothing.

"I'm actually in Nice on police business," Marine continued. "We are investigating the murder of François de Bremont. I grew up with François and his brother, Étienne. Did you know François well?"

Tatiana looked at Marine and drew her incredibly long legs up under her chin. She looked out at the sea and then at Marine and answered, "Yes, of course I knew François. He helped us, the models, at the agency."

"Was he dating your friend Natassja?"

Tatiana tilted her head back and laughed. "No way!" For a moment Tatiana sounded like an average French girl, and not a highly paid Russian model. Marine smiled to encourage the girl to go on, which she did. "Natassja was in love with her childhood sweetheart, Ivan. He's a schoolteacher in their hometown in Kazakhstan."

Marine could not hide her surprise.

"You're surprised that a supermodel would want to date a schoolteacher, *non*?" Tatiana asked.

"You're right, I guess I am surprised, and I don't know why," Marine admitted. "Is that why Natassja was so homesick?"

"Of course." It occurred to Marine that the two Russians she spoke to today both had the habit of beginning their sentences with "of course," much as the French tend to say *mais oui* when the answer is an obvious one.

"Why didn't Natassja go back to Russia, then?" Not getting an answer, Marine repeated her question. "Tatiana, why didn't Natassja go back home?"

"She just couldn't, that's all. She was a model. She had obligations."

Marine interrupted. "What obligations? She could quit modeling, *non*?"

Tatiana paused for a few seconds before answering. "Hey, it's really hard to quit this kind of money once you're used to it."

Marine continued, moving her face closer to Tatiana's. "But Natassja was so sad that she took her own life. Surely she would have given up the big salary to be with the boyfriend? She would have chosen love over money, *non*? Life over death?"

"You sound like a professor, Professor."

Marine smiled and said, "You're not going to tell me why Natassja couldn't quit modeling and end her contract with Tribeca, are you?"

Tatiana smiled sheepishly and shook her head back and forth. Marine said, "Look, Tatiana, here's my card again, with my cell phone number on it. I've written down a judge's name and phone number on it as well. He's very nice and very wise. We can help you if you need it, okay?"

Tatiana put the card in a zippered pocket in her hooded sweatshirt, and it was only then, while watching the girl get her earphones out of her pocket, that Marine noticed her stomach.

"Tatiana, are you pregnant?" No model could have a stomach like that. Marine, not an expert in such things, estimated that she must be four to five months along.

The model smiled and rubbed her stomach. "Yes. It wasn't planned, but we're crazy happy." Seeing Marine's concerned look, she said, "Don't worry, I *have* a boyfriend, and he's French. He's a soccer player on the Nice team."

The Russian smiled once more at Marine and jumped off the bench and began a slow jog toward the eastern end of the promenade.

An elderly couple, towels in tow, walked past Marine toward the sea. The Côte d'Azur, despite the glitz, seemed like a healthy place to retire. She thought of the old woman in the restaurant, devouring with much glee her plate of oysters. A thud caused Marine to stop her daydreaming. She looked to her right—it was only another jogger who had just hopped off the bench next to hers and who was jogging in the same direction as Tatiana.

Chapter Twenty-two

*T*he cours Mirabeau felt dark to Marine as they drove up it, toward the statue of King René. The leaves of the plane trees, although brand-new, managed to form a tunnel over the sidewalks and street. To add to the gloom, it was an overcast day, weather that was getting more and more frequent in Aix as of late. Marine thought of the palm trees that lined the Mediterranean, and suddenly she missed that wide expanse of water. As if reading her mind, Paulik said, "We need a body of water in Aix. We don't even have a river. At least Avignon and Arles have the Rhône."

Verlaque smiled and nodded in the direction of the rounded, knoblike fountain on their left, and said, "We have *La Moussue*." One of the four fountains that punctuates the middle of the cours Mirabeau, "Old Mossback," was an eighteenth-century moss-covered stone fountain whose warm waters steamed in the cold air during Aix's winters. Marine's father, as a child, had fetched its healing water for his mother to drink, to cure her aches and pains, and today most Aixois casually dipped their hands into the tepid water as they passed by, almost out of habit. Sylvie had once compared the fountain to an old, wet dog—steamy and pungent.

"If you want water, the sea is only thirty minutes away, in Marseille," Verlaque offered. The mention of Marseille was met with two sets of exaggerated groans. Verlaque, a newcomer to the south, quite enjoyed that city, both for its natural beauty on the sea and for its blatant refusal to cater to tourists. It's France's Genoa, he thought.

On the drive back, Paulik and Verlaque had told Marine what they had learned from their visit to the casino in Cannes: virtually nothing. At least not anything they didn't already know: François de Bremont had gambling debts, and to protect the young count the casino manager had actually barred François from playing the card tables. Lever Pogorovski was a frequent *joueur*, as were other prominent Russians; his wife, however, had never set foot inside the place. Marine had listened to their narrative, and then said, "I got basically the same noninformation out of Tatiana, except that Natassja Duvanov was in love, but not with François, nor a footballer or a tycoon, but a schoolteacher back in Kazakhstan. Tatiana, on the other hand, *is* dating a footballer, and they're expecting a baby."

"Natassja killed herself over a schoolteacher?" Paulik asked suspiciously.

"There's some opera for you, Bruno," Verlaque said.

"For some reason she felt that she couldn't go back to Russia," Marine corrected both men.

"Why didn't she just hop on a plane?" Paulik asked, returning to his role as a policeman and no longer dreaming of *La Wally*.

"That's what Tatiana couldn't, or wouldn't, tell me," Marine answered.

Verlaque inched the car along the busy rue d'Italie, careful not to hit elderly shoppers, little dogs, or inattentive teenagers. They turned right on Marine's street, and as they passed by the boutique

Agnès b. Marine managed to peek at the colorful new collection displayed in the window. Verlaque stopped the car in front of her apartment, and the two men both got out and gave Marine the *bises* good-bye. Paulik then got into the passenger seat, and Verlaque stayed outside. He stared at Marine before saying, "When can we resume our state of the union conversation?"

"Not tonight, Antoine. I'm seeing Sylvie," Marine said truthfully. It wasn't exactly a conversation, Marine thought. It was mostly Antoine mumbling to himself and trying to seduce her.

"Fine," he answered, with shortness of breath. His voice and face then relaxed, and he said, "Thank you for coming to Cannes. You were a great help."

"*C'est normal,*" Marine replied. "Étienne and François were close to me, once upon a time. Please let me know if you need anything else. I'd be happy to help." She put her key in the door and then added, smiling, "Next time, let's do the Carlton properly."

Verlaque laughed out loud, a proper gut-felt laugh that Marine hadn't heard come out of his mouth in ages, and he leaned over and kissed her on the lips. They were both startled by how nice the kiss felt, and by a sharp honking coming from a black two-door BMW that had just pulled up behind Verlaque's car. The driver of the car, a young male, who sported the slick black hair and gold chains favored by young hoodlums in the south, gestured madly with his hands in the air. Verlaque slowly walked to his car, not acknowledging the youngster. "While you were saying good-bye, Sergeant Arbadji, who taught the computer session in Cannes, returned my call. Pellegrino was there, but they took attendance after lunch, not before, Paulik said."

"Merde."

"He also volunteered that he had looked for Pellegrino during the morning session and couldn't find him. Arbadji had wanted to ask him something about a report Pellegrino was work-ing on."

"So he would have had time to go from Cannes to St. Anto-nin and back. Let's call him."

Paulik nodded and dialed the officer's number, listened for a few seconds, sighed, and then left a message on his answering machine. He turned and said, "Where are we going with this?"

"I'm not sure. What if Pellegrino gets paid to do something more than just play polo? Does he help Pogorovski? The Russian plays polo, too, come to think of it."

"For the love of the game? Pellegrino takes polo pretty seri-ously, no? Could he have killed François over that match?"

"That's a little extreme. I doubt it. What about over a girl?"

"Ah, oui. Could they both have been in love with the same beautiful blonde? I did think it was weird that he told Marine he couldn't keep the Russian girls' names straight. Wouldn't you be able to remember their names?"

Verlaque smiled and nodded. "You bet I would. There's no way I would confuse an Iréna from a Natacha."

Paulik dropped Verlaque off at the Quatre Dauphins foun-tain; Verlaque had decided to find out where the Valoie de Saint-André family lived and to pay madame a visit.

Verlaque walked up the rue du 4 Septembre, lost in thought, smiling to himself as he passed by the sputtering *Moussue*, and walked into Le Mazarin. As usual with the Mazarin, one couldn't go in unless prepared to take five minutes to greet and shake hands with about half of the patrons, which Verlaque now did. Finally he saw Jean-Marc Sauvat standing at the bar, nursing a coffee, and the two men gave each other the *bises* and pats on the back. They spoke for a few minutes about Jean-Marc's current court case, and then both began complaining of the mayor's new plans to build a shopping mall at the bottom of the *cours*. After a few more minutes, Verlaque leaned in closer to Jean-Marc and asked, "Do you know where Judge Valoie de Saint-André lives? I know that he commutes from Aix to Marseille."

"Sure," Jean-Marc answered. "I thought everyone knew," he said, grinning. "They live in the Hôtel Guimard, just north of the cathedral."

Antoine thought for a moment and said, "I walk by it almost every day. I've always wondered who lives there. Nice place." The three-story mansion boasted two things many downtown residents coveted: a walled-in garden and parking.

"Sophie Valoie, and her sister Isabelle de Bremont—what's their background? Are they from Aix?" Verlaque asked, knowing that Jean-Marc, like Marine, knew Aix inside out.

"No," Jean-Marc answered. He took a sip of coffee and continued: "The sisters are from a noble family from Nantes. They moved down here with their parents when they were in their teens. There's a third sister, Clothilde, who married a *de* someone-or-other as well. Gossip was, when we were in high school, that they were nobles with no money or property, and the parents had moved the family to Aix to marry the girls into wealthy, property-tied families. I guess all the chichi guys in Nantes were taken."

"Their parents must've been happy," Verlaque said, sarcastically.

"The girls certainly delivered, *non*? At least on the property side of things," agreed Jean-Marc.

"Does Clothilde still live in Aix?" Verlaque asked. He thought about Jean-Marc's reference to the *de*. Verlaque's parents would have given anything for a title. He was convinced that they would have paid for it, if that was still possible.

Jean-Marc motioned for the bill. "No, Clothilde lives in Paris.

Guess where?" he demanded. He then quickly added, "Or let me put it this way—if you had five or six million to spend on a Parisian apartment, and if noise and tourists didn't bother you, where would you want it to be?"

"Place des Vosges?" Verlaque ventured, not needing a second to think.

Jean-Marc didn't reply, he only nodded his head up and down, and smiled.

The two men left the café by way of the side door and parted company on the rue Clémenceau. Verlaque immediately crossed the narrow street and entered the *tabac*, where the lovely Carole was arranging cigar boxes in the humidor. She turned around when she heard that someone had entered the shop, and when she saw the judge, she raised one eyebrow and smiled coyly, a look she reserved for very attractive men or important clients. Verlaque happened to be both.

Verlaque bought his preferred short cigar, a Churchill by Romeo y Julieta, and they talked of a cigar from Nicaragua that had just been rated number one by an American cigar magazine and cost only five dollars in the U.S. Carole hadn't been able to order any from her French distributor. Verlaque paid for his Churchill and said good-bye, quickly taking in Carole's full lips, dark eyes, and ample breasts, which today had forgotten their brassiere. "À bientôt, Monsieur le Juge," she replied, raising her left eyebrow as Verlaque left the shop.

Carole's coworker then came up from the basement, carrying four cigar boxes in her arms. "Was that Judge Verlaque?" she asked Carole.

"Yes, you just missed him," said Carole, who hadn't changed position and was still staring at the door.

"Merde," her young assistant said.

"What is it about him?" Carole asked. "He isn't *that* handsome."

The assistant gently set the cigar boxes down on the counter, folded her arms, and, like Carole, looked toward the door and out onto the rue Clémenceau. "Pouvoir," she answered.

"Power?" questioned Carole, turning to face her.

"Power and intelligence," the assistant replied. "Plus that stare."

When Verlaque rang at the Hôtel Guimard, he was quite sure that Mme Valoie would be at home. Even if she did work, she had probably taken the week off to be with Isabelle de Bremont. And to do her own grieving.

"Oui?" a voice answered, heavy with a North African accent.

"This is Judge Verlaque. Is Mme Valoie de Saint-André at home?"

"Oui," the maid simply replied.

"May I come in and speak with her, please?" Verlaque asked, trying not to sound impatient.

The reply took a few seconds to arrive, and instead of a voice a loud buzz answered. Verlaque pushed open the heavy iron gate and walked through the courtyard that was paved with smooth, rounded river stones. A new white BMW was parked there. Her car, thought Verlaque, remembering that the winemaker Marc had mentioned it.

Sophie Valoie opened the door and stood in its huge frame. They shook hands, and Mme Valoie stepped aside to allow Verlaque to pass. Verlaque reintroduced himself, and asked, "Do you remember me? I visited your sister on Sunday."

"Yes, I remember. I don't know why you're here, but I do know that since you're Aix's head judge I have to let you in. Come this way, into the salon." She appeared even thinner than when he had seen her on Monday, giving her a fragility that made Verlaque suddenly feel sorry for her.

The salon was as impressive as Isabelle de Bremont's— six-meter-high ceilings, a crystal chandelier, and large French doors that let out onto the courtyard. The furniture, however, was much more conservative than that in the Bremont mansion. It was tasteful, yes, but the furnishings were the sort one bought in expensive boutiques like Faubourg or Flamant—Verlaque could never keep the names straight. The fabric was always linen: beige or cream colored. There were no bright colors, tricycles, or soccer balls.

They sat facing each other, both silent, on matching reproduction Louis Seize chairs, both upholstered in natural linen. A small marble-topped table rested between them, graced with a vase of white tulips.

"I'm here to ask you a few things about Étienne de Bremont," began Verlaque.

"*Ah bon?* There's not much for me to tell you, except that he was my brother-in-law."

"Was he anything else to you, Madame?"

Sophie Valoie got up off her chair and walked over to the wooden double doors that separated the salon from the rest of the house and casually closed them. She stood for a moment, facing the door, in order to compose herself, and then turned around and said, "What in the world do you mean?"

Verlaque waited for her to sit back down, and then he leaned over, resting his elbows on his knees, his hands folded together. "Were you lovers?" he asked point-blank.

"That's absurd," she answered. Halfheartedly, Verlaque thought.

He pressed on, "You were unlucky in choosing to spend your nights together at one of my favorite wineries in the Var."

Her face reddened, and she hissed, "What did they say? The nerve!"

"M. and Mme Nagel didn't say anything, Madame. As I said, it was a strange coincidence. Besides, they thought that you were with François de Bremont. How long had the affair been going on?"

"What does it matter? It's obviously over now."

"It matters because François de Bremont was murdered, and I'm quite sure that Étienne was as well. Plus, one of my officers did a check on TGV tickets purchased last week. Your sister Isabelle went to Paris on Saturday morning and came back to Aix on Sunday morning. So were you the one with Étienne, before he went to Saint-Antonin?"

Sophie Valoie's mouth opened and she tapped her palms against her knees a few times in rapid succession. "He left here around eleven p.m. He said he had to look for some family papers at the château."

"Did you send him there?"

"What are you insinuating?"

"Or did you go with him, and then have an argument of some kind in the attic?"

"You have no right to say such things. Of course I didn't go with him."

Verlaque leaned back and crossed his legs. "Why did you, and your sister, lie?"

"We were covering for each other . . . She knew I was having an affair, but I'm fairly certain she was in the dark regarding Étienne. I did tell her we had been together that evening—at the movies. Isabelle has no interest in cinema." She stayed silent for some time, looking down at the arm of the chair, as if deciding whether or not to go on. "We began our affair three years ago," she finally said, choking slightly on her last words. "But we've known each other since we were in high school. Étienne and I had been great friends—we joked and laughed all the time. But I went away to university, and I met, and became quickly engaged to, Henri, my husband. He too is a judge, in Marseille."

Verlaque nodded and said nothing.

"Henri and I married, and Isabelle and Étienne married, children followed for them but sadly not for us. Étienne and I always joked that we got on better with each other than with our respective spouses. Three years ago we ended up alone at my country house in the Tarn—my husband had been called back to Marseille for a trial, and Isabelle had stayed in Aix at the last minute because one of her children was sick. Étienne had been filming in Toulouse, and he came up to the Tarn house, and"—she paused, rubbing her hands along her thighs—"that was that. Isabelle has had a lover in Paris for some time. That's where she was on Saturday night. Don't think harshly of her, please. Isabelle had trouble controlling, or dealing with, Étienne's mood swings. Étienne couldn't understand Isabelle's faith or her doting on the children. Since I have neither faith nor children, we were a better fit. And my marriage to Henri, well, it was practically an arranged marriage. All the same, you won't tell Isabelle about our affair, will you?"

"I don't see any reason to," Verlaque said. He had stirred only the slightest bit when Sophie Valoie had mentioned Isabelle de Bremont's lover in Paris. He continued, "Count Bremont was moody?"

"Oh yes, up and down all the time. He had a nasty temper." Mme Valoie paused, and looking at the tulips, smiled and said, "But when he was up, oh, what fun we had."

"You must be very sad," he added, seeing Sophie Valoie looking at him. She began crying, her face softening and slowly becoming every bit as beautiful as her red-haired sister.

"Yes, it's very difficult," she said, wiping her nose on a tissue. "And I can't show my grief, can I?"

"No," Verlaque answered in agreement. "Rather like a novel by Jane Austen, isn't it? Have you read *Sense and Sensibility*?"

Sophie Valoie smiled at the judge. "Ah, Elinor and Marianne Dashwood. That was one of Étienne's favorite books." She wiped her eyes dry and asked, "What can I tell you about Étienne, besides his taste in books?"

"The obvious questions. Was there anyone who would want to hurt M. de Bremont? Did he receive any threats of any kind?"

"No," she answered, shaking her head back and forth. "Étienne was a charming, interesting, passionate man. Everyone loved him."

Verlaque smiled at the obvious reference to her own love for Étienne. "But for his temper," he reminded her.

She went on, "Strong people could handle Étienne's temper. My sister has never been strong, Judge. And the same with that caretaker at the château—he didn't know how to deal with Étienne, either." She continued, as if she wanted to build a better impression of her lover, "Even the Mafia liked him. He interviewed some of them for his Marseille documentary—of course he couldn't film them. He was quite satisfied with himself after that. You were in that film, weren't you?"

"Yes," Verlaque replied. "I was very impressed with M. de Bremont."

"As was everyone who met him." Verlaque had stopped

listening—he was thinking of her comment, "Even the mafia liked Étienne."

Verlaque got up, not wanting to keep Mme Valoie any longer and wanting to be gone before Judge Valoie de Saint-André returned home from Marseille. "Thank you so much, Madame," Verlaque said sincerely. "If you think of anything else, can you call me?" he asked, passing her one of his business cards.

She took the card without looking at it and set it on an expensive-looking antique credenza in the entryway.

"Thank you for your time," Verlaque said sincerely. "I'll let myself out the front gate."

He walked out of the Valoie house, and as he passed through the pebbled courtyard, he turned around to see Sophie Valoie watching him through the soaring French doors. She looked incredibly small.

Chapter Twenty-three

≻

M arine drew her arms tight around Charlotte's waist, from time to time resting her head on the eight-year-old's upper back. Charlotte was busy coloring a sketch that Marine had made for her; the fact that the drawing was of Antoine's terrace drew raised eyebrows from Sylvie. "Big fluffy clouds in Aix?" asked Sylvie, turning her head to look at the drawing.

"Well, you know," Marine answered, "it makes the sky look so much more dramatic."

"A storm is brewing," Sylvie said, smiling. Charlotte ignored her mother and godmother and continued coloring. She began to fill in the leaves of the olive tree with a light green pencil. "Does Antoine have an olive tree on his terrace?" Sylvie asked, looking at Marine.

"No, I do."

Sylvie, worried that Marine had begun fantasizing about Antoine, turned to Charlotte and congratulated her on her choice of green. "Are olive leaves silvery green or dark green?" Sylvie asked her daughter.

"Silvery green," Charlotte seriously replied, and her plump little hand reached for a silver pencil. The two women smiled across the table at each other, both bursting with love for the eight-year-old. Seeing that her daughter was content, Sylvie poured Marine a glass of white wine and said, "I don't see any connection between the"—she stopped herself before saying "death" and, looking at Charlotte, continued—"between the stories of Étienne and François."

"Nor do I," Marine answered, swirling the wine around in the bowl of the wineglass. "François's world was gambling, polo, and models." She went on, "And Étienne seemed to be very rooted to Aix and dedicated to his craft." Marine chose not to tell Sylvie about Étienne's affair with Sophie Valoie de Saint-André. Marine loved Sylvie dearly, but she also knew that after a couple of glasses of wine her friend was capable of blurting out the most private of secrets. "One thing that did occur to us," Marine continued, noting to herself her use of "us," which seemed, strangely, so right, "is how much the brothers looked alike, and that François's murderer may have mistaken Étienne for the Riviera gambler."

"*Not bad.* Have you figured out why Étienne was in the attic on a Saturday night?" asked Sylvie.

"No. His wife mentioned something about him needing to look at some documents, and I'm sure that the documents were in that Louis Vuitton suitcase." Marine felt silly—she had forgotten about the suitcase and now had a sense that its contents were paramount to Étienne's death.

"What suitcase?"

"Oh, there has always been this old Vuitton suitcase up in the attic. It belonged to Étienne's grandfather, and we were never allowed to touch it. Of course sometimes we needed to move it around, and it was quite heavy. Now it's empty, and Jean-Claude told Antoine that on Friday night the suitcase still had its contents."

"So the papers are with the, the," Sylvie paused, again conscious of the presence of a child in the room, "the person who was also in the attic with Étienne."

"Yes, it looks that way."

"So shouldn't you be bugging the caretaker about those papers?" demanded Sylvie. Sylvie was in one of those moods that annoyed Marine—convinced that she, though an artist, knew the intricacies of everyone's job whether they be doctor, lawyer, or waiter.

"He told Antoine that he didn't know what was in the suitcase," answered Marine, trying to make light of Sylvie's questions and shift the direction of the conversation.

"And you two believe that?" asked Sylvie, pouring more wine.

"I would trust Jean-Claude with my life."

"Would you trust him with Charlotte's life?"

"Don't be silly."

"It seems to me," Sylvie said, licking her lips after a somewhat big sip of wine, "that while the three of you were gallivanting around the Côte, you might have been in Aix, trying to figure out what, and where, those papers are."

"We weren't gallivanting, to use your word," Marine replied, somewhat vexed. "Antoine does have the murder of François on his hands, and François lived and worked in Cannes."

Sylvie looked worriedly at Charlotte, but the young artist hadn't, or pretended not to have, heard the word "murder." "Oh come on. Verlaque just wanted you in Cannes with him to show off. Did he take you to a three-star restaurant?"

Marine answered in the affirmative by not replying. Sylvie slapped her hand down, causing a few of Charlotte's pencils to roll off the table. "I knew it!"

Marine sighed, as she usually did when Sylvie was in one of

her know-it-all moods. Her cell phone rang with a text message from Jean-Marc, inviting them to Le Mazarin for a drink. "Tell him no thanks," Sylvie said. "I have to get Charlotte fed and to bed." She would accompany Marine down into the street so that she could smoke a cigarette.

"I think I'll go. I could use the diversion," Marine answered, draining the last of her wine and setting the glass on the table.

Charlotte turned around to look at Marine and said, "Do you really have to go to Le Mazarin?" Sylvie, who was taking the wineglasses to the sink, laughed and said to Charlotte, "Were you listening?"

"I heard everything," Charlotte said smugly.

Sylvie put the glasses on the kitchen counter and said, "Charlotte, what we were talking about sort of has to do with Marine's work, so you won't tell anyone, will you?"

"No," replied the third grader, looking puzzled by the question. "It was way too boring."

Marine gently slid Charlotte down off of her lap and picked up her purse, which had been hanging on the back of the chair.

When Marine got to Le Mazarin, she saw Jean-Marc and one of his colleagues sitting on the café's terrace. She asked Frédéric for a glass of white Château Revelette, and the three friends chatted about the weather and a new restaurant that had opened in an old *calisson* factory. They spoke of Étienne's funeral, and how moving it had been, and of François's murder. Marine didn't tell them about her two days in Cannes. Jean-Marc was in fine form and made them laugh with stories of his crazy elderly neighbor, who accused Jean-Marc of stealing his slippers from outside his apartment door. "That was the perfect end to my day! Then just as I was leaving the office I had to deal with a nutcase from Cotignac with a very bad henna job!" he said, draining his beer. Marine tried to hide her curiosity. She laughed and asked, "Who was she?"

"I have no idea. She had been waiting to see me, and had clearly been drinking. I told her I only had a few minutes available. She wanted to know about inheritance laws and birthrights but didn't want to give me any specific details. She said that she had papers from the 1950s but didn't have them with her." Marine got goose bumps on her forearms. She tried to look uninterested. Jean-Marc continued: "It was all very mysterious. I told her to come back next week with the papers, and she said that she would and took off. I could still smell the alcohol five minutes after she had gone. In fact, it was so strong that I actually made sure she wasn't driving all the way back to Cotignac tonight."

Marine quickly got up, bumping into the table as she did and almost knocking over Jean-Marc's beer glass.

"What's up?" Jean-Marc asked.

Marine feigned fatigue and said good-bye, mumbling that she was late to meet someone.

"Now?" Jean-Marc demanded.

"Yes! I promised him I'd stop by, and I totally forgot!"

She made her way around the café's chairs and tables as quickly as she could without knocking anyone's drink off of the table at the same time. It had been Cosette in Jean-Marc's office, Marine was sure of it. Inheritance papers from the 1950s—could that be what was in the suitcase, mixed up with a bill for two brioches from the same period? Birthrights? 1950s? Étienne and François were born in the 1960s. Inheritance laws?

She ran to her parking garage on the cours Gambetta and thought of calling Verlaque, then at the last minute decided against it. After all, she was the one who knew the Bremonts, and Jean-

Claude remembered, and liked, her. She imagined Verlaque had probably intimidated the caretaker, and so she was better off talking to Jean-Claude alone. If Cosette was there too, Marine could look at the papers and find out what the connection was.

Antoine Verlaque had gone back to his office to check messages and go through some paperwork. He was just about to close his office door when he received a text message from Paulik. He read it: *Still no word from Pellegrino,* and he walked out of the Palais de Justice, through the passage Agard and down the cours Mirabeau to number sixteen. He rang and waited. A young boy answered the intercom. "Hello, Judge Verlaque here. May I please come in? I'd like to speak to your mother." The boy said nothing, but Verlaque could hear shuffling, and Isabelle de Bremont then spoke: "Come on up, Monsieur le Juge."

Verlaque walked purposely into the salon while Mme Bremont whispered for her son to leave. She smiled. "Yes, Judge?"

"You took the 10:42 to Paris on Saturday. Why did you lie?"

Isabelle de Bremont went over to the salon's tall double doors and shut them firmly. She motioned for Verlaque to sit down; then she sat opposite him, moving her chair close to his. "What could I do? Tell you about my lover?"

"Yes, you could have. Should have."

"I am a religious woman. It is hard enough for me to have this secret life in Paris. There was no way I could tell you."

"You said that your husband told you he was going to the château late Saturday night. You do realize that you were withholding information? Your husband died that night, and his brother four days later on the same grounds."

"I was protecting my sister. They were together. Sophie said that they were at the movies together." Isabelle de Bremont let out a small laugh. "She's always thought me daft and weak."

"So you knew about her relationship with your husband?"

"Yes, for a few months now. But that didn't give me reason to kill him, Judge Verlaque. My parents had the children for the weekend, and I had just got back here when you arrived, with the news of Étienne's death."

"Where were you on Wednesday morning between eight and nine?"

Isabelle de Bremont looked at the judge in wonderment. "I was selecting which black clothes I would wear for my husband's funeral." When Verlaque said nothing she added, "My maid can confirm that—she stayed overnight."

"Thank you. Could I have your friend's name and phone number in Paris, please?"

Mme de Bremont got up and walked over to a gilded mirror, then looked at herself, playing with the gold crucifix she wore around her neck. She looked back at Verlaque through the glass and said, "Must I?"

"Yes, I'm afraid so, if you want a clean alibi. We can't go on the train ticket alone."

"Serges Tourtin, he lives in the first arrondissement," she whispered. She went over to her desk and wrote the name and phone number on a piece of paper and handed it to Verlaque, who took it and said, "One last question. You and François de Bremont were overheard arguing about money on the *cours* the other day—it was reported that you wanted to sell Château Bremont and he wanted to keep it."

She got up and went to the marble fireplace and stood before two antique Chinese pots of dried heather. Resting her hand on the mantelpiece, she turned around and said, "My God! Nothing is sacred in Aix, is it? It really isn't any of your business."

Verlaque looked at her and replied, "Madame, François died shortly after that argument. You must see the importance of my question."

"Fine," she sighed. "We . . . myself and the children . . . need the money. We are, as they say, cash poor. The properties we own won't send my children to college or give them seaside vacations."

Verlaque nodded and silently thought of the separate bank account, with the statements that went to Saint-Antonin. Either Isabelle de Bremont still didn't know about that account or she was lying. He got up and walked toward the doors. "Good-bye, Madame. Please stay in Aix, where we can reach you, until you hear otherwise." Isabelle opened her mouth to protest but Verlaque raised his hand and turned his back, walking out of the salon and through the apartment's front door. Isabelle de Bremont took the opportunity to throw a small silk pillow at the door, the thud unheard by Verlaque.

On the *cours* Verlaque tucked his body into a doorway and called Paulik. He relayed to the commissioner the information that Isabelle de Bremont had given him.

"I'll call the police station in the first arrondissement and have them send someone over to question M. Tourtin," Paulik replied.

"She also lied about that separate bank account that I told you about—or she doesn't yet know of its existence—but you would think that the bank would have informed her already."

"Not necessarily," the commissioner replied. "When Hélène and I moved our retirement plans around at our bank, it took months to clear. Hélène was so frustrated by the end of it that she said she was going to start keeping her money in a cookie tin, the way her grandparents did."

"My grandmother kept cash in an old watercolor paint box," Verlaque replied. "Have you heard how Jean-Claude Auvieux is doing? We questioned him pretty hard."

"I was just thinking the same thing. Flamant should be around the police station—you could ask him. He spent most of Thursday at Saint-Antonin, keeping watch."

"Right, have a nice evening with Hélène and . . ."

"Léa," Paulik answered.

"I'm so sorry," Verlaque said sincerely. "I should know your daughter's name."

"No you shouldn't, I totally understand." Paulik smiled and then added, "She's an angel."

"I'm sure she is. Have a nice night."

"Thanks," Paulik said. "See you tomorrow."

Verlaque walked back through the passage Agard and into the police station, then down to the ground level where suspects were held in very welcoming cells, the thick stone walls washed with a natural-based ocher paint. Verlaque had overseen the more recent renovations, and with the architect had chosen transparent plastic chairs designed by Philippe Starck and glass-topped tables. The furniture had a floating, feminine quality that the two men had agreed was needed for contrast, given the medieval stone walls and the purpose of the rooms: to extract information and at the same time make the contained person feel comfortable. The lighting was Italian, discreet, and could be dimmed. One of the older policemen had joked at the inauguration—out of earshot of Verlaque—that it would be easy to clean blood and vomit from the furniture. Yves Roussel had heard the remark and laughed.

Through the two-way glass, Verlaque saw Officer Flamant sitting at one of the glass tables, writing, and entered the room. "Do you like working in here?" Verlaque asked.

Flamant jumped up and said, "Yes, I do. It's super quiet—peaceful—if you get what I mean. And I like these tables and chairs." He immediately felt silly.

Verlaque smiled. "How was M. Auvieux doing yesterday?"

"Not too well, Monsieur le Juge. He kept insisting that he didn't hear or see anything, except the black Mercedes driving away. He knew he didn't have time to read the licence plate so he just took in the two last numbers, the 06 of the Côte d'Azur."

Verlaque looked worried. "But you say that he isn't doing well?"

"Yes, sir. I don't know if it was the shock, but he was really nervous, with his face flushed and his eyes very red, as if he had been crying."

"Thank you, Officer Flamant. I'll read the transcripts in the morning," Verlaque answered. He decided in a matter of seconds that questioning Auvieux at the Palais de Justice, or even at the château, wasn't going to get him the information he needed. In fact, he wasn't sure what he might find out, but he had a hunch that Auvieux was somehow more indirectly than directly involved, and so an indirect approach was probably best. The two men had a love of food in common, and if Auvieux wasn't well, Verlaque was sure that a good meal would help the caretaker. He then added, "Call the policeman who's patrolling the château in Saint-Antonin and tell him to go home and get a good night's sleep." Verlaque was sure that Auvieux was innocent, and thus safe at the château. The murderer, or murderers, knew that he lived on-site and had left him alone.

"Yes, sir."

Verlaque walked outside of the Palais de Justice, where the reception was better for cell phones, and dialed Auvieux's cottage. The caretaker picked up the phone in one ring, as if he had been waiting at his polished kitchen table for someone to call. Verlaque suggested that they meet for dinner at restaurant les Sarments in the village of Puyloubier, where Auvieux bought his boxed wine. The drive from Saint-Antonin to Puyloubier was always an enjoyable one, and it was Auvieux's favorite, although the judge was unaware of that. Auvieux knew every dip, every tree (there weren't many), every rocky outcrop (those were abundant). It reminded Verlaque of a stretch of Highway One in California. There were, instead of sheep, cows in California, he thought he could remember. The trip was a long time ago, with a girlfriend who was now a married mother of five, living in Rome with the CEO of some multinational fashion house.

Auvieux couldn't hide his excitement. "Is that the small, fancy restaurant on the rue Qui Monte?" he asked.

"Yes," replied Verlaque, "'the street that climbs.'" He loved the names of certain roads in France. His brother, Sébastien, lived on the rue des Quatre-Vents in the prestigious sixth arrondissement of Paris. Emmeline had always said, "We'll meet at Séb's on the Four Winds." Since Sébastien could be rather chatty, the Four Winds became a private joke between Emmeline and Antoine.

Verlaque smiled, remembering his grandmother, and said, "I'll see you in thirty minutes."

Chapter Twenty-four

❧

*M*arine hummed along to Chet Baker, who was singing "My Funny Valentine." She was glad that she had decided to go and talk with Jean-Claude, glad to be away from the dominating presences of both Sylvie and Antoine, and glad to be driving— her mother never drove when she was a child, and she still couldn't imagine her mother behind the wheel. Her parents walked a lot—they lived in a house they had built in the 1960s in a residential neighborhood that was within walking distance of the university and downtown. They came from the generation that had grown up in the damp old stone houses and couldn't imagine that those houses would ever be renovated, with central heating and air-conditioning, the way they are today. Maybe that wasn't possible back then, Marine speculated, trying to give her parents the benefit of the doubt.

She took the two hairpin turns that led to Saint-Antonin a bit too quickly and had to shift down into first gear, and at the top of the rise she turned right into the hamlet, saying, "Merci, les garçons" aloud as she passed the war memorial. Marine saw that the gates to the château were closed, but she knew a spot in the fence where she could slip through. She considered beeping her car horn, but making that kind of horrible noise in the middle of the night, in this gorgeous countryside, bothered her conscience. She parked on the road opposite the château, under some tall pine trees. She got out of the car and locked it and crossed the road to the giant gates. On the right-hand side was a mailbox, built into the limestone columns that supported the rotting eighteenth-century wrought-iron gates. She followed the limestone wall to her right until it ended, after two meters, and a chain-link fence began. This was the section of the fence she and Étienne had frequently hopped over as kids. Étienne's parents had been fastidious about locking the gates, even when they were in the château, and Étienne had routinely forgotten his keys. She threw her purse over the fence and heaved herself up, swearing as she did. At the same time she grabbed the chain-link fencing on her right, which bent toward her, giving her leverage to get up on the wall. She jumped down on the grass on the other side, which, being on a slope, was not as far a jump as it was on the road side.

She walked up the small hill and made her way to the château. Auvieux's cottage was surprisingly dark. She went up to the light blue wooden door and knocked with the brass knocker, which was sculpted in the shape of a hand. No one replied, and she peeked into a small window to the left of the door and couldn't see anyone or anything. Marine resigned herself to the fact that she had picked one of the few nights when Auvieux wasn't at home. Bad luck. But it was a lovely drive that she didn't do often enough. She tried knocking one more time, waited a few seconds, and then turned around and headed toward her car. Just as she reached the fence, something made her turn around and look back at the château. A flash of a light caught her eye. It was in the attic—a light that had been lit, and that she hadn't noticed, had just been turned off. She was sure of it. She marched over to the château's steps, smiling, realizing that Jean-Claude was on the premises after all.

The door to the château was unlocked, and she pushed the heavy door open using her right hand and left shoulder. The entrance was dark, and she felt the wall on her left until she found the light switch and turned on the hall lights. She waited a few seconds, expecting Auvieux to come down the stairs. She called out his name, but no one replied. If he was on the third floor, he probably wouldn't hear her. She remembered that about the house—it was remarkably well built, and she and Étienne sometimes couldn't hear each other even if they were in adjoining rooms. She sighed and started heading up the stairs, not excited to see the stuffed owl, who would be glowering down at her.

"Hallo!" Marine said to no answer as she reached the first landing. She shrugged and turned and continued up another flight. "Jean-Claude! It's me, Marine Bonnet!" she called again. The light switched on again, she could see it coming out from the bottom of the attic door. "Ah! I see you're in the attic. I'll come up." She went up the last flight of stairs and pushed open the attic door.

Verlaque and Jean-Claude Auvieux were on dessert now: a fluffy, light dessert that had a mousselike consistency but was like no other Verlaque had ever tasted. He normally passed on desserts, but he wanted to keep Auvieux company, for the caretaker had studied the dessert menu as if it were an exam. "What is this?" Verlaque finally asked, lifting some of the green fluff on his spoon. Both men had ordered the dessert of the day, described by the waitress only as "*une super surprise!*" "I've never had a green mousse. It isn't tart enough to be lime."

Auvieux took some mousse in his spoon and looked at it, then tasted it. "It's a familiar flavor, Judge, but I can't put my finger on it."

Verlaque ate some of the mysterious mousse, and then thought it might be a good time to ask Auvieux about the suitcase. "You know, it's funny that there isn't a safe in the château," he said.

"No, there was the suitcase for that," Auvieux replied, distracted by his dessert. Verlaque couldn't believe his good luck. "The Louis Vuitton suitcase?" Verlaque said, trying to sound casual. "Do you have any idea what was in there? Was it old documents?"

Auvieux, in awe of his five-course dinner, and warm with champagne and wine, continued eating without looking up. "They were the grandfather's papers. Philippe de Bremont."

"Jean-Claude, Marine said that you were always very anxious about the contents of that suitcase. Why? You told me before that you had no idea what was in it, and now you say there were papers. You must have had some idea of what the papers were."

"I didn't touch the important documents!"

Verlaque sat still. "What documents? Please, you must tell me."

Auvieux paused. "I was in the attic last Friday night, looking for polo trophies for François," he suddenly said, his eyes filling up with tears. "François was looking for the old polo trophies. He said he could sell them, that they are worth a lot of money, and he had a friend who needed money." He put his spoon down and stared at his hands, which were resting on the table.

Verlaque waited, but when Jean-Claude stayed silent he tried another prompt. "You liked François, didn't you?"

The caretaker smiled and took another spoonful of mousse. "Oh yes," he replied. "We got on like a house on fire. He always had a present and a kind word for me when he came for a visit, and every Christmas I'd light a big fire in the château's salon and we'd share a bottle of . . . Guess what kind of champagne he would buy?"

Verlaque smiled. "Krug?"

"How did you guess?" Auvieux said, banging the table with the back of his hand.

"It was easy for me. It was the champagne we would drink at home too. But I don't spend Christmas with my parents anymore," Verlaque said, surprising himself at his honesty.

"*Ah non?* That's not good, Monsieur le Juge."

"I know," Verlaque answered. "So did you open the suitcase that night?"

Verlaque didn't move an inch or speak. The caretaker continued: "The suitcase was in the way, the trophies were behind it, and I was in a hurry, so I tugged too hard at it and it fell. The lock broke—it was so old—and everything fell out of it. What a mess! There were all kinds of papers in there!"

"What were the important documents, Jean-Claude?" Verlaque could hardly sit still.

"Papers that a lawyer had written up, with the count, Philippe."

"What did they say?" Verlaque asked again.

"Well, I'll tell you, not because you're a judge but because I like you." Auvieux leaned forward and whispered, "They say that the count was my papa."

Verlaque's heart jumped. He remembered Marine telling him that Cosette and Jean-Claude's father had left quickly, just after Jean-Claude's birth. How beautiful and kind their mother had been. How Jean-Claude had followed the old man around everywhere. "Had you known this before?" Verlaque asked.

"No."

"You must be so pleased, no? You really liked the old count,

Philippe de Bremont, didn't you?" Verlaque noticed that he used the word "like," not "love." Did he love his own parents?

"Yes, I was so happy that I called François right away! And he was happy too. He said he'd come to Saint-Antonin and look at the documents with me, but when he did come, for Étienne's funeral, I had to tell him that the papers were missing. He said not to worry. We'd get them back. He hugged me. And now he's gone, and we can't even talk about it," Auvieux continued.

Worried that things were getting too sentimental, Verlaque asked, "Why in the world didn't you take the papers as soon as you found them, Jean-Claude?"

Auvieux looked surprised at the judge's question. "I told François on the phone that I would leave them there until we could look at them together with Étienne and Cosette."

"And François agreed to that?"

"Yes," the caretaker replied, a smile forming on his tanned face. "He said, 'You're the boss.' François used to call me that—the boss—whenever he was in Saint-Antonin. He'd say, 'You're the boss at the château—you know every square meter of this place.'"

"And Étienne? Was he kind to you?"

The caretaker said nothing, looking down at his hands again, and then picked up his spoon and began playing with the remaining mousse.

"Did Étienne know about those papers?"

"Yes," Auvieux answered, looking pale. "François told me that he would phone him the next day, on Saturday."

The chef, who had been watching the two diners through a small circular window in the kitchen door, thought he should present himself. It appeared that they were still trying to guess the identity of the green mousse, and the older, bigger guy looked quite distraught about it. The chef swung open the door and walked over to their table. "Have you enjoyed your dinner, gentlemen?" he asked.

Verlaque looked up at him, angry at first, but he quickly realized that the interruption might calm Auvieux down a bit. "Yes, it was fantastic. Congratulations," Verlaque said, holding out his hand. The young chef shook his hand, and Verlaque introduced himself and Auvieux. The caretaker was now feeling less on the witness stand and proudly gestured to Verlaque and said, "M. Verlaque is the head *juge d'instruction* in Aix!"

Verlaque smiled and looked at the chef, with one eyebrow raised. Although only in his early thirties, the chef had cooked for famous celebrities and politicians in both London and Paris, so a judge from a small city was no big deal, but he played along with the old guy, whom he had happily watched devour the five-course meal with a fervor normally associated with children and Nutella. "*Un juge!*" the chef replied. Not knowing what else to say, he repeated his opening gambit: "Welcome. I hope you were pleased with the meal this evening."

"I was, thank you," Verlaque replied. "And now, can you please settle a mystery for us? What is in the mousse?"

The chef beamed, realizing that he was right—they had been talking about the mousse. "Avocado."

"Seriously?" Verlaque asked. Auvieux slapped his head and laughed. He then said, "I recognized the taste! But to make a dessert out of an avocado!"

They chatted for a few more minutes, until the creator of the avocado mousse moved on to speak with the diners at the next table. Verlaque excused himself, to go to the toilets, and then discreetly paid the bill. On his way back to the table he looked at Auvieux, surprised, seeing him at a distance, at how big the man was. He settled once again at the table, and Auvieux asked if he could help pay the bill. "It's been taken care of, Jean-Claude," Verlaque said. "I enjoyed dining with you this evening," he added, in total sincerity. He then proposed that the caretaker leave a small tip, knowing that honest men like Auvieux liked to participate in the settling of accounts. Auvieux happily got out a ten-euro bill and left it under his coffee cup. The waitress, obviously a young girl from the village, who had had trouble opening the wine bottle and then had spilt a little on the table, would be thrilled.

The two men left the restaurant and walked down the slightly slippery rue Qui Monte. "There are no other papers that we could look at together, are there?" Verlaque asked.

"No!" Auvieux instantly replied. "Everything was in the suitcase, and now it's empty."

They chatted more about the dinner and Auvieux's plants. It was clear to Verlaque that the caretaker didn't want to speak anymore of the dead.

When they arrived at their cars, which were parked in spaces opposite the wine cooperative, they shook hands and said good night. Auvieux drove uphill toward Saint-Antonin, and Verlaque downhill toward the *route nationale* that would take him to Aix.

Halfway to Aix, Verlaque pulled into a closed gas station and called Yves Roussel. He recounted his dinner with Jean-Claude and the news that Jean-Claude was, if those papers really did exist, a Bremont.

"It's all starting to make sense finally," Roussel said. "Commissaire Paulik told me that when you questioned Auvieux he seemed to be hiding something."

"Yes, I think he was hiding the fact that he was Philippe de Bremont's bastard child."

"Maybe, but I think he's our number one suspect now. What

a motive! Kill both brothers and you get the château. It's almost as big as Dalí's château in Vauvenargues!"

"Picasso's," Verlaque corrected him. "Let's talk about this tomorrow, okay?" He had a gut feeling that Auvieux was hiding more than his ancestry. He hung up and called Marine's cell phone. He got her voice mail and decided not to leave a message. Marine had said that she was seeing Sylvie that evening, and it was still early enough to call. He dialed Sylvie's home number, and she picked up on the second ring. "Hallo?"

"*Salut*, Sylvie. I hope it isn't too late to call."

Sylvie, recognizing Verlaque's voice, said, "No, it's fine. Charlotte is sleeping, and I'm catching up on some bad television."

Verlaque snorted. He hated French television.

Sylvie ignored him and said, "I assume you're looking for Marine, but she left hours ago. She went to Le Mazarin, to meet Jean-Marc."

"Thanks," Verlaque said.

"*De rien*," Sylvie replied, trying to watch her program, a soap opera filmed in Marseille.

"But I just called her cell phone and there's no answer."

"She's probably sleeping," Sylvie said, yawning, as if the word "sleep" had suddenly given her the idea that she too was tired. She had a class at nine in the morning. Sylvie usually refused to accept any morning classes—her seniority allowed her that privilege—but by taking the nine o'clock class she had every Friday off, so she really couldn't complain.

"Thanks anyway," Verlaque said. "*Salut*."

"Yeah, bye," Sylvie answered. Feeling guilty that perhaps she was too obvious in her dislike of Verlaque, she then added, "Take care, Antoine." After Verlaque hung up, Sylvie yelled into the phone's receiver, "Snob!" She put down the phone, pulled the blanket around her on the sofa, and happily continued watching *Plus belle la vie*.

Verlaque called Jean-Marc's cell phone after getting the answering machine on Marine's home phone. "I was almost asleep, Antoine," Jean-Marc said groggily.

"Sorry. So you aren't at Le Mazarin anymore," Verlaque apologized.

"No, Marine didn't stay long, if you're looking for her. She ran away in a flurry, saying she was meeting someone—a man, I think she said. I thought she might be meeting you, as a matter of fact."

"No, we weren't meeting. Thanks . . . sorry to have wakened you."

"Is everything all right?"

"*Oui, oui*," Verlaque replied. "Just a communication breakdown."

"Okay, then, see you around," Jean-Marc replied before hanging up. He put his pillow over his head—his aged neighbor was watching some idiot soap opera with the volume turned up to maximum.

Verlaque put the car in gear and started driving, and then it dawned on him—Marine was with Arthur. He drove home slowly and illegally parked his Porsche in the cobbled square below his apartment, putting his badge in the window. He didn't feel like putting the car in the garage. He walked up the stairs to his fifth-floor flat—he never begrudged the stairs. In his teens and twenties Verlaque had been a natural athlete and more-than-adequate rugby player, but since moving to Aix and becoming a judge, his daily exercise routine consisted of climbing the stairs that led to his penthouse apartment, walking around Aix, and occasionally renting a sailboat in Marseille for the day.

He relit his 898; it had gone out in the car and he didn't want to waste time pulling over to relight it. He made himself an espresso, walked over to the stereo, put on a Miles Davis CD, and sat down in his brown leather club chair, which had been a gift from his parents for his thirtieth birthday. Verlaque drank his espresso in two sips and then took a long drag on his cigar, quickly blowing the smoke up toward the ceiling. He rested his head on the back of the club chair and closed his eyes. His legs were crossed and his right leg began to slowly rock back and forth to the music. He stayed like that for some time, smoking and thinking, until he realized that the CD had ended. He picked up the anthology of Philip Larkin's poems that was usually sitting beside his club chair and opened to a page at random. It was a short poem, and it immediately reminded him of his relationship with Marine. Only he couldn't figure out who would be reciting the poem: he or Marine.

> *Within the dream you said:*
> *Let us kiss then,*
> *In this room, in this bed,*
> *But when all's done*
> *We must not meet again.*
>
> *Hearing this last word,*
> *There was no lambing-night,*
> *No gale-driven bird*
> *Nor frost-enriched root*
> *As cold as my heart.*

He put the book down and closed his eyes for a few seconds, then got up and made himself another espresso and leaned against the kitchen counter, drinking it slowly. He smoked some more, and just where the end of the cigar starts to burn the smoker's mouth a bit, he paused and looked at the kitchen clock. It was not yet midnight but still felt too late to make any phone calls. He put his cup in the sink and set his cigar in an ashtray, said aloud, "Too bad," and dialed Jean-Claude Auvieux's phone number. Verlaque was thinking of Marine, bothered that she wasn't answering either of her phones. The knot in his stomach was getting tighter and tighter. The caretaker picked up the phone after several rings and said, "Hallo?"

"I'm so sorry to ring you so late, M. Auvieux," Verlaque said, realizing that he was now using a much more formal salutation in speaking to the caretaker than he had during their dinner.

Auvieux, hearing the judge's voice, said, "It's fine . . . I had only just gone to bed. Is there a problem?" he added, worried that perhaps he hadn't left a big enough tip at the restaurant or had done something wrong at dinner. His sister was always complaining that he ate too quickly.

"No, no, nothing's wrong, Jean-Claude. Is it nice and quiet there?"

"Ah oui," replied the caretaker. Verlaque didn't know if that was a good or bad sign.

He asked, "I've been sitting here, thinking, and I'd just like to ask you again about that night when Étienne died. I know that you were at your sister's and that the two of you ate together." Verlaque then paused, not wanting to alarm the caretaker, so he went on, lying, "And then, you watched a movie. You see, I'm pretty sure that a man I met in Cannes, a very rich and evil man, is lying about his alibi, and I'm trying to determine the time of Étienne's death. This man said that he too had watched *The Matrix*, it was on the television, wasn't it?" It was a very bad lie, one that made no sense, but it was the only thing that Verlaque could think of.

"Oh!" Auvieux answered, relieved that it was that man in Cannes who might be in trouble, and not himself. "We ate dinner and then around nine we started the movie. Yes, it was on TF1."

"So the movie would have ended around eleven, *non?* What time did you go to bed?"

"Ah! I fell asleep as soon as the movie started! I don't know why, but I was so tired!"

Verlaque had a lump in his throat, and he closed his eyes. "But, Jean-Claude, you told me all about the movie, remember?"

"Of course! I had seen it before, but I didn't want to upset Cosette so I didn't tell her that I had seen it. She has such a bad temper, and she was so excited about watching the movie with me."

Verlaque continued, but he was also conscious of being very anxious to get out of the apartment. He could not imagine Cosette Auvieux being excited about anything. Why hadn't Jean-Claude told him that he slept through the film? Did she put him up to it? Or was the caretaker playing dumb? He was a huge man, physically able to kill . . . and he was the first to arrive at the scene of the crime both times. "What time did you wake up? Were you still on the sofa in the morning?"

"Ah! How did you guess? I can assure you, *Monsieur le juge,* that I have never slept the entire evening on a sofa before! I don't know what came over me!" Auvieux didn't respect lazy people—and those who slept in, and on sofas, were lazy. He was sure that the judge would agree with him.

But the judge didn't say anything about lazy people sleeping on sofas and instead said, "Thank you so much, Jean-Claude." Verlaque picked up his car keys and apartment keys and asked one last question. "Jean-Claude, does Cosette know about the papers?"

Auvieux was silent, and then answered, "I told her . . . by mistake. When we were eating the *blanquette de veau*. Cosette was insulting Monsieur François, saying he was a good-for-nothing, and I told her that we had found the papers together, and that François was going to go to a lawyer on Monday with the papers. He wanted to help me. He was good, not like the other one."

"Do you mean Étienne?" Verlaque asked, stopping on the stairs.

"It's nothing! I shouldn't speak that way of the dead! Good night!" Auvieux abruptly hung up.

Verlaque threw his cell phone into his jacket pocket and grabbed his coat on the way out the door. Auvieux had been drugged—that's why he fell asleep as soon as the movie began, he thought as he ran down the stairs. He kicked himself for not driving to the château after he spoke with Sylvie and Jean-Marc on the phone. Marine said that she was meeting a man. And Verlaque now remembered that Arthur was away, in California. Was the man Jean-Claude? As soon as he got outside he called Paulik, immediately realizing that Paulik could never make it to Saint-Antonin in less than an hour from his home in Pertuis. As the commissioner's phone rang Verlaque whispered to himself, "She's the one. Stop it with all the others. Make up your mind, you fool."

A groggy voice answered, "Oui?"

"A thousand apologies, Bruno, but could you please call a policeman who's on duty tonight and have him meet me at the Château Bremont?" asked Verlaque, opening his car door at the same time and throwing himself inside.

Paulik put his head back on the pillow, looked at his bedside clock, and impatiently asked, "Who is this?"

"It's Verlaque!"

"Oh! Sorry!" Paulik answered, sitting up at once. Verlaque had never called him at home. "I'll call Flamant right away!"

"Good. I'll meet him there. Tell him to park his car on the road beside the château. I'll meet him there. We'll have to hope that Auvieux left the gates open. I don't want anyone to know that we are there. I'll explain later."

"Entendu!"

Chapter Twenty-five

❧

Marine blinked a few times, trying to adjust her eyes to the attic, with its oversized gilded mirrors, broken tables and chairs, and the stacks of ancient cardboard boxes that looked as though they could disintegrate at a touch. "Quoi?" Marine asked, when she didn't see Auvieux, but instead his sister, Cosette.

"What are you doing here?" Cosette Auvieux asked, slurring her words and stumbling a bit, having to reach out to an old coatrack to regain her balance. Marine noticed a half-full bottle and a porcelain teacup sitting on a wooden table next to Mme Auvieux. "The beautiful professor," she continued, looking at Marine with a clownlike smile.

"Cosette," Marine said, slowly moving toward the drunken woman and trying to make sense of the situation. "What are you doing here?"

"I came to get these," Cosette answered, her smile gone.

Marine looked at the bottle, a cheap whiskey, and then saw the stack of papers behind it. Cosette watched Marine and smiled again.

"I know about the papers, Cosette. Would you like me to look at them with you? I know a fair bit about the law. Perhaps I can help," Marine suggested.

"*Bien sûr!* I'm sure you'd like to see these papers!"

Marine stepped forward and Cosette yelled, "Stay there!" She tucked the papers against her small chest and scowled. Marine sat down on an old caned chair.

Marine wished that Verlaque or Paulik were with her, or on their way to Saint-Antonin, or somewhere nearby. The only thing she could do was to keep Cosette talking, and drinking. Perhaps if she drank more, she would pass out and Marine could call Verlaque or try to find Jean-Claude. She then realized that her cell phone was in her purse in her car, but the car keys were in her jacket pocket. Marine pointed to the whiskey and asked, "Could I have a drink too?"

"Of course. Excuse my bad manners in not offering you one first." Cosette reached down into an already open cardboard box and took out another porcelain teacup. She blew into the cup to get rid of some of the dust, and then wiped it on the bottom of her T-shirt. She poured Marine a bit of whiskey and gave it to her. Marine sipped a bit and her eyes watered as the alcohol burned her throat. The good whiskies that Verlaque bought didn't burn like this.

"Was Étienne reading the papers on Saturday night?" Marine asked.

"Yes, he was . . . but I didn't know he would be here! I drove as fast as I could from Cotignac, as soon as Jean-Claude told me about finding them. I always knew that we would find proof. Maman never lied."

"What exactly do the papers say, Cosette?"

"Can't you guess?"

"No, I'm afraid I can't," answered Marine, who suddenly saw the Annunciation's flying baby in her head. She had no idea why, but she couldn't get the flying baby out of her mind. "Is it about a baby?" she asked.

"Who told you?" Cosette hissed. Marine said a silent thank-you to the Flemish painter. She went on with her bluff. "Nobody told me, Cosette."

"I should have known—you were always a Little Miss Know-It-All. So you figured out Maman's secret . . . that Count Philippe de Bremont was Jean-Claude's father. And," she continued, tapping the papers, "Jean-Claude was to split the inheritance three ways, with Étienne and François."

Marine sat back and then muttered, "My God." She looked at Cosette, who was swaying back and forth. "And with Étienne and François dead . . . ," Marine added.

"Étienne got what he deserved! But I certainly didn't kill François!"

"You pushed Étienne!"

"He had the papers, and he was laughing! He said that he was going to destroy them . . . that nobody would believe me, a poor hairdresser from Cotignac!"

"Étienne wouldn't have said those things, Cosette."

"Are you calling me liar?!"

"You can't push someone out of an open window because he says things you don't like!"

"That's not all he said! Some of it I can't even repeat!" Cosette continued, "He said that François was stupid for wanting to help Jean-Claude and helping those models. He said that if François wasn't more careful, he would get himself killed. That's when I started to worry for François. I asked Étienne how he knew all this—and he laughed and said, 'A friend of mine in Marseille told me.'"

Marine closed her eyes and thought of her mother's words: "It's as if one brother received all the good and the other all the bad." She thought of the broken window and how François had taken the blame for it. Cosette, when they visited her in the Var, had said, "It always happened like that." Marine, as a teenager, had never been physically attracted to Étienne, but she was—if she was really honest with herself—impressed by his weird hyper-energy, his charm, and his title. The latter two attributes got them free drinks all night long at the disco in Aix.

"How was François helping Jean-Claude?" Marine asked, more interested in Jean-Claude than in any Marseille connection.

"François had been confiding in Jean-Claude, especially after they found the papers together. François had a big plan . . . and with Jean-Claude's help he could make it all happen."

"And so you and Étienne fought over the papers?" Marine asked, wanting to understand how Étienne fell.

Cosette nodded and rubbed her eyes with the back of her hand. "Yes! He kept insulting me, saying dirty things. He was standing right beside the open window, in the moonlight. But even as I was running toward him he wouldn't shut up. I meant to push him down on the floor, not out the window! He said that my mother was a whore, a cheap maid, and that's when I ran at him. I screamed when he fell out of the window, and I watched his face as he fell. It was horrible . . . because it looked like he was smiling. I ran downstairs, but I saw that he was dead. There were some papers outside, on the grass, and I picked them up and ran back into the château and cleaned up. I was so upset that I even swept and then wiped my fingerprints off the broom. I then shoved all the papers under one of the floorboards under that old bed. It's where I used to hide things when I was small. I didn't want to take them with me—I was so worried that someone would catch me on the way out. I closed up the place and ran to the *cabanon*. You remember it, *non?*"

Marine pictured the small, rough-hewn stone cabin. It was at the top of the hill behind the château, about five hundred meters past the small forest. As children Étienne and Marine had sometimes used the *cabanon* for their war games but were quickly evicted by François and Cosette, who used it for smoking cigarettes and doing who knows what else. Cosette took a drink of whiskey and continued, "François said that he loved me, once when we were in the *cabanon*. You can't believe it, can you?"

Marine looked at Cosette, and she remembered how often Cosette had been around François, trailing after him really. No, Marine thought, it was the other way around—François had followed Cosette.

"And then, after my mother died, and I moved to Cotignac to live with my aunt, François said that he would come for me, but he never did. He went to Paris to some second-rate private business school, and later moved to the Côte. And even then, when he was so close to Cotignac, he couldn't be bothered to call."

"You parked in the parking lot near the *cabanon* tonight," Marine interrupted. There was a foot path from the Bremont *cabanon* that led to a public hiking trail, which in turn finished at a small parking lot at the foot of mont Sainte-Victoire, and which the Aixois liked to keep secret. She should have told Antoine about it.

"Yes," Cosette replied.

Cosette drank some whiskey and continued, her voice cracking, "I loved François. I loved him ever since we were children.

He was so strong, so fast, so witty. Étienne told me the other night that I was just a pathetic hairdresser and could never be anything else. Nice, *hein*?"

Marine moved closer to Cosette and said, "That's awful, Cosette. It isn't true. That was a terrible thing for Étienne to say." Marine wanted to keep Cosette talking. She wanted to help her. "You said that your *maman* never lied. Did she tell you about Philippe de Bremont?"

"Maman told me everything on her deathbed, but I wasn't to tell anyone. Besides, I didn't have any proof." She drank and continued, "My father left just after Jean-Claude's birth, because he found Count Philippe de Bremont and my mother in the *cabanon* together." Cosette waited for Marine's reaction, which was what she had hoped for—the professor stared at Cosette, wide-eyed, her mouth open. Marine wanted to speak but could not. More memories swam in her head, these of Jean-Claude following the elderly Count de Bremont around the gardens and olive grove, the two inseparable, the old man teaching the eager young boy all that he knew about Provençal gardens. Why hadn't she remembered this before? While Marine and Étienne played, and François and Cosette did who knows what else, Jean-Claude had, unknowingly, been forming a rich attachment to his biological father. The count's older son, the father of Étienne and François, cared nothing for plants. He was always reading, Marine remembered. And here was the count's illegitimate son, not playing with the other children, but instead happily pruning olive trees and planting bulbs.

Cosette spoke quickly now, as if she had waited years to tell another person this story. She had probably rehearsed it over and over, Marine thought, for Marine had done the same thing when breaking up with Verlaque. "My father had had suspicions that they loved each other," Cosette continued, "and when he caught them together, he guessed who Jean-Claude's real father was. My father just left. He had class, *non*? He didn't raise a fuss. When my mother told me the story on her deathbed, I promised her that I would not repeat it. She told me that only after Étienne and François's father died was I to go to a lawyer. She said that Jean-Claude and I would be taken care of. But I knew I would need proof. Maman didn't think of that. She wasn't practical."

"How did you find out about the papers?"

"Jean-Claude found them, just last week. But François, big-mouthed idiot that he was, also told Étienne, who came in a hurry late Saturday night."

"None of you knew what was in that suitcase? Not even Étienne and François's parents?" Marine asked.

"No! That suitcase was out-of-bounds, surely, because it belonged to *le comte*. François's parents were too busy with their books to bother about things in this attic. Look at all this stuff," Cosette said, motioning around the room with her hand.

"François didn't tell Jean-Claude to take the papers and put them somewhere safe?" Marine asked.

"No, he trusted Étienne. Ha!"

Marine got up off the chair and walked toward Cosette, who was leaning on some boxes for support. "Let me help you," Marine said. "You need to sit down."

"No! Don't come near me!"

"Cosette! Don't be ridiculous!"

"Ridiculous? Ha! That's my life! Ridiculous! I could be living in Aix, like the rest of you! But Étienne turned everyone against me, especially his parents! He told them about me and François in the *cabanon*, and I was immediately shipped off to Cotignac! I owe my ridiculous life to him!"

Marine inched forward and said, "Cosette, I'm so sorry. It's not too late, you know. We need to go together to the police. You didn't intentionally kill Étienne, and you need to tell that to them, don't you see?" Marine moved closer and Cosette raised her hands in the air and hissed, "I told you, no!"

"Cosette, listen, please!"

"Listen to you? The lot of you! Born with silver spoons in your noble mouths! My brother's father was a count, and Étienne was going to take that away from me, and you're trying too!"

"Cosette, no!" A flash of red light burst in Marine's head, and she fell on the oak floor. Cosette Auvieux looked at the broken bottle of whiskey, still in her hand, and saw the spilled alcohol on the floor and the professor's bloodied head.

She took some time to drag Marine's limp body across the floor and heave it up onto the nineteenth-century wrought-iron bed—it wouldn't be right to leave her on the cold wooden floor. Marine looked odd, Cosette thought, with that big wooden crucifix hanging above her head.

She took a swig from a small emergency flask that she kept in the pocket of her sweater, careful not to put her head back on the bed. "Stay awake, stay awake," she muttered, for she had said too much to Marine Bonnet, and she needed to keep watch.

"François, you idiot," she mumbled, sitting down on the floor. "How could you be so nice to Jean-Claude but ignore me?" She got up and walked over to the light switch, flipped it off, and turned on her pocket flashlight, the same one she had used to get from the parking lot to the *cabanon*, and then to the château. She walked back to the bed, having to work her way around piles of boxes and furniture, and sat back down on the floor. Cosette didn't want to kill Marine Bonnet—Marine wasn't a snob like that judge who came to Cotignac. I've told the professor that I killed Étienne, she thought. And they will think that I killed François too. "No one will believe a hairdresser from Cotignac. I have no other alternative," she said aloud. No other alternative—it sounded quite posh. Taking another swig of whiskey, she then rested her head on the bed. Just a minute's rest, she told herself.

Chapter Twenty-six

❧

*I*t took no time to get out of Aix-en-Provence. Verlaque retrieved his car from the place de l'Archevêché and took his badge out of the car window. From there he drove quickly but carefully down the empty streets and was soon on la route de Cézanne. Once in the country he picked up speed—it was a road he knew well, and at this time of night chances were slight that he would come across another motorist. In the darkness he could not see the mountain or the wealthy homes that were privileged to have this street address, but the olive trees—as if keeping him company—shimmered and waved in his headlights.

Just as he was rounding one of the bends, at the preferred painting spot of the famous "father of cubism," five or six small moving objects came into view, just to the right of his car. He slowed down and moved the car over to the left a bit. They were walking in single file, and the last one looked up at Verlaque, its eyes red from the car's headlights. Verlaque slammed on the breaks. They were siblings—*marcassins*, or baby boars, and at the sound of the car's screeching brakes they ran off into the bushes. Verlaque slowly drove on, conscious that he needed to take two or three deep breaths to calm down.

Verlaque dipped through the hamlet of Le Tholonet, its sole café boarded up for the evening. He continued, speeding up on the straight stretches of road and slowing down on the curves, and crossed paths with no more baby pigs, nor motorists. As he approached Saint-Antonin he slowed his car down and finally came to a stop. He parked the car well before the Bremont estate—on the left-hand side, where there was a small clearing—locked the car, and started walking up the road. Up ahead, on the left, he saw Marine's Twingo and ran toward it, hoping, wildly, to find her in it, talking on her cell phone or looking around for Brazilian jazz CDs. But the Twingo was dark and locked. He turned around as he heard a car approaching from Aix. The lights flashed once, and he realized that it was Flamant. He motioned for the policeman to park behind his Porsche, and Flamant was out of his car and by Verlaque's side in seconds, a flashlight in hand.

"Let's go in quietly—the gate's open," Verlaque whispered. "Cosette Auvieux drugged her brother on the night that Étienne de Bremont fell. She's here, perhaps, with Professor Bonnet."

"Your . . . ?"

"Yes."

Flamant nodded, listening with his head down, trying not to make noise as they walked up the pebbled drive. They tiptoed past the caretaker's cottage and then walked on the grass until they were at the stone steps of the château. Verlaque lifted the château's wrought-iron door latch as quietly as he could, opening the front door just wide enough to slip through sideways. He knew, by instinct, to go straight to the attic. He pointed up the stairs, and Flamant nodded. They walked up quickly, on the balls of their feet. At each landing, Verlaque pointed to the next flight of stairs.

The door to the attic was, not surprisingly, closed, but no light shone underneath, which worried Verlaque. "On the count of three," he whispered to Flamant, who placed his hand on his gun holster, stepping aside to be ready to leap into the room. Verlaque thought he could remember that the light switch was just to the left of the door. He placed his right hand on the small porcelain doorknob and quietly turned it to the right, quickly opening the door and turning on the lights with his left hand. Both men squinted at first, and then took in the shapes of the various objects in the room—the familiar mirrors, chairs, and boxes. The only thing that was missing was Marine.

"Merde," Verlaque hissed. Flamant slowly walked around the attic, checking behind the larger pieces of furniture. Verlaque leaned against the wall and closed his eyes. "The caretaker's cottage," he said aloud. "Let's go." Was Cosette covering up for her brother? Cosette could have been the one who passed out—the way she drank marc it was entirely possible. Was Jean-Claude's shyness, and awkwardness, all just an act? François was killed by someone he knew, someone strong. Verlaque didn't tell Flamant that he now suspected the caretaker as well, but by the look on the policeman's face he knew that Flamant was thinking the same thing.

The two men skipped down the stairs, no longer worried about making noise. They ran out of the château and across the drive to Auvieux's cottage, which was dark. Verlaque was about to break in through a window when he saw that Flamant had opened the front door. "It's unlocked," the officer said, every bit as surprised as the judge. They turned on a light and ran up the stairs and saw a closed bedroom door.

"I have a gun in here," Auvieux yelled out.

"Jean-Claude, it's me, Antoine Verlaque. Open up!"

"Monsieur le Juge?"

Verlaque heard someone coming toward the bedroom door, and he motioned for Flamant to be ready with his gun.

The bedroom door opened to reveal the caretaker standing in his pajamas, holding his hunting rifle against his chest. He squinted as he asked, "Why didn't you knock? What time is it?"

"Why isn't your front door locked?" Verlaque demanded, out of breath. Flamant leaned against the wall and whispered, "*Putain.*"

"I never lock it. There's no point. This old place is so easy to break into. That's why I keep this," he said, lifting up his rifle a bit, "next to my bed."

Verlaque gently but firmly took Auvieux's shoulder and said, "I think your sister is here on the estate somewhere, with Professor Bonnet. Do you think you might know where they are?"

"Cosette?"

"Yes," whispered Verlaque. He went on quickly, "Jean-Claude, I think your sister may be in trouble. I'm afraid that she may be involved somehow with Étienne de Bremont's death. Do you know where they could be?"

Auvieux stood still, evidently stunned at the suggestion of his sister's possible connection to a murder. To get him moving, Verlaque suggested, "Perhaps somewhere where you guys played as kids?"

"I didn't play too much with the others," Auvieux answered. Seeing the frustration come over Verlaque's face, he added, almost in a whisper, "Cosette and François were always in the *cabanon*." At once Auvieux cringed, feeling that he was betraying his sister. He had always been frightened of Cosette.

"Can you show us where it is?" Flamant asked, staying calm.

"I'll get another flashlight," the caretaker answered as he turned and disappeared into his bedroom. He came back out almost immediately, dressed in his blue overalls. The three men ran down the stairs, and when Auvieux turned to shut the cottage door, Verlaque noticed that the caretaker still had his hunting rifle draped around his shoulder. "Do you need your rifle?" Verlaque asked. It was Flamant who answered, "It's in case we come across wild boars."

"Oui, les sangliers," Auvieux mumbled in agreement. The three men quickly walked around the cottage and through the olive grove, in single file, Auvieux leading with one of the flashlights, Verlaque behind him, and Flamant in the rear with the other. None of them spoke, and only when Verlaque tripped over a shallow hole and a mound of upturned earth did Auvieux turn around and whisper, "Sangliers." The olive grove was a small one, with less than one hundred trees, and it took ten minutes to walk through it. They crossed a small field and came to the forested hill that lay on the north side of the château. Auvieux pointed up the hill with his flashlight and whispered, "The *cabanon* is on the other side of this hill. There's a footpath through the forest. The boars will be out in the fields right now, looking for food and water—they won't be in the forest. They sleep there during the day."

"Let's hurry, then," Verlaque said. He was worried for Marine, and his worry became fear when he looked at Auvieux's pale, vacant stare. "We'll stop as soon as the *cabanon* comes into view," he added.

Flamant pointed his light up the hill, and they headed off, climbing quickly and purposely. The path was well traveled, and miraculously there weren't any branches in their way. Auvieux must clear this regularly, Verlaque thought. When they were almost at the top, Verlaque stumbled again, cursing as he balanced himself. He had tripped over a log and hadn't hurt himself but had made a fair bit of noise in the silent forest. They arrived at the top of the summit in just over five minutes, and Auvieux stopped and pointed to the *cabanon* that sat in the middle of a lavender field about two hundred meters off. A very faint light shone in the old stone building.

Verlaque whispered, "The policeman will go first. We won't go straight through the field but around its edge, on the right, and sneak up on the north side of the *cabanon*, since that side doesn't have a window. I'll follow Officer Flamant, and, M. Auvieux, you stay here and keep watch."

"I have to go too," Auvieux argued.

"We aren't even sure that they are in there," Flamant answered. "You'll help us more here, protecting us while we're exposed in the middle of that field of lavender." Flamant then nudged Verlaque and they were off, leaving the caretaker at the edge of the forest with his shotgun.

Cosette Auvieux heard the noise in the forest and had peered out of the *cabanon* window just as the men reached the crest of the hill and came out of the woods. The judge was with another man, probably a cop. She'd have to act quickly. A knock on the head with a shovel, and she could say that the professor had fallen and hit her head. The professor was very weak, and the job would be fast and easy. The walk hadn't been long, but it was excruciatingly painful for Marine, who had stumbled and fallen over what seemed to her to be hundreds of holes dug by *sangliers*. The walk, which would take Cosette alone less than twenty minutes, took Marine and Cosette over an hour.

She ducked her head back and turned around and looked at Marine. Marine, with an aching head that felt worse than the morning after a party at Sylvie's, looked up at Cosette and realized that she had been startled by something.

Cosette grabbed the shovel, and Marine looked at her not with pleading eyes, which is what Cosette had expected. But her fear was mixed with something else—anger. Marine opened her mouth to talk but there was only dryness, and no words would come out. The light from the candle lit up the professor's face in an eerie way, thought Cosette. She wasn't surprised to find candles in the *cabanon*—she and François had always made sure that there were a few. They would stick them in a wine bottle like the one that was still here. It wasn't their bottle—it belonged to the former gardener, who used to stash wine in the *cabanon*. Its faded date reminded Cosette of the last night she had spent with François. She paused and looked down at the professor and said, "I don't know why you insist on wearing that bloody rosary." At that moment Marine reached up and felt the big wooden beads around her neck. She had grabbed the rosary just as they were leaving the attic, and Cosette had only noticed it when they were walking through the olive orchard. Marine didn't know why she had taken it: perhaps it reminded her of Étienne, and now she was about to die, like him. Cosette walked toward Marine with the shovel in her hand and lifted it up to shoulder height. Marine closed her eyes and tried shrinking into the cold stone wall, when someone suddenly banged on the door.

A voice shouted at them. The voice was deep, and Marine thought it asked after Cosette, telling her to unlock the *cabanon*.

Cosette whirled around and faced the door, not moving. She still had the shovel in her hands, and Marine saw that this was her only chance. Cosette was distracted and, for a few seconds, had forgotten about her hostage. Marine kicked the back of Cosette's shins, causing the woman to fall on her knees. Marine then struggled to her own knees and whisked the rosary off of her neck and flung it around Cosette's. Marine pulled as hard as she could, amazed that she was almost able to stand, even more amazed that she was capable of hurting another human being. Cosette Auvieux shrieked, and struggled to breathe, trying to grab Marine's arms, trying to unclench them. Marine closed her eyes and pulled harder, but she wouldn't be able to hold on much longer. She tried calling out and managed to mumble, "Help me," and at that moment the small window crashed, and she saw the butt of a gun breaking glass. The gun changed direction and Marine saw the barrel pointing straight at her. She let go, and Cosette collapsed to the floor, the rosary still dangling around her neck. Marine slid down against the stone wall and started weeping. A voice hollered, "Marine, can you unlock the door?" and she realized that the gun belonged to someone she knew, probably a policeman. She crawled on all fours and unhooked the lock. Verlaque and another man came rushing in. "Help her, please," Marine whispered hoarsely. Flamant and Verlaque leaned down over Cosette Auvieux, who had retched but was now bent on hands and knees, swearing fiercely. Verlaque went over to Marine and held her in his arms.

Flamant took a pair of handcuffs out of his jacket and put them around Mme Auvieux's wrists. "I'll call an ambulance," Verlaque said, and he got out his cell phone and dialed 18, directing them to the public parking lot for hikers, which he guessed was just on the other side of the lavender field. He then called the police station and asked for backup, directing them to the same parking lot and describing the *cabanon*.

Jean-Claude Auvieux had run to the *cabanon* door when he saw the policeman break the glass in the window. His first thought was of the broken window, which would now need repairing, but then he remembered that his sister was in there with the professor. He had had trouble falling asleep earlier that evening, after he had hung up the telephone with the judge. The judge's questions had got him thinking about the night in Cotignac and wondering how he could have possibly fallen asleep so easily. He remembered the drink that Cosette had brought him—it was China tea, and he only liked herbal tea before bed. But she had insisted that he drink it. He stood outside the *cabanon* doorway and saw the policeman put handcuffs on his sister, and he saw the judge holding the professor. She looked like she was sleeping. He hoped that she was sleeping, and not the other thing, like Étienne, and then François. He jumped when his sister looked up at him and hissed, "You told them!"

Auvieux shook his head back and forth. "No, no. I didn't tell them anything."

Verlaque, who was holding Marine, rested his back against the wall and asked, "Told us what?"

"About the papers in the suitcase."

"No," Verlaque lied. "I figured that out for myself, with the professor's help."

Marine opened her eyes and moved slightly, blinking twice. Verlaque held her close, rubbing her forehead. He then looked into the open doorway of the *cabanon* and saw that Jean-Claude Auvieux was now sitting on the ground, his knees drawn up to his head, and his head resting on his arms, looking down at the red earth. The caretaker no longer looked like the middle-aged man that he was but like a boy, the same boy who had followed the Comte de Bremont around the gardens and orchards. Cosette opened her mouth to speak, but Verlaque interrupted. "Shut up," he demanded. They would get all the information they needed later, back in Aix. For now he just wanted Jean-Claude Auvieux to be left alone.

Chapter Twenty-seven

Xavier Régis put his sneakered feet up on the coffee table at Souleiado Films, took a sip of the machine-made cappuccino, and started watching the unedited footage from Étienne de Bremont's last film. Xavier, an intern, had been thrilled to film the bird's-eye view of Marseille with Étienne in a helicopter: the green-blue sea to the south and white rocky hills to the north. The sea and the rocks and the city's million-plus inhabitants were protected by the Baroque basilica on the hill, the one that Xavier and his buddy Georges had once visited, taking the tourist train when they were mildly stoned. Xavier had never been in a helicopter and was surprised that Souleiado Films could afford one. He had said so to Etienne, who, he now remembered, had laughed and replied, "Someone owed me a favor."

The uncut film was strangely silent at first—the soundtrack hadn't been added to that section yet. Five minutes into it the interviews started: the camera was in the Belle de Mai neighborhood, on the very streets that Xavier walked daily. Various policemen were interviewed—some in uniform, others not—followed by conversations with criminals and small-time hustlers. The location then changed from working-class neighborhoods to police stations to multimillion-dollar villas overlooking the sea. After an hour's worth of footage, Fabrizio Orsani came into view. Xavier sat forward in his chair, watched the scene, swore under his breath, and then rewound the film and watched it again. Orsani was walking through a pristine garden, blaming a recent murder on a rival gangster. He looked, and sounded, every inch a mob leader, at least to Xavier's inexperienced eyes and ears: the grimacing and scowling face, the gravelly voice. A familiar voice from behind the camera began to speak, and Xavier turned up the volume. It was Étienne de Bremont, who then came around from behind the camera and up to Orsani, taking his arm and leading him through the garden, whispering in his ear. Whether Bremont had forgotten that the camera was still rolling, or didn't care, was unclear to Xavier—at any rate he was evidently getting Orsani to do a second take. Orsani laughed and said, "Oh, I understand. Sort of like this?" and he gently took a rose in his hand. Once Étienne was back behind the camera, Orsani spoke lovingly of the olive trees and their beautiful bounty each year and how they reminded him of Corsica. The camera followed Orsani into his well-appointed home, filled with tasteful abstract paintings and African sculptures. The two men stood in front of a large painting, and Étienne said something that Xavier couldn't make out, despite rewinding the film and listening to it again. But he was fairly sure of Orsani's reply: "Thanks to my funding, your pretty film is going to get made."

Xavier knelt down, tied his dreadlocks back with a rubber band that he kept around his wrist, and rummaged through a box until he found a tape labeled "Edited, version one." He took the raw footage out of the player and inserted the new one. It didn't take much time—perhaps an hour or so—before Xavier saw that the scenes with Étienne's voice in the background had been removed. Orsani looked, and sounded like, a retired village doctor or civil servant. He spoke of his contributions to museums, an orphanage in Romania, the Marseille hospital. The murders that had been linked to Orsani, the sixteen-year-old prostitutes who worked for him near the opera house in Marseille, the car bombings—all the crimes that had been revealed by policemen and witnesses in the uncut version no longer seemed as clearly connected to Orsani. Xavier got up, tossed his plastic cup into the garbage can, and picked up the telephone, dialing his boss's office number. "M. Mad," he said. "I think you'd better come into the screening room for a bit. You won't need to watch very much."

Madani arrived in no time—he was hoping that this film would be another award winner—and Xavier showed him certain footage in the uncut version. Madani stared at Xavier in disbelief. "Why was Étienne redoing those takes? The first ones were great: Orsani seemed totally unaware of how brutish he sounded. And what's with Orsani's film-funding comment? Was Étienne's film going to be funded with mafia money?"

Xavier got up and took out the first video and then put the edited version in the player. He turned to his boss and said, with a flourish of his hand, "Watch and be amazed." Madani rolled his eyes toward the ceiling and said, "Just play it, would you, Xavier?" and they watched the edited film in silence.

After some time had passed Madani told Xavier to stop the film, and he turned on the lights. "I'm in shock. I had a feeling that they knew each other, but I never imagined that it went this far. It's hard to tell where Étienne was going with the film, since he only had the chance to edit a small part. But preferring those second, coached takes to the raw first ones . . . What was he doing?"

Xavier nodded. "You didn't know, boss?"

"No," Madani replied. "I had no idea. Étienne insisted on filming much of it alone, remember? Or if he needed a sound man, he would pick various students who were here on work terms, never the same one twice, which at the time I did think was odd." Madani stared at the screen, now white.

"Yeah, I remember," said Xavier. "I thought that he was mad at me. He only asked me to film with him a couple of times, and that was just the scenic stuff."

Madani said nothing and put his chin in his hand. He looked at Xavier and said, "I'd better call Aix. Don't tell anyone about this. Hide this footage back under your desk." Xavier stood up, and Olivier Madani looked at his young intern, a boy he had grown to like, and one who had been given nothing but obstacles in life—orphaned by ten, raised by an aunt who already had six kids, black, dreadlocks!—and now had dreams of being a filmmaker. "Come on, kiddo. Let's go see what the plat du jour is at Lulu's. My treat."

"Yes, sir!" Xavier said, smiling and saluting Madani. Xavier looked at his boss, a man he had grown to like, and one who had only been given blessings in life—a beautiful wife, born to wealthy parents who were both still alive, white, and a successful filmmaker. But that haircut!

They stopped by the stairs, and Xavier looked out of the window, as he always did. When he had first come to Madani's film company, he had expected to look out on another building or factories or a cheap apartment building. What he saw had stunned him, and now he looked out the window whenever he passed it. Madani watched Xavier and smiled. "That's the neighborhood's biggest secret. They've been there for centuries. Marseille always does this to you, just when you don't expect it—when the traffic is awful and the streets are looking too dirty and noisy—then you get delivered one of these bombshells, and it reminds you why you are here and why this town is so magical."

Xavier got closer to the window, wanting to see the details. He thought of Étienne and the film footage he had just watched. "You never know, do you?" he said into the air.

"No, you don't. Life is full of surprises," Madani answered, thinking of Étienne de Bremont's sudden death. He too leaned closer in, and the two men silently watched the black-robed nuns of the convent attached to the Basilique du Sacré-Coeur pick fruit in their walled orchard.

The late afternoon sun came in through the window from the west, and Verlaque rushed over and pulled down the blind. But the sun had woken up Marine, who, after being taken to the emergency room, bandaged up, and then discharged, had been brought back downtown just before dawn by Verlaque and Flamant. Verlaque didn't want her staying at the Aix hospital—it had a lousy reputation. He'd pay for a private nurse if he had to. Once Flamant was gone, Verlaque carefully undressed Marine and put her in a pair of striped Hermès pajamas that his mother had bought for him, as she did every Christmas. He had a drawer full of them and even more, never worn, in a box. He had considered putting them on auction at the next police fund-raiser.

Marine turned her head toward Verlaque and saw that she wasn't in her apartment but in his. "How long have I been asleep?" she asked.

"Twelve whole fucking hours," Sylvie bellowed, coming into the room carrying a coffee for Antoine.

Marine smiled but she knew not to laugh—that would hurt too much. "Take it easy," Antoine demanded. "You not only got a great blow to the head, but you're pretty bruised on your right side. Did you fall down?"

"Yes," Marine answered, trying to sit up a bit. "I kept falling in the olive grove, and I think I may have slipped down some of the château's stairs."

"Why didn't you run for it when you were walking to the *cabanon*?" Sophie asked.

"Cosette had a knife," Verlaque answered.

Marine looked at Sophie and said, "When we left the château, I saw that Jean-Claude's car still wasn't back, and so I thought that when we got to the *cabanon* I could at least try screaming. There's that parking lot nearby, where teens sometimes hang out."

"Well, while you've been sleeping I've been trying to be social with the judge," Sylvie said, handing Verlaque his coffee.

Verlaque took the coffee and smiled, acknowledging Sylvie's attempt to humor her friend. "Cosette Auvieux confessed to pushing Étienne de Bremont," Verlaque said, thinking that Marine would want an update. "Commissioner Paulik is with her now. She flatly denies killing François de Bremont, which would have been impossible anyway. She isn't strong enough to strangle an athlete, and she has the whole town of Cotignac as her alibi."

"Polo?" Marine asked, her voice strained. "The casino?"

"No, every single polo player has an alibi, except for one—but he's new to the club and barely knew François and had no motive. The Cannes casino guys are all clean too—it was so early in the morning that they were either at home, getting ready for work, or still at work, getting ready to come home."

Marine requested a pillow, which Antoine put behind her head. She licked her lips and asked for some water, and she drank more than she thought she could. "How about an espresso?" she then asked.

"No, how about more water?" Verlaque answered. Marine looked to the bedside table and saw a vase full of yellow daffodils and a box of locally made chocolates. She smiled and said, "Thank you, Antoine."

Verlaque laughed, embarrassed. "They're not from me, sorry. They're from Yves Roussel. He brought them himself."

"How sweet."

Verlaque grunted. "Yeah, sweet." He shifted a bit in his chair and stared at Marine.

"There's something else, isn't there?" she asked.

"Yes, I had a phone call from Maria Pogorovski. Can you handle more information?"

"Yes, go on."

"Mme Pogorovski left a message on my cell phone, so I called her back after I put you to bed, only to find out that she had driven to Aix early this morning." Verlaque's aching back reminded him that he very much wanted to be in bed, under a feather quilt, with Larkin's poetry in his hands. He yawned and continued, "We met at the office."

"Le Mazarin?"

Verlaque smiled. "No, my office—not yours. She told me that she was tired of the sleepless nights, and she couldn't get the image of Natassja Duvanov out of her head. The models were in fact being used as high-end prostitutes, as we suspected. But Natassja Duvanov was the prize. One hundred thousand euros a night, reserved for Pogorovski's friends when they were in New York. Natassja and the other girls were told that the escorting was a temporary arrangement, a sort of payment for their visas, which Lever Pogorovski arranged. But of course that was a lie. Mme Pogorovski claims that she had suspected the girls were being used for sex, but they wouldn't talk to her about it. When Natassja

Duvanov committed suicide, Mme Pogorovski couldn't stand it anymore. She met with François, who confirmed her suspicions. François had known about the prostitution, but at first he turned a blind eye to it because it happened only rarely. But the prostitution ring flourished, and when he found out that Natassja was being presented as the trophy, he flew to New York to try to help her."

Marine licked her lips and asked, "Was he killed for that? That was back in January."

"No, he was going to be sent to Spain, but then he tried to help another model get back to Russia, and was found out. Mme Pogorovski was there when François and Lever Pogorovski were arguing: François was wild and threatened to go to the police. She understood that her models were being forced more and more into prostitution, and she went straight to her lawyer. They were preparing her dossier together when she got the news that Tatiana, that model you spoke to, was badly beat up."

"What?" the two women asked in unison.

"Someone was watching her speak to you the other day on the beach."

Marine thought instantly of a man who had hopped off his bench and jogged in the same direction as Tatiana. She then closed her eyes and groaned, "The baby?"

"She lost it, I'm afraid." The three were silent. "Maria Pogorovski has wanted out of the marriage for years, and only now is she free do to so."

"Why now?" Sylvie asked.

"Pogorovski had something on her brother, who's a politician in Russia—some crooked real estate deals years back, which Pogorovski had the proof of. Sadly, the brother and his wife died last weekend in a car accident, so now Mme Pogorovski is free."

"This Russian guy can't be nailed on any of this, can he?" Sylvie asked.

Verlaque shook his head. "Whoever killed François covered their tracks well, and I doubt we'll ever be able to connect it to Pogorovski. But Maria Pogorovski is willing to testify against her husband regarding the prostitution ring."

Marine looked up at Verlaque. "Last night Cosette hinted at a project between François and Jean-Claude."

Verlaque nodded and answered, "François wanted to restore the château at Saint-Antonin and turn it into a luxury hotel, keeping Jean-Claude on as a partner—he'd be head of the buildings and grounds. There would be a few big deluxe rooms and an organic garden that would provide the fruit and vegetables for what they hoped would be a Michelin-starred restaurant. François needed a third business partner since he was cash poor, so he went to the Pogorovskis. Maria Pogorovski was present at the meeting, and she said that her husband flatly refused to take part in any business deals with someone who was hopelessly addicted to gambling. That was when François blew up and threatened to blow the whistle on Pogorovski's prostitution ring, calling him a pimp. It was a crazy act on the part of François, calling someone that powerful a pimp, but it confirmed Maria's suspicions that the girls were being mistreated."

"Il était perdu," Sylvie mumbled.

"Yes, he was a lost soul. His gambling addiction, combined with his wild temper and trying to help the models, sealed his own fate. Pogorovski threw him out, escorting him to the front door and into his car. That was the last time Maria Pogorovski saw François—he was killed a few days later. Lever Pogorovski had tossed aside the portfolio that François had prepared on the hotel project, and Maria picked it up and put it into her purse.

Over the next few days she read it. She said that François had done an amazing amount of work on the project, and she saw great potential in François's idea."

Verlaque saw that Marine was fading and lost in thought. "There is some good news in all this," he offered.

"I think we could use some of that," Sylvie said.

Verlaque gave Marine some water. "Since François's death, Maria Pogorovski said she couldn't get the hotel out of her head—that's one of the reasons why she drove to Aix this morning. She's touring the château grounds with Jean-Claude tomorrow. If she likes what she sees, and I think she will—Jean-Claude has kept that place in great shape despite the lack of money—she'll invest in it. She is wealthy in her own right, apparently. She's also taking in her dead brother's children, who are in their midtwenties. The amazing thing in all this is that her niece trained in the hotel business and speaks five languages, and the son, apparently he's a big guy, and guess what his passion is?"

Marine closed her eyes and whispered, "Plants."

Sylvie's eyes began to water.

"Right. Incredible, isn't it?" Verlaque replied. He tried to ignore the women's emotions and continued: "Maria Pogorovski was exhausted when I saw her but ecstatic at the same time. She'd like to sell the agency and retire to the country—Saint-Antonin, that is—and help run the hotel. She'll be able to be with her nephew and niece. They're her only family. Once all this dies down, she's taking her nephew and niece to New York, to visit luxury hotels and restaurants, and she's meeting up with some American guy who's writing a book about Natassja Duvanov."

Verlaque saw that Marine hadn't been listening.

She then asked, frowning, "Did Maria also come to Aix to plea-bargain with you?"

"Well done," Verlaque answered, staring at Marine. He glanced over at Sylvie, who had the smile of a proud mother on her face. "She came to us with information about her husband in exchange for police protection and immunity from prosecution. Paulik and Roussel are with her now."

"I'm so sorry, François," Marine whispered, and she slid back down on the pillow.

"Yes," Verlaque said. "It seems that we mixed up the brothers. One brother received all the good, and the other all the bad. They both had wild tempers, that's for sure, but François's intentions were honorable."

"François's funeral?" Marine asked, her voice barely audible.

"The doctor said you'll be able to go. It's on Monday. It's being held in the church in Le Tholonet, since there isn't a church in Saint-Antonin. Most of the polo players are coming, and Maria Pogorovski has arranged for the models and François's acquaintances from the Côte to come. It will be a packed little church."

Marine nodded and smiled. "Good," she said, and she closed her eyes. Verlaque pulled the sheet up under her chin and kissed her forehead and signaled to Sylvie to leave the room with him. As they were at the door Marine murmured, "He was an honorable man after all."

"Yes," Verlaque answered. "Flawed but honorable."

Chapter Twenty-eight

※

April 23 began with much promise—a bright blue sky with no wind. At 8:30 in the morning it was warm enough that Verlaque could open his living room windows. Little *martinets*, with their pointed wings, were circling in the sky high above his windows, on their way to and fro and in and out of the cathedral's octagonal-shaped steeple. He tried to think of their name in English—swifts, perhaps. The doorbell for the building's front door rang, and he buzzed in his visitor, saying "Last floor" into the intercom.

He had a few minutes while his visitor walked up the five flights of stairs to his apartment, and he used those to check on Marine. She was still sleeping and hadn't seemed to change position all night, her hands above her head. She had always slept like that. He had set up a bed for himself on the living room sofa and had fallen asleep immediately, but after Olivier Madani's phone call his sleep had been a troubled one.

Paulik walked into the apartment, shook hands with Verlaque, who was closing the bedroom door, and handed the judge a bag. "I come with information and brioches," he said.

"Great, thanks for these, and thanks for coming on a Saturday," Verlaque said, taking the bag and looking at it. "Where did you pick these up?"

"Michaud was too far out of my way. They're from the *boulangerie* around the corner," Paulik answered. "By the way, I finally heard from Pellegrino just this morning."

"Ah! Let me make us some coffee and you can tell me what the polo player had to say," Verlaque said, turning toward the shiny red Gaggia espresso machine and smiling to himself, happy that the commissioner was comfortable in his apartment: Paulik was touring the living and the dining rooms that opened onto the kitchen, his hands in his pockets, humming an aria. He paused now and then to look at a book title or pick up an object. He walked over to look at a small oil painting of Venice—the city and Grand Canal bathed in a mauve and golden light—that hung above the dining room table. He leaned in to get a closer look, and then turned to Verlaque and asked, "Hey, this isn't a . . . ," he paused, unable to remember the Venetian's name.

Verlaque laughed. "No, it isn't a Canaletto. But it was done by a student of his. It was my grandmother's favorite painting." Paulik whistled and looked at the painting again, and then turned to Verlaque and said, "Pellegrino wasn't at the morning computer session."

Verlaque handed him his coffee. "I was afraid of that," he replied. "Where was he?"

"Testing a horse."

"What?"

"Yeah, riding a horse to evaluate it for professional polo matches. He says he does it from time to time, and gets paid a thousand euro cash for it. The horse's owner was only available Wednesday morning, and since Pellegrino wasn't on beat duty, he rode the horse and then slipped into the computer class after lunch."

"Alibis?"

"Yes, I called both the horse's owner, and a stable hand at the polo club. He was there."

"Good for him. I'm relieved," Verlaque said. "Was he of further use? Since he's been forgetting to tell us stuff?"

"Ha! Yes. He told me who the Cannes polo team was playing on the afternoon that François de Bremont tried to rig the game. The game was against Monaco, archrivals of the Cannes club. They are unofficially owned by the owner of the Monte Carlo Casino, who hates Pogorovski."

"Why didn't Pellegrino tell us that when we were at the polo club?"

"He claims he didn't connect the fact that they were playing Monaco. It's only in the past few days that rumors have been swimming around the polo club, and in Cannes, that François, in payment for throwing the game and having the Cannes team lose, would have had his debts, or a big part of them, cleared at the casino." Paulik paused to sip some of his coffee, and then asked Verlaque, "What do we do about Pellegrino? He lied and was moonlighting."

Verlaque said nothing and only stared at Paulik over his reading glasses. He then asked, "What did *you* say to him?"

"I gave him hell."

Verlaque laughed. He was so relieved that Marine was safe, he was having a hard time caring about Eric Pellegrino. "Good! Maybe we can come up with some creative punishment. He could teach orphans polo; or he could come to Aix and clean the police stables."

Paulik's cell phone rang, and Verlaque took the opportunity to check on Marine. She was still sleeping in the same position, with the white linen sheets tucked up under her chin and her auburn hair spread out over the pillow. He closed the bedroom door and walked back to the living room, where Paulik had just got off of the phone.

"That was Monsieur le Procureur. He said that the models were interviewed yesterday, and the interviews will continue today. They're giving us more information about François de Bremont than anyone else has. Roussel says that the escorting and sleeping with clients began slowly and was initially discreet."

"Did François go along with all this?"

"The models claim that François wasn't happy about it but didn't object, either—he needed the money and Pogorovski loved having a count on board—it gave him prestige and legitimacy. But when the sex was made mandatory, and one of the girls was roughed up by a Russian client, François hit the roof. One of the house staff apparently told Inès that he overheard the last argument between François and Lever Pogorovski during which François threatened to go to the police and expose the prostitution ring."

"*Bon.* Then the account is consistent with Maria Pogorovski's story. Listen, would you mind hanging out here for a half an hour, until Marine's friend Sylvie gets here? I just have one last visit to make."

"Fine, I'll start on some paperwork," Paulik replied.

Verlaque opened the bag and offered a brioche to the commissioner.

Both men took a bite, saying nothing. Paulik chewed for a bit, took another bite, and then frowned. "I'm sorry, sir."

"What?"

"I should have gone to Michaud."

Verlaque smiled. "Yeah, these are pretty bad."

. . .

Jean-Claude Auvieux hadn't been able to sleep after they took Cosette away; he kept rehearsing the evening's events in his head: the race through the olive grove and forest, the professor's bloodied hair, his sister handcuffed.

No, he hadn't seen the green Twingo parked under the pine trees, for a fat cypress tree hid it from view for those coming from the east. That wasn't his fault, surely? He remembered that he had opened the gates with his key and then left them open, too tired to get out of his car again and lock them. Besides, he rarely locked the gates when he was on the premises. He had parked his car in front of his cottage and looked up at the *bastide*, as he did every evening, but it was dark and quiet—that's why he didn't know that the professor was in the attic with Cosette. Or perhaps they were already at the *cabanon*? He didn't want to judge to be angry with him, like Étienne had so often been.

He continued his tour of the olive grove, inspecting the trees. The wind had begun to pick up, and it was suddenly bitterly cold—strange when the morning had been so mild. He left the orchard and went into his cottage, turning on the lights and putting the kettle on to make a tisane. A little herbal tea would be good; he'd drink it while looking at the fancy gardening book that Monsieur François had given him for Christmas. He closed his eyes as he thought of François de Bremont, who had been so easy to talk to, much like the old count, Philippe. "Mon père," he said aloud, and smiled.

A car honked its horn, and the caretaker jumped. He quickly walked out, around the cottage to the pebbled drive, where he saw the judge getting out of his old-fashioned car. Auvieux smiled nervously and held out his hand. "Hello, Monsieur le Juge. How is Professeur Bonnet today?"

"She's fine, Jean-Claude, thank you. I have never seen anyone sleep so much."

The caretaker stood still, unsure of why the judge had come. Verlaque broke the silence by saying, "Ever since last Sunday, there's been something bothering me. I felt that you weren't being entirely truthful, as if you were leaving something out. I now know that you had seen the contents of the suitcase, but even the other night at dinner I felt there was more to it than your birth certificate. Is there? You specifically said, 'I didn't take anything!' Was there money in the suitcase?"

Auvieux swallowed and replied, "Not money. There were other papers in the suitcase, and I took them. They were old . . . and I couldn't read them. I just wanted to look at them, here in my kitchen where the light is better."

"Aha. Should we go inside and talk about it?"

"All right," Auvieux replied. As they walked to the cottage he said over his shoulder, "I meant to put them back! Really I did!"

The two men walked into the kitchen. Auvieux pulled out a chair for Verlaque. "I'll go and get them. I've been so careful with them. You'll see! They're fragile, that I know for sure."

In no time Auvieux was back, holding white cotton gloves for Verlaque. "I've seen them wear these in the movies," Auvieux explained. "I bought them in town."

Verlaque nodded and put the gloves on. Auvieux opened a small folder and pushed the contents toward Verlaque, who put on his reading glasses and looked, without touching, the first page. "It's a letter," Verlaque said.

"Yes, sir. Look at the date."

Verlaque leaned in and saw the date: 1776. "Ma chère Sophie," he read aloud and went on to read the first paragraph to himself. Verlaque quickly but carefully turned the page to find the end of the letter and the sender's name. "Mirabeau!" Verlaque exclaimed, whistling and looking over at Auvieux, who was now smiling. "This is one of Mirabeau's love letters to Marie Thérèse de Monnier! He called her Sophie! I've only heard about these letters. Is it erotic?"

The caretaker blushed. "Oui, Monsieur."

"Jean-Claude, this belongs in a museum."

"The Louvre?"

"Perhaps not the Louvre," Verlaque said, smiling. "I believe that Mirabeau's affairs are kept in the musée Carnavalet in Paris. You should take it to them."

"I was going to put it back in the suitcase, but then we went up to the attic together and found the suitcase empty, I didn't know what to do. I've been so careful with the pages."

"I'm sure you have. Mirabeau . . . Wow! . . . The great statesman, diplomat, and lover."

"Oh, yes! But funny they should name our famous street in Aix after a traitor!" Auvieux said, and then quickly added, "I was a good history student in school, and so I remember our teacher said that about him! A traitor to the revolution!"

"That was your teacher's opinion, but it's not mine. After the revolution, Mirabeau wanted a constitutional monarchy like they have in England." Verlaque saw the look of puzzlement on the caretaker's face. "That's a king and queen with a parliament. Too bad they didn't listen. I've always thought it a good system. If this letter is part of that series of love letters to Sophie, it's very precious."

Auvieux shuffled and looked at the floor. "I have to give it up, don't I?"

"It's up to you. But you can be proud to do so. The museum may even put a label beside the letter, saying something like 'A generous gift of Jean-Claude Auvieux.'"

"That's all right, then! I'd be happy to see that."

"Think about it. I'll call you later next week. I could go up to Paris with you if you like. I'll leave you in peace now." Verlaque stood up and put his hand on the caretaker's shoulder and smiled. "Take it easy, Jean-Claude. Get some rest."

Verlaque left, taking one more look at the mountain, a dazzling white so pure against the blue sky that it almost looked two-dimensional, a backdrop. In the cottage Auvieux sang to himself and got a tea bag out of the earthenware jar where he kept them. He realized that he hadn't been to the count's grave, nor his mother's, in months. In the afternoon he would go to the small Saint-Antonin cemetery, which stood at the foot of the mountain, and tidy up the plants.

Murder in the Rue Dumas
M. L. LONGWORTH

Another page-turning whodunit set in the vibrant and romantic Aix-en-Provence.

When the director of the theology department at a university in Aix is found dead, Judge Verlaque is dumbfounded—Professor Moutte was about to announce the recipient of both a fellowship and a coveted director position (his own). Students and professors make up a long list of suspects, but are leading nowhere.

With Marine's help—and that of her plucky mother—Verlaque uncovers a world that proves more complicated than university politics, while exploring the areas surrounding Aix, and doing his best to keep his love life above water.

Up next in M.L. Longworth's Verlaque and Bonnet series comes a surprising mystery set in a small community of theology students who seem as thick as thieves.

ISBN 978-0-14-312154-1

PENGUIN
BOOKS